Advance praise for *Trash Sex Magic*

It's to Chicago what *The Mysteries of Pittsburgh* is to Pittsburgh and *A Winter's Tale* is to New York—a winning, touching, open-eyed love letter—but with trash, sex, and magic too. Unusual and wonderfully done.
——John Crowley, *The Translator*

Jennifer Stevenson is my goddess. In this book, trash is power. *Trash Sex Magic* is a springtime bacchanalia of beautiful, wild women, magic trees and sexy men—love it!
——Nalo Hopkinson, *The Salt Roads*

Ambitious, phantasmagorical, with images that burn into your brain and stay there, even when the book is off in a corner somewhere minding its own business.
——Ellen Kushner, *Swordspoint*

This just absolutely rocks. It's lyrical, it's weird and it's sexy in a very funky way. *Trash Sex Magic* is full of people you would maybe be afraid to meet in real life, but once you've met them fictionally you are damn sorry you can't at least have a beer with them.
——Audrey Niffenegger, *The Time Traveler's Wife*

It was a proverb of the 16th Century: *On Hallowmass Eve troll notte thy broomstick bye ye caravan park, for thou wottist notte who maye mount thereon.* I had paid it little heed since learning it years ago, and planned to read this grand book one chapter at a time. I'd scarcely begun the second when I fell under the author's spell.
——Gene Wolfe, *The Knight*

trash sex magic

trash **sex** *magic*

Jennifer Stevenson

Small Beer Press
Northampton, MA

Trash Sex Magic © 2004 by Jennifer K. Stevenson All rights reserved.

www.jenniferstevenson.com

Small Beer Press
176 Prospect Avenue
Northampton, MA 01060
www.smallbeerpress.com
info@smallbeerpress.com

Small Beer Press is distributed in the USA and Canada by SCB Distributors.

Library of Congress Cataloging-in-Publication Data

Stevenson, Jennifer, 1955-
  Trash, sex, magic / by Jennifer Stevenson.
    p. cm.
  ISBN 1-931520-06-2 (alk. paper) -- ISBN 1-931520-12-7 (trade pbk. : alk. paper)
  I. Title.a
PS3619.T4925T73 2004
813'.6--dc22
                                    2004003567

First edition 1 2 3 4 5 6 7 8 9

Printed on 52.5# Perfection Eggshell Recycled in Canada by Transcontinental Printing.
Set in Centaur MT.
Cover Photography: "Roots" by Butch Welch; "Face" by Maria Daniels.
Cover Art: "Running Foxes" by Shelley Jackson.

For Rich Bynum, with all my love

Chapter One

FOXE PARKE TOWNHOUSES, BERNE, ILLINOIS
EIGHT ELEGANT RIVERSIDE DWELLINGS
ARCHITECTS: LUNT MORSE A.I.A.
DEVELOPER: ATLAS PROPERTIES
GENERAL CONTRACTOR: BAGOFF, FIMBEAU & JUICK

Raedawn Somershoe shook her mother's shoulder. "Gelia! Wake up!" She jumped back as Gelia's fist swung out of the blankets. Cold March air blew in the trailer window, fluttering the edges of quilts stapled to the walls. "*Mother!* They're cutting down the tree across the road!"

"Whuh?"

"Right now! The machines are all there!" Through the window Rae heard a chainsaw cough. She flew back outside to the edge of the railroad tracks by the road.

There they were. A big yellow bulldozer and a little one like yesterday, churning up the mud they'd made of the meadow, and today a white trailer on a flatbed truck, a big hopper with ominous whirling blades in its mouth, and, reaching up to the top of their tree, a huge crane with a man in a bucket on top. He was draping ropes over the leafless upper limbs of the tree.

Rae hugged her own arms, cold with dread. "They're really going to do it," she whispered.

"'Course they are," her mother said, appearing beside her. "They had the sign up a month ago."

Rae rounded on her. "If you knew, why didn't you do something?"

"What could I do that he couldn't?" Gelia stood watching the men at work, looking closed-up and satisfied in that horrible way she had when bad things happened just as she said they would. She turned the look on

Rae. "Well? You gonna stand here and watch? Let's get out of here."

She heaved two big laundry bags to her shoulders and stomped off toward Rimville.

The chainsaw coughed again. Rae heard a clatter as small branches sputtered away and fell. Her skin crawled. She ran to catch up with Gelia. "What—how could—"

Gelia tossed one of the bags on the ground, put her head down, and walked faster. The chainsaw roared behind them. Rae snatched up the second laundry bag and followed.

Going be like that, is it. Gelia knowing stuff and not telling. Rae tried to wrap the laundry bag around her head so she couldn't hear the growl of the saw. Maybe she could march back there, fuck every one of those men if that was what it took, or lay hands on the machines so they'd break down or, awful thought, make the machines turn on the killers.

No. Even Gelia couldn't do that. Whatever had gone wrong, it was out of their hands. A sound came like machine-gun fire. They were feeding the little branches into the shredder.

She caught up with Gelia on the climb up the hill. "You knew? When they put up the sign? What—how can he *die?*"

Gelia turned so fast, her laundry bag almost knocked Rae down. "Be still."

"What's going to happen to us?"

All Gelia's teeth showed. "We're gonna be just peachy."

"Last night—I was with him—he's been so strange—"

"Be *still!*" Her mother looked ravaged.

"You never let me talk about him!" Rae cried.

Gelia slapped her hard across the face. "That's right. And now you never will." She picked up her laundry again and toiled on up the hill, her back bent as Rae had never seen it before.

Rae picked up her own bag and panted after her. That bad old numbness got hold of her, made her sick to her stomach, made the sky dark and turned her head to a block of wood. She marched like a little kid up the steep concrete street, each step impossibly small, past black lumps of old snow and grass trying to go green. Her cheek stung. She hated Gelia putting the silence on her. *Hated* it.

In the laundromat they sorted dirty clothes, avoiding accidental touches on the hand, tossing stuff onto each other's piles. They sat at opposite ends of the room with their magazines. Blindly Rae watched the wet laundry go round and round.

He couldn't die. She shut her eyes and reached out for him, feeling for the place inside that he had colonized.

Shock slapped her, a hundred times harder than Gelia's slap. She bounced against her plastic chair and her eyes flew open.

At the sorting table, Gelia smirked bitterly.

A moment later, the cement floor shook under her shoes. *Boom.* Rae trembled with the feel of change in the air.

Gelia flinched, but she never looked up.

The manager-repairman swaggered into the laundry. "Hey, baby," he said to Gelia. "I've missed ya. Stick around and watch the game tonight?"

Gelia ignored him.

"How 'bout you, Rae?" he said across the table.

Rae twitched, trying to smile. "That's awful nice of you, Dan." Dear god, somebody was having a normal day.

Gelia put her hand on his behind, and he turned his hey-baby grin back to her.

Boom. Rae and Gelia flinched together.

"I didn't say no yet, did I?" Gelia snapped, her eyes glittering. Gelia would be proving herself number one hussy on her deathbed.

"See you tonight, babe," Dan told Gelia and swaggered out.

Gelia met Rae's eyes across the table. There was something indescribably nasty in that look. Gelia had a secret, and she was angry with her daughter, and it would cost Rae dear to find out what it was.

Boom. Gelia turned away and began stuffing her load into a dryer. Rae stared out the window at a posse of yelling crows flying hell-for-leather eastbound over the trees, and waited for the next chunk to hit the ground.

"God *dammit!*" Gelia gave a childish shriek of rage. She twiddled the knob on the dryer and her fist hit the metal panel with a bang. For the first time Rae heard disbelief and loss in her mother's voice.

"God damn machine! It ate my lucky quarters!"

Chapter Two

Rae stood under the scrubby box elder trees outside her trailer, her hands clenched in the pouch of her faded red sweatshirt. She couldn't bring herself to walk past on her way to work without looking. Perhaps there was a twig left, a leaf. She crossed the road again. Huge machines tore across the meadow, crushing the yellow noses of cattail shoots and jewelweed where they clotted the spongy wet pockets. On drier ground, the great wheels ground down the first leaves of Queen Anne's lace, black-eyed Susan, thickening mosses, and lank prairie grass.

Rae clumped over the muddy ruts, lost for the first time in twenty-five years. The meadow had been a child-high carpet of wildflowers, hummocked with interesting trash, guarded by great black-trunked trees. The ridge behind it, festooned with wild grape vines and raspberry canes and secret paths, rose only a hundred yards away.

Today the ridge was all that was left. Hot tears choked her and mud stuck in bigger and heavier lumps to her shoes. The meadow shrank around the acre of naked mud, torn beyond recognition, nothing left of chiggerweed and wild mustard, Saint John's-wort and spiderwort.

Rae staggered. The workmen paused in their ditches and watched her cry.

She found what she was looking for.

"Yo, girlie! Get off my site!"

Is this all that's left? she thought, looking down at the stump.

The site foreman said, "Foo! What's that stink?"

At their feet, the tree stump lay on its side, its huge spidery root system aimed north, the vast trunk aiming south. The roots sagged like rotting sausage. A whitish fluid oozed out of the sawn-off end and hardened, covered with buzzing and struggling flies. The stump stank of death. Rae looked for the other sixty feet of trunk, limbs, branches, twigs, and leaves.

Impossible. There should be something. A leaf, a shred of bark.

The foreman waved an arm. "Yo, Alexander!"

A big fat black workman ambled over.

The foreman pointed at the stump. "Remember that stink I was complaining about?"

"That was a big tree," Alexander said.

"Biggest tree on the site. Hadda take it out to put up the office."

Rae covered her mouth with both hands. The workman Alexander stared at her. A bumblebee flew around her head and landed on her shoulder.

The foreman picked up a twig. "Like a dead animal."

"What kind was it?" Alexander said.

"The kind that's inna way," the foreman said. He poked the trunk. The twig sank readily into the bark, and foul-smelling fluid spurted out. He jumped back. "Get this on the truck, pronto," he said and stomped away.

"You okay, miss?" Alexander said to Rae.

Numb, not expecting an answer, she said, "How can they do these things?"

"I don't know," he said. He towered over her for a long moment, so big he shut out the weak March sun, and then he left, casting another look at her over his shoulder as he went.

Rae stumbled away. What had *he* said last night?

I've borrowed a couple of spares. You won't be alone.

No, that's not what he said. Rae glared hard at the ground between her muddy shoes, trying to remember, trying to tune in to the huge, bright signal of his voice, now truly silent. But all she could hear was noise.

I've assigned a team of extras. No. *I've somethinged two somethings.* What had he really said?

She shook her head. He never said anything in words. She only understood or didn't. She listened with her inner ear for the voice that had no words, but he was gone. Hacked up, thrown away. She sucked air across her burning throat. The smell of that stump gagged her. *What's going to happen to us?*

Alexander Caebeau watched the girl in the red sweatshirt walk away across the road. She was the single most beautiful thing he had seen since he came to this cold, unfriendly place and began starving to death. She had hair that looked gold or white or tawny, depending on how the sun hit it, and her skin was whiter than white, the white that glows from inside, the white skin you saw in Nassau sometimes, even among his own cousins.

The girl in the red sweatshirt didn't seem to protect her skin much. She had a look, readily identifiable to a child of the working poor, of someone who lived with her beauty, rather than for it.

He went back to his unpleasant job. The bucketloader blade dug into the black dirt and scooped, easily lifting the bulk of the great severed tree trunk. He felt like a pallbearer.

It seemed that the whole point of the work he did was to kill the kind of life he led back home—tear down shabby old houses such as the one he grew up in, or where the girl in the red sweatshirt lived, over there by the river. His job to dig up their great trees, chase away the chickens, gouge great holes in their backyards, and then fill them up with concrete towers of ugliness. They changed the way the wind blew, those concrete towers. The old neighborhoods were passing in Freeport, as the houses closest to the beach and the heart of town were leveled and replaced with strip malls, hotels, and rows and rows of blue-and-white cement swimming pools. His own uncle owned the bulldozer company that pushed those little houses down, while grannies watched stony-faced and children hid behind their skirts. All to make what? A new piece of trash that would come falling down in fifty or sixty years.

What kind of tree was it? The kind that's in the way.

Great trees should be treasured. That's the way we do things at home. He sighed. Until Granmère relented, he would not see home again.

Meantime he was starving, living on hamburgers and growing fatter while, inside, he was always hungry. This place was soulless. The plants and trees were wrong and the sun came up too late and too cold. At the end of his last date, after he'd asked out the waitress at the coffeeshop, she had demanded twenty dollars. They all thought he was a rube. Well, so he was.

Now the girl in the red sweatshirt was standing by the side of the road, talking to a large, shambling-looking white man in overalls that flopped off his shoulder. Her father maybe, since he put his arm around her, comforting her. No, for she kissed him now. Her companion grabbed her around the waist and pulled her to him. The kiss went on and on. Alexander stalled the bucketloader, watching. The girl pulled free and ran off to one of the trailers by the riverbank.

Alexander caught a stunned look on the man's face. He understood. He would have felt the same way, had she kissed him. Perhaps the man had been in love a long time. Alexander sighed. On top of the power pole beside the construction office trailer, a crow guffawed.

Alexander looked away toward the ridge where a pair of grubby white-headed kids squatted on the ridgetop. He raised his arm. After a moment they raised theirs. To him? Or were they waving at the girl in the red sweatshirt?

Here she came, carrying a string bag. She kissed the man in overalls again. A blue convertible pulled up, its top open and its front seat full of rich, pretty girls. The man in overalls squeezed into the front seat with them, and the convertible drove away. The girl in the red sweatshirt walked away down the road. The crow on the power pole took off and floated behind her, its wings glinting in the sunshine. Alexander stared after her like an idiot.

He pulled the big lever that tipped the great rotting stump into the dump truck. "There you go, old fellow."

Sometimes he thought he was dying of the dark and cold and people's ugliness, like an orange lost in the back of the refrigerator. Maybe he would get hard on the outside and nobody would ever taste how sweet he could have been.

Chapter Three

From the road Gelia Somershoe watched with bitter satisfaction as her daughter cried. Baby. No matter what had happened today, no one would ever see Gelia cry.

Not that she felt spry today. She felt a million years old.

Men came up to Rae while she boo-hooed over the stump. Girl didn't even have sense enough to flirt. You *always* flirt. It's how you set the hook. Never know when you might need the power later. Cracker turned up, and Gelia reminded herself for the thousandth time in ten years that she'd had Cracker first, and rejected him.

She dismissed her daughter and scanned the site for likelier men. There. Some college-looking guy sitting on his tailgate over there, wearing a hardhat. Gelia took a deep breath and sashayed across the road.

Unlike many fancifully named sites, the Foxe Parke site had really once been a park, and it really sat near the Fox River. The architect, Walter Chepi, sat on the tailgate of his El Camino, a roll of drawings in his lap. It was a gorgeous site.

To his left, at the western edge of the site, a rocky ridge rose almost seventy feet straight up, covered with trees, scrub, and vines. The ridge ran along the park and appeared off and on for the length of many towns along the river. With the trees in full leaf, that ridge would make a beautiful backdrop for the townhouses. To his right stood palletloads of lumber, a four-ton dump truck, the bucketloader's little brother, two Port-O-Sans, and the mobile construction office raised on cinderblock.

Technically the first eight units would not be on the riverbank, though the river would be visible less than two hundred yards from their windows. The actual riverside site, across US 31 and a disused railroad track, would come available soon. In theory. Walter frowned.

A row of scraggly trees half-screened the river from view. Beyond them there stood or leaned or sank into the mud as ramshackle a settlement of trailers and shacks as ever appeared in a movie about brave but impoverished farm women. A hand-built hut, ugly enough to be a kid's tree house, sat right on the edge of the water. He was amazed it hadn't been swept away.

Smoke seeped out of the chimneyless hut roof, from the chimney-pipes of the two trailers, and from something that might have been a trailer or a slab house or anything, so much was added on. Next to the hut a string of fat fish hung from a clothesline, and the kind of washing machine you turned with a crank. *Resourceful, these modern pioneers.* He chuckled.

He could see one now in fact, a tousle-headed girl wearing a red sweat-shirt over a dress, waving good-bye to a vintage Mustang convertible that looked way out of her league.

The developer had made big promises to relocate these people. The trailer people didn't want to sell, but the company would soon talk them around. That was five months ago.

"You in charge of this?" said a sharp voice, and he jumped and cracked his elbow on the El Camino's cap.

A woman stood behind him—no, no mere woman: a bombshell, a vamp, a va-va-voom, a gypsy queen, a menace from Venus. Her green eyes challenged him. Her lips curved dangerously. She had on pink hot pants and a plunging neckline—wait a minute. Hadn't he just seen her across the road in a red sweatshirt? The hair was the same, collie-colored and tousled. Sisters maybe.

This one had obviously got all the sex appeal in the family. Something about her lifted the hairs on his arms.

He stopped rubbing his funny bone and stood up. "No, I'm just the architect." He offered his hand. "Walter Chepi."

Her eyes made a shell of brightness around her. He imagined he saw the air quivering.

She took his hand as if she meant to do something unusual with it. "Gelia Somershoe. Pleased to meet you, Mr. Chepi. Who gets the idea to build something like this, anyways?"

"The developer, I suppose," he said, and she seemed to relax. He retrieved his hand. "Are you from around here?"

"Grew up right on the river," she said. "I guess you know this whole area's wetter than dog stool."

He choked on a laugh, changed it to a cough. "Well, yes, I have survey maps of the region. I imagine the riverbank floods sometimes."

"You imagine aright," she snapped. "I guess I'm sitting on the roof of my trailer two or three nights, every spring and every fall." So she was one of the trailer people!

She was full of some emotion, rage or greed or hunger, he couldn't tell what. For a while she watched the bucketloader putter back and forth. When the dump truck rumbled onto US 31, she glared.

"These folks'll be mighty sorry when it all washes away," she said vindictively.

Go along with her. Maybe he'd find out why the riverbank holdouts weren't selling. "That would be bad," he agreed.

"You got book learning," she said, turning on him a look so penetrating that he realized she hadn't really looked at him until now. "What do you think? Don't you see no signs?"

He wished she'd look away again. "I'm no geologist, but yes, there are signs that the Fox River has changed its bed. This, where we're standing—" He bent and scrabbled his fingers at dead grass underfoot. "This used to be the riverbed. See? Prairie sod and moss over fossil-laden limestone. Floodplain."

She narrowed her eyes. "And when would that be?"

"Well, probably a thousand years ago. Not much less."

"Mmm-hm. That would be about right. So. We're due again."

"Due?"

She heaved a great, decisive-sounding sigh, and Walter stepped back from the bosom popping out of the top of her blouse. "I s'pose nobody's told you about this place. Not just our land, but here. It's not a good spot to build," she said. "People that live here can tell you the troubles we got with this land."

"It isn't my company, Ms. Somershoe. I think the developer owns the land. What problems exactly?"

"Call me Gelia—" She broke off and waved to someone across the road. He glanced where she waved and saw a little old black guy standing and watching them.

"That's my friend Ernest," Gelia said. "How-dee, Ernest!" She cocked her hips in a way that ought to have looked silly. Walter's arm hairs prickled. The little old black guy smiled.

Flood. Not a good thought. "Problems with the land?"

She returned her attention to Walter, her eyes glittering. "Flood, Mr. Chepi. Once in a big old while, the river changes course. Last time of change, there was Indians here. My gramma had stories from her gramma, what they remember."

She took his hand again. "Tell the developer," she said, pressing his hand. He felt a zing like a static shock.

"I'll, uh, pass your concerns along to the developer." She kept looking at him in that measuring way, as if trying to find some way inside him. He shivered. "Thanks." *I'll promise anything if you just let go.*

Gelia thought she saw a shimmer over the fresh-cut trenches. A familiar force thrummed through the mud she stood on. She listened, tuning out the architect's limp-dick voice.

Tune in. The signal was loud and clear. It set the hairs on her arms stiffening, then the hairs on her back and her neck. *Fulla all that electric.* The shimmer flowed, and the electric sang in her veins.

Then the feeling seemed to fade, flowing back into the hillside. *He's everywhere.* Her skin caught fire with his presence. A shimmer of brightness teased the edges of everything she could see. The air around her hummed.

Gelia's grief retreated. Sure enough, it was time for a change. The pain in her heart lightened for the first time since she heard the chainsaw this morning.

But how soon would it happen? His corpse was been and gone, stinking a mile in that dump truck, and his memory perfumed the ground, pushing up grass, mayapple, and clover triple-quick. The young grapevines on the hill shouted with growth.

Now the force he'd once contained burst open when he fell under the saw. It was filling the whole place. It was too much. When he had it dammed up in his body, they were safe.

Burst now, wide open. Of the mind that had governed it, and shared it through her and through her daughter, she could find nothing.

Less than ten minutes ago she'd walked across the road. The grass was already an eighth of an inch higher.

She gave the architect-feller a good looking-over. Pale-faced, limp-handshaked, he droned on about hardwood floors and breakfast nook skylights. He'll be no use. Don't feel a thing, and what he does, scares him.

Someone will have to take over.

Someone would have to *choose*. And that someone would have to teach him his job.

It'd be down to her or Raedawn. Again.

Gelia set her teeth with a click.

Chapter Four

About two in the afternoon, King Gowdy clomped over the bare mud to his family's trailer, under box elder trees bigger and more tilted than he remembered. Five years he'd been away in Alaska, first in the army, then mending the oil pipeline.

He wondered if he could stand these people this time. Their thoughts were the thoughts of birds or children, wiped clean every morning so they could do it all over again with a light heart, making the same mistakes, fighting the same battles. Hurting themselves. King had a longer memory. The army had reconciled him to futility, but home still gave him the heebie-jeebies. At the trailer door he panicked. He couldn't make his hand knock.

There was no glass in the storm-door window. Through the hole, he heard rustlings in the kitchen.

"Cracker? Willy?" Something burst out of a tree overhead, cawing, and King almost fell off the stoop. "You here?"

No answer. The rustlings became scufflings. "Mink? Ink?" he guessed. "It's me, King." The noises stopped.

He let himself into the trailer.

Even in the spring chill the windows were open, shaded by trees outside. By cool colorless light King located table, chairs, washbasin, gas-powered icebox. It was junk, like everything in this place. In front of the icebox the kids waited for him, their hands behind their backs. King lit an oil lamp.

"Hey, guys," he said.

The twins were silent.

His heart hammered. King looked around slowly. *How shabby, how same.* As high as a boy could reach the walls were black with mildew. Newspapers lay stacked in the hallway for insulation, brown with age. If he picked up the top paper, would it be from a date when he'd lived here?

JENNIFER STEVENSON

He didn't look. A sparkling plate sat on the drainboard. Willy's work, King guessed angrily. If he can wash a plate, why the hell can't he wash a wall? Even Cracker could put in a pane of glass if you handed him the glass, the putty, the puttyknife, the hammer, and the nails.

Not if I'm not here to make him do it. He felt guilty. He'd never been any good with Cracker. Willy managed Cracker better. King had thought he could trust Willy to look after things.

Just look at this place! Shoes hung by their laces right next to the clean dishes. Fishing tackle piled in a tangle on top of fishing clothes that were never washed. High on the wall over the sink, one of his mother's tiny hand-painted plates clung in its plate holder, gathering grime. Used to be a whole wall of 'em. Smashed, he guessed. He turned away, a lump in his throat.

The twins still watched him. Each wore an old tee shirt. He could see a little pair of shorts on Mink. Ink might have been naked under his tee shirt. Their faces were all pointed chin and pale unreadable eyes, hair like cottonwood fluff. They kept their skinny arms behind their backs to hide whatever they'd been stealing. Ink's jaws moved.

King smiled. "You takin' Cracker's beers?"

Ink swallowed. Mink gave her brother a dirty look.

King groped behind him for a chair and sat down. He held one hand out, then the other, and Ink smiled. Mink regarded him steadily. "Hi," she said.

King grinned at her. "Hello, monster child."

She smiled then, as if he had just arrived. "King!" she shrieked. They put their booty on the floor and swarmed him.

"You're big!" Mink exclaimed.

"Yeah. You sure aren't, short stuff. Don't they give you clothes no more? Where's Cracker?"

"Some girl," Mink said, shrugging. She had his pocketknife in her fingers before he noticed her hand in his pocket.

He took the knife back firmly. "What about Willy and Davy?"

"School. Davy—" She jerked a shoulder.

"How old are you now, anyways? Oughta be in school yourselves." They didn't answer. The rules came back to him as Mink inspected his pockets and Ink poked small fingers into his ears. Don't move quickly. Don't expect an answer. Wait.

King was tired of waiting. He seized Ink in a bear hug and squeezed him. The boy thrashed, and King laughed.

"All right, I'll let go. Quit squirming. You didn't grow a-tall, did you?" He put the boy down.

Mink had stepped away the moment he grabbed Ink. *Still beast creatures, ain't you?* "Why ain't you in school?"

Mink shrugged. There were big blue rings around her eyes, bruises or stains of sleeplessness.

"You had a bath today?"

She cast him a look of scorn and seized her thievings off the floor: a loaf of bread and a jar of pickles. She headed for the door. Ink was half a step behind her.

"Hey! See ya!" King called. No point in chasing them. Anyway, he wanted out. He didn't want to see the rest of his home right now. *Go next door and see Gelia.* On second thought, maybe he'd go downtown to the old hockey bar.

Chapter Five

Spring arrived fully that last night in March. By Wednesday night the air was at seventy degrees. The soil thawed and sucked up water left standing by melted snows and ground springs. The mud quit smelling like stale ice cubes and began smelling dirty and fertile. All up and down the riverfront, grasses and prairie plants pushed themselves above ground at an unnatural pace. Leaves burst like green fire among the twigs. A single crow rose over the early leafing trees. Its yellow eye caught the reflection of streetlights on US 31 but it was asleep, asleep and dreaming. It circled the ridge, looking for a place to rest.

Along the top of the ridge ran one railroad track, a faintly gleaming line of silver, and down there alongside the road ran the other railroad track, also silver, and out there past the trees the vast silver track of the river. Between those silver lines the crow saw the meadow as a tangle of green neon in motion. A warm wind rolled down off the ridge and the crow rode it, grabbing altitude.

Down there on the meadow, piles of human junk lay dense black, lifeless, surrounded by green fire. As the crow circled, watching, the green fire began to bend around the black spots. The wind doubled in force, lifting the crow thirty feet in one swoop. At US 31 the temporary power line rocked and fell before the wind. The night light in the construction office trailer winked out.

The large bucketloader was parked in the lee of the ridge. The sapling it had felled that afternoon lay under the steel treads, mashed flat along with grapevine, mayapple, poison oak, raspberry canes, grass, and mosses. A stirring could be heard far under the big yellow machine, like the scritch of a mouse or a rusty screw turning. Rain tinked and tonked on the cab.

The wind moved on, blowing on the No Parking signs until they flashed and trembled like a woman's earrings, flipping the lids off garbage cans and bowling them before it, peeling paper rubbish off the streets and plastering it with spattering warm rain to the sides of buildings and cars. Headlights bristled along US 31, reflected everywhere on the wet surfaces of road, tree trunk, and river. The white globe lamps in front of Water Willow Apartments shone like moons. The crow turned, barrel-rolling in its sleep, looking for the real moon through thick rainclouds, then down at the globe lamps. Wind swivelled the plastic globes, rattling them on their poles. The wind hurled a bit of branch against the brittle plastic and knocked off a jagged piece of moon.

The wind threw rain across the Fox River. Rain pattered onto the surface of the river, pockmarking the water over the heads of catfishes. The first turtles worked themselves free of the river bottom, and then, as debris and sand from upstream began to cloud the surface, the first frogs.

The wind rolled upstream. The crow flew over mulberry trees overhanging the footbridge and dreamed it saw mulberries ripening, falling to the bridge's boards like fat drops of rain. Rain dripped between the bridge's boards. The crow cartwheeled past a tiny island smack in the middle of the river, an island barely large enough to hold a leaning box elder tree and a fringe of grass.

The island stood fast in the middle of the roiling waters below the Route 64 bridge. A hot, wild smell whisked upstream toward the dam.

Swollen with rain, pent on one side by the Beard Hotel's piazza and on the other by City Hall, the river poured with greater and greater force over the dam. On the City Hall side, a fountain in the shape of a lotus flower jutted out above the water, and beside it ran a salmon race, a narrow stairway for fish. Foam poured down the salmon race, along with twigs, leaves, and crushed styrofoam cups. The lotus-shaped fountain filled to overflowing.

A clap of thunder sounded overhead. At the same moment, a turtle, accompanied by several gallons of river water, shot over the salmon race and plopped into the fountain. A gust kicked up more flying foam and another turtle flew into the basin. Then another. Then five more turtles in quick succession.

The first lightning struck the 64 bridge.

A shadow perched on the flagstone above the fountain. With nice judgment, it sprang. It seized a turtle struggling to mount the lip of the fountain, sprang back to the flagstone, every step clanking, shaking its paws fastidiously, loped to the balustrade on the far side of the bridge, and set the turtle on its feet.

The turtle crawled to the edge of the balustrade, teetered, and toppled back into the Fox, where it drifted swiftly downstream and sank into the waters under the bridge. Serene in its sleep, the crow hovered, watching with approval.

In no time the flagstone above the fountain was covered with small pawprints. They soaked quickly into the limestone, staining it rust red. The bridge balustrades were bare. Turtles continued to vault into the fountain to the applause of travelling thunder.

Upriver the wind was carrying away strings of triangular plastic flags from a used car lot and draping them in loops from the ties of the great railway trestle bridge. The river here was at its deepest and most turbulent. White whirlpools turned in opposing directions like great gears meshing, sucking whole trees under the surface. Seventy feet straight up, lightning struck the trestle bridge with a horrendous clang. The flags fluttered down like sycamore seeds.

The wind carried a red flag upriver and glued it to the roof of the *Delta Queen*. The *Delta Queen* was an old flat-bottomed paddlewheel tour boat, moored in Blackhawk Park and used only on weekends in the summer. In March her decks were knee-deep in leaves. The park keepers kept her tethered at both ends to the rotting dock.

Had her mooring lines been chain and not hemp, they would have snapped tonight. A hasty current yanked the wet lines until they stretched like rubber bands. The dock cleats rattled loose on their bolts. Every yank brought them infinitesimally closer to pulling out.

Another bolt of lightning, and the crow woke at last and dove for a treetop.

Raedawn slept alone on the big bed in her trailer.

She heard a child cry or maybe a bird and woke, lifting her head in distress. Yes, a bird, the strangest bird she'd ever seen. Her heart warmed. Hello, hello. The bird hopped out of the wet woods and onto her knee, crying in pain.

Looking up, she saw a small animal hobbling laboriously on three legs out of the trees. It joined the bird on her lap. When she looked up again the trees had advanced. They crowded black and wet around her. Small creatures pressed her on every side, huddled under her rain-plastered skirt. Her heart felt hot as a coal.

She fumbled among the creatures on her lap, trying to lift them to her burning center, but they shifted as wild things do, evading her. Every one was crying, making what small noises it could make. The sounds tore through her. Come on, come on.

The first creature stepped timidly into a beam of green fire that pierced her like an arrow, shooting through her breast like a tunnel of sound.

Green fire leaped out. She sighed and laid her head back on her pillow. An endless stream of small crying animals came forward to touch the power humming through her. It was not release, but she could sleep through it.

Alexander Caebeau, bucketloader operator to Bagoff Fimbeau & Juick, late of Freeport, Miami, and points north, slept at the Berne YMCA. He was fed up with the States. He dreamed of going home. He drove his bucketloader the whole way, bumping and churning across the bottom of the Caribbean Sea, his dreads floating around him in a sturdy halo. The scoop was turned down. Like a windscreen it parted schools of blue and scarlet fish, and the sea flowed smoothly over the big yellow machine. Sea things like butterflies rushed his head, smacked silently on the bucketloader window, or peeled away on invisible currents.

The bucketloader clawed its way up a coral hill and slid slowly over the other side. A cloud of sand puffed up as high as the cab. He felt the transmission inhale sand. The gears grated. The track jammed. The bucketloader ground to a stop.

Alexander climbed down from the cab and pushed his way through the water, one thick leg at a time. There was a way to do it quickly, if he turned his body edgewise, one shoulder at a time, cutting a path through the deeps. It was too warm for a sweatshirt. He shucked that as he climbed the coral hill, shucked all his clothes until, naked, he stood on a flat patch of coral at the top, watching the pale light from the surface turn his arms and chest slaty blue.

Home. This would be a good place to stay, right on this hilltop. But suppose waves came and swept him off? He'd like to see them try. He gained a good hundred pounds since he left. And he was home now. He stood on tiptoe, daring a wave to try to move him, and stretched his long arms toward the surface while gray light and blue shadow played over his skin.

The waters gathered at his face and pushed. He fought back, but the waves were strong. His body rippled like seaweed in the current.

Something warm slid over his ankle.

He looked down past the hard curve of his belly. The coral was smoother than he remembered, only tinged with pink. A hand the color of bright golden sand clasped his ankle. In this blue light it was the only really bright thing to be seen.

The waters pushed again. The bucketloader swept past his hill and vanished into a drowned valley.

A second hand slid up his other ankle, and a third, and a fourth. If the water seemed suddenly colder, the hands were warm, and they clung to him and held on, keeping him anchored in the stormy waves.

Alexander laughed. Underwater, the sound was loud but private. Warm hands wound around his body, higher and higher, and he raised his face to the surface and the invisible sky beyond and laughed out choruses of fishes while his storm-whipped arms fluttered like seaweed in an undersea rain.

Gelia Somershoe, her arm flung over Ernest's pajamaed back, slept through the storm in his trailer. She dreamed she was the river, a clear unlit body made of many ribbons of coolness and warmth. Her skin puckered, tickled, and turned constantly inside to outside. Her most secret currents housed millions of moving parts, alive with wild purpose.

Ernest stirred under her arm. He was dreaming about the wet earth, how it lay panting under the river's long writhing weight. She passed ceaselessly and familiarly over the sand, stones, and clay of his body, her bed.

They woke at the same time and stirred in one another's arms.

She murmured, "Hey, d'ya miss me?"

He silenced her with a kiss. She smiled and, heaving herself up onto her knees, pulled the pajamas off him as if undressing a sleeping child.

At some unnoticed point they began to dream again. The river rolled in the arms of the bank. Rain hammered on the tin roof of Ernest's trailer.

Chapter Six

Alexander Caebeau was the first man on the site Thursday morning. Today it was his turn on first bucketloader shift.

He liked starting at five o'clock. The streetlights still glowed. Unseasonably warm air lay over the river and mist rose off the water's surface. He lit a cigarette. Last night he had dreamed of going home and of tropical waters. This morning the air was wet and clean. Illinois didn't smell so bad for once. Does it good to have a bath, he thought.

He unlocked the office trailer to punch in. The timeclock didn't work. Alexander looked out the window, saw the power pole fallen, and grinned, picturing what Ike the foreman's reaction would be. He checked: yes, the phone was dead, lights out, and, catastrophe, the refrigerator had stopped running. He helped himself to a warm Coke, clapped his hardhat over his dreads, and ambled out to look at the morning before starting his machine.

The earthmovers were usually parked near the foot of the ridge. From the doorstep of the construction office trailer he could see only the Bobcat. A wall of fresh green undergrowth crawled up the ridge. It seemed to Alexander that the hill itself was closer than it had been yesterday. He paused with his foot on the trailer step and looked up uneasily at the looming face of the ridge, noticing that even the thick elderly grapevines wore baby leaves. *That's new since yesterday, surely.* How fast it grows. Faster than back home, even.

For a moment he thought of shimmering gold hands. He shivered, grinned, and sniffed the air.

It was going to be a hot day. Last night's wind was gone. The air was warmer than the ground. A smell, indescribably green, of plants and bugs and fresh birdshit and microorganisms multiplying in the black wet mud, rose like a huge kiss to his skin. Under two sweatshirts, a plaid flannel shirt and a tee shirt, Alexander was very warm. *When the sun hits this, we will really sweat.*

He couldn't find the big bucketloader. It wasn't where he'd left it, nose-to-tail with the Bobcat with the ridge on its right.

He walked the site, searching. Dump truck, toolboxes, compressor, piles of wood for the forms—no yellow bucketloader. He walked to the north end of the site, then paced back, his warm Coke forgotten in his hand, feeling foolish looking for something too big to lose. Stolen? The boss would have a fit.

But at the foot of the ridge, right where it should have been, he found part of it. He sucked air through his teeth.

The scoop stuck out from under a pile of dead brush, right next to the Bobcat. Alexander put his Coke can on the Bobcat's fender and squatted. The big scoop poked up out of the brush, piled with chunks of yesterday's cut saplings and swarming with new grapevines. Worse than the jungle, he thought. Chrome gleamed under the brush. He lifted a grapevine branch off the pile. Something clinked, clanked, rustled to the bottom of the brushpile, but he saw it before it disappeared into the leaves below. It was a lug nut. He scuffed his feet. The rock he stood on was a big sprocketed steel roller, completely buried under a web made of layer after layer of thick old grapevine. The transmission column was missing. No, here it was, sticking out from under a piece of cleated track folded over an idler roller, half buried in dirt and smothered in greenery. Knotted in among the vines gripping the track was a steering lever. Alexander recognized the Chiquita banana sticker that Jamie had stuck to it yesterday after lunch. The sticker was brand new, a sunny blue, yellow, and white. Vines bound the lever to the track cleats as if they had been growing there for years.

The hairs stood up all over Alexander's body.

He looked around. It was quite a large heap of dead brush. With one finger he picked at the vines. He found some yellow-painted steel plates, a door handle, a circle of glass sprung whole out of the dashboard, all knotted together with grapevine as tight and gray as old fishing net.

Now that he knew what was underneath, he saw the brush pile hid the whole bucketloader. It lay exactly as it had stood, only flattened, as if someone very large had stepped on it or, just as unlikely, carefully unbolted all the bolts and pulled all the pins and then let it just collapse, like a fat lady sinking into a chair. Or. Or else maybe, he thought, bending and peering, thinking hard, seeing the way the grapevines knit together around the front axle, dove into the ground, came up again *here*, grabbed the transmission at the narrow part, then down again. Could it have been *pulled* flat?

Behind him, his Coke can fell off the Bobcat's fender. Alexander turned slowly, his pulse fast. The can rolled to his feet, glugging. A thin creeper of gay yellow-green grapevine stuck to the can by tiny suckers, curled all the way around it.

When he saw this he backed, wheeled, and sprinted for the office trailer. Halfway there he remembered the dead telephone.

He stopped the first car passing on US 31. There was a little trouble at first—the driver was white, and she didn't want to roll her window down. She agreed to call the police. Alexander watched her pull away with her cell phone stuck to her ear and walked back to stand guard at the bucketloader.

The big boss arrived, Bob Bagoff, the general contractor, complaining bitterly. What kind of security did they have at his site? How come the bucketloader wasn't kept locked? Look at this pile of junk! The rental company would charge high for a rebuild, if they didn't make him buy a new machine. The utter strangeness of the vandalism didn't seem to strike him at all.

It struck Alexander. He didn't mention the vine crawling clear around his Coke can in two minutes. It was obvious he couldn't have done the damage himself, that was all that mattered, dealing with Bob. Bob liked to have someone to blame.

By late morning, work was running normally at the Foxe Parke site. Alexander took a break at 10:30 and went to clock out in the office trailer. The architect was there, and Bob Bagoff and the foreman were blundering around the office with an army cot and a measuring tape. Alexander punched his timecard and pulled a Coke out of the refrigerator.

"Oh, Alexander." Bob dropped the tape and reached up to lay a hand on Alexander's sleeve. "C'mere for a second." He seemed nervous, half-plaintive, half-angry.

Alexander allowed himself to be towed into the corner. Bob put his boot up on the cot and assumed a masterful position.

"That was really hairy this morning. We could of got burned if it hadn't been for you, you know. Quick thinking. Not enough of that around here."

Alexander said nothing. He'd done nothing. He smelled trouble.

Bob said, "Ike says, and I agree with him, that we just have to have some security in this place. This sort of shit can't happen again."

Ike nodded four times. "What we need is a security guard. All the time, tools are disappearing."

"It wouldn't hurt to have a night watchman," the architect said, sipping coffee from the corner by the pot.

Bob scowled over his shoulder. "Well, the partnership won't pay for a night watchman. The insurance is gonna go up again. Jeezus, it'll cost more to rebuild that bucketloader than just buy a new one." He shook his head gloomily, and his glance fell on the cot. "We gotta have somebody around. Keep an eye on things. What I expect, it'd practically guarantee against anything happening."

He squinted up at Alexander in so friendly a manner that for two seconds Alexander was fooled. Bob had never looked so human.

"I suppose so," Alexander said cautiously.

The boss was delighted to hear this. "Where you staying now, Alexander? Berne Y? I'll drive you back in the truck and we'll pick up your stuff. You can move in tonight."

Sleep *here?*

Once again Alexander saw the bucketloader lying in pieces, its treads sprung snaggletoothed, its cab splayed like a stepped-on toy, the pieces knotted together with vines. Something must have showed in his face.

Still jovially, Bob said, "Hey, great! See, I'd hate to have to find another bucketloader operator. Job's half-done. I like having you around." He slapped Alexander on the arm.

Alexander might have known Bob would find a way to dump this on him. He looked around the office, wondering where the vines might crawl in. There were five windows, an aluminum door with a half-glass screen door outside it, and a square plastic bubble in the roof. No proper seals there.

He thought about the other openings. Hidden ones. The heater chimney, up behind that vent in the wall. Hose connections coming in and out of the baseboard for the propane heater. Conduit for power and telephone. The whole thing was banged together out of prefabricated parts, stacked, stored, and trucked around until its joints shook loose.

He narrowed his eyes at Bob. "Your foot is on my bed."

"Oh, hey, sorry about that." Bob took his boot off the cot. "Uh, great. Good! Hey, take a break." He slapped Alexander on the arm again and made for the door.

Alexander stared after him, very nearly letting his feelings show. You nasty little man, he thought. He went out for a cigarette, and to look the trailer over from the outside.

What a cheap, ill-favored, lazy, mean-spirited little man. God, it is the truth, you can't never trust your boss. No different from home. Furiously he sucked down his Coke, walked around the trailer, and took inventory of its many vulnerable spots.

Above the furnace flue where it stuck up out of the trailer roof, a cloud of gnats had formed. They danced on an invisible column of warm air. That furnace flue—was it high enough off the ground? Maybe the hot air coming out of the flue would discourage vines from invading. All around the trailer he could see cracks in the siding, bad joints between floor and wall. In one place he could see daylight coming through a crack between the wall and the roof, shining clear through the trailer. If the vines were out to get him, maybe the bugs were too. Maybe he'd wake up to find himself being eaten alive by ants.

His imagination wasn't doing him any favors. He shivered. What would Granmère have done?

Make a whammy, he thought. She'd pick up a twist of dirt or a leaf and speak over it, just mutter it away, as she had muttered away his nightmares when he was *un bebé.* He crushed his Coke can and overhanded it into the drum by the trailer door.

On the ground beside the drum lay a stick, a thick piece of green wood as long as his forearm, with a pair of leafy twig-stubs at one end making a crowfoot. He recognized it as a piece of that giant tree and picked it up. He almost dropped it. Like touching a dead man's hand. But it was a hefty stick, club size. Something to beat the vines with when they came calling at night. He stuck it in his hammer-loop and walked on around the trailer.

I want my gran. She'd know what to do about a *mal pensee* place. Alexander felt unbearably homesick.

Bah. Don't forget the foreman at the cane distillery docking you for swearing or for smoking anytime except on your lunch break. And the tourists forgetting to tip the taxi driver and talking right in front of you like you aren't there, telling each other loudly that these islanders can't understand American accents anyway. Don't forget the cops pulling you over and taking money right out of your wallet when you go to show them your license. And the girls, who are no better than the cops. And the cloud of poison fumes that hangs over Pinder's Point in Freeport now, except in the windiest season.

Home may be a mess, he thought morosely, but it's my home. *I miss home cooking.* I wish I was sixteen again and too smart to think the world is different someplace else.

The morning got hotter. The insects became a nuisance. Alexander crushed dozens to death just by scratching his ear. The heat seemed to encourage them. Gnats rose in dense clouds from mud puddles and patches of new grass and flew into everyone's eyes and throats. They hovered near the men's knees and climbed into crevasses in their clothes. They boiled up to eye level and hung there, maddeningly motionless except for their furious, self-absorbed mating. Men bent to the cement forms and sucked gnats into their noses. Men stood up, annoyed, and coughed as their heads pierced clouds of gnats. From the ridge, gnats peeled away and fell in smoky rolling coils. The men swore. Ike handed out bug spray.

Alexander went into Berne on his lunch break and bought a length of mosquito net at the Ace Hardware.

Chapter Seven

Gelia's trailer was the nearest thing to a movable mobile home on the riverbank. Ancient hard-rubber tires rotted on their rusty axles. One time she'd hitched all the neighborhood kids to the trailer with clothesline and, braying like mules, they hauled it up the bank to higher ground.

She gave us brownies for that, thought King. First woman in America to put extra chocolate chips in brownies.

The trailer hadn't moved since then, although dirty stripes marked floodlines as high as the bottoms of the windows. King came around to the front door, scraped his boots as best he could on an iron dachshund, climbed the steps, and knocked.

Ernie opened the door, looking older and smaller. "Good day," he said politely. All the folds in his face gathered to a pink spot at his puckered mouth. "Why, King Gowdy, how do you do! Come in." He stuck his head around back of the door as King entered, and called, "Angelia, King Gowdy's come visiting you, my word he's big as a house. Come in, have a biscuit and get comfy."

King followed him inside. "H'lo, Erny."

"Come on in, King," Gelia called. Gelia was sixty, but everything about her, from her tight, freckled skin to her challenging eyes, from her collie hair to her muscular calves, spoke of youth. She stretched out on an over-stuffed brocade couch, a piece of carpet under her bare feet, wearing a very short pair of hot pink shorts with a dug-out blouse. To King she seemed not at all changed since that day he and his friends hauled her trailer for chocolate chip brownies. She brushed the gold and white hair away from her eyes and measured him, smiling. In spite of himself, King shivered under her glance.

"Well!" she said finally, as if she'd seen enough.

King grinned again. "Morning, Mrs. Somershoe." *Hell, the woman's practically my mother. Still hotter'n a pistol.*

"King, you remember Ernest Brown. My gentleman friend. Ernest and I been going steady now for some time. Thank you, Ernest," she said, accepting a cup of hot cocoa.

King sank into a squashy chair as Ernest reached him a plate of biscuits dusted with cinnamon. The old chair knew his bones. He'd run his first sixteen years in and out of this trailer. Every dent in the linoleum was as much his as theirs. Gelia's windows were covered with blankets for warmth. The living room was dim. Two oil lamps burned on the coffee table. King's ears buzzed. He spoke loudly, pushing through the strangeness.

"Still no electric yet, Gelia?"

"I won't have it." She sniffed.

It was an old argument. King grinned again. "Still got the old gas-powered icebox, then? How's Raedawn like that?"

"This place floods twice a year. We'd be zapped in our beds."

"The power comes in on a pole, Gelia," King said patiently. "The water don't reach that high."

"It's my house, Mr. Bigbritches. Day I want to burn it down I'll ask for your help." She sipped and smiled, tossing her hair off her face, showing a lot of white smooth throat. In her day she had taught every boy on the river to make love and to read. Her strong young legs were too pink and naked. She made King uncomfortable all over again, stretched out in front of him like a meal he'd never been able to refuse.

There had been a time when being home had made him physically sick, and a time before that when it was natural—painful at times, but natural. These feelings turned him over like pages of a book flipping backward, the sick and then the natural feeling, and both were familiar, but he still felt like a stranger. Five years was a long time to be away from home.

Gelia burned like a bonfire on the sofa. Ernest drank cocoa beside her as if unaware. King swallowed and looked away.

The long living room wall was lined with fancy needlework of another state and time, rusty and mildew-spotted, stapled to the masonite as a form of insulation. Near the front door hung fishing gear, most of it handmade. Toward the kitchen hung pots, spoons, a fryer improvised from a hubcap and the crucible of many a water's-edge fish fry in King's childhood days, a basket of onions and garlic, and a potted "burn plant."

The hall to the bedrooms in back was finger painted in mad colors.

The boy King had always felt Gelia's trailer to be a haven of cleanliness and hominess, a refuge from the mess Cracker made of his parents' place. There was always food here. Always a willing woman.

King rubbed his hands on the knees of his jeans. His clothes were clean now, not mended anywhere at all. They didn't even need mending. For some reason the thought made him miserable.

He fought the misery. Why should he feel bad? His hair was freshly cut. His razor was an electric one in a neat leatherette bag, bought in a big store in Anchorage. It sat with the rest of his luggage uptown, in a hotel with a big, shiny bathroom, electric lights, and running water.

"And how did you find your uncle?" Ernest said.

King breathed carefully. The air in the trailer was close and smelled of oil lamps and biscuits.

"Ain't found him yet. Twins say he's off screwing around. Why the hell aren't they in school?"

"They are small," Ernest said.

King frowned. "Why the hell aren't they?" he repeated.

"Raedawn is teaching 'em to read," Gelia said.

"As if that's all they're ever gonna need to know." Outrage was a familiar feeling, too. He bit a biscuit. "S'pose nobody's seen their mother."

"Not a hair," Gelia said calmly.

"Like every other woman of Cracker's. Least the others never left him with babies. *Fine* person to care for infants."

Gelia raised her eyebrows. "The river takes care of them. They're wild, King."

"I can *see* that," he said, spraying crumbs. "All we need in this family is another Davy." Everybody in this damn family needs watching, King grumbled to himself, only none of them knows it. He felt like a radio tuning in to an old station, one he hadn't listened to for years. He had never liked those songs.

Rage and horniness and homesickness caught up and passed him at last. The newness of his clothes seemed to be wearing off, along with the smell of store-bought soap on his skin. His home was repossessing him.

"I'm glad you're back," Ernest said deliberately. "You can talk to your Uncle Cracker about moving."

"That's right," Gelia said, as if the idea had just struck her. "King can tell Cracker the river's shifting this year."

"The river?" King swivelled on the worn chair to watch her get up. She still looked good from behind, too.

"The lines are set up. Ask Ernest. We're due to blow any day."

King shut his eyes. *Every time I talk to these people it's something crazy. Got their own world.* "Talk sense."

"The lines don't lie, King," Gelia said. She sounded near enough to touch him.

He looked up defensively. "Aw, what lines?"

Ernest paused in the act of putting on a huge rubber wading boot. He held up a finger like a sweet potato.

"Ley lines, son. What you might call the seams of the earth's skin." The finger turned like a soothsayer's until it pointed down. "Under us. Underground."

King grunted. He kept one eye on Gelia. She stood over him, examining him as carefully as Mink and Ink had done, though not with her hands, thank goodness.

Ernest said, "Any good dowser can find them. They run in pairs." He made two fingers slide over the coffee table. "Next to streams under the soil usually. The water flows this way and the ley line runs that way." The fingers walked in place.

"Huh. We used dowsers on the pipeline."

Ernest bobbed his head. "And they should have used dowsers on that building project over there." He jabbed the fingers at the wall. "Lines curling all over the place, doubled back under the hill. Could be a hell of a mudslide, pardon my French, Angelia." He leaned toward King confidentially. "The river's risen almost two foot. On the *east* bank."

"So? It always rises this time of year."

Ernest raised his eyebrows. "Didn't rise on both sides." He went back to putting his waders on. He added in a too-casual voice, "In case you hadn't noticed, there's a big new hole in the ground across the road."

King stopped breathing. *Don't tell me.* He shut his ears.

Gelia bent over King, her eyes glittering. "And nobody to fill it," she said. He sweated. *Get away from me, old tigress.* She reached out a hand toward his shoulder.

Quick as thought, he jumped up. "Where do I put this cup?" he said stupidly, like he didn't know.

Behind him, Gelia said, "Don't have the nerve?" She laughed soft and mean, and King hunched his shoulder. She disappeared into the back of the trailer.

"They want us to sell our land," Ernest said.

To hell with the crazy stuff, this was real. "Yeah, Cracker wrote me. They trying to force you all out?"

Gelia came out of the bedroom wearing overalls and looking, if possible, more feminine than she had in shorts. "Your Uncle Cracker could do the job if he weren't so blamed lazy."

King could feel her eyes on him, giving him that you-could-be-mine look. It annoyed the hell out of him. If there was one thing he was going to hold onto, now he was back, it was the notion that he belonged to himself: not her, not Raedawn, not his lost and godforsaken parents, not nobody no how.

Ernest said thoughtfully, "Gentleman from the development has visited four times. He says he can get the city to condemn us. He told your uncle he'd get the health department to take away our water permit."

"You tell him you drink river water?"

Ernest said, "Everybody knows we drink out of the river. And eat the fish. We couldn't survive without what the river gives us, King. Raedawn doesn't earn enough to feed us."

"There's nothing wrong with that water," Gelia said. "We had to boil it for about twenty years there, but the factories finally quit shitting where they eat and now it's near as good as it was when I was a girl." She eyed him with lewd speculation.

"I don't believe any of it," King said stubbornly.

"I don't think they will get around to evicting us in time. Don't you worry, boy," Ernest said in a kind voice, as if he knew King was incapable of understanding. He picked up his coat and went out, holding the door for Gelia to go before him.

Left alone in Gelia's trailer, King folded his arms across his chest, bowed his head, shut his eyes, and squeezed himself to get the bunches out of his neck and shoulders. He was home.

Chapter Eight

Rae came out of the stockroom at the Ace. A huge black man in construction worker's clothes fiddled with a hardhat and a piece of netting that lay on the counter. There was clay on the construction worker's boots, and tools dangled on his belt like toys beside his big hands. A leafy stick hung in the loop next to his hammer.

He looked familiar. *That's the guy I saw yesterday.* He'd been kind to her while she cried.

"Bugs getting to you?" She propped her elbows on the counter.

He glanced up and did a double take. Most men did. He said, "Very bad. I've never seen them so thick up here." He smiled, meeting her eyes. His face was huge and round and flat like a moon, framed in a halo of dreadlocks, and it gave off its own light in the dimness of the Ace. "Don't I see you over by the river?"

He smelled rich with sweat. Nice. "Yep. I live there."

He cocked his head. "Pretty funny place."

She grinned like a fool. She hadn't met a nice man in months.

"Something odd happening all the time." He looked at her as if he was holding back a thought. "I bet you never get bored."

Her smile fell. "Lately—lately I'm afraid things have been odder than usual." She looked into his bright black eyes. "You had some trouble today, didn't you?"

He nodded. Rae wondered how long he expected to be working at the jobsite. "What's your name?"

"Alexander," he said softly.

He held her eyes for a moment and then looked back at his hat. She watched him shake out the net.

"Don't you have to eat lunch now?" she said.

"Every day."

"My name's Rae. Want company?"

He smiled. "Sure thing." He tried the hat on.

"Let me." She fiddled with the bottom edge of the net. It lay in folds over his shoulders and spilled over his chest. She reached out and rolled the bottom edge of the net in her fingers. "Bit of wire or some fishing weights can keep this lying down for you. Cost you a dime."

"No, thank you." Deep under his veil of dreadlocks and netting, he smiled again. Rae felt her whole body heat up from the bones outward. Wow. For the first time in two days, her heart stopped feeling scooped out and sore. "This looks like as good a time as any. I'll grab my things."

They walked downhill toward the river, Alexander clasping his hardhat under his arm, the woman Rae with a string bag in one hand and a paper sack in the other. She swung along beside him with wide strides and swaying hips in her cheap cotton print dress. "How'd you come to be so far from home? Jamaica, right?"

"Bahamas. I got my first construction job in Freeport with my uncle's company, where he was clearing land for a new hotel. Learned my equipment. Then I moved over to the construction company that built the hotel. Then that job dried up and the company asked me to come up here."

"Like it here?"

He made a face. "No. Do you?"

She shrugged. "It's home."

A bumblebee zipped by and circled her head, and she put her hand out and the bee just landed there, on her palm. A woman with three small boys toiled uphill toward them. The woman stopped, glared venomously at Rae, and pulled her children to huddle against a storefront while he and Rae passed. Rae blew on the bumblebee in her palm and it flew away.

"Some women here don't like me or my folks one bit."

"No? Why is that?"

"Aahhh." She scuffed her feet on the sidewalk. "We're too poor, I guess. My mother's too good-looking. She's with Erny, and Erny's black. Cracker's a drunk, the twins run wild, Davy's a half-wit. God knows what they say about me."

He could imagine what small-town women would say about her. Her yellow-and-gold-and-white head bobbed along by his shoulder. She turned her head as a squad car rolled up the street, and the policeman inside lifted a hand as he passed. She sketched a salute in return.

"We're just too poor. And not miserable." She turned and grinned up at him. "You know? Around here, that's unforgivable. We're not—" She scowled and churned her fists round and round at her sides like a child imitating a locomotive. "We're not *trying* hard enough. Y'know? We don't *suffer* enough."

He smiled wryly back, but she was looking down, negotiating a set of ladderlike stairs from the sidewalk down to the street. He wanted to see her face again. He said, "Give me your bag?"

The smile she flashed up at him stunned him, full of surprise, appreciation, mischief. "Watch that, my friend. Chivalry is next to alimony." But she handed him the paper bag and went on down the steep stairs ahead of him.

She marched him to the bottom of the hill. He thought they would keep going across the river, but at the bridge she turned north and led him down a dirt path beside an abandoned factory, then on a path made of boards laid among tall weeds. They were always a stone's throw from the water itself, to their right.

"We're getting closer to your work again, really," she said. "Just, we're following the river, not the road. When we're done with lunch you'll be right close. You'll see."

Their shoes were loud on the old warped boardwalk. Rae slowed and stood still, and Alexander stopped beside her.

"Look how far along everything is!" The hot spring sun skinned the river with mist.

She named plants for him. She pointed out maple trees in bloom, filling the air with their nectar. "And squaw weed. This grass is scouring rush. The brown lollypops are cattail heads." Poking up between them were the brown swords of dead reeds, interleaved with new green blades.

"That's jewelweed." Rae pointed to a plant that stood waist-high to him, succulent and steaming. "If you sting yourself on nettles, rub it with jewelweed and it'll take the pain away."

Alexander realized he couldn't see any gnats here. They must have all flown uphill for the big mating dance, he thought. He could smell wet wood where his boots left damp waffles on the boards. A dragonfly skimmed past his face, dove, and grabbed hold of a jewelweed flower. Up close, the flower looked like an orchid, a round orange womanly belly dangling below delicate arms, and the sweet secret hollow inside all speckled and dusty with powdered gold, wearing the emerald shaft of the dragonfly like a hairpin.

Rae touched his shoulder.

"What happened over there with the cop car today?"

Rae saw his big round face snap shut and was instantly sorry she had asked. She said more softly, "Was it bad?"

He nodded, his eyes wary now, as if he was wondering why she had lured him here. Even the smell of his sweat changed. Whatever it was, it must have scared him.

She half smiled. "Well, never mind."

"You didn't come to look?" he said stiffly.

She looked at the ground. "No. I—well, oh, it bothered—it bothers me that they have to dig that place up and cut that—cut all those trees down. I used to spend a lot of time over there." Oh nuts, she thought, I'm gonna cry. She turned her hot face toward the river.

"It was a nice big tree, wasn't it?" he said gently.

She gasped at this. Tears spilled out of her eyes. She squeezed her arms, trying to make them stop. Even with her back turned to him, she could smell him roasting and growing in the sun, like all the other live things. She felt all mixed up inside.

He went on, "Part of the job, it is. I don't like it. Always cutting down trees for no reason, and then there's nothing but a mess."

She nodded at the river and swallowed hard. "I went up there yesterday looking for—oh, for a piece of hi—of that tree, I guess." She twisted one shoulder. "Dumb. It's gone now," she said desolately. She sniffled. Girl, she thought, you're losing your grip. You got twenty minutes with a fine, brand-new man and you're weeping on him.

He touched her arm. "Do you think this is from the big tree?" He was holding out a stick, smooth-barked and leafy.

Her heart turned over. She took the stick.

"It might be." The leaves. *Yes.* She sniffed it, her eyes closed. Something flopped in her belly like tumblers in a lock. "Oh, yes." Trembling, she turned to him. "Where—you think—"

"Sure." His face had transformed again. The brightness hidden in his deep dark face shone outward like a lantern uncovered. There was no mistaking the look in his eyes. "You keep it. I was going to use it to make a club. Ma*ybe*, ma*ybe* I will use a prybar instead. You keep it?"

She grinned happily, clutching the stick to her dress-front. Heat spread through her where it touched her hands, her breast, her throat. She felt like laughing. "Thanks. Hey, we better eat lunch or you're not going to get any." Without waiting for him, she turned and ran up the boardwalk.

He followed until she came to a chunk of broken brick wall. Alexander laid his hardhat with its brand-new netting on the wall and put her paper sack on the ground. They sat. She was so easy with him that he felt weak with unexpected relief.

"This is spring, then." With her he didn't feel that he was saying obvious things.

"Yep."

"In Freeport we don't have seasons like this. All the death and cold and silence."

She chewed her sandwich slowly. He remembered how she wept over a tree.

"And then." He gestured upward with both hands. "This! This springing up." He smiled. "I never knew the names of these plants. Thank you for introducing me."

Around her sandwich, she smiled back. "My pleasure. You go home a lot?"

Stay there.

"No. I am to stay here."

"Says who?"

"My granmère." He felt a sudden plunge of spirits. "She said it over and over. I haven't been home in five years." No point thinking about it, and he couldn't explain to Rae anyway. A movement on the sandbar across the river caught his eye.

Two small children were standing up on the gunwales of the world's oldest rowboat. They waved wildly.

"It's the twins. Mink and Ink." She raised her hand, the one with the sandwich in it. "Hey, kids!"

With hoots the twins leaped to their oars and pulled for shore.

"Oh, hell, now I've done it." She sighed sadly, looking at the last half of her sandwich and laid it down on the wall beside her. "For pete's sake, don't let them know you have an apple."

"They're so young," Alexander said, watching them row.

"They're nine."

The twins rowed the fifty yards across the river in less than five minutes. Alexander watched Rae's lips tighten and her hands move involuntarily as the children hurled themselves out of the boat into the shallows and beached it among the cattails.

"Your children?"

"Neighbor kids," she said. "Little gypsies."

Barefoot, each wore the muddy tatters of a man's tee shirt, wet to the armpits with river water. They lined up like two little soldiers before Rae. Dirt and bruises stood out on their white skin like splashes of paint.

Rae held out the remains of her sandwich. The children hesitated.

"Come on. Act civilized."

The taller child darted forward and snatched at the sandwich. They huddled over it, and, when they straightened, their mouths were full and their hands empty. Now they looked greedily at her Salvation Army sack.

"You'd think they starve," she grumbled. "All right, you can look in the bag. There's two shirts for you and a pair of shorts you'll have to fight over. And shoes you'll never wear."

The children plunged into the bag, hauling clothes and shoes out onto the ground and pawing through them.

"Alexander, meet Ink." The smaller child flashed him a glance. "And Mink." Mink looked him over, chewing. Rae said, "Cracker's kids, probably. No, Ink, that shirt's for Davy, it's too big for you." They fell back, and Rae knelt to fold the leftovers and bag them. "Kids, Alexander works across the road. You let him alone."

"He drives the—" Ink put his arms out in front of him and jerked giant levers back and forth, growling and scooping earth with his jaws.

"We waved," Mink said.

"Your hair is long," Ink said.

Alexander picked up his veiled hard hat and set it on his head with a flair, pulling the netting down.

Ink pointed.

"It's for the bugs. I don't want to eat them." Alexander peered solemnly through the veil.

Mink said, "We can make the bugs go away."

Alexander smiled. "I bet you can't." He looked at Rae. She clearly felt some responsibility for them. Like her they had an air of invulnerable assurance.

Mink aimed a backward kick of her heel at her brother. "We could. Not for free," she added. She copied exactly Rae's mysterious look, open and hidden, friendly and testing.

Alexander felt a shiver. "Suppose I pay you?" He turned his head from one child to the other. "What's the charge to lift a plague of gnats?"

The boy stared at the crescent wrench on his toolbelt.

"Payment in advance?" Alexander suggested.

Mink nodded.

He unclipped the wrench and held it forward on the palm of his hand. Ink took it with thin dirty fingers, so gingerly that it seemed to float away. The twins stepped back.

Alexander smiled down at them. "I'll be grateful for whatever you can do."

They ran off before he finished speaking.

He looked at his watch. "I suppose I must go back soon."

Rae made no move to get up, but sat back on the wall, propped on her hands, looking at him.

He studied her in return. Her face was as smooth, childish, and unreadable as the vagabond childrens'. He himself had grown up around witches. She didn't seem angry enough to be a witch, but he thought he recognized the wild power in her eyes.

"Aren't you afraid to live in this odd place?" he blurted.

Her glance flickered, but she said, "I've lived here all my life."

He didn't know how to tell her about that vulnerable trailer, so full of holes, and how afraid he was to sleep there.

As if in answer to this thought she said, "I guess I just learned to . . . I don't know . . . tune in."

"Tune in?"

"You know. Like a radio."

He licked his lips. "I don't have a radio. Some of the men, they work with music plugged in their ears. I have a hard enough time staying connected to this—" He hesitated. Looking around him he saw a dozen trees and flowers he now knew by name.

She smiled. "No, I mean you *are* a radio." Her gaze ran over him as if measuring the size of his radio, and he flushed. "I'm not explaining it right. I mean, I guess I just . . . listen."

"Listen," he repeated. He felt better, listening to her voice. It was full of messages, all of them friendly. "Explain some more? Please?" *Please keep talking. I'm not afraid when you talk.*

Her smile widened as if she were listening to his thoughts and not his words. "Well." She wriggled closer to him on the old brick wall and set her head against his shoulder, looking across the river. He held his breath and listened. "When I lie in bed at night I can listen to the river. We live real close. Sometimes it floods, so we listen carefully. The wind sounds different over cold water than it does over warm water, did you know that?"

He shook his head. Soft currents ran through her voice, warm and kind, then surprised, as if she were thinking all this for the first time.

"And the leaves rustle. And when the fish are jumping, you can hear that on a still night. Ducks. Seagulls, too. They come all the way inland from Lake Michigan and follow the river. I bet you know what they sound like."

"I'm from an island," he said. *Talk some more.* He thought about tuning in to her voice, and he felt that he knew what she meant. He became aware of a humming, very low, perhaps in his own bones. A reassuring sound. *The world is humming along all right. I can stop worrying.*

"Whenever I feel really confused, I go look at the river. Or I just . . . listen." She paused. "Makes a lot of sense, huh?"

They sat still, she with her head on his shoulder, he breathing carefully and listening.

"Do you know," he said with care, afraid to break the moment, "what it is like to feel tied hand, foot, and heart to one place on earth?"

She shifted against his arm. "Do I ever."

"No matter how far away you go? No matter how long away?"

"I wouldn't know. I've never left." She turned her face up to his. For this moment he felt the home cord loosen. There were freckles across her nose, and her eyes shone.

Through the trees, across the road at the construction site, the end-of-lunch whistle blew.

With a start, she jumped off the wall. "You gotta get back to work.

C'mon." He fumbled his lunchbox together as she slipped a hand through his elbow.

"Hey," she said, as they walked arm in arm toward the sound of traffic on US 31. "What say you come over for dinner tonight? I'll make you a turtle soup. Meet the folks." Her smile tipped at a merry angle. She swayed into him as if to remind him that he was a man.

He smiled back. "Sure." She had a mother. Maybe the mother, or this Erny, who was black, might be the witch. He couldn't imagine Rae letting him in for, what, anything too terrible.

"Here, take this to remind you." She held his crowfoot stick out to him. As he took it, he felt a tingle spread through his palm and up into his arm. They stood for a moment, smiling at each other at either end of the stick. Sending each other good vibrations, he thought. Straight up my arm into my heart.

Feeling self-conscious, he pulled it from her grasp and dropped it into his hammer loop.

"It's a date then," he said. He looked into the free pleasure in her eyes and laughed.

As they neared the site, Bob Bagoff's pickup truck screeched up beside them and honked.

Rae smiled. "Don't forget, six o'clock."

Alexander climbed into the truck. Bob hit the gas and roared away before he had the door shut.

"That's one of those people that lives in those shacks across the road," Bob said.

"Oh, yes. She say she will cook me a turtle tonight," Alexander drawled broadly, watching the boss sideways.

"Yeah, I, uh, noticed you were getting friendly. Uh, look, there's a company policy on this job that nobody talks to the neighbors. Y'know?"

Alexander chuckled. "Oh boss, her reputation is no good anyhow. Her momma got a black man already."

Bob hunched his neck. "Now, it ain't that. Fact is, it's lawyer business. Nothing to do with us—" He held up a hand. "Just—stay away from them. Til the legal stuff is ironed out."

Alexander was barely listening. He was still tuned in to Rae. He watched her sway her hips at him as she disappeared behind the trees by her trailer, and he felt that deep, reassuring hum in his bones.

Chapter Nine

By one o'clock the bucketloader bits were laid out on big tarps. From across the road, Cracker Coombs rubbernecked and drank beer. The beer was a present from Mr. Joe Stass. Mr. Stass was a talker. Cracker's head hurt.

Mr. Stass said, "Ever worry the river will flood you out?"

"Twice a year, regular." Likely more, and soon. Who knew what else might happen now? *The women must be having conniptions.*

Mr. Stass frowned. "My gosh, I hope you're insured against flood. Where would you be if all this just washed away one day? All that high water, that's dangerous, my friend."

Wonder if Raedawn knows what happened to the diggermachine over there. Cracker grunted. "True. 'Nother beer, Mr. Stass?"

"Don't mind if I do. Call me Joe. Let me tell you about a client of mine. Four kids, just like you. Lightning hit his place when he was out wor—out at a poker game, and burnt it right to the ground. Two of his little ones were inside. He was lucky. Doctor said plastic surgery'd make 'em all right, but he couldn't even pay for—pay for—" He stalled, lookng at their trailers. "Groceries," he finished lamely.

Cracker folded his beer can and tucked it away in the front breast pocket of his overalls.

Mr. Stass rallied. "Then the insurance came through. Half a million dollars, Mr. Coombs. Man's living in a palace now. The kids look great."

"Sounds like the happy ending," Cracker murmured. Free beer always cost you, though he was a master at shaving the price.

"It certainly was, Mr. Coombs. And all for a little forethought. Now, I have a policy tailormade for you." He produced a sheaf of papers. "Flood, fire, and termites, natural disaster thrown in free. Sixty-nine-ninety a year. Minute I get your first premium—take your check for five dollars this morning—you're covered. Safety, Mr. Coombs. Security, a happy future for less than seventy dollars: you won't find a deal like that anywhere else."

Cracker stuffed the papers into the pocket with the folded empties. "Beer, Mr. Stass? Don't guess I have five dollars on me at the moment but—why, hello, Henry!"

Henry Sodequist got out of his county stodgemobile, looking tight-lipped.

"Meet my friend, Mr. Joe Stass. Mr. Stass, Henry Sodequist, my good friend and poker buddy."

"This is a business call," Henry said in his official voice.

"Henry here's our county health inspector, Mr. Stass. Mr. Stass is gonna sell me some *insurance*," Cracker said, tickled. "Thinks we're liable to flood. Can you imagine?"

Mr. Stass gladhanded Henry. Henry shook like he was touching day-old fish.

"I've been telling Mr. Coombs we could insure him fully against fire, flood, and the wrath-a-God for five dollars down. Be a pity, I was just saying, if he couldn't get coverage started this very morning."

"That's the God's honest truth, Henry." Cracker peeled a fresh one off the second six and opened it. "Have a beer?"

Mr. Stass got pushy. "I must get back to town, Mr. Coombs. Can we do this deal?"

Cracker didn't like the look in Henry's eye. "I was hoping to talk to my neighbors. There's a good chance I can get that five dollars if Raedawn takes an interest."

"That's great!" Mr. Stass rustled papers. "Here's another copy. . . ." Mr. Stass trailed off.

Henry took the papers from Cracker and read them through with great deliberation.

Cracker drank beer. Mr. Stass stared in a fascinated manner at the workmen across the road.

"This looks legitimate," Henry grunted. He took his wallet out, produced a ten dollar bill, and handed it to Cracker.

"My word, that's decent of you, Henry. I'll talk to Raedawn first thing and pay you back 'fore the end of the week. If I don't take it off you at the firehouse."

Henry didn't say anything.

"Here y'are." Cracker turned to Mr. Stass. One second there was a sawbuck in his hand, the next, a pen. Magic.

"S'pose I can sign for Rae, too?" Cracker said. "Or maybe you can make change for a ten."

"Sure, you can sign for her. This is great!" Mr. Stass peeled off a carbonless copy for Cracker and pocketed the originals. "You won't regret it, Mr. Coombs. I'll phone you sometime, we'll have another beer."

"Don't have a phone," Cracker said.

"Ah. Well, yes. I'll be in touch very soon." Mr. Stass stuck out his hand to Cracker again.

"Pleasure," Cracker said, and put a cold Style in the outstretched hand. Mr. Stass moved off toward his car with the beer in his hand and the air of a man who thinks he has a rip in his pants but doesn't want to get caught feeling for it.

"Now there goes a big-hearted guy," Cracker remarked. "Fancy him thinking we might flood!" He chuckled. "Every year, twice a year. Like taking candy from a baby. Beer, Henry?"

"No."

"And thanks again for the loan in need."

"Don't mention it." Henry sniffed. "There's been another complaint lodged against your property."

"Oh?" Cracker's luck was asleep today. First an insurance salesman, now Henry countying up on him.

"This time it's serious. You're accused of using river water for domestic purposes. You're accused of improper disposal of septic waste. You're accused of housing children under your protection in an unheated building without running water or proper sanitation. You burn wood and coal without ventilation." Henry's voice wound up tighter. "Are you listening to me?"

Cracker held his beer can to his ear. "Fizzy as hell. Good beer that guy brought me."

"Your luck's run out. You can't expect me to look the other way forever." He glared at Cracker. Cracker waited. Henry squished patterns with his Hush Puppies in the muddy gravel. "If typhoid doesn't kill you people, fire or flood will."

"Who filed the complaint?"

Henry burst out, "Goddammit, what does it matter who filed the complaint? Your time's running out! I can guarantee it was pushed through by somebody in Berne."

Cracker remembered Gelia stomping home yesterday with a load of wet laundry, mad, her luck gone sour. Sour luck or sweet, it looked to him as if their protection was gone for sure.

"You've made a lot of people sick of your behavior—not just you, Cracker, but all of you. Look at yourself. You're drunk at nine o'clock. You haven't shaved in a month. The state could swoop in any minute and clear you out!"

"How long we known each other, Henry?"

"You can't trade on that forever! I'm here to tell you!"

With relief, Cracker saw Willy and Davy, grinning and muddy, come running toward them from the Rimville end of US 31. Willy was the real boss of the family. Willy wouldn't take much crap from Henry. He loped ahead of the half-wit. "Ahoy!"

"Ahoy yesself," Cracker said. "'Tcha got, Davyboy?"

Davy shambled up, his fisherman's bucket jerking heavily in his grip.

"Show him, Davy," Willy said.

Davy opened the lid. The bucket was full of frogs, not the young frogs of spring but fat, slick, green-and-yellow bullfrogs. They stood on each other's heads like commuters on a train, ignoring each other. "I caught dinner for everybody," he announced.

Cracker peeked. "Mmm-*mm*. Look at the size of the buggers."

"They're ever-so-big. We was down at Water Willow in the rushers there, and there's *millions*. We caught 'em with our hands." Davy lifted his long-fingered hands. They were grimy to the elbows and covered with small red cuts.

"What happened here?" Cracker touched the cold, sweating side of his beer can to the cuts.

Davy looked. "Oh, that's from the rushers. They're sharp."

Cracker grunted. "Soap 'em good sometime before Christmas."

"Okay. Who's that?" Davy stuck his chin out at Henry.

Cracker pulled Henry forward. "Shake hands with my nephews, Henry. You met Davy when he was a hell of a lot shorter, I reckon. This here's Willy."

Willy looked Henry in the eye. "Problem, Cracker?" he said.

"He's been getting himself worried about us," Cracker said.

Davy slammed the bucket lid. "We take care of ourselves."

"Well, I thought so, but Henry here thinks we're gonna go down to fire, flood, and typhoid. All the mud on your faces, he'll think you been eating it, ain't that right, Henry?"

Willy stood back, listening and rubbing the mud off his hands onto the seat of his cutoffs.

Davy said scornfully, "I know enough not to eat frogs til they're cooked. We can have a frog-fry by the willows tonight."

"I ain't going to clean all them frogs," Cracker warned.

"I can clean frogs. I help every time."

Henry spoke slowly to Davy. "You should stay away from those willows, son. The mud is like quicksand over there. Aren't you afraid the river will get you?"

Davy hunched. "Aw, Mom and Dad always say that."

Cracker stiffened. It was just like Davy to do this to him in front of the County.

Henry said carefully, "Your parents died, Davy."

Davy jerked his face as if shaking off a fly. "Fat chance."

In front of the County, goddammit.

Davy whined, "All the time now it's fuss fuss fuss. Change is a-coming, Davy, make sure Cracker knows. We be seeing you again soon, Davy. River gonna get you, blah blah blah."

The skin crawled on the back of Cracker's neck. He felt himself swelling up hot. "Now, David, you're getting me mad—don't you tell me—" he began.

Henry watched.

As patiently as he could, Cracker started over. "Just a darned minute. Seems there's everybody dead or alive's giving me advice this morning. Think I don't look out for you! I get all the advice I need on that score from Erny and Gelia, thank you very much. Goddammit!" he added, half to himself, "What right do those lazy good-for-nothing people have to dump a house full of childern on me?" Angrily he hurled away his half-full beer can. It smacked against a tree. Davy cringed. "And then get around behind my back, telling my boys I got no sense of responsibility? How come I got to do all the taking care of around here? Don't I get to be took care of?" His face grew hotter. He stood rigid, arms pressed at his sides and the beers hanging from his fist, leaning over the boy.

He raised his voice. Water squeezed from his eyes. "Where are they when I got four sick kids on my hands? Where are they? When the state comes down on my back for not being a millionaire? Huh?" he shrieked. "What are they gonna do about it?"

Slowly, Willy moved between Cracker and Davy, so close Cracker could feel him like a cool spot on his chest. Cracker paused to breathe.

In a perfectly calm voice, Willy said, "Cracker, can Davy and I have a frog-fry by the willows tonight?"

Cracker rocked on the balls of his feet, clutching the broken sixpack to his side, and stared across the river at the stand of willows on the sandbar. *Damn them.*

"I suppose so," he said. "Mind, you and your brother be careful with the knife." He ignored the wetness on his face.

"We will."

Davy picked up his pail, his eyes still fixed on Cracker's face, and Willy led him off by the hand.

Henry cleared his throat.

Cracker turned, snarling. "Yeah, you said your piece! G'wan home."

Henry swallowed. "I, uh, was just going to say."

"Well?" Cracker said savagely.

"You going to drink all that beer yourself?"

Cracker looked down at the leftovers. "Don't believe so." He peeled one off and handed it over. They drank in silence, watching a new baby bucketloader crawl off the back of a flatbed tow truck.

"Weird spring," Henry said.

"The weirdest."

Chapter Ten

Fourteen-year-old Rae fought with her mother every day. They moved around the tiny trailer, full of hatred, bristling like cats when its smallness forced them too close together. The trailer door kept opening and shutting: Cracker trying to come in, Gelia chasing him out. Sometimes Gelia let him stay, and Rae hid in her bedroom or lurked in the hallway, troubled, listening while they rolled on the couch and made dreadful fighting sounds. Cracker always left before dawn, and Rae would wake to find herself tangled sweatily in her own bedclothes, hearing him whistle his way back to the Gowdy trailer while her mother snored in the front room. Then back to the catfight next day.

Angry child, her mother finally hissed at her, Go cross the road and get out of my hair.

So, finally, she crossed the road.

Gelia wouldn't talk to her for days afterward. There was a long period of floating, going hungry because Gelia and Cracker ate up all the food, not knowing why she felt so hollow, or why she felt only half-afraid when she knew, she knew the world was coming to an end. Probably it already ended and she was dead, they were all dead, and they didn't even notice. She tried to ask Gelia about it, but her mother wouldn't talk. Just a phase, Gelia said. Sex and death and teenagers. You're screwed up. It's normal. Go cross the road.

Across the road, she walked on the tops of the trees that climbed the ridge. It was exhilarating but scary. The topmost twigs bent under her feet. Her new friend was inside her somehow. He kept saying without words that she was safe with him. She could feel him enter at her bleeding-place, branching and forking all up inside her, trying to follow a channel she hadn't known she had.

He didn't seem to know she was smaller than he was.

She twisted, struggling, but there was no escape, he was already here. He forced light into her eyes. She fled before him, taking wing, but no matter how long she flew he was always there waiting to catch her. There was a rope attached to her belly button, and sooner or later she came to the end of it, and he would catch her by it. This puzzled her as much as it terrified her.

How come the rope worked for him and not for her? He could climb it and follow it

47

and pull her back into her body by it, but she was tied to her body like a dog and she couldn't make sense of what he was doing to her.

He started to tell her things, show her pictures, name things not in words but in shapes, feelings, tastes. He touched her skin, touched her mind, he made a picture, more pictures.

I don't understand, she said, but eventually she did, kinda. Trapped like a dog chained up in a dirt yard, finally, she held still and let him train her.

At dawn she would climb down and limp back home to her trailer. She threw herself on the bed, feeling feather-light and unsettled, floating until her tummy turned upside down. Her skin pulsed. The pulse began deep inside her and rushed toward her skin, rushed out even beyond it, so that her skin expanded a good foot all over with every beat of her heart and then shrank just as quickly. Who am I? Her heart thundered through her body. Gimme, gimme, gimme, it said. Give. And she expanded hugely. Me. She shrank dizzyingly fast, pulsing, swelling, shrinking; it was nauseating.

She lay utterly still, just as when she lay in his grasp. Her heart beat like a hammer. Still not safe. Beat. Her skin blew itself up like a giant invisible balloon. Beat. Her skin passed right through the walls of the trailer until it touched the rainy night sky. Beat. Her skin fell in on itself, shrank and grew cold. Beat. The stiller she lay, the slower her heart beat.

Chapter Eleven

K ing spent the day sulking around the upper town, avoiding a second
visit to his old trailer. He didn't feel up to meeting Cracker or his
brothers yet. By sunset he knew he was also avoiding Rae. It
seemed madness to get anywhere within her compass.

He was getting hungry. He risked walking over to Route 64, bought a
hamburger, and carried it down to the river. The best times of his childhood were buried among these willows and box elder trees leaning out
over the Fox. King set his elbows on the balustrade on the south side of
the Route 64 bridge, his hamburger paper fluttering on a cold April
breeze, and marked the changes, one by one.

The bridge wept red rust from a million specks of iron embedded in
the concrete. Six cast-iron foxes still crouched there, each with one paw
lifted, glaring out at the water while six plumes of red rust streaked down
the balustrades below them. King eyed the foxes fondly. He thought the
long streaks of rust looked ugly, but he loved the single-minded force of
the sculptures, how they stood twisted on their balustrade, their heads and
tails at the same angle, as if snapping at fleas in unison.

He saw new neon in the window of Varlet's tavern but the same old
window seat looking out on the rapids below the bridge, the same crumbling stairway leading to Varlet's personal fishing platform, the same pillar
of old tires for sitting on.

Wonder if the footbridge is still up. He shuffled farther along the Route 64
bridge till it came into sight, a low-bottomed bridge straddling the river.
He sighed with relief. Stepping over the DANGER KEEP OUT sign swinging
rustily on its chain, he picked his way down Varlet's stairway to the fishing
platform.

Feeling childish, he hopped stepping stones along the bank to where
the footbridge sat low over the rushing water. Mulberry trees hid its

49

entrance. He ducked under their branches, already heavy with berries and early leaf. Nobody had closed up the hole in the bridge's safety fence where the links had been curled back by children's hands. He put his knees through the hole and dangled his feet, resting his hands and chin on the rusty truss.

The safety fence was as old as the bridge. Gelia used to say it was put up to keep girls from throwing their bundles into the deep spot. She should know. Such girls had been her personal friends, in her day. Years later they pointed out Gelia as a warning to their own daughters and took them to the hospital in Rimville for D&C. Kept the population down. That was Gelia's story anyway. Gelia could justify her ways by the moon.

There had to be some kind of reason. Why should his family be so piss-poor? Did they have to be weird? How well had he survived them, that he could come home all grown and wealthy, a man with a trade and a bank account, and tremble when he looked again on their private places?

King dangled his legs over the Fox and licked hamburger grease from his lips. Rae had never minded the dirt, not when she had more important things to do.

He hated dirt. The windows sat open except in the coldest weather. River air, foggy, fishy, acrid with factory wastes in some years, fresh with algae in others, came in by the windows and soaked into his clothes, his pillow and sheets, his shoes. Fried-fish smell mixed with mildew. Baby vomit and mildew. Mud, sweaty clothes, coffee brewed with chickory, stale beer, and mildew. It hadn't bothered him so much when he was little.

His mother had kept the place cleaner, or so he remembered. His father painted the outside of the trailer. A bitter anger rose up between King and those times, guarding the memories.

King sighed. Grief hung over his shoulder. He hunched and shook himself. A leaf stirred by his ear. A mulberry bounced off the back of his hand and dove for the water, plooping and bobbing, one purple eye like a fly's eye reflecting the sky on each of its shiny miniature beads.

The years he could remember, he didn't want to. There was a long floating time that began when he was thirteen. Uncle Cracker, who had come for a week to visit, stayed, immediately moving from the sofa into his parents' room as if he knew they weren't coming back, and sharing it with young women who didn't mind his drinking, his oily smell of death, his uneven temper. King waited with savage satisfaction for these girls to find out about Cracker. The girls always left, crying angrily against Cracker and taking with them whatever money was in the house. They didn't see King at all.

One of Cracker's girls carried in Mink and Ink, then nameless twin babies, and forgot to carry them out with her. Cracker tried to get Gelia Somershoe to take them, but Gelia was too busy. Her trailer was overfull of men and had no room for babies. King nursed the twins on hush-puppies and Coke. Cracker fed them hamburgers and beer. Half-wit Davy took to them like a hen adopting ducklings.

Within two years they were bossing Davy, speaking their private language, grooming him and cuffing him and sending everyone but him away from their private games. King remembered a funny notion he'd had that the twins had stolen Davy's mind and given him their bodily growth in its place.

When they were four, Mink and Ink bullied Davy into building them their own shack and lowering the old iron smokehouse stove into the pit inside. Once the door was hung and shut, they seceded from the family.

Should have done that myself, King thought. But he had lacked their toughness, their self-reliance. He never gave up craving his parents. Shamelessly, he wheedled care out of everybody: schoolteachers, the haughty health department nurses, even Cracker when he was in good humor, and especially Gelia Somershoe.

In her wayward way, Gelia had mothered King. It was one of her favorite games of pretend. She'd kept his clothes patched, and she fed him when he couldn't stand the yelling going on in his own trailer. She took him to her bed when he was twelve. She made him feel like he could grow up. King wasn't scared of her. When she lost interest in him she handed him over to her daughter, Rae, until the next time she might notice him.

It was Rae who scared him.

The powers he trusted in Gelia were too big to fit into Rae. Her thistledown hair stuck out from her head. Her eyes were too big and quick for her size. Her soft voice cut through him and commanded him. Something odd had happened to Raedawn when she was about fourteen: all the energy stirring around this place had seemed to fasten onto her, had built her up into something explosive, bright, and hungry. Rae took what King had learned of sex and shattered it into something twice its original size.

Years later King had recognized Gelia as the child and Raedawn the adult. Gelia dried his tears and invited him into her trailer for sex and supper, but Rae cooked the supper. Gelia would mend his ripped jeans, but it was Rae who went to the Salvation Army and brought home clothes for everyone. Rae got a waitress job when she was fourteen. Aside from Erny's pension, Rae brought in all the cash money they ever saw on the riverbank. Gelia's powers were harmless to King because she wasn't grown up.

Rae always knew what she was doing. Enough to scare anybody.

Dusk fell. The river gathered moisture out of its body and breathed on him. He had fallen into cool dreaming, watching coils of mist rise off the water, when a footfall rang on the bridge behind him.

"King?"

Rae. He couldn't answer. His body tightened and softened and heated up all over. "Here." He was thankful for the dark.

Her hand fell on his shoulder. "Move over?" she said.

"Sure."

There wasn't really room for two. King squeezed to one side and let her crouch and stick her legs through the hole beside him. They touched at knee, thigh, hip, and shoulder. Through her clothes and his clothes, she scorched his flesh.

"Good grief, Raedawn," he said before he could think, "why don't you just crawl into my shorts?"

She arranged herself clear of the cruel raw ends of the chain-links crowding them together. "In a minute. We ought to talk, King," she said seriously. They lay down side by side on their backs and looked at each other. Her eyes were still too big for her face. She still looked worried.

He swallowed. "So what's going on?"

She sighed. "Well." She turned her face toward the sky. "Davy's out of school two years now. Willy graduates next year. Gelia and I are teaching the twins to read."

He bit back the accusations he had already thrown at Gelia, and growled, "If you'd teach 'em to wear shoes it'd be a help."

"Gelia's pretty steady with Erny."

King grunted. "So she's given up rampaging? She was going good with the medical students at the clinic 'fore I left."

"She's slowed down anyway." Rae changed the subject again. "Your brother Willy's in the band. He practiced on the riverbank all summer long last year. He plays trumpet."

Headlights swung by across the river, blinding them for a moment, turning the river mist to silver.

"Glad Willy's having some fun," he said awkwardly. He hesitated. "Rae."

"I'm here."

"Can I—you think—how's Willy been making out with Cracker? And Davy and the kids."

Mulberry leaves cast shadows over her face. "So-so."

"So? And?" Oh, Christ, he thought, what disaster now? The wait was torture. "Well," she said finally. "He's doing better than you could have done."

King's heart stopped and started on a two-step. He blinked. He supposed, since he had been ready for a blow, that he would have felt one no matter what she said. "That all?"

It occurred to him that Rae would have taken Willy to bed by now. Nobody stayed a virgin on the river. For a dreadful moment he felt jealous of his brother. His heart tittupped again.

She put a hand out and covered his with it. Her palm was all over callouses. "I'm glad you've come home just now."

He rushed out, "Rae, I don't think I can marry you."

For a long moment she blinked. Then, to his intense relief, she laughed. "Oh! Is that so?"

She laughed so hard that she had to sit up. She slapped her knees, flopped back on the wooden bridge, shaking and holding her belly. King smiled tentatively. Her eyes were half closed. She rolled her head on the boards, chuckling. She seemed to be searching for words, and King braced himself for a Somershoe woman's retort.

"That's all right," she said in a mild voice, "I wasn't waiting for you." He waited, still braced. Her face became serious. "King, I'm twenty-four." She put her hand on his elbow and shook it. "Will you relax? What's the matter with you, you're jumpy as a cat."

He laughed uncertainly. "Oh, lord, Rae, I'm all tired out." He rubbed his hand over his face. "Coming home is harder than leaving, I swear."

"I wouldn't know."

That was right, she wouldn't. King thought of her working out her life, trudging up the hill to dirt-pay jobs in Salvation Army dresses and the scorn of two towns, trudging back down to the filth and craziness. If he could save her. Not marriage maybe, but escape. Take her away from here. Set her free.

But the words stuck in his throat. In the silence she put her hand on his fly.

He flipped over into a half-regulation push-up, his hands on either side of her head, his knees straddling her on the old wooden boards. He felt powerful. Rae looked up at him with wide eyes. Beware, beware, his memory sang. She's putting the magic on you. He smiled. He was coming home.

"King Gowdy," she said throatily, "I realize I got to give up all hope of marrying you."

He flushed and didn't speak.

"But does that mean you're never gonna give me the sweet stroke again?"

It was funny, she didn't scare him this time. At first he supposed it was because of his new years, some experience. He enjoyed showing her that. They heaved and wrestled and dropped suddenly into slow motion. He entered her once, twice. It was all somehow grown up. He had never felt her equal before.

"Nice to see you again," she said at one point, and they grinned at each other.

And then he knew she was holding back. Rae had grown up, too, he realized. She was learning self-restraint.

It made him want to cry.

She let him lead. He lifted her with his grown man's strength, and they danced on the footbridge, her toes dangling an inch above his. The river warmed and the April air cooled. The cold mist coiled off the water and fell back as dew. They made a pair of sweaty angel-prints on the wood.

As he squinted through the truss overhead, trying to see the stars, King's impulse came back.

"No kidding, Raedawn, come away with me? This place is no good for you."

She sighed. He reached out and put his palm on her breast. Her flesh was cool to his touch, but under it her heart pounded.

"Rae," he said. He felt her heartbeat with the inside of his middle finger. He had a sudden scheme. He would listen to that pulse, never take his finger off it. It would tell him the truth of her heart, whatever she might say.

She looked at him, not lifting her head. "I'm sorry." She sounded sorry, and grown up, too.

"Davy's past help. The river takes care of him. The ravens feed Cracker. Willy will leave soon," he lied. He hoped Willy wouldn't. Seemed like less of a sin to leave things on Willy's shoulders. "Gelia can mind the twins." He was trembling.

She smiled. "Those damn kids are gypsies."

"The more reason. They can look after Gelia."

That got a belly laugh out of her. "Oh, lord." She burst out laughing again, and kept laughing until she had to wipe her eyes. "It's not that simple. This is a troublesome time. I need you around for—for a while. Okay?"

Beware, beware. King swallowed. "For a while. I can't stay," he pleaded.

"I know." She sounded kind, careful, unrefusable. She could make him do anything.

Feeling somehow less vulnerable in the face of that ancient strength, he committed himself, one adult to another. "Two weeks?"

To his surprise, she agreed. "That'll be plenty."

Chapter Twelve

At six that night Bob Bagoff drove away, having fetched Alexander's property from the Berne YMCA. With mutiny in his heart, Alexander watched him go. He'd worked for Bob for five years. By now he ought to be used to Bob's micromanaging, his casual racism, and his bad manners.

What if he crossed over to Rae's for dinner after all? Crack, he'd be out of a job. If Gran wouldn't let him come home before, she'd certain-sure show him the door if he came home jobless.

So, then, stay here in the north. His heart cried out at the thought.

If he lost his job, Rae would comfort him.

He looked longingly out of the office window at the lights glowing yellow through the young trees in front of her house. A steady stream of low-flying crows stitched a dotted line in the darkening sky as if showing him the way. Maybe if he left the light on in the office. Hang a towel over the window, too. That would make Bob, perhaps driving by, think he had covered it for modesty.

Rae understood this crazy place. She might know what he had to fear.

Darkness fell. Alexander hung the towel over the window and left, locking up behind him. From twenty feet away the light showed around the towel. A good-enough lie, unless Bob actually went inside. Alexander stepped over the railroad tracks, feeling as he did so that he was crossing into another country.

Her house was all lit up. The inner door was open. Voices sounded through the screen door. His first visit in someone's actual home in the north. He drew a long breath and knocked.

A smiling, sharp-eyed, brown-skinned man came to the door. "You must be Mr. Caebeau, I'm Ernest Brown, come in, come in," he said, talking and opening the door and holding out his hand all at the same time.

Alexander sweated. "I'm terribly sorry, Mr. Brown, but I can't—I don't think I can come in. May I—may I speak to Rae?" Good smells came from the open door. His heart twisted. The first homecooked meal he'd been offered in five years. It took all his resolution to stand on the stoop and not tumble inside like a schoolboy.

Ernest Brown looked at him keenly and then stepped outside, shooing Alexander off the stoop. "Raedawn," he called over his shoulder. "Come outside."

"In a minute!" she sang out from the midst of the light and voices and cooking smells.

"Well," Ernest Brown said, and shut the screen door. Standing on the stoop above Alexander, he could put his hand on Alexander's shoulder. "Let me see you, son."

Alexander let the older man turn him so his face was in the light from the screen door. Now he felt foolish. What could Bob do? The way he had worked on Alexander to take over the night security, that meant secrets, and secrets meant Bob was vulnerable.

"What's the trouble?"

Alexander drew a deep breath. "My boss, he ordered me to stay away from here. And he is making me sleep in the office trailer at night. He says we must have a night watchman. Because of the bucketloader that was hurt."

He needed this. He needed to sit at a real table and feel not-exiled for just one evening.

Ernest Brown kept his hold on Alexander's shoulder. Slowly he looked him up and down, down and up again, nodding to himself. "That's a pity. Raedawn made a turtle soup."

Alexander almost moaned. "I must beg her pardon. Wish I could stay," he said. He wished even more that he could explain why he was so afraid to sleep in the office trailer tonight.

Still nodding, Ernest Brown touched him in the center of the forehead. "Don't worry, son. A Somershoe woman never did any man a bit of harm."

So calm and certain did he sound that Alexander felt peace radiate from that touch.

"Erny?" Rae said from inside the screen door.

Ernest Brown started. "I'll just go check on the bread."

He and Rae exchanged places in the doorway, and Rae leaned out, smiling, looking puzzled.

"Alexander?" She wore a dress that scooped deeply in front. His pulse jumped.

He came to the edge of the stoop and stood, unwilling even to set foot higher lest he throw his job away and step up into her arms.

"My boss won't let me come here," he said again, feeling more like a coward or a fool.

He turned his face up to her. It seemed the lamplight behind her shone through her, for her smile was clearly visible, and the light in her eyes warmed him like the sun. "I beg your pardon," he said. "Wish I could stay."

Her smile turned mischievous. "Maybe I'll come over with your supper."

He licked his lips. No man on this earth should be asked to say no to such a woman. "Better not." He pleaded, "I could lose my job."

She tilted her head. "There's gotta be a way around this guy. Maybe I'll run into you at lunchtime tomorrow. If you're down by the river again. Or up on the ridge? There's a nice path along the ridge, couple of logs to sit on and eat your lunch, you can see right down the hill but nobody can see up it 'cause the trees are leafing so early."

She lowered her voice and added, "I know all the secret places up there." She leaned toward him, and her breasts glowed in the top of her dress.

Alexander foresaw a long, lonely night between him and his cock. "Thank you." He backed up a step. "Thank you."

"Wait, I'll walk you home."

She didn't wait for his protest but flashed away into the house. When she came back she had her red sweatshirt on. It still didn't cover the front of her dress. She took his hand, sending pleasurable shocks through him, and led him off into the darkness between the trailers, not toward US 31 at all but along the river.

"I shouldn't have thrown the whole family at you," she said, as if thinking aloud.

She must think he was a coward. "You feed them all?"

"And clothe 'em. And pay the taxes." They walked slowly, she leading, he feeling an impractical desire to hide under her dress. "How about you?

You go home often?"

"No."

In silence she swung against him, step by step. "Sounds bad."

He didn't answer that. "My home is like yours, full of relatives. Everyone talking. Everyone eating." He thought wistfully of turtle soup. "Funny thing, I got this big here in the north." He held up a pinky finger. "I was skin and bone at home."

"Hang-ga-burgers," Rae said in a wise voice. "They'll bulk you up."

He fought back homesickness. "I have two brothers. My granm—my grandmother raised us. Robert is a concierge at a very good hotel. Malcolm works in the public gardens in Freeport."

"She get you your job?"

He shook his head. "My uncle. Well, it might have been her, too. Everyone does what granmère tells them."

Rae took his hand. "You miss her."

His throat tightened. "I worked for Bob in Freeport. He offered me work in the States. She said, Go," he said desolately. "I'm here."

"She's the boss. Huh. Must be nice to have somebody you can count on." Rae swung in front of him suddenly and he stopped, fearing to fall on top of her and nail her to the ground with the red-hot spike in his groin. She put her hand up and fingered one of his dreads. "She fix your hair like this?"

He snorted. "She would box my ears." He took the excuse to reach up and touch her hand where she touched his hair. "These used to be braids. But it is too much trouble," he lied, "to find a place in every new town. And it takes all day. This is easier." Someday he would go home all nappy and wild-looking and granmère would grieve, and repent maybe.

Not she. She wouldn't even speak to him on the phone.

"Maybe your grandma looked for a better future for you," Rae said in an envious voice. "My ma is just plain crazy."

"Maybe granmère is crazy, too." She would skin him if she knew he'd said that. Alexander laughed a little. "If she is crazy then I am doomed. She—she made me. She always said I was born for greatness. She made me leave home."

"I'll never leave home," Rae said in a tone he couldn't read. She turned her pale face up to him in the dimness under the trees. "Sorry I'm so gloomy. I've been feeling like the end of the world since yesterday. You know how it feels. When a," she hesitated, "a love affair is over."

Rae felt a charge building up between them and marvelled at his restraint. Most men didn't hold back from her unless she scared them. Must come from being lonesome. He wanted to go home so bad, but he didn't. "Erny says you got something on your mind."

Headlights across the river caught the whites of Alexander's eyes. "I have to sleep there. That bucketloader—no two pieces were left together. What will happen tonight?"

"Oh." Now she saw. He was afraid. A feeling like sex grabbed her between the legs, and she felt like wrapping them around him so he'd be safe. "It's okay. I mean, you're okay."

His hand tightened around hers. "I hope so."

The truth was impossible, how personal her disaster was. She stroked his hand helplessly. "Can you think about something if you don't know the words for it?"

"I used to. When I was a child." He sounded so homesick.

Frustrated tears stung her eyes. Had Gelia put the silence on her this strong? Maybe it was just the nature of him who had died, who said so much to her without any words at all.

As if he'd heard, he said, "Sometimes words get in the way."

They looked at each other. Rae felt like a giantess, broken in half. This guy thought he was seeing all of her. Maybe this was all she would ever be now. She lifted her hand.

"Here, this is what I mean. I saw this magazine article once about taking pictures of your invisible parts." That sounded goofy, even to her. "This guy took a picture of a leaf. It had all these invisible colors shooting out of it. Only you could see them because of the kind of camera he used." She curled her fingers. "And then he cut the leaf in half."

Alexander studied her hand seriously. He put his own hand up, stepped closer. He smelled rich and strong and a little bit scared.

"Then he took a picture of one half of the leaf." Her fingers uncurled. "The colors were still there, the whole leaf."

Alexander put his palm against her palm. A spark leaped across the gap. For an instant she felt huge and whole again. A column of sparks flew up her middle. There was no way on earth to tell him, but she could show him.

CR

Alexander put his hands out at his sides to stop himself from seizing her. She was so sure. Her palm was rough as sandpaper on the back of his neck. Slowly he bent into her kiss and gathered her up, feeling sizzling and buoyant as if he had plunged feet first into the Caribbean and then bounced up with treasure in his mouth.

She wrapped her legs around his waist. He shuffled back, seeking a tree to lean against. Her kiss was huge. It sank into his body through his mouth and shone like moonlight on shapes inside him, showing him just how they fit together, he and she. Here, a tree, found with his eyes shut. He leaned against it where it tilted toward the water and she leaned against him and he felt sex run off his body like sweat and drip into the river. *Show me*, he thought.

And she did. *Tune in*, she said yesterday. *You are a radio.* She opened up inside and showed him, pressing her open places to his to coax him open, too. Listen, she said, and he listened for all he was worth. They shook the new leaves off the tree with their vigor.

Rae felt like she was breathing for the first time in two days. She fucked him against the tree until she heard it crack, and all he said was, *More.* Maybe she'd been so lonely for the sound of that silenced voice that she heard it everywhere. Alexander's was quieter. His two big hands lifted her up and down more gently. Without words, she told him what she wanted, and without words he lifted her higher and then lay her on her back on the ground.

Oh God, this was perfect, this was what she missed. His big body covered her, every inch, and then he slid his cock into her again and she could almost imagine it was like before. But Alexander let her breathe. He kept his shoulder off her face. He drove slowly into her, waiting for her to push.

Impatient, she slapped her arms onto the packed mud beside her, and her hands sank in to the wrists, groping for the power line, pulling it up, feeding it to him through the center of her body.

And still he didn't pull back. Wow.

Alexander felt every nerve wake up, as if she'd found the *on* switch in him. He stopped pumping into her and pressed down, feeling her pussy clench around him, shutting his eyes against the flare of intermittent headlights across the river, smelling the sex and mud on her skin, sinking into her. Orgasm pulled at him as if he were taking root inside her, but he couldn't pull away. He could only go deeper.

She was perfectly right. There was no fear. He listened, and the signal was so loud, it drowned out everything else.

Chapter Thirteen

L ate that night, in his hole-in-the-mud on the riverbank, Ink lay curled against his sister, listening to the water suck at the clay walls of their house.

Their house was deep in a hole in the riverbank, seven feet deep and cone shaped, a little wider at the bottom than at the top. Makeshift wooden walls enclosed it around the top, more to keep the people from falling into their house than to hide it. At night, the hole was pitch black inside. Ink put out his hand in the darkness and felt the slick mud wall, clammy to his touch. The river was staying outside.

Yesterday he and Mink had watched the big tree come down across the road, the small branches shattering, while crows whirled and wailed overhead as if at one of their funerals.

Silently he climbed the rope ladder in the dark, creaked open the shack door at the top and shut it gently, leaving his sister asleep on the clay floor below.

He threaded his way through the trailers and the alders, across the railroad tracks, across the road, until his hard-soled bare feet stood in tire ruts at the edge of the construction site. A white trailer stood where the big tree used to be.

He looked up. His jaw dropped.

Silhouetted against the clouds, clustered like enormous black fruits or leaves, some two hundred crows slept on nothing.

Ink goggled at them.

They just slept there. Counting them, he connected the dots, tracing the outline of a huge arc, a sphere in the air like a book-picture of a human brain Rae had once shown him. Crows asleep. On a tree that wasn't there.

He snatched up a pebble at his feet and hurled it into the cloud of sleeping crows.

His pebble connected, and a bird let out a single squawk. The whole flock lifted as one, voiceless, and the air filled with the beat of their wings. They flew like pigeons in tight formation, circling the space where they had slept, spiralling slowly upward, and Ink felt rather than saw the moment when their grip on the dream let go and the whole thing splashed invisibly to the ground, sending ripples that chased Ink back across the road. On the far side of the railroad track he turned. The crows' dream rippled toward him, knocking over the lightpole next to the white trailer. A passing truck rumbled by.

At the sound, the flock scattered. The sleeping crows sped away into the darkness every which way.

Ink ran across the road, swarmed headfirst down the rope ladder, and burrowed trembling against his sister with his face against the cindery clay floor.

Alexander dreamed he was a tree.

The cot provided by Bob and Ike was much too short. Alexander lay awake trying to find comfort, and then, with relief, he felt his awareness breaking up at last, the knotted muscles in his calves and shoulders easing. He sighed. His long legs slipped off the cot. When his right foot touched the cold floor, he barely felt it. Already he was blissfully deep, listening to a faraway organ booming out a pair of notes. First one note seemed louder, then the other, and as they exchanged volume they altered in pitch, drawing apart and then crossing paths, setting up vibrations under his skin.

Trees have it good, he thought. How orderly their systems are. This ring draws moisture up, this ring passes it down, transformed by light into all the good things a body needs. Plenty of companionship—why, all the trees around were talking, commenting on the organ music, drinking noisily from the moist ground, observing spring on the river with connoisseurs' seventy- and hundred-year-old appreciation. And so much to hear! A billion night creatures moved about, twittering, their single-minded urges transmitted into his veins, rushing unbelievably slowly from one end of his trunk to the other. Never had he had such a high, not since the first ganja his cousin gave him to smoke, ten years old and crazy with it.

His limbs melted on the cot. He forgot to pull the blanket up. His right foot, touching the floor of the trailer, picked up the faint music. Two great organ notes, one cool and pure, that pulled the blood in his body from one end to the other. The other was deeper, hoarse, and stroked his body, it seemed, from the inside, making every cell fizz, making the tiny hairs quiver, making the marrow in his bones want to stand up and fuck.

He understood now why trees didn't talk to people. They were high all the time, listening to this music. It broke him in pieces. His deep roots felt it and began their noisy sucking up of water. Tiny racing tones passed with mind-shattering slowness up his length. His long sharp-nailed extremities trembled like plucked guitar strings, dividing over and over into a net, a net spread to catch the music where it floated in the air.

Every creature on the riverbank felt it. Crickets rubbed their legs together. Rabbits humped muskily in the grass. Snakes braided themselves in pairs and owls did the two-backs. He could hear it all. He could feel it all. He was too far gone or he would have laughed out loud. There was no time to laugh. When it seemed he would come apart under the pressure of ceaseless pleasure, perhaps die, fused into this new posture, he realized the music was fading. He cried out against it, and half the night creatures cried with him, but still more began to sing. They couldn't bear the louder frequencies but waited all day and half the night before coming out of their burrows and hives to praise music too faint for him to hear: cool tones, pure and unbearably hollow, drawing his life from one end to the other and back in a slow, steady pulse.

He lay frozen in that position for several minutes, losing the music, feeling the joy fade. Finally he woke up enough to discover that his right leg was numb from the knee down and his left leg was intolerably stiff. He rolled over and slept again.

Rae tossed and turned half the night before she finally got to sleep. Immediately she fell into an old dream, one she both hated and loved. Her mother was making a peanut butter and jelly sandwich for her. Rae watched disbelievingly, full of hope and traitorous joy. This is how mothers are. I always wanted one.

Gelia hummed as she wrapped the sandwich in waxed paper, put it in a bag, put an apple in with it, slid a cupcake out of its wrapper and set it on top of the apple, and piled in a handful of marshmallows, smiling mischievously at Rae because she knew about Rae's sweet tooth. Her mother's face was peaceful. Her hair was pulled back in a bun. She had a nice dress on, a clean one that covered her up and made her look like a mother. She touched Rae's face tenderly as she waltzed to and from the icebox, humming. The trailer door opened and Cracker came in. Her mother put the lunchbag into Rae's hands and put her arm around her. *You go fishing with Cracker today, honey. I got housework to do.* She turned away and started taking plates down off their shelf and laying them in the washbasin. She picked up a hammer and smiled brightly at Rae. Rae looked at Cracker.

Cracker stared down at Rae with an embarrassed smile on his face. He was tilted somehow. Rae stared solemnly back, her lunchbag clutched in her hand, wondering what was the matter with him. Then she realized he was avoiding looking at Gelia. Rae could understand that. Gelia was being pretty scary today.

Cracker took Rae by the hand, and together they went out into bright sunshiny day, while from inside the trailer came the sound of Gelia smashing plates in the washbasin, growling and screaming with rage. Rae was glad to be outside the house. Cracker was, too, she could tell. Very gently, he picked Rae up and slid her down inside his shirt. Then he put his hand inside his shirt and petted her. *Let's go fishing,* he whispered. His breath on the top of her head made her feel warm and safe.

In the Gowdy trailer on the riverbank, Cracker slept in his own bed for a change. There was flu at the firehouse that night, the police boys were out on Route 64 tending a bus wreck, and his lady friends were all booked up, or so they claimed. He had beer at home. Pack it in early, Cracker decided, and so he lay on his side half-listening to the kids breathe in the next room, sleeping lightly as he always did when he hadn't had enough to drink. His body felt wispy and full of holes. Tentacles of worry leaked out of him, leaving him hollow, worries wriggling through the night to touch all his obligations: Willy and Davy in the next room, the twins in their shack by the water's edge, and Rae, next door in her own trailer. *Don't worry,* she seemed to say in her sleep. *I'm here.* The wind whistled through all his holes.

He knew it was a dream, because she was making love to him again. She sat on his lap, laughing in his face. He laughed back. *Silly,* she said, tickling him.

In his dreams he never felt guilty for messing with a kid. He understood the mechanics of sex well enough—who better?—but it always seemed to him that she penetrated him. Light burst from her skin and lit up all his shabby secrets, scalding and purifying them. Sweetness poured from her mouth and eyes. Her lower openings engulfed him, drenched him through and through with light. She made something of him. In her arms, he transformed into himself, and for once, for once that was okay. He absorbed her as a snake absorbs the sun, almost motionless, with an occasional flexing of one long muscle in exquisite tension. Yet he felt at rest. As he dreamed, the snake circled her, winding her in his loving coils, then tied a knot at the end. *Silly,* she said. *You can't package light.* She went up then in a column of flame. The whole landscape was on fire. Green fire licked out of the ground and shot up through plants and trees in all colors.

Out of a pool of fire she rose, burning, bending this way and that, hunting for something with the most heartbreaking look in her eyes. Her expression made him weep. Nevertheless he slunk away. *Not me, darlin'. I'm not the one you want. Too much ethanol in my blood. Imagine the booze hitting all that green fire.* He flinched. *Kaboom,* he thought, and woke with a start to his own snore. Before the next breath had seeped out of his mouth he was asleep again, dreaming he was eating burning marshmallows, black and red like coals, while she giggled, fourteen again, sitting naked on his lap.

In his hotel room King Gowdy dropped off to sleep by fits and starts. A man in the next room was watching television. The noise yammered through the wall.

King, used to barrack-style sleeping, had his own devices for countering this. He wriggled onto his back and shoved his forearm behind his head. The ceiling was white, with huge dark timbers, probably fake, running crosswise. He stared up into the dim whiteness between the dark timbers and imagined that it was not a ceiling but white infinitude.

What'll I dream about? Rae's hair, all the shades of Lassie's coat. He smiled. She'd showed him a thing or two back then. He turned over on his side, smiling, and his eyelids drifted down.

He recalled the nest she had made on top of a pair of willow trees on the far bank of the Fox, and how they used to hide there, playing at sex, listening to the river murmur below, giggling and poking and rubbing each other. He slid into a dream of a hot summer day, the way her eyes looked so wild and wise as he poked her, the fishy smell of the river. His parents looked on, nodding, smiling.

The man in the next room flipped channels and King woke again. *Where was I? Rae.* She was older now. For a disturbing moment he fancied that she would continue to grow old, but her mother wouldn't. He took a firmer grip on his dream.

He dreamed he saw the entire Alaska pipeline stretched across the firred and rocky land. At the same time he could see, from his eagle's perspective, every weld on the line, and his eye lovingly picked out his own work. The pipeline could be his very body. He loved it that much.

A weight lay across his waist, like a lover's sleep-heavy arm. He thought of rolling over so it would fall off him, but he was too deep asleep now. The pipeline twisted on the frozen ground. Feeling suddenly trapped, he wriggled free of it and backed away, looking up in fear.

A mammoth paw was draped across the pipeline. It belonged to a sphinx with a thick, collie-colored mane and Gelia Somershoe's face. She smiled at him. It was the largest smile—indeed, the largest object—he had ever seen.

Alexander dreamed he was desperately thirsty. The cooler organ note had gone, but the hoarse power of the other note was growing. His fellow trees thrummed across the mud to one another and made faint adjustments in the cant of their leaves. The night creatures went off shift. Deep inside, he felt a sexual vibration start, like the shudder of the bucketloader when he turned the key. He lay still, drifting. Gradually he noticed that the vibration echoed the voice of the organ: cooled when it cooled, raged when it raged, seemed always to be talking to itself. The sound travelled up the center of his body and wrung him like a washrag with pleasure. When it seemed he couldn't tolerate any more, he burst open and grew larger, large enough to contain the pleasure. The music was always right behind him. Then it was around him, then inside him. And with a wrench he burst open again, tremendous relief, tremendous joy, room to grow. The music raked him with another surge of tingling sound.

He was so thirsty. If only he could reach the river, or bring it to him, drag it to him with his fingers. But the river was far away and he could not move. The harsh sweet organ note shot across him like a searchlight. He groaned.

At dawn he became aware of bird voices. A car backfired on US 31. Alexander drew breath for the first time in hours. He felt thirsty. Every nerve in his body was humming. He had either just had, or was about to have, the longest, most intense orgasm of his life. What was that dream? Of music? Immediately he heard the voice of the organ again. Oh, no. About to. Definitely about to. Awake, he wasn't sure he could stand it. He struggled to turn over as the sound and its wave of ravaging pleasure struck him again.

He couldn't move. Too groggy, he thought, a little panic in his heart, waiting while ecstasy passed off like a tide. Sooner or later I have to get up, get to work. He remembered then where he was. In a little while, every man on the crew would be tromping into the trailer here to punch in.

At that thought, the sound he'd been slave to all night popped away silently. Good-bye to that dream. Alexander summoned the will that gets men out of bed at dawn and tried to stretch.

His hand came up taffy-slowly. Horror clamped his stomach. First the elbow, then the forearm, then three feet later a cluster of long, long fingers. He clenched his hand. A dozen roots, brown on top and pink on the underside, stirred sluggishly.

"Uh! Uhh, uh!" In terror he jerked himself onto his left elbow. He looked down. His left hand felt twined round the metal struts of the cot. His legs had slid off the cot. His left leg, the only one he could see, touched the floor and ran off in long ropes and fleshy roots every which way, wedged into cracks between the plywood sheets, or piled up, pressed to the gap between the doorsill and the door.

His undershorts felt way too tight. Glancing down, he started, cried out, and huddled with his free arm curled over his head. His penis was nearly two feet long, as thick and stiff as his arm. When he jerked, he felt a sharp tug and straining against his toes. He realized he could still feel everything, all down this strange length. At least whatever he was was flesh enough, he thought, sickened and fascinated, glancing again at his swollen penis. The faintest movement threatened him with a paralyzing echo of that last orgasm.

He realized that the fingers of his right hand were shrinking. He bunched his toes and felt them crawl inches over the plywood and linoleum. If he watched, he could imagine he saw a change, but if he looked away and back again he discovered it went much quicker. He lay back carefully on the cot. Oh God, he thought, staring feverishly at the ceiling while he worked on freeing the long, long fingers of his left hand, You stop fuckin' with me right now. When he remembered to, he kept his right hand moving and curled his toes. It seemed to speed things up. He tried not to listen to his hands and feet slither over the floor.

Traffic sounds increased out on US 31. A sliver of sunlight touched the plywood a few inches away from what should have been his left foot. If the sun touches me, he thought, I'll start all over again. Maybe I'll fall back asleep and never stop growing. He laughed, thinking of his monstrous penis. A toe caught painfully on a splinter. The timeclock clacked noisily. "'Nother ten minutes, please God, and I won't embarrass myself," he said aloud. His voice sounded hoarse and lustful. That set him laughing again. Two minutes later he had worked all his limbs free. He dragged himself up and down the trailer, keeping away from the sun-filled east windows. His extremities shrank back to size. He went straight to the fridge, hands shaking, and drank two quarts of water standing up.

Ike pulled his half-ton onto the gravel just as Alexander, his hands still shaking, finished lacing his boots.

Chapter Fourteen

The sound of chainsaws had filled Raedawn's childhood. *Spring and summer were the worst. Guttural, merciless, biting into giant after giant with their steel teeth, their harsh voices were the measure of man's power in a world where she had no control and would never, the sound promised, be able to stop them.*

She hadn't known about tree disease. All she knew was that the mighty elms fell. Their great bodies were growled into sections, carried away in the pincers of enormous yellow-bodied machines, and then the branches were fed with a noise like machine-gun fire into the circular maw of the shredder. Their leaves, green and rough like money, lay on the ground with their pale underbellies showing, healthy-looking, out of place in all the death.

Then the stump chewer was dragged out and the stumps were reduced to a pile of aromatic chewings that children could play on. Then the city took that away, too. The sound of the saws mingled with the voices of cicadas, which imitated the saws, so it seemed to her, in high voices like children, harmless.

By the time she was ten, all the great elms were cut down or else sprayed with a germ-killer to get rid of the disease. It seemed irrational and cruel that some park district official could decide to save or slay trees at whim. By then she was old enough to know that she lived on the border of two towns. One town had chosen to spray their trees, poison the birds for a few years, but spare the proud cathedral arches over the roads. The other town had voted to spare the birds and lose the trees. To her young mind there was no comparison. The birds would come back, but the hundred-year-old elms never would. She hadn't known about DDT.

She never got used to the horrible pretense the men made, that it was only a job. Didn't they know they were putting their souls in danger? It was all in a day's work to them. She didn't know about Dachau, about Hiroshima. She didn't know that there were worse things.

It began to seem to Raedawn that a child's only hope of surviving such a world was to set down deep roots in one place, a place no one else wanted, and love it hard, until they came with the saws and tore it to shreds.

Chapter Fifteen

Suzy Wohnberg sat in the passenger seat of the company Mercedes, stuck dead in bumper-to-bumper traffic on US 31, watching crows pace around in the mud in front of yet another beige housing development project and listening to the third-highest VP in the company talk on his cell phone.

"That's right. Where do you think your loss is coming from? You scratch our backs and we both give Uncle Sugar the runaround for five solid years."

Used to be all cornfields out here, she imagined the crows saying. She supposed she should feel privileged that John Fowier thought enough of her to let her listen in. She knew John better than that. He hardly knew she was there.

"Then we sell the property and collect five hundred percent. As a limited partner, you rake your cut off the top."

She was here because she looked good in red, and because John expected to sleep with her sometime this weekend.

"You bet," he assured the phone. "You bet it's a deal. I'll have my girl send the forms. Right, Bob. Catch you later." Suzy envied the flex of his strong hands on the wheel.

She didn't even glance at him when he said *my girl* like that. Someday she would have her own girl, and she'd be cutting deals and taking names in the same way. John Fowier and the red dress were on the path. She licked her lower lip, trying to look sharp but not too smart.

"Lew! Howya doing. Stuck in traffic, it's a million degrees out here."

John opened the window so he could stick his head out. The air stank of stale truck exhaust and John's impatience. Why didn't people just turn off the damn car if they weren't moving? Suzy looked out her side window.

"What? The architect found water on the site? Wait a minute, Lew, is there a problem or isn't there? I thought you surveyed that site. Uh-huh, I understand that, but where—so your own surveyor makes a mistake—no, I *don't* see that. Your firm approved it. It's your ass if this fucks up, not mine."

Behind them, somebody slammed his car door and stomped past them to get a better view of the obstruction, and the crows rose up fussily. One crow soared to a scrubby tree at the roadside and looked straight in at Suzy. She looked back, trying not to listen to John. There wasn't much he had left to teach her anyway.

"The riverfront lots? I'm taking care of that." He leaned casually on the horn.

He had an icky blond stubble that kind of turned her on. He couldn't possibly know that. No, he was putting her in her place, like, she didn't rate a shave. Suzy wondered if crow feathers felt as glossy as they looked.

"The shit hits the fan, we have those Okies both ways."

What was that crow thinking? What idiots they all were to sit here on a four-lane highway squished into two lanes, stinking and quivering, when they could be flying. Suzy stared hard at the crow, noticing a pattern of tiny black feathers like fishscales on its head and neck. What it must be like. Just lift your wings a little and soar.

"No, no, Lew, why should it? Just a joke. I told you, I've got an attorney on that. We used him in L.A. for that mall. Bunch of wops wouldn't go. Yup. Like snails outa their shells. You don't want to know, Lew."

Suzy didn't want to know, either. She pretended she could tune in on the crow's thoughts.

"Gotta go, Lew. I need a hot assistant and a cold martini."

She tuned in harder. The crow was looking straight at her, bird-style, sideways, craning its neck in scorn. Damn thing was full of opinions. She craned her neck, too, tipping her head to one side, mocking back. John's phone rang again.

"John Fowier. Yes, Mr. Bodanza, he did say you might call."

The crow was thinking Suzy was a fool and John Fowier would eat her up and spit out her bones without even putting down his cell phone. Snooty bird, she thought. A lot you know.

"It's a somewhat complex financial structure, but the tax laws—completely legal, sir."

John might lie to her and use her but she would use him and she would lie to him, too. If she did it right, he would never know, she told the crow silently.

"That's somewhat correct, Mr. Bodanza. Of course there is always a profit—"

The crow was thinking the girl was a glistening pile of banked coals and the man next to her had a hole in his middle.

"Yes, sir. I'll send you a copy of the prosp—oh, I didn't realize you already—"

Inside her, green fire shimmered like the wet heat of a log lying in a field, slowly scorching the grass under it with never a sign of flame. Or she might explode. Someday there would be no log left, just a long charred place showing where she had lain before she made her escape. The crow had seen such things.

"Not at all, sir. We can meet you there tomorrow afternoon, and you can see for yourself—It would be no trouble—"

Inside the man, the fire stopped and started like a frayed power line, the power damming up and then arcing across the gaps, making a little spark. Every time a spark popped, his voice crackled, and the girl flinched.

"Yes, that would be fine. You won't regret—"

He ran on those sparks. Like the car they sat in, he let the fire build, and then he touched it with his anger and the spark leaped across the gap inside, giving him a burst of power. Huh, the crow thought. He better never set that girl alight.

"Thank *you*, Mr. Bodanza. See you tomorrow in Berne. And that," he said, turning to Suzy at last, "is why the red dress, babe. He seems to be deaf, but I bet he ain't blind."

Chapter Sixteen

Rae took the breakfast dishes down to the river. She had dressed for a hot day, and hot it would be, but now a cold mist lay knee-deep over the mud and seethed over the water in wisps.

She walked to a sandy part of the bank a few yards upstream from the place where they tethered their boats, knelt there, and dipped the bowls one at a time into the water. A fat carp appeared in the shallows where she knelt, moving his body lazily and making kissing faces at her. Now here came his brothers and sisters. They fought over the soggy Cheerios floating away from her bowl. Their big gray bodies looked armor plated, well-used to the cold water. They shoved and slithered over one another, nibbling at her fingertips with ghastly mouths. She laughed.

Across the road, the bucketloader's engine started, and then the beep-beep of its backup alarm. The world had come to an end, and then Alexander Caebeau, of Freeport, Grand Bahama, came along. She smiled to herself. She scrubbed the plates and forks with sand, sprinkled them with a little baking soda, and stacked them back in the basin.

She couldn't put her chores off any longer. It was time to clean the twins' hole. Rae gathered a broom, a sponge, a bucket half-full of warm water, an empty bucket, a fistful of bags from the Piggly Wiggly, and a couple of old shirts for handling things too icky to touch. Easy to find icky things when you were housekeeping for the twins.

She headed for the smelly house.

Willy's last year's band camp tee shirt hung over the window in the door, which looked out over the river. They'd have settled for no windows at all if Davy could have found them a door without one.

"Here I come, ready or not!" she yelled when she stood at the shack's doorway, lumbered down with cleaning implements. The black shirt moved in the river breeze. What a good kid Willy was, she thought, a

really decent person. Willy never complained as everybody else did when
the kids hijacked his things. Like her, he tried hard to fit in, up the hill.
Band camp in summer paid for by his paper route in winter, and all kinds
of sports all year around. Willy's stocky, solid body suited most high
school sports. There must always be a place on the team for somebody fast
and strong and not too small, who doesn't want to be a star. Rae lifted the
black shirt and peered into the gloom.

The smell inside was rank, a powerful beastly smell that said Bear: all
claws and bear-size bad humor. No bears in the Fox Valley any more.
Where did they get that smell? Rae thought of how Willy must feel about
the shirt. Should she wash it, too? Give it back to him? Leave it, they'd
steal something else before nightfall. He hadn't cried yet. Not like King,
who was a champion complainer. King's weedy frame had left him pretty
much out of sports all through school. The toughs had teased him for his
long blond hair, she remembered. The golden weediness came from
Cracker's and Gloria's side of the family, the stocky darkness from the
Gowdys.

Davy, middle child, foolish child, had the weediness but the darkness,
too: funny, that. Davy might never fill out as King had done. In her
mind's eye she fitted her body to King's, so extraordinarily changed by
just five years away. Her skin still felt the print of it. Had she changed as
much?

She set her cleaning things down, put both hands on the door handle,
and hoisted it aside. How did those little kids manage? The door was
heavy and darned awkward. It was loosely attached to the shack with bal-
ing wire that wasn't even a pretense at a hinge. The door wasn't meant to
be a convenience. It could be barred only when they were in, so they must
not be home.

It was utterly dark inside the hole when Rae opened the door. In that
moment the sun came out, setting the river all aglitter and spattering the
upper walls with reflected light. She looked down.

Davy had dug the original hole, but the kids had been at work since
then. The mud walls were black clay, as smooth as if the kids had rubbed
them with small wet hands over and over. The only furniture at the bottom was the iron woodstove. She let the broom down and then let it slip
from her hand to bounce into the darkness below. But how come it doesn't
flood? Rae wondered. Must be kid magic.

Since her last visit, they had moved the stairway of stacked crates. How was she going to get down? She stood there wondering, forgetting for the moment why she had come.

The river bounced chips of sunlight off the ceiling, and the soft watery reflections swam like fishes over the black walls, fading as they sank to the bottom. Rae looked down helplessly into the stink, toward a jumble of junky belongings, junkier even than her own, wondering if she should get a rope. Crazy kids, she thought, looking down. So, do they jump into their mudhole?

There, under her feet and directly below the door, hung a rope ladder. Its fittings were brand-new chrome snaphooks, locked around enormous shining nails hammered into the door studs and bent over to make loops to catch the snaphooks. Now, where did they steal those? she thought, but she was already swinging down the ladder, the full bucket in one hand and the rag-shirts and sponge stuffed into her pockets. The rank stink increased as she descended. Deeper down, it smelled like they'd been burning a dead skunk. She made another trip up the ladder for the second bucket and the paper bags.

Where she touched down she stopped, letting her eyes get used to the gloom, waiting politely until she could see. Some of the kids' messes were holy and some were just messes.

The old woodstove was huge in the little room. The twins had only a vague idea of the uses of furniture. Most everything was on the floor. This pile of shirts here might be dirty laundry, or it might be clean, though in general the kids let her or Cracker keep the clean clothes in their trailers and raided as they needed. She picked them up. Her nose began to filter out the skunky smell. Dirty shirts. She stowed them in a paper bag. What next?

John Fowler got out of the Mercedes and locked the door. This was exactly the kind of neighborhood where he would rather not bring a company car—construction machinery on one side of the road, throwing up dirt and stones liable to ding the finish, and an Okie slum on the other. Two little brats in bare feet ran by, squealing. One of them slipped, put out a hand for balance, and left a smear on the Merc's flank. When Fowler grabbed for him the brat slipped again and slid wetly into him. Aghast, Fowler pushed him away. "Go on, beat it!"

The brats fled, making an ungodly noise. Fowier inspected his trouser knees. "Damn kids." A few quick brushes got the dirt off his trousers, but he could still feel a chilly spot where little wet hands had got him. He set his teeth.

The woman had taken a broom into that shed over there, down by the water. Putting away cleaning stuff. Okay, he thought. I've got her cornered. He set off toward the shed.

Chicken bones, empty milk cartons, empty Wonderbread bags, empty peanut butter jars, empty pickle jars. Must have been raided from Cracker's trailer. Cracker had a hankering for pickles. One thing about the kids, they didn't leave half-et food lying around. She put the trash in bags. Glass jars went into their own bag, along with their lids, hunted up from where they had rolled away.

In the half dark, with the ever-shifting glimmer of sunlight reflected from the river, each thing she picked up smelled intensely like itself. She breathed deeply. Chicken bones. Breathe. Milk. A big sniff at the jar, licked clean. Pickles! What a trip! Now she thought about it, she realized that the bear-or-skunk smell had vanished. Gone. Not just lying under or over everything, like smog or chitterlings that you filtered out to save your sanity. *Smell tricks. Huh.* She wondered how they did that. Animal children living in the dark, they know all about smells. Their sense of smell must get 'em around this hole. Their eyes sure wouldn't.

She squinted, then closed her eyes, breathed slowly and deeply, willing her pupils to dilate. In that deeper darkness she could smell the river now, even feel it a few yards away like an enormous animal sleeping poorly, shifting its muscular body back and forth against the mud. She brought her attention inside. The black mud walls felt smooth, dense and rich and fertile, as extravagant as if they were walls of gold. *Black gold, maybe. It's so dark in here.*

She looked up. Outside, a cloud passed over the sun's face, and the schools of sunchip fishes vanished into darkness on the ceiling, a ceiling now unimaginably high above her. What's it like up there, fishies? As the unseen cloud passed, the world dimmed and brightened, and her skin shrank and breathed again, even though the sunlight was not falling on her or even near her. Up there, she imagined, the surface of the river would be seething, shrinking and expanding like her skin, changing under the sun, shifting with the sun's movement as quickly as water shifted in its deep-folded watery guts.

For a while, in her mind's eye she watched the river surface puckering. A footstep on the ground outside brought her back. That must be Cracker looking for her, or Davy wondering why the door was standing open. The children would come silently. It couldn't be anybody else.

The woman's face looked up like a ghost in the dark. What was she doing kneeling on the ground? Shit, what a smell. John leaned in the low doorway and squinted.

"Hi. Got a minute?"

His own voice sounded loud in the shed. The woman moved, and he realized she was actually standing in a hole. The whole damned shed went down, way down. He saw the business end of a broom sticking up against the wall down there. Cleaning the outhouse by hand, Jesus Christ. Obviously they were dirt poor. He'd find her price.

"My name's John Fowler, I'm the Atlas exec in charge of the development over there on US 31. Can you come out? I'd like to talk to you."

She didn't say anything. Deaf and dumb? His eyes adjusted to the darkness in the shed. There was furniture down there, or stuff anyway. Not the outhouse. He felt relieved. He'd just got himself cleaned up from where that kid ran into him. He didn't feel up to negotiating with a woman covered in shit. He crouched, and more light came in past his shoulder. Criminy, he could see clear down the front of her dress from here. He grinned. May as well get a closer look. If he jumped right *there*, he wouldn't fall on anything. Look out for those buckets.

She made a sound as he jumped. He fell farther than he expected and landed with a bone-jarring thump right in front of her, but she didn't back away. They were almost touching. He smelled something else now, some kind of perfume she was wearing. *I know how to talk to a woman who wears perfume while she cleans the outhouse.*

"Okay, let's talk turkey. You know I'm trying to buy these lots for Foxe Parke. Now, there's no reason we can't reach an understanding, you and me."

His own voice was deafening. Must be something with the acoustics in here. "As I see it, we have what you need and you have what we want. If you prefer, you can get payment for the lots in shares of the deal. Hold 'em til we sell out. Five hundred percent profit on your money in five years, what do you say? Some little savings account!"

She took shape in the dimness. Her throat was shockingly white above her housedress collar. Her face came into focus only gradually. Eyes first. Like that cat in the movie, he thought confusedly. Jesus, what's that perfume? It soaked into his skin like bar smoke. Made him tingle all over. He'd have to have this suit cleaned. He squinted. Wow. Didn't she wear a bra?

"I have an offer right here," he said, leaning closer and putting his hand inside his coat. He crackled the papers. Her smell seemed to sneak all over him, around the back of his head. It was even making his butt feel hot. Phew!

He thought she shrank from him a little then. Maybe not quite enough. Push it.

"Light a fire in here and I'll show it to you," he said, his voice dropping. He hadn't meant it to. He felt himself expanding into her smell. *That perfume's giving me ideas.* Go with it. He took a tiny step closer.

She squared her shoulders and looked up full into his face. Her breasts touched him, just a few bits of cloth away. *Holy shit.* He felt hard all over, huge and hard and light-headed. *Hang on, cowboy, keep your grip.*

He leaned over her with his hand in his coat, like a mobster in a movie about to produce a gun.

So what have we here? she thought, looking him up and down with that inner eye. The outline of his true form took shape in the darkness of the hole.

Fire. Lots of it. Her skin came alive here and there and tasted his fire.

God, I'm good, he thought, but his head swam. He spoke huskily. "You have title to the place, I know that. Think I haven't done my homework? The deal's yours to make." She didn't retreat. *Driver's seat, boy, don't you forget it.* The sound of his own voice seemed to fade. His heart was too loud.

He talked and talked. Rae paid attention to the sounds *inside* his voice. There was a kind of top-heavy sound in it, as if he wanted to bring a big weight down on her and silence her. His body was shouting, too, with shouts of fire, but that fire didn't go all the way through him. There were blank spots in his middle. Hm. How come, d'y'spose?

She opened herself from throat to crotch, letting herself grow wide enough to catch all of him as he came to a boil. He stiffened immediately in response. But not horny. But yes. Or maybe. Huh. She watched his pale hair bob back and forth in the dimness, leaving a trail of visible echoes. *All that power is locked up in the top. But the fire's all down below.* She felt for the gap, broadening her reach until the heat of her body touched him everywhere.

He breathed in so far that her perfume clanged through him like a huge bell. Was she really going to do it with him right here in a hole in the dirt? *Seal the deal in the dirt.* The words echoed in his head over and over. He shook his head to clear it, then shook it again. He could have her right now.

John Fowier knew he was going to do it. Gonna be standing up, girlie, that's for sure. I'm not kneeling down here in this suit. Her smell made him feel short of breath. His stomach felt funny. *This is just a little bit crazy.*

Found it, she thought triumphantly. Just then she sensed a spot in his navel that began trembling like the heartbeat of a bird, tiny and quick. *A hole.* A bad hole right in his middle. Good grief, however can he walk? The top-heaviness was getting bigger and bigger, as if all the sex in him rushed out of his lower body and up into his head, making a thundercloud as he bent over her. Give me a headache, that would, she thought. Man's nigh about to fall over. And that big old hole in his middle.

Maybe I can close it for him, she thought.

She put both hands out at her sides and braced herself against the circular mud wall. *Slowly now, don't spook him. Bring him close.* The twins' tricks with smell began to make more sense to her. The knowledge came to her like a string sliding through her hand, a string of smells coiling around the two of them in this circular hole. With a gentle tugging she drew him to her, pulling slowly until their hips were bound, tied tightly together like feather and fishhook on a fisherman's fly.

John Fowier felt very odd. Sex usually made him feel tall, high up or something. God knew he was taller than this bimbo. She just stood there, braced against the dirt, looking up at him while he raised her dress and unzipped his fly in the same movement.

She smelled like the first woman he'd ever had. He felt a pang as he heard his trousers hit the floor with a chink, probably filthy as sin down there. Then he was sliding into her. God, she was ready! Wow! He held her by the ass and made his moves, *son of a bitch, that's good,* and felt himself pulling down somehow, or in, away from his usual high-up feeling. His belly felt hot and runny. Unsettling.

He let go of her and put his hands against the wall behind her, leaning into her. She stood braced, firm, and motionless, like the best kind of whore. Oh yes. God, that felt weird. A fireball was building in his groin. The smell of her hair seemed to drag him down. He stiffened his legs and locked his knees. I don't do that stuff, honey, he thought, sorry, but still he sank into himself until he felt bigger on the inside than he felt on the outside. It made him dizzy. It made him want to get away. *Am I nuts?* Her hair stank. He turned his head aside with a wrenching movement.

His hips pumped on their own. He wanted to come and then get the hell out of here. He felt huge and small at the same time, a horrifying inside-out feeling.

Explosively, he came. Then he threw himself back, away, out, *get me away!*

His pants were still around his ankles. He bounced off the muddy wall, lost his balance, and came back almost on top of her. A quick scramble got him away again. He trembled violently from head to foot. What the goddamned fucking Christly hell! That smell was driving him crazy.

"Who do you think you're trying that stuff on?" he yelled. The sound of his voice was tiny, absorbed in the thick air in the hole. His pulse thundered in his ears. He didn't know if he wanted to rip her dress off or get the hell out of here fast.

Rats, she thought. Panicked him. She hadn't moved slow enough. Time to give him some space now. She'd had that great big gap in his innards all but closed up, but she'd used too much force, and now everything inside him was all mixed up. She was turning into Gelia. An awful thought.

He squinted. What was she doing? He pulled his pants up. She moved until she stood half-hidden behind that black iron dingus in the middle of the hole, while he scrambled shakily with his belt buckle. Scared of me now? he thought. About time, and a little too fucking late. A quick glance around showed him that a rope ladder hung just behind him. Got you, he thought savagely, hardly aware of himself any more. He grabbed the rope ladder and watched her while he jerked, jerked it down. *Christ, I'm twitching all over.* He was still so horny he wanted to tear his pants down again. The rope in his fist made him feel better. His hearing had come back. That stink was fading, too. All he could smell was his anger, reassuring, like metal in his mouth.

What was she doing? She seemed to step toward him, putting out her hands. He backed a pace. "What the fuck are you doing?"

Then he saw she had taken hold of the iron dingus. She was climbing up on it. Her skirt swayed as she rose, brushing his face and dousing him in her smell, making him so dizzy he staggered back. What did she think she could do? Jump on him from up there? He braced himself.

"Come and get it, honey," he crooned. His wrist flicked of its own accord, and the rope ladder wrapped itself around his fist, the steel fittings slapping hard against his arm. All his anger rushed into his head. Anger blackened his sight and made his ears ring.

For a moment she crouched over him, bent double like a ghostly monkey, grabbing the top of the iron dingus with both hands and both feet. That intolerable smell poured out of her dress onto his face. His knees bent, his arm flexed, and he felt the rope bite into his palm.

He breathed, "Ready when you are."

She jumped.

He swung.

The rope ladder fittings clanged into the iron dingus. She passed clean over his head, flopped into the wall with her legs hanging half out of the doorway, kicked and missed him, and then she was gone.

Rae landed in the doorway on her stomach. She scrambled her way up out of the hole and rolled over onto her back, puffing, on the mud outside the twins' hut.

Well, good grief, what was that all about? I've messed up good. No sense trying to talk to him now. I've scared him. Rats. I'd better get Cracker. Ignoring the clangs, bellows, and curses coming from the depths of the hole, she brushed herself off shakily and headed up the bank to Cracker's trailer.

At John's touch the black iron dingus rocked, and something separated from something else, and the damned thing collapsed onto his foot in two parts. Cast iron, heavy as sin. "Ow!" Soot showered up in his face. "Fuck!" The soot filled the air and made the hole completely black.

He heard a kid giggle.

"Goddammit! Get that bitch back down here! Somebody get me a ladder!"

The kid answered with a deafening shriek that echoed in the darkness. John swung a foot and connected agonizingly with a piece of iron. The soot began to settle. At the same time he felt a chilly weight on his ankles. When he stooped to massage the sore foot his hand splashed into cold water. He was ankle deep and hadn't even noticed, he was so fucking mad. Fuck, had she thrown a hose into the hole? His calves prickled. His pants seemed to clasp his legs. The water was rising fast. Smelly, too. He splashed at it, as if to hold it back. There were things floating in it. Paper bag? Don't even ask. The black water reached his knees. He panicked.

"Shit! Get me out of here!"

More giggles. He looked up. The shaft of light from the doorway lay heavily in the sooty air overhead. The roof was nailed onto a grid of timbers, and those two little shitbags from out by the road were hanging from the grid like fucking monkeys, like their fucking sister, laughing at him. He glared wildly around the hole, looking for something to throw.

He saw now where the water was coming from: it seeped like a million tears out of the mud walls, beading up and trickling down in streams. Something wrong with that. It ran too slowly to fill the place up like this, if he just thought about it—if he could just think straight and calm down! But surely it's coming in too slow to flood like this. The rising water reached his undershorts. He gasped. Spinning, he lost his balance, tangled his feet in another chunk of that damned iron thing, and fell. Cold black water pressed around him, wet his hair instantly, soaked his clothes more slowly. The water lifted him. He surfaced, sputtering. Soot and grit coated the water, and now it coated his face. Soot slipped between his buttons and under his shirt, soot down in his waistband, soot in his shoes. He trod water and spat crumbs of soot.

The water was considerably higher now. He was floating well above the bottom. His temper had cooled with the dunking. He realized he would be within reach of the doorway if it came up another foot. Grab that nail-head sticking out. "Ow!" Missed it. "Shit!" With an effort he buoyed himself once and grabbed for the mud sill. His hand slid off it and he sank over his head again. He surfaced, blowing soot out of his mouth. Try again. A couple of bounces to get his height up, and he could get the door frame.

Like a porpoise he shot up and grabbed the frame. He lay with his upper body supported on the sill while his legs still hung down, floating in cold, noisome water.

While he lay there trying to pull himself together, the two kids swung one at a time, upside-down, out through the doorway. He heard their footsteps on the tin roof, with more giggles. Little shits. The water kept rising. A trickle leaked from the doorway and ran past his head. John dragged himself groaning to his feet. Which way had he parked the damned car? He tramped north, squishing, as fast as his dignity would allow, while giggles followed him and crows yelled insolently overhead.

The damned car had four flat tires. The caps to the valve stems sat lined up in a perky row on the hood.

Chapter Seventeen

I can't do it!" Eugene stopped moving. He grunted.

"Do you want to stop?" Willy held still, though it drove him crazy not to move. He was gasping and his heart thundered. *Oh, go-go-go!* He waited.

They had chosen Willy's hideaway at the willow nest on the sandbar for this meeting, ostensibly for trumpet practice. Eugene had brought a jug and some reefer.

"I'm—" Eugene grunted again and pushed gently back against Willy's cock. "Oh man, I'm—" he panted. "Going—" and suddenly he relaxed. Willy slid into him all the way, and immediately Eugene clenched up again. A whimper and then a cry of joy escaped Willy.

"*TO*—" Eugene yelled, and in that moment they moved together, pistoning at first, bucking away from each other and then colliding with a force that knocked half the air out of Willy's lungs. And then they moved in unison for what felt, even to Willy, like a long time.

Their nest sprawled across the tops of two weeping willows whose limbs had been bent and knit together young. Their trunks had been planted less than a foot apart, many years ago. Now the willows were thick-bodied giants, their trunks intertwined, their feet plunged side by side into the loamy edge of the sandbar where the river lapped their ankles. Their big branches supported a huge nest made of old foam mattresses, sacking, egg cartons, plastic packing pellets, dog fur, dried grasses, and aromatic weeds. Somebody had gone to a lot of trouble to make it.

Eugene rolled over very slowly. Willy clasped him. Eugene laid his head on Willy's breastbone. A tremble passed through him.

"What?" Willy said to his hair.

"It's so strong. I feel all this stuff." Eugene pressed his sticky face and hands to Willy's body.

"I know." Willy stroked his friend's bright hair.

Eugene sighed. "I don't know how people stand it."

Willy shut his eyes. He tried to remember how it had worked for him. He would have to translate. There weren't any words, really. He moved his chin on Eugene's bony blond head.

"Well, it takes time to get used to it. This is the strongest thing in the world. Better than wine."

"Better than pot," Eugene said to the few hairs on Willy's chest.

"Too strong for lots of people, even older people," Willy said, thinking of his uncle, and his brother. Cracker managed better than King. Cracker drank to damp it down. Willy felt for the jug where it had rolled up against him.

He said, "They think all this stuff about it, like loveydove and romance, or maybe they get scared and violent. But that's just so's it makes sense to them. It's not supposed to make sense," he said, wondering if that was true. "Mostly they don't do it at all." He shrugged. "Sad."

"It's just so scary," Eugene complained. He sounded happier now. "They don't tell you that. Why is it?"

"Why's it scary?" Willy sat up, giving Eugene a squeeze as he unstuck the other boy's hands from him. "'Cause it is scary. It's scary and—" he paused. He had a rule for this. He never put words on it for somebody else.

"Makes you feel like you're out of yourself," Eugene finished for him dreamily. "And *in* yourself. It's like God," he added with surprise in his voice.

Willy sidestepped. The sun burned on his sticky spots. "I guess so, yeah. It's scary and it feels like that." He never knew what people thought they meant when they said God. It was like trying to figure what they meant when they said sex. "So it's kind of like that, in you and outside of you and scary sometimes. All by itself. People don't have to *add* any more God or scariness or romance to it, but they do. I guess it helps 'em feel like they're in charge of it."

"Even for when you do it with girls?"

Willy thought about Cracker and Gelia, Cracker and Rae, Cracker drinking before he went up the hill to his far-scattered harem. "Oh, yeah."

Eugene burrowed up against him. "It shouldn't be so hard," he said in a muffled voice.

"It gets easier."

"I mean, it won't be like this *forever*, will it?" Eugene sounded worried but awed. *What if.* Always like the first time.

Willy smiled. He felt a hundred years old. "I dunno. I haven't done it forever." The thought of all the boys he knew at the high school made his mind ache with weariness, but his heart leaped, and his cock heated up stiff. Stupid thing, he thought. Aren't you tired? And his cock said, Never. Willy groaned.

"You been doing this a long time," Eugene said as if reading his mind.

"Since I was twelve."

"Didn't you feel, like, weird?" He tried to reach his left ear to scratch it. Willy scratched it for him.

Weird. There's another word, Willy thought. Like God and sex. "Yeah. I guess. It took a while to get my body to put stuff together with my head. You know. You feel something and it makes pictures in your head, and then the pictures make you feel some more. Like your body talks back to the pictures with feelings that make more pictures that make feelings. That's how you find out what you like, and how your insides work." Was it, though? "You're making this map." He shrugged. In the voice of their prissy old gym teacher, he said, "It's the mysterious process of *maturity,*" and laughed.

But Eugene didn't laugh. "I mean, like when did you know it was— wasn't girls you liked?"

Oh. That. "From the beginning, I guess." Of course that's what he's worried about, Willy realized. The least important part. How come none of his friends from school ever thought about the whole miracle of how it felt, how they were growing and changing with it? All they worried about was that they should do it with girls. Should, should, should.

The miracle itself was enough for Willy. Every time, when he thought he'd learned something, the mystery got bigger and filled him all up until he was bursting open with it again. There was never any end. Once he had hoped he would figure it out when he was King's age, or Cracker's age. But King was back, and according to Gelia he still didn't know anything. And Cracker was Cracker. If he didn't know now, he never would. Didn't care to, maybe. Willy wanted to know. It was why he kept going to school, kept trying to learn, long after his brothers had quit.

"I mean, didn't it get you in trouble?" Eugene persisted. Still on the girls thing.

Trouble with who? Willy thought. Good question. Who had even noticed him?

He said drily, "Well, I don't talk about it to my family." He didn't know what else to say about that.

Abruptly he said, "I had a friend." Two hot tears ambushed him. He lay his head back on the crushed egg cartons. "A really good friend." This part he couldn't tell, either. But it was the whole answer that answered all Eugene's questions. *I didn't have to be scared of being different. I didn't have to wonder and worry. I wasn't alone.*

He pulled away from Eugene. His throat tightened and he turned over on his stomach, covering his head with his arms.

A *good* friend would admit all these things to Eugene. How it's okay to be scared of being different. How alone Willy felt now, worse than ever. The sun felt burning hot on his shoulders. But. But he just couldn't make himself say it. It didn't seem okay at all, not to him. Some of this grief belonged to him alone, dammit. It was personal. Wasn't he allowed to have a personal feeling? He couldn't be everybody's buddy all the time and never feel—not just cry— Willy held still and stopped thinking, and the bad feelings went away for a while.

A clink told him that Eugene was at the jug. Eugene said, "Want some?" Willy propped himself up on his elbows. "Yeah." He drank.

While Willy had another pull, Eugene rolled a joint. They wriggled on their stomachs and peered over the edge of the nest. Directly below them, a cockleshell of a boat bobbed against the bank. It was empty, tied to an alder sapling. River rising again, Willy thought. Funny I didn't notice it at home.

"Somebody's here," Eugene squeaked. They wriggled to the other side of the nest. There was a clearing below, ringed with baby willows and box elder. Somebody was moving around down there. "Who's that? What're they doing?" He passed the joint to Willy.

Willy sucked smoke and then craned his neck over the edge of their nest. Below, Ink and Mink had something in their hands, a dead bird? A pigeon?

"It's the twins," he whispered.

"I used to play in the hobo jungle near my house." Eugene let the smoke go. "Before they extended the subdivision. Is it their place?"

"My brother's."

Ceremoniously the twins held the dead bird between them at arm's length. They took turns plucking feathers and throwing them in the air. Then Mink climbed a rickety edifice of crates and five-gallon pails, placed the carcass on top, and clambered down. She backed away, fingering her chin in a mock-adult pose of contemplation. Ink copied her.

The clearing did look like a hobo jungle. A broken chair, the ashes of a fire on a flat stone, a pocket knife stuck into the crotch of a sapling, a bleach jug cut for bailing hung upside down on a broomstick thrust into the mud, a wine bottle with violets wilting in it. The children walked solemnly around the clearing, touching things: a dangle of bones and feathers strung on monofilament fish line, a pink bare-ass doll with outrageous breasts and collie-colored hair standing up to her knees in a pile of tiny eggshells, broken porcelain cups, and loose sequins.

Down under the trees, the twins were almost invisible, a pair of shocking white heads over ghostly tee shirts. They clambered into their cockleshell boat, dipped their oars, and spun away out onto the river.

In the nest above, all was hot and bright. Willy shoved his wadded clothes and trumpet case with one foot and squirmed deeper into the matted stuff. "I'm sleepy," he said. "Gimme the jug."

The boys rolled over and lay on their sides face to face. Eugene opened the screw top, swigged, and tipped it over to Willy. "I think I'm falling asleep, too," he said apologetically.

"'S okay."

"Finish the joint?"

"Sure." They passed it back and forth one more time, and then Willy pinched it to death and ground the shreds into the mat under him. "Sleep tight." He kissed Eugene on the cheek.

"Boy, am I." Eugene was asleep in seconds.

Far away upriver, a crow was calling. Willy tried to turn his head toward the sound but he was too full of cheap wine and reefer to do more than flick his eyelids. In the sun, comforted by the wine and reefer, he could imagine that instead of the cold, angry, narrow Fox, it was the Mississippi that ran under him, a mile wide and warm as milk. If this were the Mississippi then the trailers across the river would have to be a mile away. Maybe more, since the Big Muddy rose further and wider than the Fox. Miles and miles, maybe.

That yelling crow was nearer. Willy could imagine it pumping its broad black shoulders over the flatness of the Mississippi. He could build a cabin in these woods, like Huck Finn. No, Huck Finn's dad built it, that was how the story went. Willy's dad had bought a trailer and towed it to the banks of the Fox, and then one night he fell in. Him and Mom.

Willy winced. Awful thoughts lay that way. He fled them into sleep. He dreamed he lay on his back in the nest beside Eugene, feeling sorry for himself, planning his own cabin on the Mississippi.

The crow swung noisily into a nearby alder tree. It made a chuttering sound deep in its throat. In his sleep, Willy swallowed, his tongue rough and foul with reefer smoke. He would be an orphan, like Huck. Only there would be books in his cabin. Electricity. Tap water. Central heat. No more running away from four muddy walls and a life of loneliness and dirt, taking care of an old drunk and a lot of kids.

He twitched, suddenly overwhelmed with self-pity. There was a thump next to his leg. On the floor of the nest, the crow stepped and pecked.

"Aw, hell," it sniffed. "Snivelling again."

"Lemme alone," Willy moaned.

"'Lemme alone,'" the crow moaned in a little old man's voice, a child's voice mocking. "'Lemme alooone.' Wassamatter?"

Willy rolled over onto his stomach and buried his face. Knowing what was coming, he hunched his shoulders. He felt a breath of breeze. Two sturdy claws thumped onto his back.

The crow nibbled his ear. "'Samatter, hmm?"

Willy felt boneless. The sun and wine had drained all the strength out of him. The cold river ran below, tugging at the long fingertips of the willow trees, making them whisper. For a moment he sank downward into deeper sleep. He left his body and ran like mercury down the willows' fingers, touched the cold water, *Brrr*, and then ran back up to his body where it lay in the hot sun. "I was just thinking," his own voice said in a muffled way, and almost woke himself up.

"About," prompted the crow.

"My folks." His forearms smelled of sunshine. Willy licked sweat off his wrist and rubbed his cheek on it. "Where they are now. If they think of me." His eyes stung. *Shit.* His belly muscles clenched. He was not going to cry.

"Sure they do." The crow shifted on his back, hunkering down so that its stiff tail tickled him below the shoulder blade. "You're tired," the crow said.

"Tired," Willy breathed. "So tired and lonely." He opened his eyes with difficulty. His hair lay thick and black over his face. Each individual hair was outlined in red fire as if the sun were gilding it. "I want to die."

In its gravelly way the crow crooned, "Naaw, you don't. Cummere, lemme tell you a story." It craned its neck over his shoulder until it was eye to beady eye with him. "You go back to sleep and I'll tell it."

Obediently Willy shut his eyes. The crow shifted on its scritchy feet and settled. Willy could feel it rising and falling on his shoulder as he breathed, a light creature, lighter than a cat, but more compact of power. It felt like a hand on his back, patting him, the gentle hand of a giant bigger than the river, bigger than the sky. There, there.

He sighed.

There, there. The dream was getting better now.

The horrible feelings seemed to leak out of him all up and down his body. He might never be strong enough. So what. Nobody needed him right now. His eyes rolled up into his head and found a place where all was dark and safe.

"There." A wing whispered briefly. The hand rocked on his back and stilled again. "Okay. Once upon a time there was a kid who had a best friend. His friend was so big nobody could see him. The kid really loved his friend, because his friend taught him how to fly."

No fair, thought Willy. I was feeling good there for a minute. A ripple of black grief came and went in his belly, seeping slowly out of him into the rough stuff of the nest.

"His friend sure was big. Everybody for miles around knew his friend. The kid had a good thing going there. He was special. His friend wanted the best for him."

Another sigh fell out of Willy. His back rose and fell.

"So about ten years ago his friend was getting kinda old. Worried about it. Somebody hadda look after his kid. So he said to the kid's parents, 'Giddover here,' he said, 'don't you know trouble's coming? Gummint inspectors! Lightning! The chaos of an accumulation of unmediated vital waveforms!' Well, the kid's parents didn't know diddly, but his friend soon set 'em straight. 'Somebody's gotta do my job when I'm gone,' he said."

My parents couldn't have done that job, Willy thought. He would have said so, but he was asleep, too tired to open his lips, too tired to swallow.

"Well, the kid's parents cried and fussed, but his friend was very convincing. 'Sheesh,' he said, 'you think *this* will be hard! You just try taking care of all them kids.'"

That's right, Willy thought. Now you're talking. That's the truth. Oh, it really, really is. He drifted deeper and floated slightly out of his body. The crow roused fastidiously. "Don't interrupt." It stepped off Willy's shoulder and paced back and forth between the two boys' heads. "So the kid's parents bitched and moaned and then they tried to run away. Yellow. A'course if they'da stayed where they were told, they'd be dead by now. To tell you the truth, kid," the crow said confidentially, taking a liberty, "they wasn't good for much annahow.

"They tried to run away. They went across the river in a boat, but their feet got too big. They stomped holes right through that boat. And they sank up to their knees in the mud. Where they stand to this day. Waitin' to get ee-lectricked and draggin' the river around their feet.

"And in doo time it gets to be now, and the shit has hit the fan. Ee-lection day comin' up, kid." The crow cooed with malice. "They thought they was running away, but they didn't run far, kid. Trust me on that."

It turned its canny eye on the west bank of the river. "Now the whole river is gonna move. Unless the new guy settles down where he belongs, those folks gonna be ee-lectricked, no doubt about it. They'll drag this river clear up around their ears. Better not be sleepin' here that day, kid." The crow paced thoughtfully, like a stout man walking with his hands clasped behind his shiny black coat. It glanced back at Willy.

"Mind you, they left all the heavy work to you. A'course you know that. 'Course you do," it repeated, its voice falling off in a soothing drone. The crow tilted its head at the boy's face, deep in its curtain of black hair. "Out like a light. Good kid." It hopped onto the trumpet case and shat.

Below in the clearing all was still, except for a single feather turning on a monofilament string. The crow cocked its head. What was that heavenly odor? Pigeon, flattened less than three hours ago, by the smell. Delicious! Definitely check this out. The crow inflated itself and let out a couple of yells. Neither boy stirred. Half-spreading its wings, the crow tipped itself over the edge of the nest.

Chapter Eighteen

O ne thing King would never put up with again was the squalor, everything smelling of damp all the time. On the pipeline he had seen empty houses abandoned among the firs. The crew would climb the rocks into these houses, the walls tumbled by fallen firs and larches, open windows covered in poison ivy. There they could eat their lunches while it rained; play cards, or look at the back numbers of Playboy that accumulate in such places. Patches of mildew stank in corners and coated the pictures of pale-pink breasts and bottoms in the magazines.

Sometimes a whole wall would be black with mildew. A translucent fungus grew from that, miniature forests of pale-white penises curling toward the light, turning themselves inside out into breasts, then ribby umbrellas, blackening, rotting, falling away in slimy sheets. The smell could stop him in the doorway. King always ate his lunch outside. The crew twitted him for being countrified.

The truth was, it stank of home.

One time he and Rae, exploring the upstream river islands, had come on a house even more abandoned and smelly than those in the Canadian mountains, oh, eight, nine years ago it must have been, a couple of miles upstream from here. The lumber had long since been stripped off the outer walls and floors. Nothing but lath and wilted plaster enclosed the place.

They stepped across the floor joists to a box spring. Rae laid swathes of new grass on it. She came there often.

She had showed him some things that day, he remembered. At length King had rolled away from her, his skinny chest heaving and running sweat. Wilted grass stuck to his back. He stared cross-eyed up at sunlight pouring through the ruined window frames. His head spun with what she had done to him. He closed his eyes and panted until the spinning world slowed. When he opened them, he saw a huge patch of black damp huddled in the one shadowy corner of the ceiling. He thought at first that hornets had built a nest there.

"Look, King." She pointed at the corner. "Toadstools."

"Naw." He heaved himself to his elbows and looked. There was a hot, scary feeling in his groin.

Rae stayed on her back. "Don't they grow funny!"

He squinted against the light. A bunch of white and yellow fungus grew in a hump out of the mold. He could see Time working while he watched: here's a brand new white button of a fungus, and right next to it a bigger brother, and a bigger one than that, then the biggest with its shining wet tip already aged. And then the terrifying descent down the wall, each fungus expanding, blowing outward, turning from penis, all tip, into breast, all swollen flesh and nipple, then collapsing, exposing bare black-and-white ribs to a harsh dry shrivelling light. Dozens of them. He shivered.

"That's death," he said. He turned away and lay down beside her, pushing his face into the crook of her shoulder.

She snorted. "That's life." She tried to turn his face. He stiffened and worked his nose into her armpit. She shook him. "Look. They're alive, King. Everything's alive."

"Not for long."

Chapter Nineteen

At lunchtime Alexander clocked out quickly before Ike could draft him to spend his lunch re-erecting the temporary power pole. He slung his veiled hardhat into his toolbag, shut the toolbag in his locker, and walked into Berne to buy lunch.

Then he ran down to the river boardwalk where Rae had led him yesterday afternoon. She knew all about this place. She would comfort him and tell him the truth. Maybe she would know a secret spot, and he could lose his fear in her body again.

His heart throbbed like a car radio. Her crowfoot stick swung in his hammer-loop. He touched the stick with his middle finger and felt a jolt.

How was he to find her if they couldn't be seen together?

He worked his way along the boardwalk to the broken wall where they had sat and parked with his hamburger. The noise inside him rose to a buzz while he thought about last night's dream, which he couldn't remember without a thrashing panic.

He would lurk, that's it. Wait. Maybe she would come this way today. He couldn't afford to lose this job, not so far from home, not with two checks out of three flying back to Gran. He glared across the river, chewing his burger furiously.

He became aware that he was not alone. When he put his hand down he found his fries had disappeared, and when he looked up he saw Mink, the wild girl-child, standing within sight and out of reach, wiping her hands on her tee shirt. She chewed quickly and swallowed. Her dark-ringed eyes were on him, alert and calm, like a crow who knows she can fly out of reach quicker than a man's brain can tell his legs to get after her. She half smiled.

Her brother was nowhere in sight. He put his hands down on his hips, near his toolbelt, just in case.

Behind him, Mink's brother leaped away and scuttled behind his sister. Alexander was aware of a cool place on his shoulder. The boy had actually been leaning up against him.

Wonderingly, Alexander found he was at peace inside now. The utter stillness of these wild things was as reassuring as the birdsong around him: No hawks nearby, no traps of man. He realized he was smiling. He waited.

"Show you something," Mink said.

Slowly, Alexander got up. He laid the rest of his hamburger on the wall behind him and did not look back.

They led him upriver to a swampy place. Mink scampered barefoot over the board path, Alexander treading carefully after her, his workboots leaving a damp waffle print on the whitened wood. His clomping started a frog. It squeaked and shot across the path, belly flopping into the open water. Alexander shook his head. Should not frogs be under the mud until next month?

He turned to ask Ink, who followed, the remains of the hamburger tucked into one cheek. The boy glared at him. Alexander blinked and said nothing.

Obey their rules. Be quiet. Wild things know what they have to know already, just by smelling you. Pay attention. You won't learn by asking. The boy had come close enough to smell the hairs in his ears.

At that thought Alexander felt covered with a warm, safe love. A ridiculous feeling, but it belonged here among the weeds and wild creatures.

They turned off-path and aimed for the water. Alexander's boots crunched over treacherous spiky reeds. The children marched ahead, their bare feet as tough as his own feet had once been, when he ran along the trash-covered beach on the bad side of Freeport. Where the cattails grew greenest and tallest, Mink stopped. Alexander and her brother caught up.

At their feet was a hole full of water. Mink looked up at him expectantly.

It looked like a blue hole, or a big land crab hole. Slick mud surrounded it. There were mounds of little mud balls the size of marbles around the rim, like cannonballs made all alike and stacked, then knocked over and scattered, like soldier-crab mudballs, only big. Some wet spots made him think something had been drinking here, maybe a raccoon. Many raccoons, by the look of the smooth, packed mud. The river itself was only a yard away behind the thinnest veil of new reeds.

Mink prompted him with an impatient gesture, her lips pressed shut. *Look.* Alexander hunkered down.

It was much too big to be a crab's hole. It was three feet across, and water filled it almost to the brim. Alexander glanced through the reeds at the river. The water in the hole was higher. Was it a spring? But this was dirty water, not clear, full of little floating bits and particles. It gave off a powerful fishy odor. He thought he saw a fish flash up and out of sight again. The surface moved as though working itself up to a boil. He reached a hand out.

"Don't!" Mink jerked his sleeve with a skinny hand of authority.

Alexander watched.

The sun passed behind a cloud. Suddenly Alexander could see that the waterhole really was boiling: dimpling, humping, and sinking, flecks of stuff making curls and whirlpool patterns half out of sight. The fish flashed by again, and then a turtle surfaced, carried on the strange current rather than swimming. All its legs stuck out, and its hooked mouth strained. It thrashed mightily and made the bank, crawled ashore and sat for a moment. The sun came out. The turtle bent its yellow-and-green-striped head toward the sun as if taking a bearing and then set off purposefully for the river, its sliver of tail leaving a shining wet pencil line on the packed mud. Alexander watched it, fascinated, until it plunged through the reeds and tumbled into the big water beyond.

Mink tugged his sleeve again. She pointed at the hole.

A five-inch snakeling wriggled frantically to the surface. Alexander's heart clutched in sympathy. The water's boiling action carried it to the edge of the pool, and with a convulsive effort the snake hurled itself out onto the mud. In the sun, the gunmetal colors glittered for an instant. Then the snake streaked into the rushes toward dry land, leaving a wet S-curve in its wake.

"Where do they come from?" he marvelled.

Another fish appeared. Two, three, five, Alexander lost count. He stared into a cauldron of fish, a fish-boil in reverse, where the main dish rose to the surface alive and thrashed to get out. The children named them for him.

"Bullhead."

"Crappie."

"Catfish."

This is kind of creepy, he thought. He remembered his Gran had a story about how all the animals had been born in one place. For the life of him he couldn't remember if the story had included water creatures. Must have. Look at them.

"What happens when it fills up with fish?" Fill it must, at this rate.

He heard a rustle behind him. He looked around.

Mink flourished a plastic milk bottle that had been cut and punctured to make a sieve. She elbowed him aside.

Solemnly she waited, her milk bottle poised, as the water thickened with fish. Finally, when they began leaping gape-mouthed clear of the surface and Ink was squeaking in wordless urgency, she plunged the bottle in and brought up a wriggling load. The sieve-bottom cascaded water over her tee shirt. Carefully she turned and scuttled the few feet to the river. Ink rushed ahead to part the reeds for her. Sploosh-splash, bright blazes of silver light poured out. Then she handed the milk bottle to her brother.

Bemused, Alexander watched them bale fish for ten minutes, strictly sharing turns. "But where are they coming from?"

Ink shrugged. His colorless eyes shone and skittered, his little arm was drawn back, his milk bottle aimed for the plunge.

"I would surely like to know," Alexander murmured. He watched Ink carry his load to the river and dump it. "Give me a turn? I'll reach down full deep. My arms are longer."

Mink said, "No."

Ink handed the bottle off to Mink.

Alexander smiled. "Oh, so you can play and I can't." Maybe Rae was keeping an eye on this miracle. Where was she? He remembered his own miracle. His urgency rose in him again. He stilled it. Be with the kids. Learn something.

The fish stopped boiling up. Mink hooked the milk bottle over a stump of cattail and flopped down on the mud to watch. After a while another turtle drifted up, and after that two frogs. Alexander squatted by the hole. The questions he needed to ask! They're kids, Alexander. Go slow. "How long have you been doing this?"

Mink lay on her elbows, puffing and looking pleased. "Yesterday and a lot of times at night. We *have* to. They can't get out."

Ink spoke for the first time. "Yeah. We found it! All fish like—" and he spread his arms out, swinging in a circle at the trampled mud round the hole. Alexander imagined the waterhole overflowing with fish, the ground covered with flipping flopping gasping silver creatures, slipping into the rustly dry reeds and wedging there, so near and yet so far from deep water. Ink pantomimed how he had grabbed fish barehanded and thrown them toward the river, giggling and shrieking and sucking his fingers when a gill or a scale cut him. Alexander felt sorrow and at the same time a solemn joy, as if he had missed the larger part of the miracle, and yet there was still some left for him to see.

Someone yelled nearby. Pounding footsteps approached. "God*dammit* now I've got you!" The children scattered. Alexander looked up in surprise.

A white man in a suit, a sopping-wet, filthy, but very expensive suit, burst into the clearing. He missed Mink, but he got hold of Ink in an instant, shaking him and shouting before Alexander could jump to his feet. Mink danced around them, making snatches for her brother's ankles and the stranger's punishing arms. Ink screamed.

Alexander stood up and put a hand on the man's arm. His hand was shaken off.

Adrenalin poured up through Alexander from his feet. "Hey, man. Let go," he said. "Let go!"

The white man snarled and, still gripping Ink with his right hand, swung at Alexander with his left. Mink hurled herself at the man's back and grabbed his hair. He roared.

Alexander caught him by the shoulder. "Shut up!"

In a convulsive movement Mink flew away off the white man's back. He finally let go of her brother to attend to Alexander.

There was a splash behind them. Then a long scream, shrill and desperate, descending on and on, lower and lower, to grief, disaster, horror. Alexander couldn't turn round to look. He had his hands full.

"Cut it out, man! Now stop it!" He took the man by both arms. Sopping wet! What had the kids been doing to him?

The sopping-wet white man was in a berserk fury. He had an inch on Alexander but nothing like the bulk. He settled down fast. "Don't touch me, nigger!" he said through his teeth.

Alexander kept his grip. "You going to calm down?"

The fight was going out of the fellow. His glare cooled as he got a good look at Alexander, twice his size. "Okay! Okay, okay," he grumbled. He tried to jerk himself free.

Alexander let go. Ink hurled himself sobbing against Alexander's leg. Alexander looked down. "Okay, little man," he said. "Maybe you should go."

The white man narrowed his eyes at him, taking in Alexander's work boots, the layers of plaid shirts and tee shirts that were his uniform. "You work for me, fat boy?"

Alexander bent over Ink. The child pointed, hysterical.

Alexander threw himself to the ground beside the hole. He plunged his left arm into the water. It was surprisingly warm. His fingertips touched something—a root? a foot? and he snatched, but it slid away from him. Ink stood by his ear screaming encouragement, horror, anxiety.

"Jesus," Alexander said under his breath and stretched until his shoulder was immersed, until his ear touched the water. The hole was a tunnel, slick and smooth as if polished by a water-animal. He twiddled his fingers around its smooth wall until they found a bend in the tunnel. He reached around the bend. Nothing. The boy's screaming came to him in two notes, through the ear in the air and through the ear in the water. Alexander thought he heard a third voice in the water and cursed under his breath. "Shut up!" he said, and warm fishy water slipped into his mouth. "I can't hear her!"

The white man squatted over him. All Alexander could see was a pair of soggy Italian shoes. "Get back to work, nigger. If you want to keep your job."

Alexander rolled an eye at him. He didn't move. "You knock the kid in the water. She drown, is your fault," he panted.

Where was she? He stretched another inch. The angry wet white man still squatted over him.

"Child killer," Alexander panted. His fingers brushed something again and he grabbed, a leg this time for sure, but it slid away again. Alexander cried out and lunged, feeling the tunnel bend again, the elusive foot just out of his reach.

The white man backed up. "Prove it," he said, but he didn't sound confident. Alexander heard him wheel and run away.

Ink clung to Alexander's side, peering into the hole. Alexander shut his eyes. The water was colder down at the deep end of the tunnel. He was afraid his fingers would go numb and he wouldn't feel the child even if he touched her. He felt a rush of current over his fingers and panicked: the open river lay down there somewhere. With a lunge and a prayer he grabbed out, until he thought his shoulder joint would pop. Her foot came into his palm neatly, and he gripped it. Just another few inches. He plunged his head under the water, jamming his shoulders in the hole, and slid his grip higher on her leg. He pulled gently.

Down here under the water the river voice was silenced. The boy, whom he could feel through his back, was a warm heartbeat. He pulled. Somewhere down here, too, he could hear a roaring. Just the engine of a truck far away, he thought, tugging gently on his catch. But it was a wonderful sound just the same. Layers of bright rich sound, setting up a vibration in his chest. He pulled and pulled. He realized that he was intolerably thirsty. He opened his mouth and sucked in the fishy water. The best he'd ever tasted. He pulled.

The child's second foot came into his hand. So he needn't fear she would tangle herself in her own limbs and get stuck in a bend of this tunnel like a breach birth killing itself in the very doorway of the world. What a lot of bends there were down here. He wrapped his long fingers around the little ankles in his hand. With some regret, for the roaring was louder now, stabbingly sweet and harsh like the voice of a lion in ecstasy, he withdrew his shoulders from the mudhole, pulling gently.

The air burst on him like a bucket of cold water in the face, ripping his streaming skin. He pulled gently. The boy laid small hands on his arm and helped him pull, hand over hand. Together they brought up the boy's sister. The boy helped drag her up onto his chest.

Alexander's ears rang. He let his arm slip back in the hole and sagged onto his back.

Mink thrashed and choked, vomiting water on his cold wet shirt. Alexander couldn't move. He lay on his back, listening to her gasp and heave in the air, while his burning body poured heat into her cold one. He realized, too, that he was still listening for that faraway truck sound, though for sure by now it would be long gone down the highway. The sweetest sound he could ever remember hearing. His eyes closed, listening for it. *Ah, there.* Nearby, a red-winged blackbird trilled as if to sing along.

A tug on his arm made him open his eyes. Alexander turned his head and saw that Ink knelt beside him. The boy jerked on his hand where it dangled into the warm water.

"Come on!" Ink choked out, as if language were a torture that

Alexander imposed on him by his enormousness and his stupidity.

Obediently Alexander drew his hand up. He hated to do it. The water was so warm, and the air was cold. He came back from dreamland to realize his hand was still half-in, half-out of the water, still moving. Slow motion, he thought muzzily. I must be sleepy. The boy had hold of his wrist and was hauling at his hand like a sailor hauling rope, though his little hands could barely encircle Alexander's wrist. Alexander felt the rasp of the reeds on his palm, the warm water on his knuckles, the smooth mud wall of the tunnel sliding down, curving and bending toward the deepest, coldest water, where his fingertips dangled and brushed against each other in the current.

Mink stood beside her brother, laboring at the same work. Alexander opened his eyes fully and watched with detachment as the sun dried her mud-slimed hair. The white wisps peeled away from her head and floated up like thistledown in the breeze. The sound of that huge roaring voice filled his chest as if he sang it himself. How beautiful was the intent frown on her face, her brilliant, pale eyes almost hidden by her sun-whitened hair as she squinted, her teeth sunk in her lower lip, as she hauled and hauled on his slack hand. Clouds sailed behind her head, throwing shadow over the sun's face and then passing. The girl saw him blink his eyes. She pivoted ever so slowly. Her scowl of concentration turned to annoyance. She pulled her leg far back and kicked him hard in the side.

Alexander came up onto his elbows with a jerk. His hands clenched. "What for you kicked me?" he tried to say, but water ran out of his mouth. Suddenly he realized he couldn't breathe.

His body came back to him all at once. He curled on his side, coughing and retching. He was cold, now that his hand had at last come out of the warm water. His right arm lay bent under him. The elbow was in agony where he ground it against the mud. He retched. His side throbbed where Mink had kicked him. Agony pulsed in his elbow. His left arm wouldn't support him. It was clammy, tingling, useless as a rubber crutch. Fucked up my elbow, he thought. That's going to make it hard to work. He curled the wet arm and clenched his hand experimentally.

At that the children let go of him. His arm fell slowly back. The fucked-up elbow stopped hurting. His wrist hit the mud, fingers slapping the dry reeds and coiling around the new reeds, fingertips splashing into cold running water.

Crickets sang in the reeds. The river lapped the bank. His left arm tingled unmercifully, like the worst crack his funnybone ever had. Even his palm, even his fingernails felt it. He scrabbled at the ground.

Alexander didn't dare look at his arm and hand. He lay still, his sodden dreads lying against his cheek and trickling water down his face and neck. The packed mud under his face was the richest thing he could ever remember smelling. He tried wiggling his left elbow. It flopped horribly. Lie still. You'll scare yourself to death, he thought.

Alexander lay still.

The blackbird sang its whirring song again, ending on an upward shriek like a hiccup. He listened intently, trying not to notice the slow drag of mud and reeds under his palm as it moved over the ground. That was the wind in the reeds, not his fingers slithering and shrinking. The children stood nearby, their bare feet within sight. How still they are, like small animals, he thought. The crickets' voices deafened him.

From where he lay, he could just see through a chink in the old and new cattail reeds. The little sandbar where the children had been boating yesterday was right in his line of sight. The yellow heads of its willows shone bright above the choppy water. Something was caught in those willow branches, a big something, like a dirty bird with its wings stretched out to dry, or else, but a ridiculous thought, an enormous nest.

An insect landed on his ear. Thoughtlessly he slapped it.

At his sudden movement the children leaped back and fled.

He held the hand up to his face. The fingers were three inches too long, like the fingers of drummers embroidered on his Gran's big skirts. He flexed them. The tingling intensified. He clenched his hand. When he opened his fist, all was as it should be.

He blinked. He sat up. His head was stuffed with the noises of the riverbank. Behind the railroad tracks, across the road, less than five hundred yards away, the whistle blew for the end of lunch break.

Alexander sighed hugely. He had heard of people dying and having adventures until they were brought back by the doctors. Perhaps he had drowned, and the child brought him back from dreamland by cracking his ribs.

The lunch-whistle stopped. Real life. He hauled himself to his feet. His hair dripped fishy water over his face and shoulders. He was wet down to his waist. Can't go to work like this, he thought, light-headed. He remembered that there was another flannel shirt in his toolbag. Okay.

When he stood up, he found a packet of wet papers almost at his feet. There was much fine print, and the Atlas Properties logo. So that's who the crazy white man was. He glanced across the road to the site. The chimney pipe of the construction office trailer stuck up past the trees between him and his job.

Carefully avoiding another glance at the hole, he turned and headed back to work.

Chapter Twenty

Wisely or unwisely, John Fowier decided to cross US 31 to the development site to get a phone, since his was ruined with water. From there he could call a cab and maybe, though he was nervous of the scene with those kids and the big fat nigger, a cop. Nobody messes with John Fowier and walks away from *that*. He squelched up to the construction office trailer.

Ike the foreman didn't recognize him, but Walter Chepi, the architect, did. Fowier was intensely aware of his filthy wet state. Introductions took place without a handshake, and he declined to tell them how he got that way.

He used their phone. Triple-A, impressed with his voice, promised a towtruck with a compressor. Then, wishing the foreman and Chepi would go away, he dialed another number. He should have called from a more private phone, but he was too fucking mad to wait another minute.

"Did you get the prelim paperwork done?" he barked.

"Yup," the voice of Joe Stass said.

"I'm through dicking around here."

"You want me to proceed?" Joe was a bagman's bagman, but he was discreet.

Fowier thought about the Mercedes, all four tires flat, and the nigger glaring up at him from that puddle, accusing him of killing the kid. *Burn the fuckers out.* "Yeah. Soon." He hung up.

He didn't want to go outside to wait, but Ike, unhampered by his boss's presence and unimpressed with the developer in his current soggy state, expressed himself freely in the Brooklyn idiom about wet chairs and puddles in the office trailer and guys who held the door open to let the bugs in. Fuming, Fowier went outside.

A squad car was rolling slowly by on US 31. Burning with a sense of his wrongs, John Fowier marched up to it.

Right away things went wrong.

"So let me get this straight," said the cop, who had gotten out of the car more because Fowier was dripping into it, Fowier felt, than because he was intimidated. The cop was grinning. "You jumped into a hole with Raedawn Somershoe and got all wet."

He exchanged glances with his partner in the squad car, who was obviously trying not to giggle.

The first cop shrugged. "It happens to everybody in this town. Some of us like it."

His partner broke up completely. The first cop watched with interest but no alarm as Fowier turned ugly colors.

John Fowier tried to explain what had happened without making himself look like a prowling tomcat. The laughing policeman was putting him off. Twice he described his arrival, his negotiator role, his attempts to communicate, her silence, the unpleasantness of the hole, and then stuck, unable to explain why he had lost his self-control and unwilling to admit he'd porked her or why she had left him there. He felt himself heating up red-hot with humiliation. All but his legs of course. His legs were ice-cold, and so were his feet, his back, his chest, his arms, and the back of his neck, where the wet gritty clothes stuck to him. Black gnats whirled in front of his face. Rage and pride kept him from pawing at them.

The cop interrupted him in the middle of the third go-around. "Yes, I got that part. What I don't see, I don't see how you got all wet and she didn't. I never heard of that happening, not in all the years I been in this town." Fucking cop thought he was funny. He said kindly to Fowier, "Maybe you should go back home and get into some dry things, huh? You'll catch your death out in the open air."

Fowier jabbed his forefinger at the trailers across the road. "That bimbo goddamn near drowned me, I'm telling you! And what she did to my car—"

"She may be a bimbo, Mr. Whosis," the cop said, suddenly standing very close to him, "but she's our bimbo. Who are you? Are you accusing her of doing something to your car now?"

Fowier looked into his face and backed up a foot. "Well, her kids did it. Let the air out of my tires—"

Looking past the cop's shoulder, over the hood of the squad car, he saw the big fat nigger with the long hair crossing the road with long strides, coming straight toward them. The nigger was wet from the waist up. Fowier met his stony black eyes and shut his mouth.

"Can you prove they let the air out of your tires?" the cop said, pounding home his point.

Fowier opened his mouth and shut it again.

The nigger came straight up to him and, without a word, handed him a packet of soggy papers. He looked Fowier hard in the eye. Fowier took the papers, looked from the cop to the nigger, and backed up another step. A car beeped behind them.

Saved by the cab. "Uh, that's my tow. I'll just go tell him to wait."

They stood watching him while he moved stiffly to the tow truck. His clothes were revoltingly cold and clammy. Black bugs flew up into his face as he walked, and he could barely move his legs. "Gimme five, will ya?" he said to the driver.

The walk back gave Fowier time to think. The nigger must have got the kid out of the water or he'd be running for an ambulance now. He shuddered, imagining the nigger carrying a dead kid in his arms straight up to him and the squad car, with that same look in his eye. Christ, that would have been a fuckup supreme.

When he got back to the squad car he said quickly, "Time I got moving. Let's just drop the whole thing, okay? I'm getting pneumonia out here."

The standing policeman looked him over, and then looked at the nigger, wet to the waist. He raised his eyebrows. "Okeedoke. Next time, pick a woman you can handle. Then the police don't have to get involved." The cop gave the nigger a friendly leer. "You have fun with her in the hole?" The nigger gave the cop a long strange look and stalked away.

Fowier, his rage threatening to overcome him again, turned on his heel and headed for the tow truck. Halfway there he swerved and went back to the construction office trailer.

"Hey!" Ike said, on seeing him.

Fowier stopped in the doorway, his knuckles white on the door handle. He looked around the trailer. That Chepi guy, the architect, was standing over the table looking at drawings. "You. Come outside for a minute."

Chepi came out and the two of them walked to the cab.

Fowier talked fast. "Here's the scene. We're not getting anywhere with those Okies across the road. Mike at Scadwell says you know 'em, is this true?" Mike at Scadwell was the senior architect partner, as Fowier knew Chepi would know. He was strong-arming Mike's boy, he realized, but in his condition he felt he had to make a point with somebody or else he'd explode.

"Well, I met the woman, Gelia Som-somershoe." Chepi did a double-take at the look on Fowier's face.

Fowier realized he was still losing it. With a superhuman effort he tried to simmer down. "Okay, great. I've had it with that bit—with those people. You give it a shot. Here's the documents—no, you can't use that." He handed the soggy paperwork to Chepi and took it back in one movement. *Christ, I'm going loopy.* His head and hands felt hot, and the rest of him was icy inside and out. Catching pneumonia, too.

"I'll have my girl Fed Ex you a set by tomorrow morning." He batted a gnat away from his eyes. "Go talk to 'em. Loosen 'em up, y'know? I'll send you a memo explaining the offer. Read it carefully. Don't fuck up. And keep me posted, okay? This deal has got to get settled sometime this century.

"Here's my card." He reached reflexively for his wallet and paused with a sinking feeling, but it was there, and the inside of the wallet wasn't very wet, either. "Call me tomorrow. If you have to date 'em up, take that— that woman out for dinner, send me the bill."

Chepi looked smart but fuddled, which was just how Fowier wanted him. He looked like a weak sister. Just the kind of guy to seem harmless to a bunch of horny Okies. Fowier repeated, "Call me if you make contact. You got it?"

Chepi nodded, then said, "Yes, sir."

Atsa my boy, Fowier thought. I need somebody to say "Yes, sir" to me for a few minutes. Or hours. Suzy's back at the hotel, he remembered suddenly, and so's a hot shower and a nice big bed with a river view. Well, hell. This day *can* improve.

Chapter Twenty-One

Ernest Brown and Angelia Somershoe shared a truck garden. The land they worked was almost certainly past the extreme edge of Angelia's property, hacked out of a cattail-choked marsh by a Somershoe woman of a previous generation, and filled with such waste and soil as Somershoes had seen fit to include. Nobody had challenged her use of the land yet, probably because nobody wanted it.

Ernest had no formal agreement with Angelia about sharing it, either. He didn't mind. The garden was the least irregular thing about their relationship.

This morning they had turned the spring compost into the earth, and this afternoon they would lay out the rows. By mid-June the bramble beds would yield early berries; by the end of June, they would have tomatoes and squash, earlier than anyone else in town was able to grow them. Rae would sell these to her coworkers at the library and the hardware store. Later yields would go into Angelia's formidable August and September canning sessions.

Now was the season for planning, the most enjoyable part of a garden, Ernest thought, setting aside what the digging did to his bursitisy shoulder. In recent years Davy had dug for them, when they could keep his mind on the work. This spring the boy seemed unsettled and flitted away whenever one of the adults spoke to him. Ernest remarked on it as he unwound the old gray string and paced off the rows.

"Davy's gone fritzy," Angelia muttered. "And no wonder." She wasn't as athletic as she used to be. Spadework left her puffing and red in the face.

"Do you suppose he understands the situation?" He bent with a grunt, poised his stake deliberately, and thrust it into the black dirt with satisfaction. Best dirt he'd ever worked. Better than in Virginia.

She crept to the right another two feet. Together they measured off another row.

"No doubt. Mind the raspberry canes. He can see the signs. Gramma Romy used to say the simple knows stuff quicker'n we do. Wish my daughter had a inkling," she added dispassionately.

Ernest wasn't fooled. Angelia was jealous as hell of Rae's new status. It was a big job, finding a new man to put his feet in that hole in the ground across the road, and it seemed to be running Rae frazzled. Nor did her mother seem inclined to smooth Rae's path for her. Well, what Angelia saw fit to keep from Rae, he wouldn't speak of.

Straightening his back with a grunt, he said drily, "She has a few things on her mind." Such as feeding and clothing the bunch of us, he did not say. Keeping an eye on Cracker and the boys, putting pants on the twins when she can catch 'em, and living in Angelia's shadow as number two Somershoe hussy. He bent and set the next stake.

"Her new young man stood her up," Angelia added, her smugness obvious. "S'posed to come to dinner last night."

Ernest said, "I was there." They changed positions. "He didn't want to lose his job."

Angelia took up the string and began to lay out the cross-rows. "She's gonna have to fall back on King Gowdy."

Ernest shook his head. "King won't do. He's just a baby."

"All men are babies." She poked savagely at a clod with her trowel. "Don't know what's so all-fired innersting about some dude from Jamaica." The wet clod got a smack with the flat of her trowel.

"Bahamas, I thought she said."

She jerked a shoulder angrily. "Whatever. What's the matter with our coloreds, if she wants one? The dirt don't know no different. And don't—" she squinted up at him and pointed her trowel at him, "Don't you even think of it, Ernest Brown. I got a better use for you."

He blanched. "Perish the thought!"

She laughed at his dismay. "Aw, I didn't mean it."

Didn't mean it. Didn't think he could handle the job, or didn't want to give him up? He wondered which. She poked at her end of the row, while he at the other end worked toward her with the claw, breaking up clods and smoothing the surface.

She said, "We got, what, a few days? King's been around his whole life, and she's gonna break in some feller who never set eyes on the place 'cept to plow it up with a bulldozer?" She sat back on her knees and surveyed the fresh-turned earth. "A heap of growing here this year."

He wondered if she actually saw something there, a shimmering or a burning, like the burning in her own bones that made her such a lustful thing. Angelia and that dirt had a lot in common.

She said slowly, "I'm remembering. Must have been eight, ten years ago. Gramma used to say, they does that sometimes, marks somebody to take their place when they feel the end coming. I could of swore he told me he done that. But if so, where is it?"

He pursed his lips. "Likely torn down with all the other trees across the road."

It wasn't his business to talk about. Only the ley lines had been dancing all over the place for the past three days, first veering toward the river, then back toward the ridge. And the river seemed to be following them.

It wasn't his business. The women had always dealt with it. He held his tongue.

"S'pose so." She winced.

Footsteps. Rae's voice called, "Gelia?" Rae steamed up the path, astonishment and outrage in her face. When her toes touched their new rows she stopped, her hands on her hips. "Gelia, do you remember telling me about that city man who came and tried to buy our land?"

Angelia sat up on her heels, a warlike look in her eye. She owned the land where they all parked their trailers. "Back, is he?"

"Back and gone. If he's the one." Rae's dress was wet at the hem, and she was sooty all up the back, on her palms, and on one shoulder.

Angelia said, "Tall, blond, brittle, fancy suit, lots of gold jiggers all over him?"

"That's the one."

"What did he want?" Ernest said.

"Same old same old, money in the bank and a share in the new buildings. Did he offer you that last time?" Rae looked at her mother, and Angelia shook her head. "So that's new. He had papers, but I guess they got drowned."

"Did you tell him no?" Ernest said.

Rae chewed her lip. "I don't think I said anything."

"So? What's the fuss?" Angelia said impatiently.

"He was awful, awful mad." Ernest hoped she wouldn't panic. Rae was all that kept them together. "What's going to happen to us? We can't leave this place. Can we?"

Angelia hesitated, and Ernest turned an amazed face to her. Angelia said, "Tell me what happened."

Rae heaved a sigh. "He's a very peculiar fellow. Got a hole in his middle, keeps himself all up in his head. I was cleaning house for the kids, and he came right into it with me. At first I thought he kind of liked me, but, you know, the more he talked, the stranger he got, talking real fast and kind of bulking up at me. And angry? Hoo!"

"Did you push him?" her mother said, her eyebrows up.

Rae flushed. "Maybe. I didn't *say* anything," she added defensively.

Oho. Now they would argue about sex. Ernest thought it was time he got out of the line of fire. He faded back and went up the path to lay out their lunch on a blanket. If he had to, he could take his sandwich down to the river. He listened.

Angelia tut-tutted. "Them kind is brittle."

"That's not the point, Gelia."

"Well, get to it then."

"You know how that old shack is. I've never been in it with more people than just me before. How it *smells* at you. Today it was so much *stronger*." Rae paused. "Everything was stronger." She chewed her lips. "First he was horny and that was okay, and then he was just furious, and the place started to flood. Well, I got out of there and went to get Cracker, 'cause I didn't want to pull him out of that hole all by myself. Didn't find Cracker, but when I came back he was gone. Looked like it flooded clear to the top. He must have been *mad*," she added, sounding awed.

"You tell a story all beginning and ending and no middle, Daughter," Angelia said.

Ernest unwrapped his sandwich and edged toward the water.

"Did you *listen* to him?" Angelia said, needling.

"Of course I was listening to him! I didn't say anything! Good grief, Gelia, the room's smaller'n an outhouse nearly, we was standing on top of each other. I told you, he was all head and shoulders, and this big hole in the middle. I don't suppose," Rae added with surprise, "I don't suppose he even knew he was feeling thataway."

Angelia mm-hmmed. "One of those. I bet you pushed him." As if Rae were the pushy one.

"Oh, shut up."

Ernest took his peanut butter and pickle sandwich to a stack of old tires twenty feet away, behind a stand of cattails, and sat down. Their voices faded. He could hear fine from here, if he had to. He bit in and chewed, listening instead to the pickles crunch. Crunch, crunch. His joints might be going back on him, but his teeth were still good. Thank goodness he could drink milk, it probably saved his teeth for him. Plenty of folks in his family couldn't drink milk at all.

"What's that got to do with it?" Rae was close to shouting.

Ernest winced. My Angelia, she knows where every nerve is.

"—keep a hold on a man," came Angelia's voice, softer but getting hotter. "—rushing this Bahama feller, and now he's gone panicky and won't come over."

"He's the night watchman over there!" Rae protested.

"Uh-uh. You oughta use a little finesse."

"Finesse!" Rae hooted. "You should talk. You just want to try for him yourself!"

"Now, before you get all riled at me, just listen. I ain't after this feller of yours."

Oh, Angelia, you liar, thought Ernest. He shut his eyes, his belly shaking with silent laughter.

Angelia's tone softened. "'Stead of you just jumping out and trying to drag the feller home first night, give him a little space. Some fellers is scaret of meeting the folks right off."

"I don't bring 'em all home," Rae said sulkily. "*You* know what happens when I do." As did Ernest. Angelia liked to keep a snug hold on her number one hussy position.

"That's true," Angelia said in a peacemaking voice. "I was wondering why you wanted to this time."

Ernest held his breath. The firefight might have come to an early halt, though it took Angelia lying her pants off to do it.

There was a pause. "I like him," Rae said.

Hearing Rae's tone, Ernest wondered suddenly if she had the faintest idea where she and this young man would likely end up.

"I guess so. Now you listen to your old ma." Angelia was at her least convincing when she came over all motherloving and wise, in Ernest's opinion. "Just—just go easy a little. Back off. Let him stew. He's gonna wonder what you think of him, and you just let him. 'Nother day with no word from you, and pure curiosity will bring him right around, and to the dickens with his boss. You'll see."

Would Rae swallow it? Ernest stood. Time to break this up before Angelia lied herself into any more trouble.

As he rustled loudly through the cattails, Rae said skeptically, "So you can put the moves on him."

Angelia came into view. Her right hand was raised. "As God is my witness, I won't even look at him," she said solemnly.

Ernest bustled up with his hands full of sandwiches and gave one to each Somershoe.

"Well, you better not," Rae said. She gave her mother a dark look but said no more. "Thank you, Ernest."

They stood and ate peanut butter and pickle sandwiches while Ernest, somewhat thickly, explained what was to be planted in each row, when it would bloom, when it would set fruit, how much they could expect to put up in cans by the end of summer. He chattered until the sound of his voice nearly put him to sleep.

But it worked. Rae simmered down. "Thanks for the samwich, Erny. I'm going to the Piggly Wiggly now, since I can't get into the kids' hole til they drain it. I just hope to God it's safe for them. Gelia, did you use up the peanut butter?"

"Nope," Angelia said.

"You sure? This sure is a lot of samwiches, and it was near gone this morning."

"I fwear," Angelia said, her mouth full.

"Well, all right. See you." Rae left.

Ernest turned a reproachful eye on her mother. "Angelia, that wasn't so. Why didn't you tell her she's out of peanut butter, for goodness sake?"

With a completely straight face, Angelia said, "I didn't want to distress her any more."

Ernest shook his head. "You are a caution, miss." He wiped peanut butter off his chin. "You lied to her up and down."

"Well, she could make a mess of everything."

"And your untruths will help that?" Ernest looked down at the rows of strings and the tidy barrows of earth ready to cover the hidden seed. "It's occurred to me, Angelia, does she know what she will have to do?"

"Goodness knows." Angelia reached for a bit of waxed paper, licked it clean, and folded it in four.

"Have you *told* her?" When he got no answer, he caught his woman's eye. "Well?"

Angelia turned her shoulder. "She's addled in the head." He frowned, and she put her hands out. "She needs *guidance*. I'm going to *guide* her."

Ernest put his hands on his hips. "Angelia, you have no more control over that child than I have. Less. She's been putting the pants on in your house since she was fourteen. Why should she trust you to guide her? You never have before. You need to tell her."

Angelia just turned her shoulder again. With the green and gold light of the spring sun on her, she looked like a girl. They ought to have been sisters, Ernest thought. Though they'd still be fighting over the same men. Was Angelia really going to sneak around Rae's new man? Looked like it. There would be trouble this time, more trouble than Angelia could handle.

He said instead, "She won't take King Gowdy." He took the folded papers full of seeds from their box and carefully removed the rubber band. "Tomatoes, beans, carrots, spinach, peas."

"I s'pose not. Pass me some tomato seeds. She wants this new feller. Big strong young dude."

Ernest heard the wistfulness in Angelia's voice. It hurt him in spite of all his wise years with her. It was clear enough how different they were, himself and Alexander. The boy was big, bigger than Cracker, young and strong. Earnest knew how a youngster like that would look to Angelia, next to her little old shoe. He feared she might decide to steal this man from Rae and put his feet in that hole herself, risks be damned. Gloom descended on him.

"Well, I've *told* her I'll keep hands off," she grumped. After a minute of setting tomato seed she said, "D'you s'pose he's another weenie?"

"Angelia, your language."

"You know what I mean, Mr. Mealymouth. Every time she's took a real fancy to someone, he's turned out limp."

"We don't know she has a fancy for this one," Ernest countered.

"Oh, don't we!" She put a goofy look on her face and spoke in a baby voice. "'I *like* him!'" She poked tomato seeds into the earth. "Idiot child.

How any daughter of mine can like so many pansy-ass boys. And it ain't only boys. That Cracker."

"You can't call Cracker a pansy," Ernest objected. "Great heavens, he'd be offended. What do you say, beans? Or peas?"

"Peas for a change. Shorter stakes, which is all we got. No, I guess he ain't a pansy." She mounded dirt over her row of tomato seeds, pressing it to leave the print of her small gloved hands. He watched her bottom rise and fall as she crept along the row. "He just don't put up much of a fight no more."

That made more sense. Ernest knew she liked the chase nearly as much as the consummation. Maybe the new man wouldn't appeal to her. He hoped not. He bit his lip. If the thrill of competition didn't draw her in. She'd already started something with Rae over this one. That was usually the kiss of death. They'd be fighting like cats for weeks.

Only they didn't have weeks.

"Cracker's nice enough," she allowed. "Only—here, pull on that string again, I went and got it all crookt—only he's, I dunno, he's *too* nice. I like 'em toothy."

That figured, too. In her own way Angelia made plenty of sense, enough to get her through her day. He watched her set peas. The same lock of tawny-and-white hair brushed her shoulder in the same place each time she bent, covered, pressed, and sat back. It occurred to him that both she and Raedawn had been brought up from babies here, under the shadow of the same great power. It had never before occurred to him to wonder about its quality, its personality. Not a very friendly one, he guessed.

It took Rae different from her mother. Looking at them both, he could see it, clearer than if he looked at just one woman or the other. Angelia must have got off the easier, with her short attention span and her lightmindedness. Gelia was a child raised up without law. Yet you had only to look at Rae to know more. Raised in exactly the same spot, forced to be mother for both Somershoes, Rae was hungry for justice and serious things, and you knew she wasn't getting them.

Whatever that thing had been, it wasn't lawful, and it wasn't gentle. Angelia took to the roughness like a puppy playing with all its teeth, and Rae, though she wanted gentleness, didn't have any training for it. Where would she have learned?

He supposed Cracker was a gentle sort. Angelia had used him and dropped him ten years ago. Cracker wasn't much use perpendicular. Ernest's guess, guessing from Angelia's sneer and confirmed by Rae's taste, was that the old toper managed pretty well in the prone. He hoped so. Rae needed nicer men. And if ever Rae found a nice one, her mother would chase him off. Too bad Cracker was such a bad match in every other way. It occurred to Ernest that Cracker probably served Rae just as he, Ernest, served Angelia Somershoe, who needed a nicer man for everyday use no matter how much excitement she craved, and got, across the road or up the hill. He guessed it was harder on Cracker than on himself. Cracker was an Angelia in his own right. He hustled women all up- and downriver. Not much comfort to a working girl, Ernest thought, and smiled thinly to himself.

"Dammit, Ernest," Angelia said suddenly, waking him from his thoughts. She stood up with a groan, stretching backward and pressing her knuckles to her kidneys. Her shirt rode up, and Ernest, kneeling below her, could see a curve of breast. The smooth white flesh of her calves was marked with the print of her sneaker treads. "I'm getting old."

Ernest looked up at her openmouthed.

She stared fixedly down at the new rows, then east, as if trying to pierce the veil of willows and cattails to the river. She spoke decidedly.

"I'll tell you something. I'm glad Raedawn's taking over this time. Hell, I don't even care if he's a weenie." Glancing at him affectionately, she added, "Gonna be sticking to my own old weenie, I guess."

He winced. It was one thing to think it, and another to hear her say it to his face.

She said with sadness, "I just don't have the energy to tackle the job at my time of life."

She looked down at him so mournfully that he found himself standing and taking her in his arms, even while the pain she had dealt him spread through his chest and brought tears to his eyes.

"Angelia, Angelia," he said shakily, patting her back. *Old weenie.* She didn't mean anything by it, but, oh, it hurt. He kissed her ear. "You're never old to me."

She threw her arms around him. "I miss him so much!" she wailed.

"Yes, yes. Shh, shh." He felt a sudden lightening of his heavy thoughts as the meaning of her grief sank in. He laughed. "Angelia, you're so rough with me." His tears wet her neck.

She sniffled. "Aw, did that hurt?" She tightened her grip on his back and kissed his neck. "Old shoe. Old fubsy Mr. Mealymouth. Old stay-at-home." Her voice caressed him. Her hipbone ground against his trousers.

"Indoors, if you don't mind, madam," he said, muffled against her hair.

He had only just now realized that, out of all this grief and upheaval, he alone might come out a winner. He felt he had earned her full attention.

Such as that was, he thought affectionately but without illusions about his beloved.

Chapter Twenty-Two

Late Thursday afternoon, King came back to the riverbank to find Cracker. Time for that long-overdue reckoning. For five long years he'd avoided it.

He'd convinced himself that it was all Cracker's fault. Cracker moved in. King sometimes had trouble remembering which happened first, his parents vanishing or his uncle moving in and taking over, but he remembered now. Cracker came first. Then it happened. And then only Cracker was left. The Cracker reign of terror.

And King was the only one who'd noticed. Davy didn't even seem to realize they were gone. He kept talking about them like they were still around. Willy coped.

King was the one who resented Cracker. Cracker had told him to be a man and face up to it. They were gone, and he, Cracker, was trying his best. *You'll just have to face up to it, King,* Cracker kept saying with that worried, don't-hate-me look. *Just face up to it, they're gone.*

What was the point of facing it? Cracker was a bastard. He drank and whored and never worked. Sometimes King had dared to suspect that Rae preferred Cracker to King.

So when he walked across the tracks, the first thing he saw was Rae standing by the shack. She faced the twins, looking guilty.

"You broke it!" Ink said.

"I didn't mean to," Rae said. "It got really strong in there."

King sidled up beside Rae and peered into the hole inside the shack. It was brimful of water.

"Can't you fix it?" Rae said weakly.

"Don't look at me," King said. Junky old hole. Be good for those kids to sleep in a real bed for once.

Mink said, "Hmph." Ink squatted at the doorway and peered inside with the doubtful expression of an auto mechanic examining a wreck.

Shrugging helplessly, Rae turned to King. "Come to my place and get warm?" She looked sad and approachable.

Without hesitation, King let her hijack him.

In her trailer, she changed into a fresh dress, and they sat down on the old broken-backed couch. "Cuddle me, King?"

She was chilled through. He wrapped himself around her and squeezed. "Those kids getting to you?" She shook her head. "Gelia, then?"

"Oh, no more than usual. It's just things. Yesterday—when they cut—when they cut him—" She choked.

King clenched his teeth. He didn't want to hear about it.

"They're after Cracker to put the kids in school. Davy's getting wilder. Ernest's Social Security don't stretch for beans any more. They want our *land*. Where we going to *live*, King?" she said, and he saw with horror that she was starting to cry. Her voice stayed level and practical.

"And all I get from Gelia is her competition, though what we got to fight over now I can't imagine. *She* won't worry."

Tears ran down her cheeks while she spoke. Far worse than Rae putting the whammy on him was Rae in tears, talking calmly and sensibly while her face swelled up and the tears ran out.

"You're the only responsible person around here, that's what you are," he said in a firm voice. "It's too much to ask of you. What I said last night. I mean it, Rae. Let's get out of here. Find the world. *I'll* see you get what you want."

She sniffed, peeped at him, smiled, and shook her head. "I can't even think about what I want. Afraid to."

He handed her the roll of toilet paper that sat on the coffee table. She peeled off enough to blow her nose. Between honks, she said, "It's so horrible. That mess they made across the road. The river turning over. These *damn* developer guys coming around, trying to take our land." He jumped to hear the cussword in her mouth. "I've probably made a mess of that myself. One of 'em came around today—and I don't know what I did, but it sure didn't help—"

"Rae, Raedawn, what do you *want?*" he whispered to her hair.

"I can't say. I *dasn't*. I ain't going to wish. I try hard not to dream. Woke up the other night," she said, choking again. "I had this dream—oh,

King!" she wailed. She pushed her crumpling face into his neck. "It's just so hard without him!" She sobbed like a little kid.

King held her. Stop talking about that! He wasn't going to ask *who* and he didn't want to know *why*. There was a big hole across the road. He'd avoided thinking about it since he arrived. He shut his eyes tight.

He was so confused. What did he feel? Vindictive. Smug, angry, unsatisfied, empty. One night ten years ago his mother had crossed the road, and then his father chased after her, and when they came back they got into a boat and disappeared out onto the river. And yesterday somebody got his revenge for him. Now nobody would cross the road any more. He was damned if he'd think about it.

Rae babbled against his neck. Every few words, she broke up and cried some more. King patted her on the back, not listening.

Why ever had he wanted to come home? Why face up to it all over again? When Cracker used to say *my boys*, King turned his face to the wall. *I don't care how good he's doing. I don't care if he's a great guy just for trying. He's not Mom and Dad, and it feels like hell.* His brothers seemed almost not to notice.

King alone had failed to adjust. That's what the letters said that came home with his report card. "Failing to adjust." The damned school counselor had a crush on Cracker, if nothing worse. They put their heads together over him, which infuriated him—wasn't he the oldest? didn't he see the most of what was going on?—but he was eighteen years old finally, and before he knew it he was packing a satchel and stomping out, headed for the bus station, leaving yelling, yelling, yelling behind him.

Rae moved in his arms. He realized she had been weeping, and he, selfish creature, had thought it was the personal sound track to his sad story. What was she saying, something about losing their land. Oh, right, the building development across the road.

Awkwardly he petted her head. "Hey," he said. "Hey now."

The panic was still in her voice. "—roll right over and squash us if we don't clear out. And King, I don't know what's to become of us if we go. I just can't imagine!"

He rocked her. "So don't go. How about I get you a lawyer? I can pay for somebody to come and sit in with you long enough, 'til things are ironed out. He'll talk to the city man. Lawyers cost money, but I'm flush now. Back pay and clean living." He smiled down into her hair. She probably had no idea of the money he'd made in Alaska, but he had sixty thousand dollars sitting in a bank account in Anchorage. Finally, he really could help.

"What good's a lawyer gonna do?" she said hopelessly. She shook her hair out of her eyes and looked up at him. "King, I wish you'd face up to this."

He went cold. His arms dropped from her and he sat, swelling with anger. "*Face up to it.*" Damn, that made him mad.

She saw his face and slid out of his lap onto the couch. She said, "Gelia says it's all gonna come right, but whatever the heck that means only Gelia knows. There is *such* a smash coming up. I feel it. What if she's got it wrong? The worst of it is, I can't ask her. You know how Gelia is when she knows something you don't."

King fought for control of his temper. He should have been paying more attention. He bit his lip. "What makes you think things are going smash? Why now?"

She stared at him wildly.

Oh good grief, Rae. He spoke slowly. "You been limping along for years, Raedawn, the lot of you. I'm off your hands. Willy'll be growed up soon." He smiled a tight smile. "Who knows, you might get married. Somebody'll come along and put those wild kids in a home, and then where'll you be? No more wild ones of any kind to look after." He paused. "Except Gelia," he added, and waited for her to laugh.

Rae pulled herself to her feet. The lot of you, he'd said. Talking so easily about putting Davy and the twins in a home. She stared down at him. What had happened to King out there in Alaska? He'd always been a little dense, but she'd put it down to his age. Plenty of boys she knew were in their own little world. They got it knocked out of them, unless they were too rich or spoiled. She'd never thought King was spoiled.

Now he was trying to josh her along, like it was nothing, like the life she lived here was nothing.

He said, "C'mon, what's the matter?" and took her finger and shook it.

"I've been telling you," she said.

His face darkened. Angry, she thought. She couldn't remember a time when King wasn't angry.

King, she thought. You're gone for good, probably was gone before you even left, and I never noticed. I've been in my own little world, too. She was too wrung out to grieve over that. She had learned by now that she was old enough to make mistakes that could never be undone.

"I come home," he said in a hard voice, "and I find you-all ain't done *nothing* to better yourselves. Erny's still letting Gelia run around off the leash. Kids are wild in the dirt. Cracker's got 'em living like pigs over there, I've seen it. Got a thing or two to say to *him* on that subject." That reminded him. Time to face up to Cracker. He said through clenched teeth, "So just don't say to me, I've got to *face up* to things."

His anger boiled over. He bounded off the couch and glared into her eyes. His jaw champed. "It's not your fault," he said finally. "You don't know anything." He turned and stomped to the door.

Let him go. He's all full of something, girl, and you didn't even see it. Her heart had a stone in the middle. *Too late.* He's been full of anger all his life, but you figured it didn't matter, heck, he had shoes and clothes and food and you. You've used him up.

"King," she said anyway.

In the doorway, his silhouette was black and hard. "I'm going to talk to Cracker. Been putting it off." He left, slamming the door.

Rae wondered if there was a single person left in the whole world who liked her the way she was.

One, maybe. She'd looked for him and missed him on the ridge at lunchtime. *Go and look now.* She dragged herself off the couch. Maybe if she just went up there and looked at him awhile, she would feel better.

Chapter Twenty-Three

At two-thirty Ike the foreman announced a break.

Alexander decided to sit it out on the ridge. He was one of the senior men on the site, but that wouldn't stop Ike from putting him to work picking up trash—anything to keep a black man from looking idle in front of the white workers.

Besides, Rae might show up. He took his Coke and climbed to the top of the ridge.

Water ran down the slope in rivulets that cut across the path. Beside the path, silver saplings broke bud among the black-trunked trees, footed in a layer of dead leaves. Baby plants poked up: three-leafed, fiddle-headed, moss-backed, and the occasional single spike of green with a curling white tip, furled tight as a cigar.

The path was worn smooth by children's feet and continued the length of the ridge as far as he could see. He walked along looking for a place to sit down. Here was a stump, and right in front of it a clear space through the underbrush that looked down the slope. A puffball the size of a coconut grew at the foot of the stump. Alexander touched it gently. Its flesh was firm and unbelievably white in the sun-dappled dimness of the ridge.

He moved his feet so as not to kick it by accident. "I'm just visiting," he told it. He sat on the stump and sipped his Coke, his thoughts on the island.

About now the whole island would be in bloom. The cormorants would rise from their diving and pose like proud brown ladies drying their throats and bare breasts in the sun. The herons would muster for the winter fish runs, spearing fish with their long beaks, hunting land crabs as big as your fist. The claws and legs would thrash as they disappeared down the long windpipe. The banyan trees would put out new leaves. Their roots would drip like candlewax down the trunks of their hosts, and the seeds of air ferns would drift by and alight, to borrow life from the highest branches.

Floating clouds of dragonflies would be mating, he thought watching gnats dance over the office chimney flue. And pitybirds, the voracious little hawks of the night, flicking over the treetops, eating dragonflies and screaming. Everything and everyone would be mating in a frenzy while the good weather lasted.

His homesickness seemed faded today. It must be because Rae had shown him the river. The jewelweed, the cattails. The maples, heavy with yellow-green flowers that dripped sticky sweet nectar. He'd never known their names before. Five years in this awful place and he'd never even noticed spring or known the names of its many lives.

Yet Rae got him thinking about the beauty he had left behind. She and those tow-headed children reminded him of a story he had read in school about fairies stealing away a child and leaving a changeling in his place. I am that changeling, he thought, staring at the leaf mold on his boots.

Rae made him think of sea turtles mating on the beach, slow, relentless, brave.

Rae made him think of mating.

A woodpecker snapped through the air under his nose and stuck to a tree trunk. It wore a jaunty red cap on the back of its head. The black-and-white bars of its coat dazzled him. The woodpecker took a tentative whack at the tree and then sidled until it was out of his sight around back of the trunk. Then something rustled on the path beyond, and the woodpecker hustled back into view.

"Why, hello, Alexander. Fancy meeting you here!"

He leaped to his feet. Rae climbed the last few feet to his side and stood smiling up at him like a miniature sun. Instantly his heart filled. "Hello."

She turned her face up to him. "Missed you at lunch." She put a hand up and parted his dreads where they hung over his eyes. "Peekaboo." Their gazes locked. "You're all wet."

"I—" He held his breath. If he touched her, he wouldn't say anything. And he had too much to say. "I met the children by the river—"

Lord, what to tell? That he had heard a lion underwater? His chest tightened. He needed to be in the circle of her legs where there was no fear. A man who woke up with his cock a yard long had more than hearing trouble.

"Well, hello," said another voice. "Mrs. Somershoe, we meet again!"

Alexander froze. Rae looked over her shoulder.

The architect, Walter Chepi, climbed up the path. "You've got quite a view from here." He looked at Rae, blinked, and looked again.

Rae flashed him a brief smile. "You've met my mother. I'm Rae, her daughter." She turned back to Alexander. "You were saying?"

Words failed Alexander. Her hair was all red-golds and yellows and white. Her lips parted in welcome.

"Gosh, I do apologize. You look a lot like her, don't you? And it's Alexander, isn't it?" said the architect. He took up a position beside Alexander and gawked down on the site. "I'm Walter Chepi. Architect on the job."

He stuck his hand out between Rae and Alexander. Alexander had to take it, though he wanted to throw the man down the slope.

"Hello," Rae said. She shook Chepi's hand and dropped it. "Alexander was just telling me about his lunch on the riverbank." Her body kept turning toward Alexander, heating him up, making him lift up like a turtle turning its head to the sun.

Don't do this to me, he thought, with this man here. "I wanted to ask you how—" *How a man can stretch like taffy.* "How things grow here. All the, the plants. I'm from the tropics," he rushed out, feeling Chepi ready to interrupt with some banality that might force Alexander to choke him and hang his body in a tree. "It's all so strange," he finished lamely.

She brightened. "You've asked the right person. C'mon, I'll give you a little tour."

"I have ten minutes," Alexander said.

"That would be great!" Chepi said. "I'm from Phoenix. I don't know a thing about the native plant life."

Rae walked up the path. She pointed.

"That's trillium. Don't confuse it with poison ivy, another three-leafer over here. That umbrella thingy is mayapple. This tube with the little weenie sticking up is skunk cabbage. All of these like it wet and dark—see?" She gestured overhead. "But not too dark. When the rest of the leaves come in, these guys will be done blooming and on their way to seed already."

Alexander committed the names to memory.

"Wild geranium. Watch out for those raspberry canes, Walter." She pointed, and a bumblebee lifted up off a thorn and buzzed the architect.

"Yowch." Chepi stopped to disentangle his sweater, swatting the air.

Alexander took the opportunity to get closer to Rae.

"The trees," he said urgently. *Do you have one made out of flesh?* The closer he got to her, the less he cared. His mind went blank with a rush of desire.

"These little ones with the purply pink flowers are redbud. White flowers over there, dogwood. That's a magnolia over there, don't know how that got here, it's not native."

"Today I noticed something," he said, to shut Chepi out and to bring her closer. "Back home life and death are like the surf, moving with every breath. Here the seasons don't come like waves, but like the tsunami. One big, long, slow crash."

Perhaps that was what he heard under the water. The great life of spring in flood. The thought of those falling tons of water made him thirsty. He drained his Coke.

All her attention was on him now.

He said, "Back home the forests have flat floors, not all this brush, and the colors of golden beaches and pink and yellow orchids. Not like this, this wet, black-footed place."

He thought of the hole by the water, issuing baby turtles, baby snakes. "Here it is all full of secret hollows. Dead things take longer to rot away here. In the islands, when a bird or a fruit falls, it is dry-dry in a day. Then some new plant grows up through the carcass and eats up every scrap of it. There is no end to growing back home. No winter. Even bones are gone after a month or two."

Her lips parted. Shadow set a patch over her right eye, and her left eye seemed full of dazzle. Alexander lowered his voice.

"Spring in this place is—is more violent. The soil is so rich that every seed that falls must germinate. I wonder why the land was not choked with their lives."

She leaned close to him, looking down at the black soil, her body warm in the brisk air. She smelled delicious.

"One big, slow wave, you see?" Alexander said huskily. All the tension left his body. She was here. That was enough.

ℚ

Rae stared around her with new eyes. She could see plants that shouldn't be up for weeks. The raspberry cane that bit that dumb architect was fully leafed. That was ridiculous. She looked down the slope. The box elders around her trailer were also in leaf. Across the river, the willow heads were crowned with bright yellow and turning faintly green. Two months early.

"A big wave?" she echoed. When she turned back to Alexander she realized how it must look to him—the eruption of life from death. "Everything's a lot farther along than usual." She hadn't even noticed. She'd seen the death, but not the life.

She watched Alexander slide the edge of his hand along the deep-furrowed bark of a cottonwood trunk. He looked back at her, and his dreads swung around his face like a caul, dark and shimmering, his eyes like secrets peering out.

"We took down a monster tree in the middle of the site, couple of days ago," Chepi said cheerfully. "What kind was it?"

Rae looked at him with sudden revulsion. "The kind that's in the way." She turned her shoulder to him.

"What's the matter with her?" said Chepi, dodging a bumblebee hovering near his face. Rae ran off down the path.

"Yo, Alexander!" a man yelled, waving from the torn-up meadow below. "Break's over!"

Alexander watched Rae out of sight. Then he picked his way back down the hill.

With the bigger machine he began clearing brush and fill from the north end of the site. His hair was still wet and fishy-smelling. His mind was far from his job.

He had planned to think of Rae all afternoon. Instead he found himself remembering playing with his brothers on the beach back of Pinder's Point. They collected smooth bits of blue and green bottle glass and threw dead fish at each other. How angry it made Gran! She had to wash the fish guts out of their hair and put medicine on the cuts where the fish-scales sliced them.

That was a different fish smell, of course, from the way his hair smelt now. Freshwater fish smells different. That crab hole over there was full of river water, fresh but not clean, full of baby fish, baby snakes, baby frogs and turtles. He remembered the boy Ink screaming down at the murky water, and Mink's glowing face staring thoughtfully upside down into his eyes, right before she kicked him.

Alexander shook his head violently, and the tips of his dreads stung his cheeks. He put the bucketloader into reverse. The backup alarm beeped. *Work.*

Yet he kept circling back to that moment when he had stuck head-downward in the hole, one hand frantic for the child's ankle, while his breast filled with the music of that faraway truck. He felt swoony just remembering it. He recognized that music now. It was the hoarse brassy voice from his dream this morning, the one that had roused him and teased him until he—

The blade clanged hard against a chunk of concrete the size of a small car. The machine bucked under him. Alexander threw it into reverse and backed up slowly, suddenly aware of his own harsh breathing in the stuffy cab.

Lord, he was thirsty. For the fourth time that morning he sucked at his water bottle. This time he drained it. It didn't help.

It wasn't just that he wanted Rae. The wanting was so strong, he should be miserable with it. But he felt content and joyful all the time, even sitting in this diesel-scented, sweat-soaked bucketloader cab, even when Bob Bagoff was screaming in his face. Even knowing that he had to sleep on that cot again tonight.

The sun poked its fingers through the window into his bucketloader cab, throwing river-glitter in his eyes. He should be worrying about what might happen to him on that cot. He glanced across the road at the glitter coming off the river, so close and cold and deep. So thirsty he was right now, he would like to plunge into that river. Bliss. His eyes drifted shut on the thought. For a moment he felt keenly aware of the nearness of the river, the way it saturated the soil under his bucketloader. So close.

An odd thought occurred to him, exquisitely sweet and satisfying. *Tonight I might grow long enough to touch it.*

His eyes opened. What would become of him then?

The world slowed around Alexander.

He had a choice. He could run. Or he could wait and see. What am I? he thought, not for the first time that day. Who is Alexander Caebeau and where is he going? He was thirty, alone, far from home, living in a shantybox like a squatter, doing work he didn't like to think about for people he despised.

That train of thought would do him no good.

He opened the cab door to let in fresh air. After a few deep breaths, he wiped his hands on his shirt, took the levers in his hands, and peered hard through the dirty window. Pay attention. He focused on clearing landfill. Here was an old stove half-buried in the mud. When he thought he had a purchase, he eased the machine forward. The stove tipped up, slumped suddenly as its oven door slid open, and wedged itself against the blade again. He drove forward steadily, and the stove toppled out of its hole and flopped onto level ground. He scooped it up and drove to the waiting truck.

His hair stank of freshwater fish.

About now, the sweet apple trees and the fragrant guava would be blooming along Fishing Hole Road.

Bah. Why was he still thinking of Freeport? He had worked hard to break that habit. Barring a note to Gran at Christmases, he hadn't written to her for three years. She never wrote back. That hurt him bad.

He dumped the old stove into the waiting dump truck and smiled grimly at the bang. They paid him a lot of money for that. And they weren't polite about it.

He canted the bucketloader blade another two degrees and drove forward, slicing at a deep angle into the earth and cutting loose a surprisingly large root mass at the bottom of a scrubby sapling. The sapling's thick yellow roots were tangled like snakes. That got him thinking about a big tree in Gran's backyard behind the cement plant.

It was a banyan tree. Gran said that once upon a time there was a coconut tree under the banyan. A hurricane or a bird brought the banyan seed and put it on top of the coconut tree, she would say in her storytelling voice, and then the banyan put down roots that ate and drank the air. Then it ate and drank of the coconut tree. Its air-drinking roots trickled down the trunk like streams of gray molasses, reaching for the ground. When the first trickling root touched the ground at last, the banyan suddenly grew very fast, smothering the coconut tree, putting out big branches, piling up roots like ship's cables on the ground around its foot. And one day there was no sign of the coconut tree. Only the banyan.

He never saw anything like that banyan tree here in the north. The one in his Gran's yard had roots that grew up like a skirt out of the ground. Some of those roots were as thick as his legs, as big around as his body.

The body of the tree was short, like a man's body. Then the branches began, and the branches looked just like the roots—smooth and thick and twisted like snakes, like arms and legs, like vines that had grown as great as trees. The whole tree looked like an hourglass. The bottom was like the top. The little hard fruit was good for throwing down on your friends.

He had thought a lot about that tree when he was a boy. Maybe the sun and lightning passed down through the top and ran out the roots into the ground. Maybe the rain came up through the bottom and fed the leaves until it dried away at the top. He imagined the tree must have felt very crowded in the middle. He supposed that it must have up-going tubes and down-going tubes in it the way sugar cane had, so that the sun and rain didn't mix.

It now came to him suddenly why that image should be in his head now: the banyan's roots lengthening, stretching toward the ground, thickening and lengthening and stretching.

The bucketloader blade slammed into a chunk of concrete. The machine bucked again. Alexander came back to himself and swore, glancing over his shoulder at the office trailer. Bob Bagoff stood on the steps. Slowly now, Alexander admonished himself. The boss is looking. And pay attention.

Bob walked over, and Alexander stopped his machine.

"Hey! Watch it, Alexander! You wanna break up another bucketloader for me?"

Alexander knew he should appear to be paying attention, but his mind wandered. *Those banyan knees made a good lap.*

"The damn thing cost me two thousand dollars just to pick up the pieces," Bob whined.

Alexander's stomach knotted up. *What if I just said yes?*

"I can't afford this shit!"

I wish Rae would come. Come, he must focus. Bob would rant at him for fifteen minutes if he didn't make eye contact. Alexander opened the cab door.

"Two hundred thousand dollars worth of equipment! Just like that! There's too much carelessness—"

Alexander threw the netting back off his face. He caught Bob's eye. "I didn't break your bucketloader, boss."

Bob stopped. He took in a big breath. "Well, see thatcha don't. I can't afford it." He stomped off.

Alexander shut the cab door again. He was ashamed of cringing for that bag of noise. But within a minute he had forgotten Bob, and in five minutes he was lost in dreamy recollection again.

He felt ten years old, alive in a joyously familiar way. For the first time since he was a boy he could smell every growing plant and *name* it, not just with one of Rae's words but with a more true and loving name that came from direct knowledge. It was knowledge he might have touched before, while he dawdled home from school to snatch at the curly tails of lizards and dye his tongue purple with guava. But then he had only touched it. Now he was drowning in that loving knowledge, blissfully at home at last.

I wish Rae would come.

What an odd notion. How could he be at home here, in this icy alien place? For the first time since he came north, he felt he knew everything he needed to know. His fear seemed to have faded completely. This feeling was so wildly at odds with the facts that Alexander laughed out loud.

What if I just said yes?

Chapter Twenty-Four

King slammed into the Gowdy trailer. "Cracker!" he bellowed. *We're gonna have a little conversation here.* It was dark as hell in the trailer. He nearly jumped out of his skin when Cracker's voice came close by. "Don't need to shout, son, I know you're home," Cracker said mildly. He was sitting at the card table in the kitchen end of the trailer, using a tall stack of newspapers for a chair while he ate his lunch. As King's eyes adjusted to the dark, Cracker slid the table gently to one side and stood, chewing slowly.

King noted with distress that Cracker was still bigger than he was. Right away he began to settle down. Can't very well punch the man when we've just said hello after five years, he reasoned with his angry self. His grievances stuck hard in his throat. His fists hung hard and tight at his sides.

"Didn't see you there," he said gruffly.

Cracker bobbed his head. "I'm here. You et lunch yet?"

King fidgeted. "No!" He was damned if he was going to let Cracker do a Gelia-and-Erny number on him. "I—" His voice whiffed and then hardened. "I got a few things to say."

"All right." Cracker looked him up and down. "You going to set?"

King sucked air in through his nose. There was a bad smell about Cracker. Like an old man. Cracker's old, he thought with surprise. "I guess."

Immediately Cracker turned his back and reached him a folding chair off the Peg Board.

The smell was stronger. Cracker's coming apart, King thought with alarm.

Cracker slid behind the table. He looked up at King without, this time, any of that infuriating phony patience that King knew well could slip away fast as a beer can falls from a man's hand.

King unfolded the chair and sat. Cracker picked up his peanut butter sandwich.

"It's like—" King tried to recover his grievances in some kind of order. All he could think of was Rae's face, all over tears and surprise, staring him out of the family. "Things were bad enough when I left, but now they're all different and they're *still* bad. What you all been *up* to while I been gone?" he said, finding a starting place for his feelings at last.

Cracker swallowed sandwich and took a swig of beer. "That's a big little question. What part you want to hear first?"

King stared helplessly around the trailer. "Well, say, like what's going on with Willy? Been home three days and I ain't seen him yet. He been looking out for you?" A tactless question, he realized, but he let it stand.

Cracker put his beer can down empty. "Going for to be an alkie."

It hit King like a blow to the throat. His eyes prickled. "Come on."

"Think I don't know the signs?" Cracker put his elbows on the table and hunkered down, looking King square in the eye. "Yes, he's been taking care of me. And Davy. And Rae if she'll let him, which she mostly won't. Twins won't, either."

Willy, the good brother, drinking. Shit, this is no good, King thought, forgetting himself, we got to have one success in the family.

"Gelia been at him yet?" he guessed. He figured he knew that answer right enough. But boys got over Gelia; she was like the measles. He didn't want to find out if Rae had done it to Willy.

Cracker glanced down at his hands and up again. He spoke deliberately. "No. I don't reckon so." He put a huge hand behind his head and scratched what was left of his hair in perplexity or sorrow, King couldn't tell. "I 'spect liquor's just in his blood, King," he said finally. "His daddy was thataway, and Gloria probably gave it to him on the Coombs side, too."

"Willy didn't start—" King choked on guilt. "Start drinking because of the kids. When I left?"

"Naw, a burden don't make a man drink." Cracker's eyes were wide-open. The crow's feet around them were deep. That old-man smell exhaled from his overalls.

King's heart clenched. History was being made. Cracker was admitting for the first time that raising five kids didn't make him drink. King had come ready to wring blood from a stone, but Cracker was bleeding of his own accord.

Things surely had changed.

King couldn't stand to look in that face. He closed his eyes. There's one score settled, he said to himself. Wait the old man out and he'll come around, wasn't that the plan? What's the matter with me?

But his anger burned too strong. Raedawn staring him out of the family. Revenge in a hole across the road. Revenge for his parents gone missing ten years this very spring.

"What happened to them, Cracker?" he burst out.

Cracker blinked. King could almost see him fitting all the *thems* he knew into the question, until he was stuck, dammit, stuck for once with the toughest one. The question nobody would ever answer.

"Gloria and Carl," Cracker said. Time stood still. "Well. I was drunk at the time." He was dodging. Cracker *knew*.

King half stood. He shouted, "Talk, goddamn you!"

"All right." Cracker winced. "Hold your horses. Let me reckon awhile. I don't like thinking about it any more than you do." He gave his sandwich a look of revulsion and put it down.

"The thing is," Cracker said, bending his head, putting his hands on the back of his neck, and squeezing. "I don't know how much you knew about things between Gloria and Carl. Right there at the end. And I don't want to be yelled at about it." He glanced up. "Was a lot you didn't want to think about in those days, King."

Cracker waited a moment, but King didn't answer that. Cracker got up, pulled another can of beer out of the freezer, and sat again. "You didn't drink to put it aside. More fool you, you might have stayed home if you could. Or more fool me," Cracker mumbled, putting his chin down.

King felt a rush of nausea. He put his palm on the table to push it down. "I get you."

Cracker heaved a sigh. He popped the top off the beer can. "Gloria was getting fed up with Carl's temper. She didn't mind the booze. She was bred up into that. But he had a wicked temper. Worse'n mine. They were fighting every night. Carl was mad further because Gelia Somershoe had been telling him no." He grinned at King's expression. "She says *no* more'n you might think. Don't get me off onto *that*." He rolled his head on his shoulders. "Well, anyhow, Carl was fixing to leave, pack the whole famdamly up and shift 'em to Detroit, where he thought he might get a job making cars. He said it a lot those days."

Ugh, this is nasty, King thought. He remembered those fights, when he'd hide in the bathroom, waiting to hear the door slam. On real bad nights he'd hide under the bunk bed.

Cracker said, "It didn't mean anything, all that Detroit talk, it was just what they picked on to fight about." He swigged beer. "Where was I? Detroit. She didn't see it. They had a humdinger that night, and I guess Carl hit her—I wasn't in the house when it started, you understand. I was out there across the road, waiting for a lady friend."

"I was here," King said in a small voice. He was in two places at once, here, now, watching the people in Cracker's story run across the road, but he was a boy, too, lying under the bunk bed, listening to their footsteps fade. A grown-up self watching and a boy self listening. It made him feel cross-eyed.

Cracker nodded briefly. He looked at the table again. "So you know better'n me then. Anyway, first thing I know Gloria's running across the road to me, with Carl yelling his lungs out behind her. I shinned up the tree fast." He spoke quicker now. "They kept it up for ten, fifteen minutes, up and down the decibels, Carl smacking her and Gloria boo-hooing. Somebody else must of come along then, because they got quiet."

Cracker got quiet, too. He said, "Couldn't hear his voice, he spoke too soft, but I figured it was a cop who'd drove by. I kept shut. Let Carl knock a cop's block off, I figured. That'd work fine for me. Either way Carl's took care of, hauled off to jail or lighting out to stay out of jail." He raised his eyes to King's again. "I don't conceal it from you, King, I had no particular use for Carl. He was your father, and you had a right to side with him."

"I didn't!" King burst out. His heart hammered in his chest, sometimes fast, sometimes horridly slow. He remembered, he remembered. "Go on."

Cracker pressed his lips together. "More complicated than that, ain't it? Always is." He sighed heavily. "I was good and high up the tree. Never did hear what was said to 'em, but sure as shit, Carl quit yelling at Gloria and the two of 'em starts arguing with the . . . with the cop. From what Carl was saying, I guess the cop was telling him to shape up and settle down, and Carl wants to get out of town, and she's with him for once. Nothing like authority to bring the childern into line, is there?"

He grinned sourly. He opened his mouth and made a stopped sound. "That's about it, I guess. They yelled and pleaded and got fractious and I guess the cop must of laid down the law, and eventually they went back across the road. I sat where I was till everybody left. Waited to hear the cop car to pull away, but I never did. It was starting to rain, so I came down and slunk off the back way to the firehouse for beer and checkers, and the next thing I know I'm home, Willy's shaking me and waking me, you're boo-hooin', and young Davy wants breakfast. No Gloria, no Carl. I don't know any more, King, and I swear, I *swear* I ain't heard any more."

There was something in Cracker's eyes that left King in doubt about the truth of this, but he didn't say so.

"They got in the dinghy," King said abruptly. The memory of that night was alive now. *That's not how it happened!*

He could almost remember the next part himself, how he had crept out barefoot and rounded the corner of the house and peered to the west, across the road. The boy King had known what he would see, and he didn't want to: the silhouette of a huge span of branches blotting out the sky. It was a rendezvous, a betrayer. It blotted out memory.

Cracker leaned back and crossed his legs. The man smelled really bad. All my enemies are dying, King thought, and hated himself for feeling sick and glad at the same time.

King shut his eyes. Cracker's account lay there in his mind, stuck there forever now, ready to catch the boy King walking barefoot across the mud, following his parents' voices, with his heart doing terrible things in his chest. King could remember what his feet had felt, but then Cracker's story took over. He could no longer remember what had happened when he crossed the road. Cracker's version intervened, with the imaginary peacemaking cop, and Cracker up the tree like the betrayer he was from the start—dammit, there was something wrong with that version! King's fists squeezed on nothing where they lay on the card table. His throat felt hot.

Cracker had got up and was standing by the refrigerator, opening a can of beer.

"Want one?"

King reached for it with both hands.

For a few minutes they drank, King in his chair, unable to get up for the moment, and Cracker by the fridge ready to pop a fresh one out of the freezer. The beer was ice-cold. It settled King's stomach.

"You were waiting for my mom, weren't you?" King said.

Cracker eyed him for a long time.

King waited him out.

Cracker said finally, "Yeah." His tone said, Oh hell, and now I guess you're gonna make something of it.

"Your own sister."

Cracker kept up with that measuring look, as if to say, How smart are you, boy, or was you ever? But King waited. He'd figured out how to pump Cracker at last.

Cracker lifted his chin. "Wasn't no your-own-sister about it," he said deliberately. "She wanted to know how to fit in. She'd finally come around. I don't say she was just like Gelia, I mean, who is? Just, this place gets to you sooner or later, and I have to say my sister was slow on the uptake from a child. Didn't take *me* more'n a couple months to figure it out." He conceded, "And Raedawn explained it to me." He watched King for a glimmer.

King stared. "Come on," he said flatly.

Obviously Cracker didn't know what to make of him. His head tipped to one side.

Oh hell, he's gonna lie now, King thought. Explain it so's the idiot boy can understand, only then it won't be true.

"It takes the women, mostly. Makes 'em horny and crazy. I'd figured Gloria wasn't in it, for she was always a coward, a good woman I guess, but weak as water. But then Carl turned mean. And she started to get the *feeling*. She wouldn't talk to Gelia about that, or anything else. A good woman like Gloria wouldn't. She'd lie to herself first before she'd admit there was any truth in Gelia. *Which* there ain't. And that left Raedawn, only she didn't think much of Raedawn neither, who was only fourteen." He wiped his chin. "She asked me. Her own brother." Cracker's palms came up spread out. "What was I supposed to do?"

King kept shut. Black anger rose in his head, thundered in his ears, until he could barely hear Cracker speak.

"So I says to her, come across the road and find out. I sure as hell can't explain it by myself."

King said, "I don't want to know!"

Cracker shut up. After a minute he said, "That's what I thought."

He opened the fridge and took another beer out of the freezer. "Here." The pop-top hissed in King's hand. Cracker sat down again and fiddled with the pop-top on his own beer until it tinkled down inside.

"You were a good son, King. All you boys were good. But you especially. It's because you're a square. Always trying to act regular, like those half-dead folks up the hill. Willy, too, but the funny thing is, he's better at it than you are, and he's faking. You never faked. You wanted to *be* regular. Don't know how you come to be that way in this family, all you had to grow up with. Raedawn had a spell of it from when she was twelve or thirteen until I took up with her, but she grew out of it. Gelia said it made her awful hard to live with, while it lasted. You might remember. You were here and I wasn't."

King squinted into his beer can. There was ice floating in it. He drank, closing his eyes and pressing the ice against his palate with his tongue while he swallowed the cold, cold beer. "No." I don't remember anything, he lied, just as hard as ever he could lie.

"This is hard for you, coming home, ain't it?"

"Don't say it!" King burst out laughing. His eyes were wet. "Don't say it! And don't say how I've gone and filled out, either. I had enough of that crap from Gelia, and Erny, and that wild child Raedawn, and besides I can see you're still big enough to lick me—god*damn* you, Cracker." He grinned feebly.

Cracker grinned back. "Well, shit, don't ask me to prove it. If you young roosters gotta test yourselves, do it on each other."

Chapter Twenty-Five

John turned up at the inn in a perfectly astonishing state. He was so furious Suzy didn't dare ask why he was all wet and dirty. She stood in the door while he ranted and threw things around his room.

He actually took all his clothes off right in front of her and stuffed them in the wastebasket. His pale hairy back was covered with cinders. "Call Pat in Chicago and tell her to fax the buyout packet to a guy named Chepi at the site office." His phone rang. John said "Yes, Sir" a lot, glaring at her. Then he hung up. "Go put on the red dress. Be ready in ten minutes."

Now the setting sun was raising steam off the river as John drove Suzy in her red dress, and the investor, Mr. Bodanza, to the Foxe Parke site. He hadn't said another word to her.

It was hot. The air was full of bugs. She waved a hand in front of her eyes, feeling sweat pop out on her bare shoulders and trickle down her backbone.

"Bugs. That means water. I hope this location isn't damp. Modern construction techniques are disgracefully shoddy."

"No, I'm certain it isn't damp, Mr. Bodanza," John said. "It's just spring out here in the suburbs, sir. Just a little phenomenon of nature." They got out of the car, and the men stood staring at the muddy mess of the construction site.

Suzy wandered away, fighting bugs. Either her makeup or her perfume was keeping them off her face, but the cream she'd put on her hands was apparently a gnat aphrodisiac. She tried putting her hands in her armpits but decided this looked unladylike. Columns of bugs rose like campfire smoke out of the mud. She looked up. The bugs climbed high into the still air, whirling around each other, mating like fiends. They were doing it all over her hands! Yuck! She let her hands hang at her sides and tried to ignore the tickling of little gnat feet.

That man driving the bucketloader over there wore an actual veil with his hardhat. Smart guy. She smiled at him and caught a flash of white teeth behind the veil. She ignored the sales pitch and instead watched him jockey the bucketloader. His head turned toward her. He waved and she blushed, but then she saw he was waving at a pair of children she hadn't noticed before. One of them circled a hand in the air.

"Riverside property, too. This is close, but I hardly think you can bill it as riverside property. Not that you could get *me* to live any closer to the water. These insects!" Bodanza squinted across the road. "I thought you said you own that property, Fowier. There's houses over there."

He pointed. Suzy looked. Two people waved from across the road.

Suzy turned away, embarrassed for John. It would only make things worse for her that he was fucking up in her presence. He hadn't forgiven her. She would have to apologize.

She'd have to do more than that, obviously. She would have to sleep with him tonight. For the fiftieth time in two days she wondered how badly she wanted to be a vice president.

John flicked her with a cold look.

Directly over her head, someone screamed. Something whistled through the air, missing her hair by inches. She gasped, ducked, and covered her head. A few yards away, a construction worker did the same.

A workman behind her laughed. "Incoming!" he sang out. She turned in a crouch to look at him. The scream came again, and he threw himself to the ground, his arms over his head.

Another hoarse and furious scream swooped out of the clear sky. John Fowier swore. Something came whizzing down on them with a noise like a crossbow bolt ripping the air. Suzy quivered, crouching. Her high heels gave her ankles hell. Right above her head it screamed again and missed her. She heard it slice the air, not so closely this time. Wobbling on her heels, she found her balance and looked up.

It was a bird. Lots of birds. They had wings like gulls and the heavy legs and hawk-bills of hunters. Each wing had a white band across its underside. Ten or twenty birds stirred the air overhead. They were eating the gnats.

Suzy fixed her eye on one bird as it wove in and out of the flock. It climbed as if the sky were a spiral staircase, one stair at a time. When it was high, high up, the bird wheeled in a tight circle, tipped over onto one wing, and stooped. The sickle-shaped wings arched and touched each other over the pointed shoulder blades. The curved beak was wide-open like a funnel. From the bird's thick throat came a triumphant scream. It hurtled head-down through a black cloud of gnats.

Almost at the ground, the bird pulled its wings down into a menacing bat posture. The air tore and whistled, and the hunter shot upward again like a boomerang.

Suzy lost track of it in the flock. From higher up, more birds approached, rowing the air. Still more skimmed nearby treetops, jerking to and fro like water beetles. They missed each other and the trees by a flick of the wing. They turned so sharply that Suzy could hear the feathers snap.

John Fowier and Mr. Bodanza hunched over, staring and dumb, their shoes squishing in the mud. The construction workers lay on the ground or huddled against the big yellow machines.

Suzy became aware of pain in her shins. She had been crouching in high heels for five minutes.

The dive-bombers screamed and stooped deeper, lacing their paths together. The dark columns of gnats shredded.

The veiled bucketloader operator held his sides and giggled. He shook his fist—at the birds? Suzy followed the gesture. The two children on the ridgetop danced and pointed. The bucketloader operator put his hand under his veil to wipe his eyes. Suzy smiled in spite of herself to see a man so fat laugh so hard.

John Fowier grabbed her by the arm. "Get Mr. Bodanza out of this!" Walking in a stoop, they coaxed Mr. Bodanza back to the Mercedes, where he took a pill from his pocket and swallowed it.

A few gnats flew up from Suzy's hands where they'd been fucking their brains out and dispersed around the car. She didn't have the energy to squash them.

Chapter Twenty-Six

Some devilment. Those kids," Gelia said, watching Mink and Ink dance along the ridge and the nighthawks swoop screaming through the air over the construction site.

Ernest pointed. "There's Rae's friend, laughing on the machine."

She looked. *He's a nice big one.* Not scared of the nighthawks, either, she noted with approval. Good gravy, that girl's lucky. She wanted a closer look.

"Have you met him?" Ernest said, as if he'd read her mind.

"I ain't yet." She grinned at Ernest. She was wearing the pink hot pants, and she knew she looked her best. "Shall we?"

Ernest glanced sideways at her. "Raedawn will have something to say about it."

She raised her eyebrows at him. "And? So?"

"And so I would appreciate it if you quarrelled with her *out* of my hearing," he said in his most precise manner. "Wait til the whistle blows. They have to work yet awhile."

The old sweetie. Adorable when he was jealous.

They waited. The workmen clambered among their two-by-four cement forms. The bucketloader bumped around. Gelia felt disgruntled. Construction workers look so darn good in blue jeans. She'd kept her hands off this bunch, though it tested her sorely, on account of Rae's claim and the urgent business at hand. Rae's claim, Rae's man. She watched him handle his machine. The long lever-controls of the big machine looked just the right size in his hands. It depressed her all over again to know she wouldn't be breaking him in. Thing like that didn't happen every day. How could she trust Raedawn to manage it?

She scowled. Everything changing, the river rolling over any day now probably, and she had to step aside and let it all pass her by. Ernest knew how she felt, bless him. She wondered if he didn't just pretend to be jealous to keep her spirits up.

Big feller, Rae's choice. Her mouth watered.

According to Ernest, he was about to get fired. Fine thing that would be, his boss lose his temper and send the feller away. That would leave them all looking no-how. And then what? She, Gelia Somershoe, would have to step in and sacrifice someone she couldn't afford to lose, like Ernest, or that worthless bum Cracker, or one of the children, which would be no fair to the child and probably prove out a bad choice later down the road, or King, who would be a terrible choice. The more she thought about it the more resentful she felt, because Raedawn's choice was the best choice after all. And she didn't deserve to make it.

Nevertheless something would have to be done to save Rae's choice. May as well go and be done with it. Show that mean old boss who the real power was around here. Show this Alexander feller who he would have to deal with if it was up to her.

She was damned if she'd feel old.

"Any second now," Ernest said.

Gelia stepped forward. Every head on the construction site turned, as they damned well should.

With a flick of her head, she threw a glance at the bucketloader where the black man in the veil sat.

His head snapped toward her. She couldn't see his eyes through the veil, but she sure could feel them. Got you, she thought. She held her pose for a calculated few seconds and then looked away at the office trailer.

The whistle blew.

"I'll be along for supper," she murmured to Ernest.

"No rush," he said drily. She didn't feel him leave.

It went to her heart to do it, but she let her head sag, let the wanting leak out of her like water out of a bucket with a hole in it. By the time she had crossed the tracks and the road, she felt almost as old as she must look.

There she is, Alexander thought. She was wearing shorts this time. That must be her stepfather with her. All of a sudden he was hot and trembling, trembling so hard that he almost drove the bucketloader straight into a pallet of lumber. The end-of-day whistle blew. Relieved, he parked the machine and wrenched the key out. She was coming to meet him! Oh boy.

But when he had walked across the site she looked different. Her hair was whiter, with less yellow and brown and gold in it, and her carriage was different somehow. More supple, less fiery, more wiggle to her hips but less—what? Not the same woman at all. Getting Rae on the brain, Alexander thought. As they came together by the roadside he realized what should have occurred to him before: this must be the witch, Gelia Somershoe, the mother.

But she put him at his ease at once. "My, ain't you handsome?" It didn't sound silly, coming from her. They shook hands and said their names.

"My daughter, Raedawn, said you might be around," the witch said. "Maybe you'll come for supper sometime. Whatcha say?"

She reminded him of the bleached-blond barflies in the Port Lucaya hotels where his brother worked, too old to be loose women any longer and too lazy to try very hard. Her eyelashes were gooped thick. Her painted lips made her skin look parched.

He shifted uneasily and looked over his shoulder. "I would like to come. Only this boss of mine, he has said he'll fire me if I talk to you."

"Ain't never met this boss of yours." Suddenly her voice was like hot molasses.

And before his very eyes, she turned into another woman. Alarmed, Alexander stared.

Her skin grew pink, all that makeup seemed to disappear, and her eyes began to glitter. She glanced around the site at the men heading for their cars, styrofoam coffee cups in hand.

As one, all their heads turned.

She smiled.

Alexander went cold. *Witch.*

"Maybe I should talk to him," she purred. Why did she want him to think she was just somebody's mother?

"You see," he said, beginning to sweat, "I have got to work here all day. At night I stay in the trailer for security."

"You poor baby," she cooed. Her attention was on him again. The voice was the changed voice, the steamy young voice, but the light had gone out of her eyes. "Why, I'm sure that's against the law. Making a man work day—and night." Was he imagining all the double entendres? She flickered on and off like a light bulb. "And you cain't even get away for a beer?"

Alexander knew he was in her hands. "That's what I'm saying, Mrs. Somershoe." He was stuck. He'd have to trust her. "You see," he lowered his voice, "things have been happening at night, where I am sleeping—"

"I thought I told you to leave these people alone!" Bob Bagoff had found them, as Alexander had feared, and he was furious. "Now git back inside and punch out. And you, lady—"

Bob rounded on Rae's mother and stopped. He actually rocked back on his heels. Alexander smiled to himself. "This is a hardhat area," Bob said, more mildly. He swallowed.

She didn't look like anybody's mother now. A smell like the smell Alexander remembered on Rae came from Mrs. Somershoe, too harsh and persuasive to be perfume. She cooed at Bob. Her hands fluttered. Every time she almost touched Bob on the arm or chest he took a gasping breath. What she was saying, Alexander noticed, had nothing at all to do with the big come-on.

"I just been telling your friend here that he can sue you-all sixty ways for locking him up day and night on the job. Is he gettin' overtime for all this work? He even gettin' the same money these other fellows make? I bet he's not even in the union. Does the union know that you don't pay him right?" In midseduction she stopped cold and stood nose to nose with Bob.

Old Mother Somershoe, I don't think, thought Alexander.

When she changed back into an old woman again, Bob's eyes narrowed.

Alexander backed up a pace. A prudent man would go to the trailer and punch out, he thought. He stayed put.

"You're interfering in my business, lady," the boss grated. Someone came to stand behind Bob. Alexander tried to glance that way and was astounded to realize he couldn't turn his head. "The nigger stays here."

"You're interfering in *my* business." Her voice was soft and sweet. It filled the sky. It thundered with bone-rattling power. He couldn't say how she did it, because from where Alexander stood she looked cinder-cold, an overly madeup old lady in a pair of cheap pink hot pants and a torn blouse. He was watching witchcraft at work, he knew that much, more brazen than his Gran would ever have dared.

It's working on me, too, he thought. He summoned the initiative to back up another pace. Then he looked around to see who had joined them. It was the architect.

JENNIFER STEVENSON

Rae's mother turned to the architect where he stood behind Bob. "I thought we didn't call people nigger to their face no more."

The architect blinked as if he'd been slapped.

"'Specially not if they're your own employees." She drove her point home. "In front of witnesses."

Released from eye contact with the witch, Bob spun toward the architect. "Oh, it's you," he said hoarsely. "Tell," he swallowed and cleared his throat. "Tell this b—this lady we got orders to talk to nobody who lives around here."

The architect looked at his shoes and then at Rae's mother. "Well, as a matter of fact, I've been told otherwise by the developer himself. Apparently the policy has changed," he added. "Just today." Alexander was interested to note that the architect suffered from none of the paralyzing effects of the witch's force.

"If you'd wait a moment, Mrs. Somershoe, I'd like to speak to you later, if I may?" The architect herded Bob away.

Walter was pleased to see that Bagoff was calming down.

"Anyway, she's got to get off the site," Bagoff complained.

Fowier was right, Walter realized. The situation needed a mediator. Walter shrank from intervening, but somebody had to, and Fowier had anointed him.

"I know, Bob, I know. Last week Mr. Fowier was adamant against contact with the locals. Mr. Fowier seems to be a—a man of quick decision sometimes," Walter said.

That was putting the best face on it. Fowier was out of his mind, showing up at the jobsite drenched to the skin in a two thousand dollar suit. But Bagoff was impressed with Fowier. And who can blame him? Walter thought. Fowier scares me to death.

"We need this lady's land," he said in plain English.

Bob's jaw worked. "What's it got to do with my nigger?"

Walter cringed. "Really, Bob!" He bit his lip. "She's right, you know. If an employee takes offense at that language, your company could suffer legally. And he could call on both me and Mrs. Somershoe as witnesses."

"I'll fire him," Bagoff snapped promptly. "The bitch leaves him alone."

"He can still sue." Walter sweated. Bagoff didn't fear lawyers as he should. That was destined to change. *But please, please,* Walter prayed, *not on my project.* "Look at it this way, the lady's husband is black. She's probably sensitive."

Comprehension crept over Bagoff's face. Somebody at home in there after all.

"So perhaps it's a good thing that your workman makes contact with these people. It could turn out to be helpful. They have a ready-made point of affinity."

Bagoff nodded slowly. "They're both black." It sounded much stupider coming out of Bagoff's mouth than it had coming out of his own, but Walter felt that Bagoff wouldn't notice that. Bagoff shot a hostile look at Gelia Somershoe. "If he balls that bitch over dinner I guess I'm cool. Long as he's back on the job by dark." He strutted off to deliver the good news to his workman.

Rae's young man wasn't making very good use of his time with her mother, in Gelia's opinion. Was he a man or a mouse? Gelia bet that he would have snook back to his job if she hadn't been there and stood up for him, the big fat chicken.

Hafta show some ginger if he wants to play with my Rae.

She bantered him, giving him a hard time, answering none of his questions, so's he'd know a Somershoe woman is hard to please.

Under her banter, Gelia felt sad. She hadn't had to pander for Raedawn since the child was fourteen and Cracker had started to get on her nerves. She thought wistfully of the interns in the clinic in Rimville, the ever-changing faces at the high schools, and her old steadies at the power plant, the courthouse, the Berne firehouse. All those men seemed far away now. Counting the roster of her personal favorites and Ernest Brown, the man who kept her sane, it seemed to her like they was all used-up old shoes. Old. She felt old, and it made her sad.

With disfavor she watched the man of Rae's choice fumble the repartee. He kept looking anxiously at his boss, kept trying to be *serious* with her. As if he didn't notice she was a woman.

I could make him want me, she thought with a flicker of glee. But she had promised Ernest she wouldn't. Rae wouldn't be pleased neither. She was already sick of pleasing Rae, and it hadn't even begun yet. So tempting to take this one, just once.

Well, it wouldn't mean much if she won. They'd had that out years ago—which of them could take a man away from the other.

No, it wasn't worth it. The consequences would be a dilly.

That was all she needed at her time of life, Gelia admitted frankly to herself for the first time, to put her brand on this feller right before he got filled up with all that electricity. Besides, he wasn't her type. If she could have another one like the old one—

But that wouldn't happen, she thought with regret. Never in a million years. There'd never be anybody else like him. That was the meat of it.

She wanted the old one back, not some young football-player-size stud with no experience and a attitude like, well, what was *wrong* with this feller anyway? Didn't he just want to reach out and *grab* her? What's men coming to these days?

This line of thought headed straight for feeling old again, and she veered off it. He's just not the same, she thought. Guess I'm a one-man woman at heart.

She flirted with him, tweaking the heat, dodging his questions, until the shouting boss came back to lay down the law.

While Bob Bagoff talked in a tense, insincere undervoice to his workman, Walter reopened negotiations with Mrs. Somershoe. She made him nervous.

"Why, I surely would like to talk to you some more, Mr. Chepi." She batted her eyelashes at him. "Why don't you come over and we'll have a little set-down? We'll be all alone."

"Um, tomorrow, perhaps?" It was pure funk, but Walter felt a powerful need for air. "I'd like to dress a little better before calling on your home. And find a florist." Happy thought!

She slapped him playfully on the arm. "Well, ain't you the perfect gentleman?"

Chapter Twenty-Seven

Mink led Ink to the golf course at the northernmost end of their territory. The late afternoon was too cold for all but the hardiest golfers to be out. The children came to a tall grassy hill all over holes, a rabbit warren, and they sat utterly still for perhaps an hour, waiting for the baby rabbits to come out and lip-lop around the golf course lawn.

Several times she heard Ink's tummy growling. She ought to get them some food. For some reason she didn't want to. He'd just have to control himself and watch rabbits.

She felt funny inside. She felt as if her skin had become very porous and the millions of tiny pores were expanding, making her bigger inside than outside, so that smells and sounds and sights could fly around inside her. She had chosen to watch the baby rabbits because they would run away if she moved, and she needed to be utterly still. Maybe the feeling would go away.

It didn't go away. She felt hollow inside. The rabbits hopped around, scratched, sniffed, chewed grass, but mostly they sat. She thought maybe she knew what that was like. The longer she sat still in one place, the more she felt herself opening up, and the world rushed in at a million tiny holes all over her body, making her feel like she could see out of the back of her head or look out of her heels down deep into the ground she squatted on. The smells got so strong, they talked to her whole body, not just her nose. There was too much to see, and it was moving way too fast. She could feel the rabbits getting ready to hop before they did it. Even with her eyes shut she knew which one would hop first. The rabbits knew, too. They could tell when you moved even if they weren't looking at you. Maybe they're all open holes like this, too, she thought.

Probably she was just hungry. Willy probably had a loaf of bread back at the trailer. She stayed where she was.

The rabbits had a zillion different-colored hairs on them, even on their faces. Brown, black, tan, gray, red, gold, white. Their whiskers flipped forward and back, sometimes both sides at once, sometimes one at a time. She imagined having whiskers. Probably it would help you see behind yourself. In her mind's eye her whiskers were stiff and strong where they stuck into her upper lip. She twitched her upper lip around, moving imaginary whiskers, and finally sat motionless, letting the fine tips of her invisible whiskers tell her what was going on around her.

The air got colder as the sun slanted lower. Cool air seeped in through her million pores, and her skin shrank and swelled with every heartbeat.

The rabbits chewed grass. The grass smelled rich, full of sunshine. She could imagine pulling it up and eating it herself. *I'm hungry, too.* But if she moved, the rabbits would run away. So she held still. Her stomach wanted to rumble. She breathed carefully so that it wouldn't. Smells came in through a million holes all over her body. New grass, saliva, musky momma rabbit. Baby rabbits smelling like baby everything, new and fresh and good. Rabbit poo: hot and musky momma rabbit poo, sweet baby rabbit poo. And that was just the rabbits themselves. Beyond them she smelled her brother, so much like herself that she didn't really smell him at all. Then the sycamore overhead, and the worm-cast dirt below, and the river down the hill, a single speedboat way out there, putting out diesel fumes and growling.

Sounds, too. Sounds entered not just at her ears but all over her body. Sparrows rustled among fallen leaves, squirrels chased each other and, far away at the other end of the golf course, there came a whack of some-body hitting a ball with a club, then the thock of the ball hitting a tree, and an anguished cry: "Fuuuuck!" That throbbing up there was a plane, going to the local airport. She let the sound carry her upward, rushing up and out through her own pores into the air, higher and higher, until she knew how the sky must feel where it pressed down on the pointed tops of trees, all tickly with new leaf.

She knew a moment of panic. What am I? She wanted to move, scratch, rub her nose, smack her lips, fart, anything to find her body again. She swooped back into her skin and stopped herself just in time from moving. *Baby rabbits nearby, don't scare them.* Maybe, she reasoned, maybe this is why animals are always hopping around eating and pooping and scratching and sniffing and licking theirselves. Tweeting and pecking and biting under their feathers with their beaks. If they stopped still and just listened, just *listened* and felt and smelled and looked, they'd be in trouble. They'd fly out of their bodies and be everything and never move. And then a fox would get 'em.

Ink's smell changed. She ought to have expected his touch. But when he touched her arm, she leaped convulsively, rounded on him, and socked him good in the eye. He cried out and clapped his hand over his face. The rabbits scattered.

She snarled, "What!"

Ink whimpered, his hand over his eye. "I'm hungry."

Now that she had moved, she found she couldn't sit still for another minute. "So go eat!" she yelled.

Leaping up, she darted off into the woods between fairways. When she looked back, Ink was staring at her. It was her job to find food, she remembered, fuddled. She didn't care. She was hurt or scared or startled or something terrible.

Mink turned and ran again. She heard her brother follow her. He called out to her once, but she ignored him and kept running. She felt the beginning of the grandmother of all itches coming in through the soles of her feet. She ran on.

Chapter Twenty-Eight

Her daughter was waiting for her when she crossed the road. It was nearly dark. Rae stepped out of the box elder trees in front of their trailer and came to meet her. Gelia could see the fire in Rae's eye from twenty paces away.

"Let's you and me have a little talk, Mother." Rae took her by the arm.

"Don't grab me so hard," Gelia complained. Her voice sounded weak and whiny, but she felt a great reserve of power left over from that unsatisfying talk with Rae's young man. Ready when you are, Daughter, she thought, and clicked her teeth. "Where you been?"

"Watching you. We had an agreement, Mother," Rae said in a steely voice.

"I remember."

"Do you?" Rae let go her arm with a little shove.

Gelia was comforted to recall that she knew where to find every one of her daughter's sensitive spots. Looks like we're gonna need 'em tonight. "Well, goodness gracious, don't let's have a scene," she lied, high glee in her heart.

"Shall we go under the hill?"

"I'm agreeable."

Gelia headed across the road with a fresh spring in her step. Nothing clears the air like a good knock-down-drag-out. A little tussle and she'd feel like a new woman.

Walter watched the two women stalk across the road, make a half-circle around the site, and head straight at the ridge where he was standing. He sidled behind a bush with his thermos, trying to be invisible. He could practically hear the air crackling as the Somershoes, mother and daughter, strode past.

They walked straight past him without noticing him, slap up to the ridge where it rose like a wall out of the meadow.

And then they simply disappeared, mother and then daughter, the elder as if fleeing the younger. They disappeared into the black hillside, spinning sideways through solid ground. His mouth fell open.

Then he heard their muffled, angry voices.

"You said you weren't interested in Alexander. Was that a lie? Are you? 'Cause I'm about fed up. I'll lay off if you want him, but you got to be honest with me."

"You know I don't want him."

"Then what the hell were you up to out there today?" Rae sounded furious.

Walter stepped closer to the ridge. No door, no gate. Just a wall of dirt and trees. He leaned and laid his ear against the hard-packed soil.

"Getting your boyfriend out of the trouble he's in. Tried to find if there was some gumption in him, too, but there ain't. He's a-scared to come calling on you, child. That boss of his got him working twenty-four hours a day. I had to go shake the law at them like a newspaper at a dog."

Rae's voice wobbled. "Shaking your bottom at him, more like. I say again, do you want him? Do you know, King Gowdy has asked me to marry him? I am that close to giving up, Mother. All of it. And all of you."

"I don't want your man, Daughter. Surely we don't have to have all that out again?"

"I don't want to have it out. I know you and your fights. You purely love it. Well, I don't! I'd rather give Alexander up than go through that again, and you know it. I'd rather leave town with King."

Gelia's voice turned to a whine. "Why don't you believe your mother? I said I don't want him."

"You lie."

"Not this time."

"*Yes* this time. And every time. You swore to me."

"I was just looking at him. At a time like this I got a right to know who you're taking up with."

"What do you mean, at a time like this? Well? Cat got your tongue for once in your life?"

"Since they cut that tree down, since you just got to know."

Tree? thought Walter. That one got past him.

"What difference does it make what man I'm with any more? It's over. He's gone. Nothing'll bring him back."

Mrs. Somershoe sounded oily. "The more reason. You better keep that Bahama feller. You're gonna need a man now."

"What do I need a man for? To get married? You want me to leave, don't you. You never wanted me around, and now you think you can just chase me out of here."

"Not at all—"

"Yeah, I heard you. I like this guy. It's not because they cut—cut down—it's just because I like him, so you want him!" Rae yelled.

"Child, there's more people involved in this asides just yourself and your fancy. This thing's big. We all got to exercise some self-control."

"Fine one to talk about self-control! Who can't keep her knees together for twenty-four hours at a time? Who forgets to feed the kids?" Her voice rose higher and harsher. "Who sleeps half the day and prowls half the night like a bitch in heat? Who ends up feeding them and cleaning this place and working every crummy job in these two towns while you're shaking your thing?" The mud against Walter's ear trembled with the force of Rae's scream.

"I don't want this one."

"I am so sick of hearing that lie!"

"Why can't you believe in your mother for once?"

"'Cause you're a liar, Mother!" The hill trembled again. "How can I trust a *liar?*"

"Quiet, child, you'll bring the hill down on us."

"You just spread yourself around like a cloud, and if it's a happy cloud I guess we're all lucky, and if you got a bad mood we all suffer! You don't even know what's you and what's the world! 'Be quiet, child.' Well, I *won't!*"

The soil crawled under Walter's hand. Water oozed out of the dirt and ran over his fingers. The whole ridge shook, and the hairs rose on the back of his neck. A rush of droplets spattered on his head.

"And now you got me screaming again, damn you!"

Gelia sounded syrupy and understanding. "I know you hate me, darlin'. Oh, not all the time, I know. Children have their bad tempers. It passes. When you've seen what I've seen, you won't question your mother so much."

"Shut up!" Rae shrieked. "Just shut up!"

"Tsk. You used to have better control of your temper."

"What's the matter with you? Why won't you let up? I've offered you the guy. You said you don't want him. Not that I believe you."

"You'll be wiser someday."

There was a pause. Walter considered running for his El Camino. Maybe if he locked the doors and hid under the dashboard.

Rae's voice came more quietly, "Come on, Gelia. What do you want from me? I got nothing else, you know that."

"It's no use talking to you once you've lost your temper. I remember when you was fifteen. Lordy, the way you'd scream."

"I stopped screaming and started just giving you the man."

"Oh, yes, you had contempt for your old mother, you just let go of the rope with that snooty look on your nose—"

"That used to be enough for you. What's changed, Gelia?"

"Don't use that patient tone of voice with me."

"Is it because they cut him—cut him down? No use taking it out on me. It won't bring him back, Gelia. Not fighting, not crying, not nothing."

"Catch you crying over him!" Gelia laughed scornfully. "You done nothing but make hay since Wednesday!"

"Look, I've had it. I don't know what you want or why you're goin' after me like this. If you're grieving, fine, but don't take it out on my hide. And I changed my mind. I take it back about Alexander. I'm keeping him. I'll fight you for him. Let him decide which of us he wants."

There was another long silence.

"This ain't the same old fight, Daughter. It's different."

"Oh, baloney. That's lame, too."

"Don't you feel the change in the ground?"

"I have. What about it?"

"Listen! Can't you hear the whole river groanin'?"

Gypsy stuff again. Walter felt a powerful need for shelter. He tiptoed away clutching his thermos to his chest like a shield, slid behind the wheel of his El Camino, locked both doors, and poured hot cocoa with shaking hands.

Rae caught her breath and listened for the river. The living night hummed. Her mother had that lying look again, but this time Rae felt the truth nearby in spite of Gelia, coming to her out of her own skin. She would have to get alone if she was going to figure it out. There'd be no thinking with Gelia attituding at her like a dose of poison gas.

She murmured, "It shifts every day." She felt the hum in the ground, in the fingers of trees around them. She thought about how the river shifted west at night, closer to their houses. "West at night."

"That's right. West by night, east by day. He was holdin' it, you understand? Holdin' it westerly. Now he's gone, the rubber band's gone an' snapped, and it wants to go back. We're gonna see a flood like there's never been, child. If we're lucky we'll gain land when it settles. My proppity line goes way to hell out in the water."

Rae listened with one ear, trying to puzzle through whatever Gelia must be leaving out. Of course he'd held the river close. He was always thirsty. Now he was gone, and the river had shifted east—by day. By night it rose to the west bank. That bespoke indecision. Why? What was drawing it back and forth?

With the other ear she attended to the night. Out there, beyond their temporary hole in the hill, beyond the site, beyond the railroad tracks and 31 and their tumbledown trailers, the river groaned against its banks.

She needed to be alone. "We better get out of here."

They bowed their heads low and stepped toward the wall. There was a smooth folding. Rae felt it like a sheet of paper with a cool side and a warm side, like rolling over in bed. Then they were outside.

The night sky spattered them.

Rae stomped home to get ready to be picked up for her ride to work.

Gelia headed for Ernest's place. Tempers were still a little chancy yet to be spending the night at home.

Walter watched a half-moon came out from behind a cloud. Up on the ridge a child wailed with abandoned grief. He squinted up. Something white moved along the path up there.

A white figure ran surely along the path, leaping, scrambling, flickering among black tree trunks, disappearing only to reappear higher on the ridge. A second followed more slowly. As he watched, the second figure stopped and wailed again.

If he hadn't been looking at the ridge he would have missed it when the two women came out of the hill.

In the darkness their clothes floated, ghostly. They marched out of the hill as if out of a cloud, separating and walking around either side of the site as if they couldn't stand to take another step in one another's company. Walter slid under the dashboard of his El Camino, spilling cocoa on himself. The better part of valor, he thought. With his head tilted at an unnatural angle and his arms stretched out painfully, he screwed the top back on the thermos. Footsteps crunched by on the gravel outside the car and disappeared into the night. For the second time, Walter emerged from cover, quivering, and at last he did as he should have done half an hour ago—took himself back to his hotel before he got involved with any more furious people.

Chapter Twenty-Nine

Cracker sat in the tree and waited for his sister. He hadn't much idea what to do if she did come. What he could say to her. Maybe he just needed to get her to climb up here and let things take their course. Slip away, leave her with it. Then he heard the shouting and crying and Carl chasing Gloria across the road toward him. What do I do now? He patted the tree's big limb under him and whispered, Up to you, big guy.

And the limb answered him. Gave him a hell of a shock.

The tree said, At last. You're old enough. You'll do.

Lord, what a weird feeling. Made him feel big and open like his auntie's old screened-in front porch, with a nice wide sofa for spooning on. Suddenly he felt he could handle Gloria, and great godfrey he had a hard-on like yesterday's biscuits, brrr. He could show her what it was all about. He even thought about showing Carl. We're all the same. Second time in his life he'd had such an inclination. Room for both of you, he thought as if they could hear him. He called silently, feeling that big open sweet porch-sofa feeling, come and get it, my darlings, oh, welcome. So much sweet horniness rushed up in him, he almost fell out of the tree.

He perched there, listening to Carl and Gloria fight below him, waiting for them to go away so he could get off this tree and get out of here before he turned into another Raedawn. He could feel it happening already.

A strange weakness that was like strength came over him. He wondered if this was how Rae felt when she was getting, well, intimate with the thing. Kind of wild and thirsty and powerful. His hands and feet throbbed something fierce.

The sound of a smack saved him. Gloria shrieked. He roused to find himself draped over the limb like a sleeping leopard. His arms and legs hung down around the limb, down and down, dripping over the branches below him like poured honey, dangling like old rope, reaching thirstily for the ground. He jerked wildly, tumbled clean off the limb and fell ten feet, landing thump on the ground with the wind knocked out of him.

At first he was too winded to move, but then he heard Carl and Gloria talking to somebody new. His hands and feet still throbbed. He sucked air into his flattened lungs and

*strained to hear a third voice. Not a sound. His heart pounded in time with his throbbing
hands and feet.*

He began to hear the big voice again. It was talking to Carl and Gloria. At last.
You're old enough. You'll do.

*Galvanized into flight, he crawled away on elbows and knees, his fingers and toes
dragging behind him like loose shoelaces.*

To this hour he couldn't remember where he went next.

Chapter Thirty

Willy and Eugene had finished the jug with the reefer, but Willy always kept a beer stash at home. He had been abandoned before. By now he knew just what to do.

He headed home at sunset. The western sky flamed pink and red against the black body of the ridge. The ridge prickled with black trees sticking up into the ugly colors. Once upon a time there had been a tree so tall that it stuck up into the sunset, even with a sixty-foot ridge behind it. Shambling south along US 31 from the footbridge, Willy looked for it, then looked away.

He felt flat and sad. The fun was going out of his job. He wondered if this was how Cracker felt all the time, a kind of black hole inside, eating up his good times before he'd properly finished having them.

Eugene's face rose before his mind's eye. Eugene had learned tenderness quickly. Willy craved that more than anything. How much longer would he have Eugene? He counted the months until they graduated high school and Eugene went off to college. Dumb, because it just made him sadder to know how soon he would lose him, but Willy couldn't help doing it.

The fact was, even his dead best friend hadn't been all that tender. Kinda rough, really. Too busy being the biggest thing around, he guessed. Willy'd had an inkling sometimes that everything he cared about had always been at the mercy of this great power. And now the power itself was gone. It was finally getting to him that he didn't know what would become of him, of his family and his life, all that, now that his friend was gone. Vanished in the back of a dump truck. Not even a decent coffin.

His parents had never been found or buried, either. The half-assedness of it got to him.

He checked his stash, two warm six-packs hidden under Ernest's trailer steps. Cracker hadn't found it, so this was still a good hidey-hole.

He circled his own trailer and its added-on back room, listening for Cracker. Nope. Another circle around to pick up the beer and he was inside, in his and Davy's room, with the lamp unlit and the bolt thrown on the door.

Cracker's doing, that dead bolt. It baffled Willy how the man could be such a slacker in some ways, and yet in others he really seemed to understand what it was like to be a kid in this family. What Willy wouldn't have given to have a lock on this door when he was little! He sucked warm beer through the mouth of the can and stared fiercely at the gloaming light crossing his bedroom ceiling, not-thinking about his mother screaming while his father rampaged through the house, hitting everyone and everything.

Braver now with a couple of beers in him, he returned to his earlier train of thought. Not gentle, his friend. Willy tried to imagine what it must have felt like to have all that stuff rushing through your body all the time, not just when you're with a Willy or a Raedawn or a Gelia, but all the time. Enough to make anybody a little on the rough side, probably. Willy tried to temper that roughness when he passed the good stuff along to his friends in high school. Too many guys were rough with each other as it was. Somebody had to show 'em the difference.

He found he had finished both six-packs. It wasn't quite enough beer, but close on an empty stomach. Somehow he got all the empties gathered up, and the little pop-tops, and the plastic collars, and hustled them out of the trailer to toss them under the front steps.

Davy came home while he was performing this perfunctory act of secretiveness.

"Anything to eat?" Davy said.

Remorse stung Willy. "I'm sorry, I didn't even look. Pee Bee an' Jay prob'ly." He followed Davy inside.

Davy stuck his head in the refrigerator. "Good," he said into it.

Willy hovered behind him uncertainly, wondering if he should stay and make sure the kid ate something. Davy kept his head in the fridge. Willy waited. Davy seemed to be waiting, too, refusing to take anything out of the fridge or just shut it.

Mad at me for being drunk, Willy realized. He hung his head. Darned if he would apologize again. "G'night," he said bleakly to Davy's back.

He had shambled to his room and was standing, humiliated and repentant, staring at the bunk bed, when Davy came up suddenly behind him and seized his hand. When Willy lurched around, surprised, he almost fell into his brother's arms.

"Here." Davy pressed a sticky jelly sandwich into his hand.

Willy choked on a laugh. *Criminy, the kids take care of the kids around here.* "Thanks."

Chapter Thirty-One

Bob Bagoff didn't leave the office trailer until six-thirty that evening. He fiddled with the insides of his briefcase and made calls and shuffled papers.

Alexander suspected Bob of trying to stop him from crossing the road to Rae's place, after all. Rae's mother had set off the worst of his pig-headedness. *You can talk to 'em I guess, but do it on your own time. I mean, dinner break or something.*

Alexander thought, Sure, my dinner break is an hour and a half. Ninety minutes out of twenty-four hours. Bob was engaged in a tug of wills with Rae's mother, and Alexander was the rope. Not that it mattered, he thought gloomily. He'd made a bad impression on Mrs. Somershoe.

Irritated beyond endurance, he said, "Do you want me to go outside while you finish your paperwork, boss?"

Bob looked guilty. "Hey, no, you're not disturbing me."

Alexander rolled his eyes and puttered noisily with the can opener and hot plate, pointedly preparing dinner for one.

At length Bob packed up his briefcase and clumped out. Alexander propped himself in the trailer door and watched him drive away, sucking his teeth and thinking hard thoughts.

Presently he began to worry anew about his own predicament. By God, if I go crazy you will fire me anyway, you ugly man you, he thought as the taillights of the half-ton disappeared. He couldn't imagine what Bob or Ike would have to say if they found him tomorrow morning rooted to the floor, his cock a yard long and the eyes rolled up in his head like a lunatic's.

On the other hand, it was as Rae had promised—nothing had tried to kill him here in the trailer. Yet. Alexander was far from satisfied with this thought. As he spooned up baked beans, he wondered if it was safe now to cross the road and knock at her door, angry boss and witch-mother be damned.

Out in the night, a man came whistling up the road. He paused at a pallet of lumber. Alexander stepped outside onto the gravel.

"Hey! You! Quit pissin' on the wood over there!"

The other grunted. "'Lul-lo.'"

Alexander went to meet him. "Go home, man, you are drunk."

"Situation modus operandi," announced the other. "You Raedawn's new boyfriend? She said he works over here."

Alexander hesitated. "I—my name's Alexander Caebeau."

"Cracker Coombs." The man wiped his hand on greasy overalls apologetically and extended it. "'Scuse me. Chokin' the chicken. Alexander, yeah. You know, you missed a good supper the other night."

Alexander gripped him by the arm. "I told her, I'm real sorry. Yesterday my boss says he is going to fire me if I go over there. Now maybe today it is okay, I don't know. He says lawyers are all over the damn thing."

"Wouldn't surprise me," Cracker grunted, taking him literally. "Got everything else, including rats, mice, bugs, fish, frogs, wild childern, and horny women. Got 'ny beer?"

"I wish I did."

"Tell you what. Bring you some."

Alexander sighed. "Lord, that sounds good. Can you—would you like some beans? Sit and talk? Maybe you know something about this place? Why a man gets crazy dreams here, things happen?" He shivered. "I don't mind a man with two fists. That's something you can see."

Cracker scratched his head. "Got a hot poker game a-waiting, but I can stand here a bit, I guess." His eyes lit up. "Queer story about the hole-digger. Who did it, d'y'know?"

"No." Alexander didn't care to explain, but he didn't want his new acquaintance to leave him yet. An engine roared down the street. He flinched and watched until the headlights passed. "Hope my boss doesn't find you here. He'll fire me, sure."

Cracker put a paw on his chin. "This guy's a menace, know that? How about I come by in an hour or so? Knock on your window. Make a sound like a hoot owl."

"Okay."

"Going to a little card party up to the firehouse. Done in half an hour or two. Mind, if you conk out before I get back, I'll drink all the beer. Only fair to warn you."

Alexander agreed to these terms, and his new friend whistled himself off up the road.

Maybe Rae would be home. Maybe he could just drop by her house, as Cracker had. Perhaps that was done here. Alexander stepped out past the circle of light by the trailer door and looked up and down the road. Fifty yards down the road, under a streetlight, a big pickup truck sat pointed in his direction. The driver's distinctive hat showed in silhouette. The boss.

What was *wrong* with the man? If he wanted to watch the site himself, why make Alexander sleep here?

Alexander went inside and lay down with the lights on. The day's filth scritched between his clothes and his skin. He smelled filthy, too. After ten minutes he got up and took a shower in the tiny cabinet next to the water closet. That felt better, but now he was even sleepier. He tried sitting up in Bob's canvas chair, but it was miserably uncomfortable for a man his size. With misgivings, he lay down on the cot again.

In no time he was dozing. Panic jerked him awake. On an inspiration he laced his boots onto his bare feet. If his feet tried any funny business, he was sure to wake up. As extra insurance he laid his horn-handled knife in its sheath beside him.

Chapter Thirty-Two

Another fight in the Gowdy trailer. In the boys' bedroom King cringed, paralyzed and sickened, listening.

The slap. His mother cried out. The screen door slammed so hard it bounced open, and their voices faded into the darkness, his mother fleeing, his father pursuing.

From his bunk, King listened to the wind slam the door against the outside wall until he couldn't stand it anymore. He climbed down past Davy whimpering in the lower bunk, past Willy motionless in the cot, and walked barefoot to the door to stand listening to the dreadful darkness. Saplings swayed at the river's edge, the young branches bending until their tips made rings on the streetlight-smeared water. He thought he heard his mother's voice. His bare feet were cold on the linoleum.

After a while they came back, his mother clinging to his father, the two of them stumbling over the tracks jerky and slow like runners in a nightmare, as if their feet sank into deep mud at every step. In the dark, from the way he held her and bent away from her at the same time, his father looked like he didn't want any part of his mother but was too scared to push her off.

They walked right past the trailer, staggering because his mother wouldn't let go of Carl, and Carl either couldn't or wouldn't push her away, though he wanted to, King could tell. They hauled each foot from the ground as if the foot were a lead weight. Come home! King shouted in his mind. Why aren't you coming home?

They disappeared around the back of their own trailer, not stopping, not going in the door. He walked after them, his bare feet slow and numb with cold. There was something weird about the way Carl held onto her. Was he dragging her to the river? Full of awful thoughts, King could not make his legs move any faster.

He rounded the front of the trailer and saw them. His mother already sat slumped in the dinghy. Was she holding her head in her hands? King peered through the patchy darkness, dumbfounded. Carl threw the anchor chain in the dinghy, and now he was climbing in, kicking off, pulling at the oars almost before he sat down.

King ran to the edge of the water too late. The sound of Carl's oars splashed away into murmuring blackness. Deep in the hard-packed mud, his parents' footprints glowed in the dark.

Chapter Thirty-Three

The people were going to bed. Lights went out upstairs in all the houses, and smells of food faded away. Mink had shaken off her brother hours ago. Since then she had covered almost every inch of their territory, from the golf course in the north to the abandoned bear cages in the south.

She itched. Her skin, her nerves, her bones all itched. They tingled as if they were shouting, the way her hand tingled when she touched Willy's blaring transistor radio. Every now and then a wave or bubble of restlessness would form in her groin and inflate itself horridly fast, ripping through her whole body to pass out the top of her head, leaving her light-headed. Sometimes the bubble flew up and stuck in her throat, so that she had to let it loose in a scream.

She screamed now. The bubble of restlessness flew into the sky. Free for the moment, she leapt up onto the Route 64 bridge's concrete balustrade and ran, hopping over each iron fox in turn and slapping it on the head as she passed.

Far down between her legs, further inside than she could have imagined, the itching began again. She ran.

Ink almost caught up with her at the bridge. His sides ached with running. As his feet touched the bridge at the east end, Mink leapt off the balustrade at the west end and disappeared around the corner toward Second Street. Ink fell to a walk, to a standstill, and wailed his confusion into the night air.

Why was she running away? She *never* ditched him. It was part of their bargain: us against the world. She'd *ditched* him! Sobs of abandonment and misery jerked out of him.

Something heavy hit the bridge at his feet, like a chunk of concrete or a car engine. Ink looked up.

The balustrade in front of him was bare. He frowned, sniffling convulsively. Little clinking sounds drew his eye downward. Something ran away from him on quick trotting feet, not silent, though the creature seemed to float along above the pavement. Chink chink chinkchinkchinkchink: faster than he could count, the footsteps fell. Another animal jumped down off the balustrade and followed the first.

Ink watched open-mouthed as the cast-iron bridge foxes left their perches on the balustrade. The foxes at the end were waiting on the pavement by the time the first two had trotted the length of the bridge. For a moment they milled around like dogs meeting in the park, sniffing butt, caroming off one another's shoulders with clanking sounds, and then they turned and pattered off in the direction Mink had taken.

Mink couldn't tell if she felt hot or cold. She ran blindly through the short streets that bordered the river, splashed through new-flooded shallows, clambered over fences to run across parkland, wasteland, the grounds of the abandoned nail factory, hopping without thinking over the nail-strewn gravel on the hard bare feet of a country child.

She tore at her itching skin, rolled in grass, in sand, but found no relief. Mostly she ran. She could not run and tear at her skin at the same time, so she gripped her hair while she ran, bending her head and pulling, pulling her hair hard as if to pull the battery right out of that radio. That was how she happened to trip and sprawl painfully across the asphalt of US 31.

Sobbing, she rolled over on her back. Her skin was on fire where the asphalt had scuffed her sides, her shins, her elbows, and her knees. For an instant, while the pain lasted, she felt cool. The night was quiet compared with her slamming heart. She heard tires coming on the wet asphalt. She scrambled onto the shoulder and wriggled down into the grass.

A slug pulled its suckery foot across her sore knee, and she sat up to watch it. The knee burned. The slug felt cool. When it stopped to lick her with its rough tongue, she yelped and picked it off and put it down on a dock leaf.

Deep in her middle, she felt urgency. Almost home.

Her hands and feet tingled. It felt like a fly was caught in her grasp, the biggest fly in the world, held in both her hands and both her feet and buzzing unmercifully. She wrapped her arms around her folded knees and sat clenched, forehead pressed to her knees, willing it to stop. In panic, she actually formed words, pulling a sentence out of that compartment where she kept the unimportant business of people.

What are you telling me?

The buzzing in her hands and feet roared up, angry bees released from a jar, roared up her arms and legs. In an instant it was through her, past her heart, past her shoulders, rising in a black wave through her throat and up over her head. Submerged. All was silence.

Something enormous, very bright in the blackest eyeless darkness, was watching her. It asked an enormous question.

Who?

The darkness filled up with starlight, street light, moonlight. Her body came back from the outside in, and with it, the tingling itch. Mink tried to shout, but she only made a weak kittenish noise. The burning spread from her skinned knees and elbows to fill her up with cool electric fire. It ran along the insides of her arms, up her legs, down her sides, into her groin.

She leaped as if stung, and ran. This time she knew where she was going.

Chapter Thirty-Four

In Ernest Brown's trailer, Angelia read aloud, sitting up. Ernest lay feverish on the bed beside her, listening to her voice but not the words. Angelia's voice rose and fell, a different voice for each character, signalling the jokes, the tragedies, the bits of marvel, soothing and charming to listen to. Later she would talk about those people as if they were real, and Ernest would mostly not listen, because he wouldn't remember what the story had been about. Books to him were like pictures, only coded, as the welding manuals he had used in technical college were coded. Angelia loved a puzzle, but it seemed too much like work to Ernest. Best for him were the books about something you could see. All this he-said she-said, it was transitory.

He suspected Angelia enjoyed reading the way she enjoyed sex, for the thrill of the moment. Himself, if he was going to stuff his head with a lot of words, they would be names of the parts of a metal lathe. Something he wanted to keep.

He was still getting used to the notion that his place with her was safe. Maybe it had always been safe, and he, gentleman or fool that he was, had refused to know until she said it herself. There was a child in Angelia that no man saw but him. That was his secret. He couldn't deny she made him feel more of a man than any woman he'd known. It was a proud thing to be her chosen.

It didn't bother him, how far he'd come down in the world. Ernest had set his sights on what he wanted and kept them there. His mother might say he'd turned himself into a humble nigger, but he had never stepped back from his desire, either. There were plenty of people who thought to discourage him. Most of them meant it kindly. Most were afraid of Angelia. In the end they couldn't drive him away because they would have to get closer to her. The fire was too hot for them.

That's something his mother would never have understood. This was a terrible place in some ways. The women had had to bear it all. He pitied them.

He saw the marks it made on everyone here. There is a thing in the eyes of men who have been to war, or children who are mistreated, or dope fiends. The ones who survive. You knew it when you saw it. Ernest saw it in his Angelia and her daughter. Those brats of Cracker's had it, and young Willy. Davy was safe and still innocent, but he was witless. A bullet would pass through him like a charm. Cracker had that understanding, and it had shipwrecked him. Carl and Gloria had lacked it. King had run from it.

Ernest might have run, too, only this—he could not imagine living someplace where he couldn't feel the size of it over his shoulder all day long. It felt like living near a mountain. It meant something. A man will tolerate a lot of inconvenience to be near what is genuine.

Gelia could tell when Ernest had had enough reading. He got restless. She interrupted herself. "It's hot."

Ernest reached over, shut her book, and leaned to blow out the lamp.

"'Lectricity in the air," she said. Thick curling white hairs stuck to her neck. Together they slid down under the sheet and found their places in each other's arms.

Gelia thought about the boy across the road. So young. She wasn't accustomed to feeling the difference in ages. It made her think of dying, a thought she objected to. She shook herself.

What difference could age mean anyway? There was ripe or green. Accustomed to knowing the electricity of it in a concentrated form, like frozen orange juice in a can, she knew that a boy had the same man-power in him that a man had, only not yet grown. It was her privilege and her responsibility to grow it and grow it right, so that when he made up into a full man, he'd be somebody worth knowing. Too many of the sad creatures she took to her bed, she met too late. Momma's boys trapped in fifty-year-old bodies, with a momma-weight hanging around them to keep the old trouser snake from standing up like it wanted to. Letting things hold them back. Even worse was the ones who'd been started up wrong, scared witless, confused about the difference between sex and fighting. They had to be taught not to pour it out in destruction. It was a delicate business, and one she'd become expert in. This new man of

Rae's, now. What would become of them if he was a holder-backer?

Outside, a nighthawk screamed like a cat in anger. Gelia raised her head from Ernest's shoulder, straining her ears. She could feel the river shift, as if it had just got a new idea about downhill and uphill and, snake-like, decided to move all its parts, one by one. It was shifting nearer to her bank, to the place nearest the construction site. She lay down again. *That's all right then.* Get him wet and he'll do.

It was against her religion to worry, but her worries got bigger all the time. That tree-cutting across the road had really put a dent in her outlook. Then Rae, so stubborn and lawful, trying to make her feel guilty, another feeling that was against her religion. And then these fellers from the development, full of contracts and money, two things she'd managed to do without most of her life, thank you very much. She stirred uneasily. What did it mean that King came home? What did it mean that the river didn't just flood and be damned, but instead wavered, wobbling back and forth like a politician? She wouldn't trouble Ernest with all this. He had enough to contend with.

Her awareness of the size of things was getting bigger. She didn't like it. It made her uneasy.

A spark shot through her, and she flung an imperative arm over her lover's legs.

"You scared?" he whispered.

She pressed her face against his nipple. "I'm only human," she said, her voice muffled.

"What?" He paused in his stroking and moved his chin on her hair. Then he said, "Oh." He heaved a great sigh. Gently he worked his hands under her armpits and pulled her up onto his chest. "Come on, woman. Looks like we got time for one more."

Angelia Somershoe's power rode her like a saint. Ernest thought briefly of the ecstatic revival meetings of his childhood and women falling down in fits, and the men handling cottonmouth snakes, eyes rolled up in their heads, shaking the way Angelia shook now.

She writhed in his arms, and as he thought "snakes" she twisted, and suddenly he found himself on top. They could do it a thousand times. She always took him by surprise.

Chapter Thirty-Five

They fell asleep eventually, Angelia's head cuddled on his shoulder. Ernest dreamed. In his dream, she sat up reading to him, and the bed where they lay skidded along a tightrope of years wound together very fine, one moment twisted together with the next. The tightrope sagged and swayed over a parade of the many men Angelia had had, but for a mercy she didn't notice them. She read aloud with all the lively humor and pathos of her real life, but it was only a story, a library book Raedawn had brought home. Just some book.

The sky darkened around them. Big chunks of land fell off the ridge across the road and tumbled down over the park, where somehow no construction work had ever been done. The landslide splashed mightily into the river. Angelia turned a page. He saw their trailers tipped over by a wind, blown until they were stacked up on end like toys. A wall of water felled the stack, scattered the trailers and smashed them apart, and he marveled that it didn't bother him. He was here in bed with Angelia, listening to her read to him, and soon they would turn out the lamp and cuddle up like always.

A long column of half-naked men came marching up the road carrying shovels. They were going to fix the landslide. Angelia's lovers of bygone years, and he worried that she would notice them finally, for they marched right beside her elbow while the bed swayed and jounced on its eternal tightrope. But she never did. At last he knew that all the world was going by, floating, tumbled, disarranged, and this bed was fixed and safe because Angelia was in it, and she would never leave him.

Beside him, Gelia slept heavily. In her dream, her mother was dying. Aw, Ma, do we have to go through this again? That face was awful, coming apart and changing every day, though the voice never changed. It gave Gelia the willies.

The old lady rotted in her nest of quilts. She poked her finger at Gelia. Gelia dodged, not wanting whatever cuss the old lady was putting on her now. The finger came right off her mother's hand and flew through the air. It caught Gelia hard in the ribs. Poke. Gelia twisted, crying out, and the finger became a knife that slid into her and made her bleed. Her life came leaking out of the hole it made. Stop that! Gelia cried.

It was too late. Now you're next, her mother said.

Gramma Romy sat behind her mother. *She* had died at a hundred and twenty-one, diabetes, the stubbornest kind, and Gelia had lived in a succession of men's cars for a year while it lasted. Gelia's mind twisted from the memory lest it invade this dream and come alive here, too, oh, not again. Gramma Romy nodded while Gelia's mother cussed her, telling her what aging and death was like, and Gelia clutched her side where her mother's knife had gone in and out. There was another old lady behind Gramma Romy, and another behind her, curving away like Gelias in a restroom double mirror, and they all nodded, their heads bobbing, laying the cuss on her. She felt the hot blood run away out of her side and go cold on her fingers. This dream is no good, she thought angrily.

She turned over in bed. Ernest, give me a good dream, she commanded, but he was asleep. She lay her cheek against his warm back and listed to his heart, tuning hers to the same beat by breathing with him until her heart stopped pounding and gentled its pace.

Then it seemed that Ernest shut her book and turned the light out for her, and then they slid down into a bed surrounded by every man who had ever wanted her. They lined up in ranks. They sang to the sound of two organ notes, one hot and raspy, one cool and sweet, sang so seriously, like a choir, that she started laughing and almost woke up. O Gelia, O Gelia, they sang. She smiled in her sleep. She was darned if she'd wake up from this one.

Walter lay in his room at the White Fence Inn, his window ajar and the river's chuckle rising to a louder and less good-natured sound under his window. He slept.

In his dream, the woman Raedawn was on all fours. Her ears were laid flat against her black velvet skull because she was leashed and the leash was bound to a tree. She couldn't get far from the tree on the leash, and she couldn't jump up into the tree because the leash was too short. Her tail lashed her sides. There were men standing around her, just out of range, trying to catch hold of the leash to tame her. Walter knew they were fools.

A man who looked like John Fowier came too close, and she reached out one paw like a black catcher's mitt and laid him flat on the ground. Just pulled him into her lap and settled on him. John Fowier lay like a broken doll under her body. He looked pathetic, but it was his own fault. The man knew she was tied up. Don't taunt the animal.

Walter came up to her and stood just inside her reach. Very carefully, he showed her his hands. She padded up, her eyes glowing, and sniffed him all over. She spent a long time smelling his hands, and then his shoes, his legs, his crotch, his behind. His skin prickled all over. She sniffed his shoulders, his ears, the back of his head. Walter felt exquisitely alert but calm. Finally she rose up daintily on her haunches and looked into his eyes. He wondered what she saw there. He was tempted to lie flat on the ground before her, but that would be a mistake. Instead he sat.

She lay down with her back to him, leaning against him, and started to write a story in the dust with a forefinger. Walter read, and heard her voice in his head as the words ran past his eyes. She turned a page and showed him a woodcut, a very tiny woodcut, and when he bent his head to peer at it the woodcut grew large, turned into a photograph, grew larger still and became a movie. The movie grew and grew until it swallowed him up.

Inside her movie, the men were changed to dumb beasts. The woman Rae stood on her hind legs and walked among them, touching each one and quieting it, all the while talking to Walter, instructing him. To his embarrassment he realized that everything she pointed to was sex: the long fiery backbones of the men gamboling at her feet, the perpendicular spines of trees and buildings, even the stones and the black deeps of the river, with its occasional flashes of fish like lightning: all about sex, a sexiness that was bigger than the world itself, so that finally it swallowed the world and knew it through and through. Hard, eager quivers ran up through his body while she spoke. Yet she kept her distance.

After a time he realized that she was protecting him from his own excitement. So you can be my friend, she said to him, meeting his eyes. In that moment he recognized how lonely she was.

When she turned away from him, he found that they had slid inside one skin together.

For the rest of the night he walked through the dream forest as Raedawn, seeing what she saw, feeling what she felt, going where she went. The core truth of her secrets became known to him in this way. A sense of arrival and joy grew in him. He decided not to wake up.

Cracker didn't get home until the wee hours on Saturday morning. He remembered his promise to bring Alexander a drink, and he had the beer with him all right, but as he trudged up US 31 from downtown Berne he found himself shying away from the construction site and its great gaping holes and piles of lumber and Alexander's office trailer. The beer'll keep. Bring it to him tomorrow.

The fact was he didn't like to go near the place, not after he'd spent the afternoon telling King about Carl and Gloria. The memories percolated up. He wished King had let well enough alone.

Cracker lay back on his bed, shuddering. He ought to bring that beer over to Raedawn's boyfriend. Later. Tomorrow.

He imagined Raedawn in her own trailer over there. He imagined her lying beside him, as he often did when he had trouble sleeping. He wished he could just forget everything.

Something throbbed outside like a big car radio, like a hole where a tooth has been pulled. Oh, right. It was the hole where the tree used to be. He slid slowly into a dream where he put his tongue into that hole, tasted the dirt and the cut-off ends of the roots all bloody and sawdusty. He winced, felt the hole itch and tingle. *Uh-oh, don't get too close.* He pulled his tongue back, worked his jaws a bit. He sucked at the hole and put his tongue in again, unable to let it alone. He sank deeper into sleep.

Willy slept across the hall from Cracker. He dreamed a wonderful dream.

He was playing trumpet from the highest point on the ridge, right opposite his home, looking down on the place where the great tree had stood. Instead of lumber piles and trucks, there was the old lumpy meadow restored again, carpeted in flowers. Instead of a squat little white construction office trailer, there was a hole, deep enough to take the echo of his trumpet and return it many times, like a clangor of brass bells growing out of the dirt.

His trumpet called, he called, he called. He was trying to imitate the song of a gray goose, which, he'd learned just today from a film in school, takes a mate for life and sings over the body when one of them dies. It could be no coincidence that the gray goose also sometimes takes a mate of the same sex. Willy relived over and over the thrill he had felt, his eyes glued to the classroom screen, when he heard the voice-over say that. *A mate of the same sex.* He played the movie over in his dream, that same part. Rewind. *A mate of the same sex.*

The gray goose stood over its fallen mate. Its long neck bent and twisted while it sang. Some of the kids had laughed, but Willy might have been at the opera watching fat old people pretend to be young lovers and not doing a bad job of it, either. Nice work. He wove his body back and forth like a goose neck, pouring grief through the trumpet in an effortless stream without needing to draw breath. His music clanged across the meadow and ran down the hole.

And now the good part of this dream, okay, here came the good part, his heart got big, something was growing out of the hole. Willy let a cascade of notes fly out of his trumpet, and lightly, because he knew he would be okay if he moved quickly, he stepped off the ridge into thin air and ran down the stairway of his music, tooting and hopping, hopping and tooting, one step ahead of the dissolving echo, until he almost fell the last six feet from laughing instead of playing. There it was, a big tree growing right out of the hole, its crown foaming with new leaf like a thunderhead. Willy stood at its mighty foot with his head and arms thrown back in amazement. Music passed through him, coming from the tree and running into the ground in a circuit: two notes, one bright as his trumpet and a thousand times stronger, one cool and secretive that beat to his pulse. It was alive, and it knew he was here.

As long as I'm wishing, Willy thought. He would wish this dream until it was all wished out. *What do I want?* Two great limbs reached down for him, and it took him up in its arms. It lifted him higher and higher, until he could see its huge face, and the tree looked carefully through him into the marrow of his bones. With one delicate twig-tip it traced a line of green fire running from the soles of his feet right up through his body to the top of his head. Because it was a dream, he could see his whole body from all directions at once, as he used to do when he was with his old friend. From two vantages, outside and inside, Willy gazed up like a happy baby into the giant face looking down. What a big face. It took him a while to gather all its features close together enough to understand its single huge expression.

The tree was amazed with him. Willy felt heart-full and peaceful.

Rae dreamed that her lover came back to her. She was sitting next to a pile of mending: crickets with one leg off, blackbirds minus a wing, cracked turtles and severed earthworms, hopeless, all of it and her fingers were numb from the prick of her needle. And here he was, bigger than ever. Until this moment she hadn't known that she too wanted mending. Hope and joy blazed through the loosened seams of her heart, and she ran to put her foot on the worn place on his trunk.

Her foot went right through him. Just a ghost.

At that, Rae broke. Her patience broke, her courage broke, and, most terrible of all, the rope that bound her to him and never let her get away, the rope came back in her hand, frayed and worn and bleached and dead. She threw herself onto the mud and beat it with her fists.

Alexander got down off the bucketloader. *You okay, miss?* His shadow was enormous. He glowed. Rae tried to explain, but there weren't any words.

His big warm hands turned her by the shoulders. Look at this. Green fire streamed away in their shadows, illuminating the perfect beauty of a bumblebee crawling on a leaf, the pattern of tiny feathers around the wise yellow eye of a crow. Look.

The wind slapped the office trailer door against its latch while, inside, Alexander dreamed he was listening to organ music and watching the sun rise continuously around the curve of the planet, shooting colored light through all manner of skies, misty, clear, half-clouded, overcast, while land and sea raced by so fast below that he could not imagine setting root in it. It was safer to stay aloft and watch the sun rise forever.

Outside, the wind blew over the temporary pole again, and its array of cheap halogen bulbs popped out. Pop, pop, pop, darkness, and the crash of the pole on a stack of plywood.

Alexander dreamed his way across the world. He skimmed like a waterbeetle along lines of music that he could feel but not see, one harsh brassy note, one cool liquid note. The brassy sounds cracked across the spinning horizon like rays of sun breaking through cloud. I'll bet I can get all the way to Freeport, he thought, speeding over the waters of the Pacific.

Quick as the thought, he saw the long lazy curve of Panama coming closer, with the glorious colors of sunrise gilding its palms and mountains. *Slow down, slow down!* The home island approached, the tops of its pines making streaks in the golden light. *Slow down!* Alexander reached out a hand and grabbed a treetop, and then he was holding his granmère by the hand, and they were standing under the big banyan tree in her hen yard, only between the hens at their feet lay a whole world of whirling sunrise colors and glittering ocean decked with islands. He clung tight to her hand.

Every ounce of the past five years' homesickness came rushing into his throat. His head grew heavy with unshed tears. His throat ached with grief. *Oh, Gran.* He drew a long breath for weeping with, but with that breath came the organ tones, and his grief turned into a shout of startlement and joy. He put down roots. He sucked up water. Fishes nibbled the fine ends of his toes. He shrugged. No matter, I can always grow more.

She held his hand and looked him up and down. A dab of whispering oil shone on her forehead. So there you are, she said, and he felt a huge relief that she had come looking for him. There was deep power in the seams of her face. Good, she said, looking at him narrowly. You have used your chance well. You have not wasted it.

He was so surprised that he half woke. Muzzy-minded, he lay still, feeling his naked body sprawl over the cot and pour like a ton of loose hemp rope onto the trailer floor around him. Some part of his mind was still holding Gran's hand in his dream, and she saw every bit of his shameless opening and growing. She nodded again, Good.

Oh, good, Gran. Because I don't think I can stop. He thought perhaps he should cover his body, dreaming that he looked down at his penis. It was the size of a telephone pole and twanged like a guitar string. For shame. Cover up before your Gran! he scolded himself.

She tugged his hand at that, and at her summons he slipped deeper into sleep. This way, she said, turning him firmly by the shoulders, as if he were ten again, to look downward at the sunrise and the world turning and turning under the banyan tree, while the hens scratched up whole islands and pecked. Up close the hens' heads were scaly with tiny overlapping feathers, each feather perfect, the size of the moon. Turn your face to all this, she said.

With her hands on his shoulders he looked, taking it in, the sunlight, the sea, the beauty of the hens, the golden-leafed banyan sprawling over-head. Every part had smaller parts of great power and beauty in them, and he could smell them, hear them, become them. He was a bubble rising in a hen's throat, buck, buck, a bubble of joy. He felt his Gran standing behind him, with her hands holding him comfortingly by the shoulders, long after she had faded.

Chapter Thirty-Six

Under half a moon, a line of clouds ran furiously west to east, like a fat jet trail huffing and puffing against a crosswind. There was wind at ground level by the river, too. Styrofoam cups flipped into the air and rappelled across the mud, clinking. It had rained early in the night. The mud glistened under the moon in wheel ruts, in lumps, in the wide grave plowed up by the bulldozer to make room for a foundation, still clayey and puddled with rain. Some white animal was splashing through the mud puddles, making crying noises.

The mud on the site was cool. As Mink pelted through it, mud splashed her naked body and stuck, making each muddy part of her disappear, hiding her from the white eye of the moon. Here. Somewhere near here. Her feet throbbed. She was feeling for the right place with her feet. They felt twice their natural size. The ground throbbed back at them. She came to a sudden halt, sunk to her ankles in thick black mud. She threw her head back, shut her eyes against the moonlight, and throbbed back with all her might. Yes, here.

The ground almost had a voice. She could hear it, expanding with that huge heartbeat in her groin, until the acre of torn mud and the ridge rising glacierlike overhead all throbbed and shouted, asking, asking.

If she could explode it would end. But she couldn't. She didn't know how. She was boiling away from the inside out and nothing would make it stop.

Words finally came ripping out of her. "I'M TOO *LITTLE!*" she screamed.

She threw herself into the mud and grovelled in it, rubbing herself against the big wet clods until they disintegrated in her fingers, rolling, crying, until she ran out of breath and had to lie curled into a ball in the hollow she had made.

It occurred to her that she hadn't tried lying perfectly still. She locked her arms around her knees. Be still. She forced her breath to move evenly. Oh, no. Now she remembered. Yes, she had tried this, many times. She whimpered but she didn't move. Fearfully she waited for the buzzing to drown her, listened for the sound of nothing to steal her ears.

What she heard was splashing. Then came a powerful smell. A cold wet nose pressed itself against her shoulder. Her eyes flew open. She held perfectly still.

A low doggy shape picked its way delicately around her, giving her more space as it came within her view. She recognized it: a fox, a particular fox in fact, one she had patted on its cast-iron head as she crossed the Route 64 bridge tonight. It had never moved before.

A second fox stepped into view, and from the other side a third. She felt another cold nose on her calf. A shudder of wonder shook her. The tingling itch reawoke. At any other time this would have been an excellent miracle, good enough to keep her occupied all night. Now she turned her face to the mud and wept tears into it.

Something extremely cold and heavy touched her arms where she clutched herself. It pressed against her knees. She didn't move, though her skin screamed and her bones buzzed. The fox whiffled, curled itself as she was curled, and settled with its back against her. Soon she was surrounded by small, incredibly heavy bodies. They packed themselves around and over her like littermates, pressing their sides and their stomachs to her bare skin, at first chilling her, for they were made of cast iron, then warming her as her small body poured its heat into them.

A car backfired on US 31. Six iron foxes and a naked child leaped to their feet. Mink watched the car pass and then turned to the foxes where they crouched behind her, hiding behind heaps of mud and the odd pallet of lumber or brick. She put her fists on her hips. One by one they crept near again.

She itched. She wanted to run again, but she knew it would do no good. Her bones were trying to sing their way out of her.

To take her mind off it, she bent and seized the nearest fox by its rust red ears. "What's happening to me?" she screamed into its face. The rusting iron eyes half closed, and the ears lay back. The iron fox crouched, cringing, before her. The others scattered and then returned, slinking.

"Woooooo," she crooned to the fox in her hands. Her hand found the spot where a real fox would want to be scratched. She stroked it. The fox made a sound in its belly. Another fox came out of nowhere and nipped the ankle of the one she touched, making a clanking sound. She petted her fox. It stilled, smiling like a dog. Then it threw its head back and yipped. She jumped. All the foxes sprang to their feet, laughing silently and yipping aloud.

Under the half moon Mink played fox with the iron foxes. She danced when they danced, hopped when they hopped. Soon they were all laughing, the foxes making uncanny sounds, Mink imitating them. The buzzing rose into her knees, into her groin. The foxes tussled like puppies.

She felt unbearably sorry for them. They clanked when they wrestled and fell over one another, and their feet hit each other like hammers. *Be wild,* she would have said, if she had needed words to say that. The poor things had been made to sit frozen forever, but maybe they could learn to be wild. They whirled around her in a circle, tearing up the mud with their iron paws.

Fearless of their iron teeth, she squatted and grabbed at their hard brushes as they hurtled by, nipping and yipping. The itch came and went in her bones, and her feet tingled no matter whether she stamped or stood. She caught hold of a tail and found herself yanked off her feet. She tumbled in the mud, laughing fox laughs.

The itch worked its way outward from her bones to her skin and stuck, half an inch from the surface, making her crazy, until she had to abandon the game and roll in the mud, laughing hysterically, rubbing herself all over with mud, while foxes snatched at her hair and ankles. One of them connected a little too hard, and she yelped. Instantly they backed off.

She sat up. They hung around her in a half circle, watching.

Mink pulled herself into a crouch, rubbing her ankle. The rust red iron foxes were coated with mud. They looked more like real foxes now. Poor things, they still didn't know how to be wild. They ought to be tearing her to pieces, since she was the first one to cry out and call quits. She wouldn't have minded. Her insides were tearing her to pieces anyway. She felt wilder than they, by far. It would be easy to show them how.

She bent, reaching for her ankles. A growl formed in her throat. The buzzing began to condense into her chest, in her voice. All the itching worsened at the same time, but this time she had it by the tail, down in her voice somewhere, in the center of her body. She reached into herself with her voice and grabbed herself by that tail. She pulled, growling, roaring, pulled with her voice on the itch in her tail, pulled until she was ripping herself inside out.

The itch exploded at last, and then receded. Exquisite relief! She yawned until her tongue wrapped itself around her nose. She stretched. She shook herself all over. She sneezed luxuriously, picked up her four paws one at a time and licked them. She sprang into the air and fell, laughing and dancing on her hind legs, whipping her head from side to side, wheeling in place, chasing that marvelous tail and never, never getting dizzy! The iron foxes circled her in a big slow iron ring while she chased her brushtail faster and faster. "Let's go," she said, the call rising easily to her throat, easier than people language ever had. In an instant they wheeled, all seven, leading with their shoulders and not with their heads as stupid people do. Seven foxes flew up the ridge into the underbrush.

Chapter Thirty-Seven

Of all the wild and fey people he lived among, Ernest Brown called himself the tamest and most down to earth. He woke suddenly in his bed in his own trailer with Angelia heavy beside him. Now what? He listened for a few minutes, waking slowly to the river air coming in the window, wondering if he had heard a sound or only dreamed it.

His bursitis was playing up. Getting old. He felt for the hot tender spot in his heart where Angelia had bruised it the other day, telling him that he was old, that she was old, and that her rowdy days were almost over. His mouth twisted by itself in a smile. Love, his daddy had used to say, was a b.i.t.c.h. That would appear to be the case, Daddy. Oh, indeed.

He lay in bed a moment longer, thinking of waking Angelia. Best not. This was her hour for intense dreaming, and she was jealous of it. He imagined her dream as she might describe it to him when she woke: perhaps she was flying without wings, without her clothes of course, over the river and the furrowed brow of the ridge beside it; flying over Chicago, Toronto, New York, the Atlantic, Paris, Constantinople, onward to the cities of her fancy in the east. She had always wanted to see Bangkok. She never would. Probably best to scandalize them in her dreams, he thought, the idiot smile of love still gripping his face. Lord only knew what they did about barenaked Somershoe women in such places.

The bed was getting uncomfortably hot. That was age for you. Woke you up stone-cold and near death, got you horny, and then you couldn't lie still. Might as well get dressed. Go see the doings on the construction site.

He took his dowsing twig from its hook on the wall and let himself out of the trailer.

It seemed to him that the river had come closer during the night. Shifting again. This time the water came halfway up the bank toward his door.

Mink watched Ernest moving slowly the way people did among the clods and furrows and long straight boards. He looked quite different through these eyes: a huge person powerful and cunning with seniority, the sage of his pack. He smelled even more like himself when she sniffed him with this nose. Sometimes he shuffled along, sometimes stood still, turning this way and that with a twig in his hands, clucking and shaking his head. She crept nearer until her nose was almost against his pants leg.

Once, he looked down, as if he could see her small brown body camouflaged against the mud, but his hands stayed steady and he went about his business. Yet he must have seen something. His smell altered: surprise, then a greeting. At the change in smell, she leapt back. Did he know her like this? A powerful craving for his warmth overcame her, craving for the safe hollow she knew he could make if he sat down and took her in his arms.

Yes, but *people!* objected her animal nature. She had come back here because it felt best, or worst. Some dangerous naked wire in the center of her body came home here, a wire such as Ernest had once shown her and warned her against while he was working on a car. Maybe he knew about this wire. Thinking about the wire made the hairs on her body wriggle and try to grow inward, even the hairs between her toes. She shook her head until her ears flapped.

She began to itch again under her skin. Her pelt bushed out, every hair separating from its fellow. She imagined she could feel her skin expanding, sizzling outward until it swallowed up her hairs to their tips. She planted her tailbone in the cool mud. She pushed with her forepaws, her back arching and rippling like a sick dog's, not to throw something up, but throw it out. Out! Inside out! Now that she had acknowledged it, the tingling tingled harder, the buzzing buzzed louder. Faster! Louder! Harder!

Her hackles bristled with the strangeness until her hackles themselves seemed to sizzle their way over her head, rolling the way a wet tee shirt rolls over your head to fall stinky on the ground. Only there was no dirty pelt on the ground. She knew where it had gone. Inside, right under her skin. She could feel it there if she let herself. Itch. Tingle.

Don't think about it.

With a cry she launched herself at Ernest.

Ↄↄ

Ernest waited for her to come to him. Woodcraft told him to leave open that odd place in himself that he could not see. When he relaxed and thought welcoming thoughts, it brought small birds and animals to him and, once, Angelia Somershoe. Still, he nearly fell over when Mink cannoned into him out of the darkness. In the dim predawn light she appeared suddenly on the ground before him. She seemed to squat and pull off a shirt, revealing herself palely naked on the mud. He knew better than to trust his eyes. His nose, old and spoiled by pipe smoke though it was, had not failed so badly as that. He knew fox when he smelled it.

She wept against his legs, smelling rank and muddy, reaching her arms up to be held like any ordinary child. He knelt.

"Here you are. My, my. Yes, yes." The twins hadn't asked to be picked up since they were, oh, three and a half, it must have been. He said soothing things and thought peaceful thoughts of the past, to keep her from bolting. *Mink at one, nursing at a Coke bottle. Mink at two, her hair already thistle-white, splashing in the river shallows.* She quieted in his arms.

"Okay. Easy does it. Okay, baby," he said softly. He made a lap. She curled up small in it. With difficulty, for she was pressing hard against him, he unbuttoned his outermost flannel shirt and wrapped it around her. "Where's your shirt, child?" he said, more to be making a comforting sound than to get an answer.

"I threw it away," she said clearly.

He looked up in amazement. The wild child had spoken! Actually answered a question!

"What—what's the matter?" he said, bending his head over her again.

She squirmed and pressed her face against his shoulder. At first she only grunted. Then:

"Bad things." Some long hard breaths heaved in and out of her, then she said, again quite clearly, "I fell in the fish hole. And then I came out."

"Wait, wait, what fishing hole?" Ernest said.

"And I was like this, and I couldn't *stand* it."

"The fishing hole down by the Berne dam?"

"No! It's a *fish* hole. Where all the babies come out. And now my skin is wrong. Just *listen!*"

It took some minutes for Mink to assemble enough words to say her piece. Strange times we're living through, he thought. How do I even know this is our Mink? Almost more likely that a fox full of clever speech would pretend to be her, than that our silent wild child would start babbling.

"And it's time to go," she said finally. "And tell Rae and all the others."

"Go?" he said in the same calm voice, though his heart clenched around the word. Angelia had been talking like this for three days.

"Go! Get out! And the river will come and make everything wet and—and wreck it. So *tell* them."

"Put this shirt on, you're shivering," he said, to give himself time to think. Good gracious, what next will befall us? She permitted him to dress her in the flannel shirt and wriggled in her old impatient way while he buttoned it up to the collar and rolled the sleeves up to their armpits, so that her hands could come out.

"There. Suppose we take a walk to the bridge and look at where your foxes li—used to live."

She gave him a long look at that.

He stared her down. "I'm old," he said gently. "You go slow with old people."

She tossed her head, but put her hand in his. "You go slow with *people*," she said.

"That's right." They started walking toward downtown Rimville and the Route 64 bridge. "Now tell me more slowly. What's the matter with your skin?"

Her story was full of strange things. As they walked he looked around him, wherever she pointed, to the places where this or that miracle had occurred to her, and he realized how wrongheaded had been his years of careful self-blinding. Really, he was nearly as bad as King. In the middle of this poor life, we are surrounded by mystery, and the pity of it is that we would rather just be poor. No real tolerance for mystery at all.

Where was Ink in all this? He interrupted her to ask, but she would not be diverted. Something radical had happened there, too. The twins were a single animal. This terrible accident in the fish hole, and what on earth was that?

He thought of his woman asleep in his bed, glowing like gold under the coverlets. He felt for the invisible radiance that flew outward from her in all directions, which he could feel even now.

"Mink?"

She drew breath, silenced for an instant.

"Did you ever go play in the big tree across the road? You and your brother?"

Her shoulder jerked. "No."

He chewed his lower lip. "Are you sure? That was a mighty excellent tree for climbing."

"Come *on!*"

He blinked at nothing and walked on, shuffling a little in his old work boots so as not to step on her bare feet. The sun was rising over the eastern bank of the Fox River. Heavy clouds cast pink light down on the asphalt of the Route 64 bridge, tinting its balustrades. Ernest was not surprised to see that the balustrades were bare. A few fat raindrops fell at their feet.

Mink gasped and let go Ernest's hand. He looked down. She stepped away from him, shrugging out of his shirt and squaring off.

Her brother appeared five yards away. Ink's tee shirt was filthy. There were tearstains on his face and a great blue bruise over one eye. He looked at Mink with abject reproach.

She said nothing. Her stare was like stone.

The boy twitched and stamped in place, his fists opening and closing by his ribs as if beckoning or questioning.

Mink didn't move. Her face was a mask. Ernest became aware of an intensely bitter smell: musky, acid, as unbearable as a whole bottle of perfume smashed at once. Skunk? Ink blinked as if he'd been struck. The children stood still for a long minute, not moving, while they argued in their animal language of glance and twitch and stink.

Then Mink leapt toward the bridge. At the foot of it, where the stairs led down to Varlet's fishing landing, she seemed to trip and rolled fluidly down the old broken concrete steps. Her dirtied white hair flashed past her heels. She caromed off the bridge abutment where it met the stairs and plunged over the steps into the darkness toward the deep water, disappearing in the black shadow of the bridge only to reappear, gliding halfway across the river now, fleeing wingstroke by silent wingstroke toward the trees on the far bank. It seemed to Ernest that she landed and looked back once with a face startlingly round, her huge white-rimmed eyes glaring with grief or refusal. Then the face turned and the broad wings stroked away, farther into the trees.

Ink hunched at the top of the steps, staring after her. His eyes bulged wet. His mouth gaped.

Slowly, for his old bones were feeling the morning air again, Ernest hunkered down on his knees. The boy might want to be held.

Chapter Thirty-Eight

lexander woke to the sound of rain spattering lightly on the trailer windows. He was thirsty, so thirsty. His work boots, he could see by rolling his head on the pillow, were lying on the floor. Dimly he remembered kicking them off last night, when he half-woke and found them uncomfortable.

He was again bound to the cot. It felt as if all his fingers were locked white-knuckled around any number of strange objects on the floor below him. He traced the path of one finger, lying on his back, sweat coming out on his forehead, and thought: This is my wrist. This is my hand. This is my first knuckle. This is my second knuckle. Oh God! It's bending again! No wait, I have three knuckles to each finger, right? Go on. Third knuckle. No, this here is third knuckle. It's still bending! Wait, I've lost count. Start over.

His hands were cramped, and they responded nightmare-slowly to his commands. He concentrated on the right hand. With effort he withdrew each finger from its entanglement and flexed it, trying to ignore the long, soft, whipcordy extraness, pretending he couldn't feel the cot struts with his dreadful flopping fingertips, and also the floor, the door, and the cool smooth edge of the distant refrigerator.

When the last finger on his right hand came free, he placed the knife-sheath in his teeth, wrapped his palm around the hilt, jerked the knife free, and lurched over, slashing at his left hand.

There was an instant of shock, then blinding pain. He shrieked. The knife fell. The instant the pain began, he felt all his many fingers and toes curl convulsively in protest. They shrank rapidly in short, hideous spasms. He seemed to be falling, falling backward into blackness. He gasped in agony.

I am a man, he thought. I am not a tree. Cut again: I will be a man.

Still the animal Alexander, half-pinned to his cot, oozed blood out of his weird mutilated extremities, rolled back and forth and howled. Come on, Alexander, be a man, he scolded this creature, but there was no doing anything with him. Tears ran down his face and puddled on the canvas under his nose.

When the pain subsided, he sat up and rummaged under the cot with his right hand for a tee shirt, meaning to bandage the hurt fingers. Fearfully he examined the damage. There was a deep cut across the base of all four fingers.

He watched with fascination while the cut flesh and capillaries turned gray, then pink. The cut closed. The flesh mounded slightly over the faint red line. And then the wound was gone. There was not even a line of white scar. He sat rigid for another ten minutes, glaring at the hand, but it didn't hurt and it didn't grow anymore.

He showered and dressed for work in a daze. Cars rolled onto the gravel outside. He wadded up his bloodstained blanket, folded the cot, and went to the fridge for a drink of water.

The screen door slammed open. Ike stomped into the trailer. "Ain't you made coffee yet?" he said aggrievedly.

Chapter Thirty-Nine

The rain spattered off and on past dawn. When Rae woke up after sunrise, the river had risen to within four feet of her doorstep. The crawdaddy traps had rolled until the stones weighing them down fell off. Now the traps floated free on their tethers. The clouds hung low, heavy with unshed water, and tangled themselves in the branches of trees on top of the ridge. She waded out up to her ankles over the drowned mud to the clothesline and pulled wet shirts and jeans down onto her shoulder.

A shout nearby made her look up. Forty yards downstream, Davy stood up to his thighs in the river, glaring across the water to the sandbar with the willows on it.

"S'amatter, Davy?" she called.

He pointed across the river, not turning his head to her. "I see ya!" he shrieked.

She looked. His little canoe was half-floating at the willow sandbar, bumping against a naked yellow root. Davy danced back and forth along the bank, working himself up. She squinted. The current had eaten away the far bank under the willows. The willows tilted slightly, so that the nest on top dribbled stuffing.

For the second night in a row, the water had shifted. West at night, east in the morning. Rae tried to imagine the ley lines as Ernest perceived them, pulling the water west, east, west, east, slopping higher and higher from side to side until the bank was bared on each side of the river in turn. She herself couldn't see the ley lines. She shut her eyes.

Oh, there they were.

She could feel the lines like heat in the soles of her feet. A rush of fire sizzled over her skin from her feet upward, so hot she imagined she could hear the river hiss against her ankles. Rae threw her arms around herself, hugging clammy laundry and pressing her hot cheek against its rainy-smelling folds. The air was cold and sweet in her lungs. She could smell last year's leaves in the water where she stood, and bitter laurel twigs broken off and rotting. She raised her head and saw new green leaves everywhere: on mayapple, on cattail reeds, on swagged grapevines, on sycamore and alder already in bud. *What are you telling me?*

She closed her eyes and let the heat rush out of her again. She fancied she could hear a chuckle like the sound of the trees around her slurping up the flood, not cruel but only natural, only doing his job. The fresh greenery across the river blazed against gray sky and black branches.

"I hear you," she muttered. "Only what the heck are you saying?" Her feet felt cold again. She saw that the water had risen even while she stood here.

Davy shouted to his boat again. "Stay! I'm a'coming!" His long arms sawed the air in excitement.

"Davy!" she called, "Don't you swim over there! Walk around by the footbridge!"

He looked back at her for the first time. "That's half a mile! It'll float away by then!"

"Probably not. Just go around by the bridge. Hear?"

He twisted his mouth at this, but he did as he was told. As he passed, wading calf-deep and well out of her reach, Rae saw that he was only wearing shorts. His long bare thighs were hoary with flood scum.

"You wearing shoes, Davy?" she said, but he put his head down and slogged by. Ten feet past her he picked up his feet and ran through the water, showing his bare soles with much splashing. He threw a laughing look at her over his shoulder.

She shook her head. "I love you, Davy-boy!"

The sound of a latch made her turn her head. More Gowdy boys up and around this early! No, it was Cracker. To her amazement Rae saw that he carried a small suitcase. He had his winter coat on, too. He seemed not to see her, but turned and slipped around the back of his house.

Rae didn't waste time calling out. She ran after him as he skulked along the row of trailers. He seemed to be heading for the Rimville end of US 31.

What in the world? He must have heard her following, for his shoulders hunched, but he didn't speed up, either. She threw the wet laundry to the ground. Her bare feet slithered and slid in the mud. *God almighty, what has got into this family?*

She caught hold of him, and he jumped and twisted like a trout.

"Now, Raedawn, don't you talk to me," he warned, as if they had been arguing for hours. "Don't you even say nothing, because that's *it.*" He made an umpire's gesture, *safe,* and his suitcase thumped to the ground. She threw herself into his arms.

"No, don't you try to talk me out of it," he whispered to her hair. She clung tight, and his arms moved around her and locked. "Stop it. Just. Stop it." He was shaking all over.

She held on for dear life. *What in the world?* He squeezed her harder and harder. He lifted her off her feet and squeezed until he grunted.

"Cracker," she said, but he shushed her.

"Leggo," he said.

Her heart pounded with terror. "You first."

"All right." He let out a whoosh of air.

He set her feet on the ground. She thought he must have been up all night, for he looked a mess, pale and shaky, dressed in half the clothes he owned.

Rae grabbed up his suitcase and dragged him back, unresisting, to her trailer.

In the doorway, Cracker paused. "Your mother in?"

"Nope. We had a fight. Now get *in* here." She pulled him in and shut the door. "And *talk.*"

When she tried to take his coat, he wouldn't let her. "Ain't staying. And don't you try to make me."

"We *settled* all that," she said, as if they had. She coaxed, "C'mon."

They sat on the sofa.

Cracker threw his arm around her and pulled her into his lap to press his face into her hair again. They sat that way for some time, he sniffling in her hair, she motionless for fear he would run. She could barely think it. *He's* never *tried to leave. Not even when the twins were babies. Cracker, don't. I need you.*

He was afraid, she realized. She could feel it, smell it on him. Scared out of his mind. Not drunk, either.

"I'm hot," he said abruptly, and she twisted where she sat on his knees to let him wrestle out of his coat. "Let me up, girl, I want to get this off."

"No." She turned on his lap, locking her ankles around his leg and thrusting her face into his neck. She ferreted her hands under his layered shirts and sweaters.

"Hey! Quit! That's cold!" He giggled. They grappled for a few minutes, she tickling him, he pushing her hands down and shucking his layered shirts and sweaters, until they were both sweaty and laughing.

She didn't yet dare speak. Her body talked to him the way she used to when she was a kid, when they were just starting.

"Darn it, Rae," he murmured, "you might give a feller a chance."

She put her burning hand over his chest.

It never failed to amaze her how much he could absorb. No matter how much of the fire poured through her, quaking her, making her hair stand on end, he took it. Where was he putting it all? No use asking. Amazing capacity. She guessed it was probably what made him such a slut. She giggled to herself.

"You laughing at me, miss?"

"Yes. Shush, now."

Obediently he put his hand between her legs and took her ear in his teeth.

She asked him later, "What do you do with it?"

"What, darlin'? This?"

She stroked his hand where it lay on her breast. "I dunno. That feeling. How strong it is."

He rocked his hips on hers. "Mostly just let it go by."

"Really?" She couldn't imagine that. She shoved a couple of throw pillows under her elbows, so she could prop herself high enough to look at his face. "I can't."

"I bet you can't, either. Poor little girl," he said, stroking hair out of her eyes. She felt the fear come back on him.

Afraid herself, she took his chin in her hand to make him look at her. "What?"

The whites of his eyes showed. "You know," he said. "You Somershoe women."

Angrily, she sat up on his hips. "I do not!" she hissed in his face. He flinched. "I do *not* know, either."

"Well, I don't wanna say," he grumbled.

She accused him, "You have to! You and Gelia. Always keeping secrets," she said bitterly.

"Hey. Ain't ever been a me-and-Gelia, bar a long time ago," he protested. With a long sigh he pried himself out of her embrace on the old sofa and sat up, pulling a folded quilt over his lap. "Okay. I'll tell." He looked small and scared, clutching the quilt, with his long knees poking up out of the sofa. He took a deep breath.

"I woke up early. Remembered I promised to look in on your boyfriend this mornin'." She wanted to hurry him, but he stared stolidly ahead. "Still dark. Thought I heard some noises over there, like screamin' or cryin'. I felt bad, because I told him I'd bring him a beer last night and then I forgot. So I drug myself out of bed and went to the window, but it was only Erny and Mink walking down the road, and then I thought, it ain't neighborly to promise a man a beer and stand him up. I wasn't thinking too clearly myself, y'understand." He pulled himself together with a visible effort and rubbed his face with one hand. "Long night at the stationhouse."

"Yes?"

He looked at her strangely. His easygoing voice tightened until he squeaked.

"I got the beers out of the freezer and brought 'em across the road. Went over to th' trailer. I looked in the window." He swallowed.

"He's all stretched out on the floor, Rae. He's comin' out of his clothes," Cracker's long arms let go of the quilt and stretched out, fingers wiggling. "His arms and legs is all over the place, comin' right across the floor and goin' down into the cracks. Then I looked down and seen a thing coming right out of the trailer wall, by the door where there musta been a crack, coming through right next to me like a snake, or a finger, or *something*. Rae, it was *moving*."

Rae trembled. "No."

"Yep. It's happening. My gawd." He shivered. "Somebody hadda get the job. Thank the stars it wasn't me." He eyed her narrowly. "You didn't know?"

She shook her head, stunned.

Cracker snorted. "That Gelia. She was supposed to of told you. That's the big idea, see. The old one dies, and right quick somebody else has got to take it over, or else this whole place'll just shake itself to pieces." It struck him swordlike with sadness that he had to be the one to tell her, when he might lose her forever. "It—" He swallowed. "It wouldn't hurt for you to go over there. Mebbe tonight. Tell the poor guy what's happening. Kinda, well, ease him into it."

She found her hand on the door before she realized. Her hand was on the cold aluminum doorknob, and Cracker was standing naked holding her by the shoulders and shouting in her face.

"Rae! Wait! Raedawn, put some clothes on! Rae, you gotta wait til he's off shift."

He wouldn't let her out. First she must dress, and then she had to wait for him to dress, and then he said he was going to run away after all and she realized that she had to do something to stop him, keep him here. He was being unkind. He was pulling her in half.

Her heart was calling to Alexander like a church bell, while Cracker thought up things to distract her from crossing the road to see for herself. She tidied the kitchenette while he stood over her. He made her fold all the extra clothes he'd been wearing and try to pack them into his suitcase, and, when they wouldn't all fit, he made her help him put them all back on his body. He buttoned his shirts wrong and made her help him button them back right.

He was being so silly. Tears fell out of her eyes now and then, and, every time Cracker made a joke, she laughed. All the time she listened to her heart. Sooner or later he'd have to leave her alone. She ached with hope.

A shrill mechanical whistle cut the air. Cracker was ready and had hold of her, his broad back against the door, before she could get out. "Now, Rae. They've started work. I been waiting and listening, and I didn't hear no ambulances or cop cars or nothin'. Whatever happened, it's over for today. Everybody's come back to work. Listen, Rae! There's his machine going."

She stared into his face until her eyes hurt. And then she heard it, too: the backup alarm of the bucketloader.

"Your mother'll be back for breakfast, I expect."

Gelia. Rae went cold. "Don't tell her!"

He gave her a funny look. "I ain't told Gelia Somershoe the time of day for ten years. What do you take me for?"

She put her hand on his sleeve. "Just don't," she pleaded.

"Rae." He took her hand in both of his. "You ain't thinkin' she wants any part of him, do you? 'Cause she don't."

Rae croaked, "Cracker, you don't know what she said to me last night. How she lied."

"Nor does she," he said ruthlessly. "What that woman says and what she means don't shuck no peas, and you know it. He's safe from her. Lord!" Cracker laughed unkindly. "See Gelia walkin' in there?"

"See Gelia walking in where?" Gelia said from the door.

Rae's hand squeezed on Cracker's.

He looked down at Rae and winked. "I'll prove it to you," he said in an undervoice.

Gelia wore a hard, bright manner. Rae could tell that she'd braced herself to come home and look her daughter in the eye, a sure sign that she felt ashamed of herself and wasn't about to admit it.

Gelia assailed Cracker instead. "And what you dressed up for like Nanuke of the North, you Cracker? It's spring!"

He turned to Gelia with Rae's hand in his, picking up his suitcase in the other. "Rae's runnin' off to get married with me. I thought we'd go back to Georgia."

Whatever Gelia had been about to say was sucked back into her throat on a gasp of fright.

Rae watched with interest. She saw her mother glance from Cracker to her and back to Cracker, saw Gelia get the joke, saw the relief flooding back, and then hot anger, quickly stifled. How odd. Gelia Somershoe, scared to go off on her own daughter. What a marvel, Rae thought. And more miraculously still, she saw her mother start to think.

Gelia's eyes narrowed. "What you up to, Cracker Coombs?"

He turned his back on her. "Remember the man who needs you," he said to Rae, drawing her close to him.

Her mother's face was terrifying. Rae felt she didn't have an ounce of fight left in her. Understanding came to her at last. What Cracker saw in the construction trailer. What Gelia had never said. Rae held on tight to Cracker's hand. Everything, everything in her life righted itself, like a boat foundering and then turning right side up again, face to a clear sky.

Gelia looked back at her, her eyes snapping. "Well!" she said in the same bright, brittle voice. "Guess I know when I'm not wanted." And she banged right out the trailer door again.

℞

Cracker let himself out of the Somershoe trailer. He felt whipped. He figured Rae was going to be all right. She ought to know what to do, if anybody did. If he hadn't screwed up by telling her.

What have I done now, he wondered, remembering the guilty thrill he had felt that day long ago, when Gelia first put Rae into his hands. Just a kid, she was. And he had taken her greedily, full of wicked desire. He could remember like it was yesterday, the shameful hunger that he poured over the kid, how gentle and slow he did his crime so's only he would have to feel bad about it. She gave so much. And she never blamed him. Wrong is wrong, even if the kid never blames you. Guilt clutched his heart.

Well, he was paying the price now. The image of Alexander on the cot stirred him with horrible fear.

That could have been me, he thought. He shuddered.

Maybe he had better go over there with some beers tonight. Just to make sure.

Lordy, he wanted to run away so bad.

Cracker shook his head, stumping across the mud to his own door, his imagination following his own shadowy shape toward the bus station, toward the freight line, picturing all the routes out of town.

Oh, well. Those escape routes were closed to him now. Rae had taken him back. His suitcase weighed a ton, and it didn't have anything like his whole life in it. Just a few spare underwears and a beer.

A beer. Now there was a thought.

Chapter Forty

All morning Rae tried to imagine Alexander "coming out of his clothes." She longed to see for herself. He was over there now, walking on the dirt where she belonged, and she imagined that the dirt called him, welcoming him.

He'll grow good, she thought happily. How he'd scared Cracker! She giggled, remembering the horror in Cracker's voice. Fool man, lived across the road from it for ten years and evidently never thought much about it.

She'd been silly, too. He was gone but not gone. You don't kill something like that so easy.

It would come upon someone new. That was the part Gelia had been hiding from her. And he'd need help, too. Company. Some good advice, if she had any in her. Poor guy was probably in a swivet, wondering what was what. Rae smiled. She would tell him all about it.

And *that* was what had made Gelia so jealous. *She could have told me.* Talking her into keeping away from Alexander. Rae thought of all the men her mother had taken away from her. She wouldn't be Gelia if she gave up power easily.

Yet she'd given it up. Rae had seen that in her eyes. Gelia didn't want the job. For the first time in ten years, Rae had caught a true glimpse of Gelia. Why, she's old. Grudgingly, Rae spared her mother a drop of pity.

Well, it ain't too late for me.

Rae dragged a comb through her hair. As she stared into her own eyes in the mirror, her face seemed all parts. Just a box of parts waiting for the missing piece. A humming feeling started in her chest, moved around in her body, warming her feet, her hands, the long bones of her thighs, the back of her neck, then sizzling and shooting up her backbone. The pieces came together. *There's* that face. She smiled at herself in the mirror. That girl looked so happy.

The construction workers' lunch hour was ticking away. She dragged on a pair of Willy's old tennis shoes, grabbed her hooded sweatshirt, and banged out of the trailer.

The sky was lumpy and bruised-looking. A warm southwesterly wind whipped her hair into her face. Tornado weather. She fairly flew across US 31.

It was a minute before she could take in what she saw. Shocked, she stared. Two workmen turned to look at her. In a trance she walked up as close to the trailer as she could get.

A fence. They'd put up a chain-link fence all around the office trailer. Her heart did jumping-bean things in her chest. It's because of Gelia's visit yesterday. That woman. Rae ground her teeth.

The fence was a temporary one, already leaning a bit on metal feet stuck into long wooden shoes. It circled the trailer and a few pallets of lumber and brick, and the opening was on the far side of the circle, farthest from her where she stood with her fingers clutching the chain link, farthest from the edge of the site, and farthest from her home.

On a pile of cinder block by the trailer Alexander sat, drinking a Coke, while his shrimpy boss stood over him with one foot propped up on the blocks like a great white hunter standing on his dead elephant. When Alexander saw her he stood up, dropping his Coke on the mud. He came straight to her. The boss stared after him with his mouth open.

Their fingers locked through the chain link.

They stood that way, smiling silently at each other, for a long time. It seemed to Rae that she was telling him everything, and he was saying just what he ought. When she realized how ridiculous that was, she also became aware of shouting, quite near. She tore her eyes away from Alexander's dark moon face and looked.

His boss. Goodness, he was red.

"What's with the fence?" she said.

Alexander looked as if he had been listening to something else, too. Rae felt him separate from her a little, and then he glanced from her to his boss.

"Oh, he has a thorn in his underpants, my boss. A woman made him look foolish and now he must be having the last word."

Gelia. I knew it, Rae thought. A bumblebee droned past her ear, right through the chain link, and landed on Alexander's shoulder.

Alexander turned and interrupted the noise his boss was making. "I'm on my lunch break," he said.

The boss paused for breath, glaring. Rae carefully avoided meeting his eye. Alexander seemed to swell a few inches all over. He spoke louder this time. "Go away."

Rae felt the ground give a little shake, as a horse shakes to get rid of a fly. The boss went away. Alexander looked at her again, and everything was all right.

She giggled. "Is he gonna fire you?"

"No." Alexander realized this finally, and in the same moment he understood that it didn't matter. "Bob? I'm his prize possession. Without me, he can have no one to put a fence around. Nobody else will take his temper seriously. After today," he said, smiling, "not even me."

He looked at her, every bit that he could see without ungluing his body from the fence. The look on her face was his reward: hungry and anxious and naked to the bone. He swayed toward her, and his hammer clattered against the chain-link fence.

Rae looked down. "You still got it! Let me see."

He looked down and saw not his hammer but the forked stick in his hammer loop. "Sure," he said, feeling light-headed.

He pulled one hand away from hers and fished the stick out of its loop. After a few pokes, he said, while she giggled hysterically, "It won't go through the links." The fence was almost higher than she could reach. "Can you get it?"

It was only seven feet. If he stood on tip-toe he could easily put his arm over and hand her the stick. He touched her hand again as he did so. A shock ran through him. He heard the sound again, the sound that had pulled him headfirst into a hole full of fishy water, the same sound that drew him deeper into a glad sleep every night, no matter what sleep did to him.

"What is that?" he gasped. The wind came up and blew her hair through the fence to tickle him on the chin. Even his heavy dreads flew around his head.

"What?" she said, bringing her face closer.

A Styrofoam coffee cup sailed by. "That sound." He felt it in his own voice now. His throat and chest vibrated as the music rumbled through his bones.

She said, "I don't hear anything." Her body swayed to the fence and touched him again. The faraway music called him like a choir of horns.

The stick slipped from their fingers.

"Rats," she said, and parted from him, stooping. "Well, I guess you can keep it." She stretched to hand him back the stick.

He felt foolishly grateful to have it in his hand again. He took a step back, only to be brought up short with a yank on his scalp. "Ow!" One small dreadlock was caught in the jagged links on top of the fence.

Rae laughed. "Easy, easy. I'll climb up and get it. You hold still."

He fumbled for his horn-handled knife. "Ow! Here, cut it, cut it."

Ike and Jamie were watching him from forty yards away. The stick at his side sent hot tingling through his body.

"Hurry up," he whispered. If he didn't come to earth soon he would be rooted to the spot.

She cut him loose. The wind seized the bit of hair and whirled it away. She slid the knife through the fence. Their fingers touched again, thrilling him.

"I'm sorry about your hair," she said shyly.

He burst out, "Something crazy is happening to me. At night."

She looked up eagerly. "I know." A shadow passed over her face. She said, "I guess—I guess you must be pretty nervous."

"Yes, you could say that."

"Are you—" She raised her eyes to him. They were full of worry. "Do you hate it?"

That shock ran through him again. He flinched.

She saw it. "I'm sorry," she said in a small voice.

"Don't look like that," he blurted out. "It is only, you are so strong. How you can bear all this feeling running through you? It is like a—a wind that tries to push you over."

She looked serious. "You mean I'm trying to push you over."

"I mean," he said softly, "I mean, I am a slow creature. I can't go so quick as you do."

Was he too slow for her? His breast filled with a sharp pain at the thought. He didn't mind being bewitched, if it was by her. But he needed to *know*.

He pleaded, "Wait with me?"

"When do you get off work?" she said.

"I don't," he said. "You have to come here."

Alexander stood over her with his fingers laced into hers through the chain link, smelling so good. Oh lordy, what a day to pick, she thought. Her traitor hands wouldn't let go.

"Wait with me," he said again urgently.

She gasped, "Ain't no waiting left." Her fingers tightened on his.

The whistle blew for the end of the lunch break. He clutched tighter. The workmen were moving back to the office to punch in again.

"Come see me tonight," he commanded.

She wanted more than anything to hold him properly in her arms. Tonight? She had to work until six.

"If I can," she said, but then she saw his stricken face. "I swear I'll come."

He wrenched himself away from the fence and strode to the trailer without looking back at her. The piece of tree branch swung in his belt loop. The bumblebee crawled along his collar. Enviously, Rae watched it ride him across the site.

Chapter Forty-One

It took Davy several hours every day to straighten his room. Sometimes he got distracted and had to go off to attend to other things, or eat lunch if he thought of it, or it rained and Raedawn made him come home. This morning he got to work early, mostly because his boat had got caught and he had to rescue it. He pottered among the alder saplings, restacking stones, tying a feather tighter on its string, deeply satisfied, while the sun shot a flare of hot pink through a crack in the clouds.

The Lassie-haired Barbie doll had tipped over for probably the zillionth time. Davy contemplated her long plastic legs. Feet too small? Or did she just want to get out of there? The teacup fragments he'd stood her up in were kicked every which way. What she wanted, he decided, was the right thing to stick into.

This was just the kind of problem that took him all day to solve. He looked long at it. Her huge breasts stood out like G.I. Joe's guns, shooting straight ahead. Ought to know not to point at people. 'Tain't polite. Still, it shows she likes to know where she's going, he thought. He took her by the legs and jammed her feet-first into the loam. The doll fell over, her blue eyes staring at dirt. Nope. He turned her head. Round and round, she could go round and round like an owl until she came right back to the beginning. Straight ahead. Boy, she was stiff. It did make her easy to work with.

Well, okay, that's just how she is. Good. He experimented with that feeling, feeling good about her stiff, straight, easy-to-work-with legs and her straight-ahead stare. Sure. That meant the problem was just sticking her into the right thing. He wriggled happily on his bottom in the sequin-scattered dirt. Now what?

Well, could he move her? He turned and stared around. Young alders marked out the walls of his room. Once he had strung string and old plastic netting between trees to make better walls, but wind and bad boys tore it down. Now he understood that the walls were there if you knew they were. The trees made the room out of their own shape, along with that rock there, and the hole you wouldn't find until you stepped in it by mistake, and other secret walls. And since he'd begun feeding the crows, there had been no more trouble with bad boys. He got up and went to the feeding station. Wind had knocked over the topmost pail. The twins' latest offering lay scattered on the ground outside the room, looking shabby from rough handling, although crow food was never at its best by the time the crows got to it. He poked a finger into the cavity in the pigeon's smashed head where a big black beak had pecked through the eye, hunting for brains. Still plenty squishy in there. He set the pail bottom-up on top of the stacked apple crates and laid the pigeon carcass on it. That'll keep, he thought, remembering an expression of Cracker's. Funny way to say it. He said it aloud. "That'll keep." He giggled. "That'll keep!"

At the sound of his voice, an animal leaped and crashed among the dead leaves outside the room. Davy's head turned before his thoughts did. He saw a flash of white. "Ink?" The crashing went on, as if Ink were running, maybe, oh yeah, running in a circle around the room. Going to the front door. Davy turned, following the sound. Don't be too tall, he remembered. He sat down. Ink barrelled through the front door, between two trees, and slammed into Davy's chest, nearly knocking him over.

Davy held still. Ink clutched at him, trying to squeeze up handfuls of Davy's bare shoulders in his small hands. His eyes were wild with grief.

Davy sniffed him. What? Davy closed his eyes and listened to the boy's smell. It made him feel hollow. Someone gone. Mink, Davy guessed. He hated being ditched, himself. When he was younger it had happened all the time, if King and Willy didn't want their stupid brother tagging along with them. He smelled himself going all salty, trying to tell Ink not to care. Didn't work. Impossible not to care.

Ink rubbed his face against Davy's chest. The boy wanted to tell him something and Davy was just too slow. Ink was kinder than his sister, so he didn't often tell Davy how slow he was. Instead Ink wriggled out of Davy's arms and stood on his long shinbones, grabbing both Davy's ears and pulling. Ink's face worked frightfully. Finally the words came.

"Tonight. We got to go 'way." Ink had a swollen eye.

Holding on by the ears, Ink shook Davy's head until it rattled, but Davy just wasn't getting it.

"She goned! We go tonight!" Ink almost pulled Davy's ear off in frustration. "Oh, you *stupid!*" Then he was off, running into the new green of the woods, running upriver toward the footbridge.

Davy went back to his housekeeping, filled with disquiet. Rae would come and tell him if something needed to be done.

He stood on the bank watching branches rush by in the swollen current when a bit of black fluff sailed across the river and straight into his hand. What was it? Ash? Knitted wire? He sniffed it thoughtfully as he turned back to his room. Musky.

It worked nicely to fasten the Lassie-haired doll to her place.

He waded out to the willows, climbed into the big nest and curled up, drawing one of Willy's abandoned shirts over himself. From where he lay, he could watch the clouds march along. He named their colors after crayons: cornflower, periwinkle, charcoal. Later, when his stomach began to rumble, he named their shapes after foods: macaroni and cheese, mashed potatoes and gravy, boiled peas. He wriggled into a hollow made just for him. "Mom, I'm hungry," he whimpered. His eyes closed. While the sky filled and lowered, he slept.

Chapter Forty-Two

By six o'clock Saturday night the sky was black with swiftly moving clouds. The streetlights rattled on their poles along US 31. Mr. Stass stood at the foot of the Townhouses sign, marshaling his plans, wearing his accustomed shabby suit and a raincoat. He patted the pockets of the raincoat: pistol, whiskey bottle not quite full, cigars, matches. Two gallon-sized cans of gasoline were hidden in a bush across US 31. *First thing, get this night watchman out of the picture.*

A large man lurched out of the darkness on the road.

Mr. Stass said, "Why, hello, Mr. Coombs. You're out late tonight," and the man wheeled round.

"Wo boy! You surprised me." Cracker wore overalls and apparently nothing else. He cradled a pair of six-packs. Mr. Stass slid the whiskey bottle out of his pocket and offered it to Cracker. Cracker took it without remark and drank.

Mr. Stass said, "Just came by to hand over those policies." He took them from his coat. "One for you and one for the Somershoes. Put your copy in a bank, 'smy advice," he added, watching Cracker slide the papers into a gaping side pocket. He waved a hand as Cracker tried to give the bottle back. "Keep it." He tapped his head. "Got to drive back to town tonight."

"Aw, you can't do that," Cracker said pleasantly. "First off, I owe you a drink or six already." He waved the six-packs in his hand. "And second, it's early. Come along and meet my friend Alexander. He's over here in the ghett-toe, pining away for conversation and beer. And whiskey, I shouldn't wonder."

Mr. Stass pretended to hesitate. "Maybe I ought to see the night watchman. I thought I saw prowlers around that machine." He pointed to the bucketloader in the ridge's shadow.

"No shit?" Cracker peered through the dark. "They been having a bit of that lately. C'mon." He grabbed Mr. Stass's coat sleeve and towed him across the mud to the office trailer.

The inconvenience of the lock on the chain-link gate cost them some time. Cracker waved Mr. Stass aside. "Hang on, hang on. I used to be good with these." He pulled out a ring of old keys and twiddled with the padlock while Mr. Stass fidgeted. "Rats. I'll get it. Gimme a minute."

At this point an even bigger man, the night watchman, Mr. Stass guessed, came out of the trailer, shining his flashlight on them where they stood at the gate. Cracker hailed him gaily. The watchman seemed pleased to see them and invited them into the trailer.

After Cracker's lengthy and overly particular introductions, Mr. Stass delivered his message about the prowler.

"All right. You go inside. I take a look." The watchman thumped out into the night.

Inside the construction trailer, Cracker got comfortable in the canvas chair by the card table. "And there goes a very fine reason t'beware of a steady job," he said.

"Amen," said Mr. Stass, in high good humor.

"Whisky?" Cracker leaned across the table with the bottle.

"Not for me." Mr. Stass put his hand up. "Gonna be rain tonight, weatherman says. Wouldn't say no to a beer," he added. They drank quietly until the watchman returned.

"Nothing there," the watchman said.

"That's what I figured," Mr. Stass said. "It's too dark out here in the burbs. Give me the city lights." He looked at his watch. "Darn. I gotta go right now, or my wife will yell at me." He shook hands with both men and departed.

Chapter Forty-Three

John Fowier stepped out of the shower in his room at the White Fence Inn. What a miserable fucking week, he thought. Through the bathroom wall he could hear Suzy brushing her teeth. She'd ducked him all day long and then tried to drink him under the table at dinner. She knew it was pay-up time.

He heard her open a window next door. After a day like today, he better get something out of being the boss. He put on his best satin pajamas and headed for the door communicating between his and Suzy's rooms.

It was locked.

Suzy put the finishing touches on her makeup. Just how she had come, over the last three months, to be in a hotel room preparing to have sex with John Fowier, she didn't want to think.

Dear heaven, I feel sleazy, she thought. Who is this bimbo? I'm not even going to be me in the sack.

Maybe if she opened a window he wouldn't expect moaning-in-ecstasy. She rattled the casement as wide open as she could.

A gust of fabulous-smelling air puffed in the window, smelling like rain and sweet earth and fresh river water and new grass. Suzy leaned out on folded arms and sniffed. All the good smells of a farm and none of the yucky stuff. The air was warm, making the river seem more like inside than outside. The water ran just below her window. Some ducks looked up at her in the waning light, making soft quacking noises, bumping each other like bumper cars.

"Sorry, guys. Cookie hava no."

Leaning on the sill, woozy with after-dinner margaritas, she could see a park downriver, with fingers of sunset-colored water and fingers of green islands interlacing, and the black bare branches of some trees veiled by willows already in leaf. One warm raindrop fell spat on her arm. Lovely evening.

Upriver was the cute little bridge that served Berne's main street, all arches and wide cement handrails. A naked child ran along the handrails, arms flailing, laughing or crying, and a dog jumped up and followed. She could hear each small dog-foot patting the concrete. The sound carried a good thirty yards.

That settled that. Better shut the window. She couldn't stand the idea that passersby might know that someone in this room was having sex. The window didn't want to close and then it did, with a bump that bounced it half open again and broke one of her nails. That was the last straw. Tears stung her eyes, and she let out a sob of frustration.

On impulse she unsnapped her lace teddy, jerked it over her head and threw it in a corner. She caught a glimpse of herself in the mirror: naked, crouching, furious. Suzy snarled at the mirror. With a quick hand she slathered on cold cream. A few tissues took care of her lipstick and the goo on her eyes. Feverish energy pushed her on. She bent over, her hair dangling between her knees, and savagely messed the blow-dried curls with her fingers. By golly, she thought, he'll get it, but I'll give it to him my way.

Then she head the most uncanny scream outside. At first Suzy imagined that the little kid had fallen off the bridge, and her heart missed a beat, but it wasn't that kind of scream. It started with wailing, then coarsened to rage, and trailed off rhythmically, as if between blows, or footsteps. Horrible, trying to imagine what could get someone make that sound.

The sink taps turned off in the next room. John was humming some song. Ravel's *Bolero*?

The scream came again. She couldn't ignore a scream like that—she had to look out the window. Halfway to the window she remembered she was naked.

There was a clank next door, like a towel on a towel rack.

John would be here any second.

Suzy clutched her hair. She stepped to the communicating door and locked it.

Instantly the doorknob rattled. *I can't believe I did that.* She held her breath.

John's voice came loudly from the other side of the panel, only a foot away. "Hey!" Rattle-rattle. "Hey, sleeping beauty, what the fuck?"

The doorknob rattled again. John roared. Suzy reached for the door-knob and held on. The scream outside came from much closer now, as if the screamer were running through the park.

What could be *happening* out there? A child or a woman, running and screaming.

The door crashed, as if John had thrown himself against it with his full weight. "You bitch, I'm not kidding! Open up!"

She went to the window. *I can't do this with that going on outside. I have to know what's happening. I have to stop it.*

"Are you all right out here?" she called into the darkness.

She threw on her kimono and belted it, watching over her shoulder as the door bounced under John's blows. Opening her window further, she slipped one leg over the sill, then the other. Two cool fat raindrops spatted against her kimono-back. Her toes dangled into the river. The river was startlingly warm.

John slammed against the door and swore.

The scream, weaker now, came from the woods.

She let go the sill, and dropped knee-deep into warm rushing water and mud. "Hello?" she called.

John slammed against the door one last time and leaned there, panting. Twice was too often. It would be her job. He'd damn well see to that.

A window went up in the room next door. John turned his head. Suzy's voice called out—a greeting? Goddammit, he thought. God*dammit.* He ran through the bathroom to his own room, where his window stood ajar by three inches. By peering sideways he could just see that no one was standing outside her window. Duh, that's because the river's out there. He looked down. Directly below their two windows was a two-foot drop and, below that, the river. He couldn't quite see the water. Maybe she had a midnight caller waiting down there in a boat.

He slid his window up another inch, then jerked it open wide. Suzy, practically naked in a flimsy kimono-type thing, was standing in the river. Her hair stuck out every which way. She looked up and down the river. Someone out in the darkening woods or water cried out, and Suzy called in answer.

Had she seen him? John pulled back.

Silence.

When he peeked again she was moving out of sight, wading down-stream through the shallows toward the park.

John watched as she sloshed away. He swung his knees up, scrambled through the window in his pajamas, and came splashing down in warm water. Where'd she go?

There, out in the water, Suzy's long, pale kimono glimmered in the dark. His heartbeat rang in his ears. His pajamas were wet to the waist. He waded after her.

Now where had that scream come from? Suzy stood in the river, her toes squishing in the mud. She didn't know what to do. Except stay away from the inn tonight. Maybe she should go to the lobby, call the cops. It was their job to look for trouble in the night. She waded downstream toward the wooden stairs up to the patio, followed by pestering ducks.

But when she got to the empty patio she hesitated. The screaming had stopped. Sure was nice out here. Occasional raindrops splashed on her feverish face, cooling her. Her feet were warm where they sank into the riverbottom silt, and her panic attack over John kept her skin on the sizzle. She squished mud between her toes, wavering, while her before-during-and-after-dinner drinks burned in her stomach.

Right now the thought of sharing her state of mind or even the inn lobby with another human being appalled her.

And she was still mad at herself. What was she thinking to get into this situation? Stupid, stupid girl. Her knees slashed through the shallow water. Time to face facts. She would never rise higher at the company. She was nothing in John Fowier's world. Never really one of the players. Just a prop.

The realization of how completely she had fooled herself made her madder. She took a swing at the water, sending a satisfying curl of spray into the air. Something behind her made a great shlooping noise, as if she had frightened a beaver or a big water rat, but when she looked back, there was only the dark, enigmatic surface of the river and the silhouette of a single duck, twenty yards back. She turned and waded on.

John Fowier surfaced carefully. She was looking right at his head where it stuck out of the water. He scrooched down a little more.

He couldn't think why he wanted to hide from Suzy. That bothered him. Maybe because she looked so pissed off. A woman crazy enough to climb out a window into the river in her bathrobe was probably bad news. God, she looked good though, stomping through the water, throwing her arms around in that wet kimono. Best view he'd had so far. Maybe she'd take it off. He pulled himself off the sucking muddy bottom. Keeping low, he followed.

Suzy stomped and splashed her way along the shore. Between silver fingers of the river, the strips of parkland were laid out with benches and empty black flowerbeds. To Suzy it smelled terrific, wet and fresh, woodsy. She splashed again. *That* for John Fowier, and *that* for the makeup-counter girls at Niemann Marcus, and *that, that* for *me.* Dumb bunny. Stupid, dumb girl.

Listen to me, I don't even swear in my head! She swore aloud, every filthy word she knew dumping through her mouth like a mud bath, cleaning out all the pink fuzz in her head.

"*This,*" she growled, and stamped into the muddy riverbottom, "*this* is *real,* and *this* is *my* cunt, and *this* is *my* fist, and if John Fowier ever gets within a *mile* of the one he'll get the *other* one up his pretty *nose.* If I can't reach his *asshole!*"

She giggled, feeling dizzy. Her anger left her. *I am sooo drunk.* The mud was gentle on her sore Achilles tendons.

She threw her head back and wandered, watching the racing clouds, shuffling along the squishy bank, feeling a loosening in her legs and shoulders, making her hips wiggle and her breasts wobble. *Wobble wobble.* The clouds ran this way and that. I've got to get out of the city, she thought. This beats hell out of looking up the Sears Tower's nose.

She walked up a finger of the river until she stood among trees. She could hear the water better now. It seemed as she waded along the bank that the water was retreating, lengthening the little fingers of land and leaving the good, gooshy mud exposed. The exposed silt was up to her ankles here, warm and black as molasses.

She looked down at her ankles, totally invisible where they were smeared with mud, and her legs, white as peeled bananas sticking up out of nowhere. Standing on her right foot, she smeared her left knee with the sole of her right foot. I'm invisible! She giggled. She smeared the other one. Look, Ma, no legs! Her muddy legs felt hot and tingly. With both hands she scooped up mud and rubbed it up her legs, over her butt, tearing off her kimono to get at all the bright white skin underneath. Her belly disappeared, and the poky white points of her hip bones, then her breasts, goosh, moosh! She laughed out loud. Mudpack treatment, she thought, and laughed and laughed, holding her sides. Her hands tingled and her muddy armpits felt as hot as if she'd been dancing all night. She flicked her fingers. Mud spattered across the water. Black spots appeared on her arms and shoulders, and she felt it spatter across her face, first cold, then burning hot. It smelled good enough to eat.

She could hear and smell a lot of things, now that she was away from that horrible inn, away from John Fowier and his dumb hard-on. In the middle of rubbing mud into her hair she paused to listen and sniff, moving her invisible toes in the black squishy mud. Crickets. Frogs. The river noise, making splishy ripply sounds. Smells of sycamore trees, smells of kerosene as a truck rumbled by across the upriver, then rainy air after the truck exhaust blew away. Absently she stroked the back of her neck. The mud was as smooth as talcum powder. It went on cool and then heated up, as if her skin somehow turned the mud into a giant margarita that made you drunk when you bathed in it.

The invisible woman stood stock-still, up to her ankles in the river, one hand on the back of her neck, one foot on her other knee. As she breathed in, she drew the mud's warmth up into her legs, just as trees drew it up, making her skin tingle, making the buds swell on a million twigs. As she breathed out, the water's voice carried away all her anger and sorrow, all her mistakes, leaving her a single quiet moment without breath or thoughts, only her pulse bumping on her skin. The breath came in, with smells of fishy water and clouds and mud and sweet tree sap. Then a tiny pause where the world was huge, the world was tiny, and she was both inside it and filled so full that she was outside it as well. When she couldn't hold it any longer, the breath went out, and joy came with it.

Upstream, thunder rolled. She felt it between her legs, like the old locker-room joke about sitting on the washing machine in the spin cycle. Rumba time. The wind was picking up. Suzy started to dance.

Chapter Forty-Four

N ow there goes a big-hearted guy." Cracker laid his all-purpose blessing on Mr. Stass's back.

"Is Miss Somershoe angry with me?" Alexander said. "I asked her to come visit." He wished fiercely that they had not had the fence between them today, nor Bob and Ike and the whole crew watching. "If only she is not angry."

"I doubt it. Somershoe women don't let go. Very often," Cracker said, with an inward look.

Alexander winced. Wind rattled the screen door. "Big storm coming," he said.

"This? Naw. It's th' calm before the storm." Cracker eyed him. "This place getting to you?"

"You said it," Alexander said in a heartfelt voice.

"Did to me, too, at first."

Alexander waited for the older man to say more, but he didn't go on. "I thought you grew up here."

Cracker peered into the bottom of his beer can. "Came here ten-'leven years ago. Dropped in on my sister, liked the place, liked the women— you should of seen Gelia ten years ago, my word. And Rae."

Alexander didn't say anything.

Cracker said, "And I hadn't been here a month before my damn sister and her husband just upped and disappeared. And about a year later this girl caught up with me, she's got *two* infants with her, mine she says— 'your seed' she calls it, like I just throw it on the ground and it grows. Won't say it don't," he added comfortably, as if flattered by the idea.

He was revving up, Alexander saw. Telling all, the way a drunk does at a certain point. Maybe he would tell everything Alexander needed to know, too.

"So then she blows town," his voice rose, "and here I am holding *her* babies. So there I was with five kids! Well, when I say babies, King was sixteen and his brother was what, twelve. Davy don't need much watching, but who's gonna *feed* these kids, I asked myself? Raedawn couldn't manage, she hadda go to work. Gelia wouldn't. Erny was still workin' then." He brooded awhile. "You ever feed an' change twins? Gave me gray hairs, so help me. Right here." He pointed.

"What happened to your sister?"

"Time for whiskey. Some?" When Alexander shook his head, he said, "Right you are. Never mix whiskey and beer."

Alexander badly needed to be told things. "Not my business," he suggested.

Cracker took a pull and then rubbed the bottom of the whiskey bottle on the table restlessly, watching the bottleneck move. "Ain't that. Dunno where she went. Her and her husband, too, just snatched up inta the air. I'd say they ran away, only Gloria never had the imagination. Nor the fool she married, neither."

Alexander wondered if Cracker's sister had ever fallen asleep in this meadow. Thunder smashed into itself in the sky outside.

Cracker said, "Raedawn sorta likes you."

Alexander looked up, startled to find himself being regarded with lewd speculation. Now what? Was he supposed to preen, or backpedal? Some sober undercurrent in Cracker's manner left him in doubt. *That's all I need, to be in trouble with this man for making up to a white girl.*

He swigged beer and looked back at Cracker. "Is she someone's girl-friend?"

Cracker pulled at the whiskey without looking at it. "She's everybody's girlfriend. *You* could be something special to her, I'm saying." He waved ten fingers at him. "Now it's true I'm overstepping my bounds here. Raedawn conducts her own amoors, as I damn well oughta know." He drank. "I was just trying to encourage you," he said to the bottle.

"And?" And warn me, Alexander thought. Here comes the other shoe.

"Well." Cracker paused. Hail spattered on the trailer windows while he thought. "It ain't easy bein' special to Raedawn," he said finally, as if dissatisfied with this opening but stuck for another. A huge explanation loomed in what he didn't say.

Alexander waited. He could do with an explanation, any explanation.

Life had gotten very complicated lately, and he had completely failed to keep himself from rolling roundheeled into love with Rae Somershoe.

It was only because she had been nice to him, he told himself. He reflected with self-pity that she was the first woman to be nice to him without reaching for his wallet since he came to the States. The first to sit on his cock while he lay in the lap of a tree and fuck him until his mind turned inside out. How had he got here? He could have left days ago. There was a bumper sticker on the back of Bob's pickup that said, *Watch my tail, not hers.* Alexander had long ago stopped watching where he was in traffic.

Cracker was looking at the floor now.

"It could confuse a man to be her boyfriend," Alexander said.

"Yep. Yes, it can. See, you're more her speed. Young guy. You got the look," and he paused to hold up a hand, *don't get me wrong,* "you look like the marrying kind. I never was. She wants that special someone who can," he paused again, a double meaning in his look, "who can take it all on. Big shoulders kind of guy." Cracker smiled weakly. "Not my thing. Cripes, when I think what she's laid on me." He brooded.

Alexander felt the pressure of sexual frustration, his loneliness for Rae, and his fear of sleeping in the trailer mixing together, building up like steam or an electrical charge.

"What Raedawn has, her and her mother, see, some folks don't understand it. I could feel it in her, but I never tried to understand it, see. Anyways, it kind of made what I did not much matter.

"Women up the hill, scared sissy women who look down on Gelia and Raedawn and call 'em names, I had them," he said without boasting. "They never come within a mile of that. That kind of special thing. Gelia's the same, but she's selfish. She's drawed the line. Got to me a bit when I found out she had put Raedawn up to it. Got to King, too. I think he left home over it, among other things. Not that he'll face up to it."

Following maybe a third of this but still patient, Alexander passed over the second six-pack. Cracker peeled one off, opened, and drank, scarcely pausing for breath.

"I didn't know about any of that the first month or so I was here. There was Gelia, wild as horses, and my sister with her family letting me sleep on the sofa—I was a halfway decent carpenter oncet, and they always needed that. And there was Rae."

Cracker put his hand on the breast of his overalls as if feeling for his heart, and Alexander thought, Now we come to it.

"Mink reminds me of her a bit. Hair like cotton, eyes too big for her face. Rae was a princess growing up too fast, gonna be queen of a troubled country. I always wondered if Rae really knew what she was in for. Living with it. Dishing out her thing to two whole towns. She crossed the road at fourteen. Wasn't as if Gelia gave it up, mind. Just handed over the heavy work to that little girl like always."

He put his head back and looked at the trailer's suspended ceiling. "She was little, but she burned. Not like some of those skinny truck-stop waitresses 'at's burnt-out at twenty, not Rae. She burned all right. Nor she didn't draw the line like Gelia. There was always more of her. She growed into it. She took everything I thought I'd learned about kindness from women, and she—she laid it on me like a curse."

Cracker shook his head. "It's not like she ever told me, you got to stay with the kids now with Gloria and her husband gone away. I could have run for it. Almost did." He spread his hand over his breast again. The words poured out.

"It was like her heart was too big for her body, and when she'd caught me, and taught me, she made mine the same way. I'm not cut out to be a daddy. I'm not anybody's kind of hero or solid citizen. But she—she bulked me up somehow, like the way they put a flower under glass and it swells up bigger'n nature made it. Or a cow that always needs milking. I didn't *feel* good unless I had the kids under my eye. Made me nuts. I'd run away sometimes, get clear up the hill and halfway into town before I felt all sweaty and had to stop in at the Dew Drop, or one of the boys'ud say, Come play checkers, or some woman would drop her bag of groceries in the parking lot and before you know it I'm showin' her how to cook 'em Southern style." He smiled.

A wave of hail sputtered against the windows and walls, hissing like radio static.

Alexander said softly, "Fourteen?"

He had thought Cracker lost in his own confession, but the white man shot him a look that showed he was completely awake.

"I know. I said Rae had me. I was forty-five and she was fourteen. Still, I'll say it, *she* had *me*, and a sorry creature I was before I gave in to her." He fell silent, seeming to listen to his insides, or to the past, while shock spread through Alexander. Fourteen when this man had her, and by then she was already *across the road,* whatever that meant. Alexander thought he knew, maybe.

Cracker said, "I know how pathetic I was, because I can barely stand myself today and I been pulling in this harness for ten years. My kids are big and wild, and she's all over the county with younger men and older ones, too, and I fill in the cracks with women I meet up the hill til she notices me again."

Here Cracker met Alexander's eyes. Instead of a sordid, failing old man's defiance—she's my girl, too—Alexander saw a strength, the largest strength he had ever seen in a man's eyes. I won't be in the way, Cracker seemed to be saying. Less trouble than most of the men in her wayward path. You'll find out.

Alexander's heart jumped, sending a burst of sweet heat through him. She wouldn't be faithful to him. Did that matter? That was Cracker's warning, wasn't it? Or was it? And if not, what in hell did the man want? A promise that Alexander would tolerate him, leave him a corner in his, Alexander's, woman? This whole line of thought was running way too fast. He'd slept with her once, hadn't even talked with her more than an hour. They were strangers.

But something in his bones, or deeper, said *Yes.* His body was sure, anyway.

"You're a good listener, bub," Cracker said softly. "What do *you* want?"

"Jesus, man, I don't know," Alexander burst out. He wrung his hands. His roughened palms rasped on one another, and he listened: the sound of a snake passing over a linoleum floor, a root dragging in sand. "Some slack. To go home. At one time I could not." He thought of hens pecking up islands while his gran held him by the shoulders. "Perhaps—no. No, never again. But I am mightily tired of this life on the road."

Cracker put his hand out. Alexander, not knowing what else to do, took it and shook.

As if he had forgotten asking Alexander a question, Cracker said, "I don't know that she's the sort *I'd* want to marry. She's not a restful woman. There's too much of her, for all she's more honest than that mother of hers. I could use some rest. But I ain't dead, and I don't plan to be til I'm no use to a lesser woman, even if Rae won't have me. She belongs with a young guy like you, or King, or—or somebody straight and—and strong like that." He passed a hand over his thinning hair. "My heart's about wore out with belonging to her and these damn kids, and with them the strings get even longer, so there's Gelia on my conscience, too—Christ, that's a funny notion, ain't it? And Erny. We're not exactly family, but we're all we got."

He's inviting me into the family, Alexander thought. Uncle Cracker's blessing. Tears stung his eyes, and he smiled. He was so very ready to belong somewhere.

He wouldn't know if he belonged here until he saw Rae again. "Let the woman decide. I just got here." To change the subject, he said, "What do *you* want?"

Cracker put his arms behind his head and stretched, leaning back in the director's chair. He yawned. The cheap wood cracked.

"Aah, I don't know what I want. Cold beer, hot women, good friends. Got that now. Maybe just somewhere to sit and soak up the sun. Just *be*." He scratched under the waistband of his overalls. "Yeah. Let's start with that."

Chapter Forty-Five

Davy woke to a sizzle of lightning, a crack of thunder. He cringed. It had been full dark for an hour, he realized. Rae would be worried.

The knitted willow trees under him quivered. The nest-hollow where he lay shifted shape. The wind was right down here on the ground with him now. The clouds were lower, too, close enough to touch, and all-new colors: graygreen, mustard, lavender, sienna. He kept his arms inside Willy's flannel shirt, curled around himself. It wasn't raining very hard yet. A bit of egg-carton separated from the parent body of the nest and flew away in the wind. As it left, it seemed to take warmth away with it, and Davy said under his breath, "Tornado." Another gust grabbed the edge of the whole nest and heaved. The mattress on that side rose up, lifted itself perpendicular, and then flipped away to splash down in the river below. The temperature fell another notch. Davy cried out in terror.

A second mattress, loosened now, along with dog fur, old flannel shirts, matted cottonwood fluff, egg cartons, Styrofoam peanuts, and rags, peeled away and flipped out of sight. Hail and rain stung him. Davy hunkered down in his Davy-sized hollow, clinging to the crumbling foam rubber between himself and the bare branches of the willows.

The river below him sounded different. Much closer. Now and then the two willows under him shook with a tremendous thump that rattled debris out of the nest and opened gaps in its floor. Through one of these gaps he peeked. The wind was lashing up whitecaps on the river. A huge chunk of something floated by—part of a house? a boat dock?—and again the trees thumped under him. A big board wallowed there, almost drowned in waves, as if it could barely keep itself afloat. The current smacked the board against the willows a few more times and at last succeeded in prying it loose, whirling it away, end over end, like the needle of a compass.

Chapter Forty-Six

Rae should have gotten off work at six, but the children's reading room was a mess, and then the head librarian had got his wheelchair stuck in a crack in the parking lot. By seven she was puffing down the hill. She figured she had just time to change clothes before the last of the busybodies would have left the construction trailer, and then she could see Alexander. Her heart went hot at the thought.

The sky still looked bruised. Tornado weather. Up there somewhere, she knew, the layers of clouds ran crosswise against one another, warp and woof, hot and cold, fast and slow and fast again. Somewhere a few miles away was a wall of cold, pressing on the sky. She could feel it leaning over the whole river valley. Gusts of warm wind puffed her skirt into her face and swirled her hair into the air so that it floated, faintly electrified.

Her trailer was dark. No Gelia. Just as well, Rae thought. I'd like to smack that woman. The lamp wasn't on the table where it should be, and the sofa was pushed back—where?

"Damn!" She barked her shin, fumbled in a drawer in the sink, came up with a candle and a box of matches, and lit it.

The trailer was empty.

Rae stared around her home, stunned. The living room furniture was piled up against the back wall, near the doorway to the rear rooms. All the quilts were off the walls, gone. She lifted the candle. A coat hanger lay on the floor. Shoes were tumbled in the sink. Litter everywhere, things that belonged in boxes and dressers in the bedrooms. Her mother's old winter scarf. A broken cup. What on *earth?*

Her hand tipped, and hot wax spilled over her fingers. "Ow!" She ran to the back rooms of the trailer.

The bedrooms were emptied, too. The dresser drawers stood piled on beds stripped of sheets. The curtains still hung on the windows. The curtains were stapled on, she remembered. Everything that would move quick had gone.

A bang came from outside. Sounded like a bucket blowing over. While she watched, the curtains were sucked hard against the windows. Her ears popped. When the curtains let go, three long heartbeats later, the trailer was ten degrees colder inside.

Tornado coming.

She remembered to grab the matches and a handful of candles from the drawer on her way out. The wind whipped the door out of her hand and smacked it against the wall. She hesitated, then pulled the door to and locked it, and ran next door.

Ernest's trailer was emptied of its movables, too. His furniture had always seemed much nicer than her mother's. That was before it was stacked against the windows in the southwest corner of the room. *Is this what our lives come down to? A few heaps of junk?* She ran outside and circled the place, pulling shutters down over Erny's windows and locking them in place with the bent nails Erny used for that purpose.

She found her mother and Ernest crowded in the doorway of the twins' shack. They stood over the hole, looking down at the iron stove inside. Heat and woodsmoke shimmered out of the glowing slots in its crown. Ernest took an iron bargehook from the wall. Gelia was holding a pail of water. At their feet lay bundles of their valuables: Gelia's jewelry, some glass dishes and bric-a-brac rolled in the family quilts, kitchenware, fishing gear, a couple of bales of off-season clothes, and some old books wrapped in plastic bags.

Reaching down into the hole with the hook, Ernest flipped the stovelid open. Red light bloomed in the shack.

He said, "Go ahead."

Gelia poured the water onto the coals below. They hissed, and the hole was instantly dark. By feel they lowered the bundles, with muffled clinking, into the space between the stove body and the curving mud wall.

"You think this'll still be here when the water goes down?" Gelia said.

"We've just got to hope we can find the spot," Ernest said.

"Cover it?" Gelia said.

Ernest shook his head. "No time." Lightning ripped the air outside. The sky shattered. A handful of hail clattered on the tin roof of the twins' shack. In the close darkness and the smell of wet coals, he said,

"The river will fill it up, but I dare say nothing will wash out of it."

When their valuables had all been lowered into the hole, everybody went back to the Gowdy trailer. Ernest seemed brisk and businesslike, and Gelia was in high good humor as always in the presence of disaster. By lamplight they waded into the business of stripping Cracker's place. Gelia avoided Rae's eye.

"Do you have room in that box for these?" Ernest said to Gelia. He handed her a tangle of unmatched socks. "Someone should go look for Mink and Davy," he said to Rae.

"Cracker know you're messin' up his place?" Rae said. She could make no sense of the piles of Cracker's belongings heaped on the bed, of what they were saving or leaving. "Where is he?"

"Firehouse, I think," said Gelia. "Outa my hair." She threw a sock out of the box in front of her. "These things are full of holes."

"They're all he's got, Angelia," Ernest said mildly.

She grumbled and retrieved the scorned sock.

Someone banged in at the door out front. "That's Willy with Ink," Gelia said, and skipped out of the room.

Ernest put down the socks he was holding. He turned to Rae. Their eyes met.

"Tonight's the night," Ernest said softly. "Mink says so." Rae couldn't argue with that. She'd known it already. He gave her a gentle looking-over. "Have you seen her today?"

"Mink? No." The air pressure changed again, and the wind whistled and buzzed as a bit of paper blew against the windowscreen outside.

Excited voices, Ink's and Willy's, came from the front room.

Ernest tipped his head toward the door. "Hear the boys? The river's rising. We need to find Mink. She's in trouble, Raedawn."

Rae ran a hand through her hair and pulled distractedly. One more crisis. Everybody was trying to keep her from going across the road where Alexander, shining like a jewel in her mind, was begging her to come. Ernest stood before her with his hands full of Cracker's unfolded underwear, not saying anything. She sucked in a shuddering breath and rubbed her face with her hands.

"Okay. What about Mink?"

"She came to me this morning." Ernest went back to packing his box. "Did you ever see that hole out there, south past the garden?" She shook her head, mystified. "Well, I did. I took a look today after Mink ran away." He hesitated. "Raedawn, you were fourteen when you crossed the road."

She gaped at him. *How dare you, Ernest Brown?* It occurred to her only now that no man in the family had ever even sideways-mentioned the tree across the road.

"Isn't that right?" he persisted. She nodded. "It was a big change for you, wasn't it? I remember you had a few nerve storms with your mother. Things changed between you and King, and you and Cracker, too. It was never my business—"

Darned right, she thought indignantly. What's got into Erny tonight? He's never tampered with women's business before!

"—But I imagine," he said in his most precise, careful tone, "that it must have felt mighty unusual." He smiled impishly at her scandalized look. "My land, Raedawn, the way you ladies have been carrying on all these years, and yet you never speak of it. Your mother neglected you more than I thought." He put the box aside and stepped closer to take her hands. "It was nearly too strong for you. And you were older. Mink's just a little thing. It has knocked her all endways," he pronounced slowly.

With difficulty, Rae blinked and tried to see into his face. "Someone did something to Mink?" He's right, she thought, laughing hysterically. We don't have any words.

"Some thing." He was looking meaningfully at her. "It's a hole—just a hole in the ground. There's no time to show you. She fell in. That was probably just Mink's bad luck. But Rae, it's this *place*. You know things have been strange."

She squeezed his hands in hers. "Mink fell in a hole and she got—" She stopped. It had felt almost the same, this past week, like when she was a girl and had just crossed the road for the first time. Her whole life had turned inside out. Only then it had been so good. Scary but good. Mostly good, anyhow. And now, with his body felled and cut in pieces and gouged out of the earth, the whole place seemed covered with his blood. Or something like it.

Ernest said, "Mink is just a baby. You were mighty wall-eyed for a while, I remember. Think how scared she must be."

It turned me inside out, she thought. It made my nerves stick out of my body a foot and a half all over. Gelia rubbed me wrong every time she come close. And, to be fair, most other people did, too. It made me feel like lightning stood on my shoulder. He was always inside me from that day on, pushing on me from the inside out.

"Poor Mink," she said, thinking not of Mink but of young Raedawn.

"Someone has to look for her. My hands are full with Angelia and all this baggage. Willy's found Ink. Angelia will keep an eye on Ink now, and Willy's got to look for Davy, and I've got to keep an eye on Angelia."

She frowned. "I still don't understand how—"

He turned her around with both hands and guided her to the door. "Go south past the garden and look along the path on the riverside. It's a hole in the ground full of water. Look for the child, Rae. She might come to you."

But when they came out of the trailer, Rae found it wasn't going to be that easy to get away. Willy and Ink were struggling with a wheelbarrow full of boxes and loose gardening tools, and Gelia was trying, without much success, to put a whammy on a furiously shouting King Gowdy.

When she saw them come outside, Gelia abandoned King in mid-coo. "For pity's sake, Ernest, talk some sense into this boy. I got work to do."

King turned on Ernest. "What the goddamnhell are you doing? Where the hell is Cracker, to let you go tearing up all my family's things—"

Rae stepped in. She put her hand on King's chest. "I'll tell him, Ernest. King, there's a tornado coming, and your brother is missing."

Distracted at last, King glared down at her. "What?"

The wheelbarrow wobbled in Willy's hands. He tried to steady it, but a rake toppled off the top of the load and fell on Ink's bare foot. The boy let out a scream of frustration. Quickly Willy knelt to him and held him. Ink wailed. One eye was half-closed, leaking tears, and the other was swollen with a dark bruise.

"What happened to you, kiddo?"

Ink howled.

"Why don't we go in for just a minute? It's kinda noisy out here," Willy said, glancing over his shoulder to where Raedawn worked on his angry brother.

Ink stood stolidly before Willy, his arms hanging at his sides, his wailing face lifted in an ecstasy of grief. Shrugging, Willy picked the boy up. Ink didn't even struggle.

"It's all been a little too much for you, hasn't it?" Willy said, and carried him into the trailer.

There was one big chair in the living room that wasn't stacked, up-ended, or covered with discarded junk. Groping feet-first in the dark, Willy collapsed into it with Ink on his lap. "Tell me about it?"

Ink subsided into hiccups.

Guess not, Willy thought. He put his cheek on Ink's dust-saturated hair. "There once was a boy," Willy began, feeling that weird time-machine feeling that comes when you know that somewhere in the future you are remembering this moment and reliving it, "Who lived in a hole by the river."

Ink's snuffling became a wail again. He twisted in Willy's lap and threw himself on Willy's neck. Willy felt a wet spot forming on his collarbone.

"And one day a big storm came from a long way away. It was a mile high and a block wide and it had a long black tail that gobbled up houses. It sssucked up the houses," Willy put his face on Ink's wet neck and made a raspberry noise. Ink giggled and flinched. "It ssssucked up the cars." This time Ink giggled but he held still. "It tried to ssssssssuck up the river, but the river was too big. Nyaah nyaah, said the river. Nuts! said the storm. Well, I'm gonna get that little kid in that hole there!"

Willy blew raspberries all over Ink's neck and arms, until the boy squealed and thrashed. "Ow! Careful what you kick, it's attached. Now where was I? The little boy heard the storm coming a miiiile away, and he grabbed his best toys, and his favorite burglar tools, and his cousins and all their stuff, and he carried them awaaaay up the hill where the storm couldn't go."

"Why?"

"Why what?" Willy said indignantly.

"Why couldn't the storm go?"

"Beee-cause, it was full of water. It had a big fat belly full of water now, from trying to ssssuck up the river." More raspberries. "And it couldn't get up the hill!"

"And the boy said, Nyaaaah!"

They sat quietly, listening to the wind rise outside. Willy heard Gelia and Ernest clanking around between the wheelbarrow and King's old red wagon, trying to decide what to keep and what to leave behind, and Raedawn's soft voice persuading King, persuading and persuading.

Willy shook his head. Three whole families in a wheelbarrow and a kids' wagon. Would King help?

It had taken only Ernest's straight look to convince Willy. Deep in the pit of his stomach he'd been waiting for something to happen. The world was finally going to acknowledge the horror that had happened when the chainsaws cut into his friend. He didn't have to know what it was. He hoped it would be something really big. The whole *world* ought to know what had been done.

Even if Ernest hadn't said, Willy would have known by the way Gelia was frisking around like a puppy at a picnic, tearing her own house apart, throwing her favorite clothes on the floor. In Willy's opinion, Gelia loved disaster. It made her as giddy as a teenager, and yet it focused her wandering will. She had taken a positive outlook when Willy's parents disappeared. Gleefully she had bullied Cracker into staying on with them, and tackled the police and the state's family inspectors. She had even got through to Davy in a way that mystified Willy, accustomed as he was to Davy-logic. Speak the same language, those two, he thought.

Where *was* Davy? And where was Mink?

"Hey, where's your sister?" he said to the little boy.

Ink began gasping again, as if working up a head of crying. Too dark in here, Willy thought. "What's on your mind? Mink? Okay, okay. Rae's going to go look for her in a minute." He hoped. He remembered Ink's black eye, so noticeable outdoors, invisible here in the fuggy dark of their trailer. "Did you two have a fight?" He felt Ink nod. "What about?" It was none of his business, Willy thought at first. Then he shook his head at himself. Everyone treated the kids as if they were grown up. They weren't. Little babes in the wood, he thought, forcing back self-pity. If things came off the way Ernest and Gelia were talking, he realized, things could be extremely bad for Mink. If she was out there alone. And Cracker. Where the hell *is* Cracker when this shit hits the fan? Doesn't anybody else take care of anybody in this family? And Davy. Where *is* that kid?

"She hit me. And then she ran and then I catched up with her. And then she jumped on me."

"What for? Was she mad at you?"

Ink squirmed in his lap.

"Hey, take it easy, I said."

"She did this!"

Ink grabbed him in the crotch. Willy's eyes watered. "Ow, hey! That stuff's not for you yet." He loosened Ink's grip and pulled him up so that their faces were on a level in the lampless dark. "Know what, scout? I think we better go find our family."

The wind was whipping up now. A long fold of paper flew off the top of the wagonload. Rae caught it on its way to the river.

"Thank you, Rae," Gelia said, taking it out of her hand. "That's my deed to the land."

"Well, for gosh sake stick it away safe, will you?" Rae watched her mother stow the paper in the bosom of her shirt. A clothesline snapped and snaked through the air over their heads.

"I will. Hurry yourself, too. This all is gonna go bang any minute," Gelia said blithely. "Ernest, you ready?" She took Ink by the hand. "I'll watch him, Willy. You get after that half-wit brother of yours."

Ernest stood up from stooping. "Feel this ground, Angelia. It's full of something," he said in a troubled voice.

"'Lectrified fulla all that stuff," Gelia said.

"Can you manage?" Rae frowned at the wobbly piles on wagon and wheelbarrow.

"We will. We're going to the storm shelter at the Beard Hotel." Her mother's face was full of the two-faced warnings she'd thrown at Rae last night under the hill. "Don't dawdle."

"I won't." Rae watched them move off, Ernest and Ink steadying the wheelbarrow, Gelia towing the wagon. She ran her fingers through her hair. " Where's Cracker?" she said to King.

"I'm more concerned about young Davy." King was scowling across the bloated river at nothing. "He been gone long?"

"All day." A shrill yipping floated toward them from inland. Rae started. Dogs going nuts. Air pressure changing in their ears, she guessed. "I better get going."

She fled south down the river path, feeling guilty for leaving her family to haul all that junk up to the Beard Hotel, then forgetting, because she was coming closer to Alexander.

Mink's fish hole wasn't hard to find. Yards before Rae came to it, the ground was littered with dead and dying fish, fingerlings all. They were thicker and more lively toward the center, where the silvery bodies pushed up like rice boiling over in a pot. Rae bent and squinted, trying not to flinch as live fish slithered over her ankles.

The first flash of lightning came, then the thunder a moment later, along with a curtain of black water. The flash had showed her a young snake wriggling hard, forcing its way up through the mounded fish and then slipping toward the corpse-littered ground, slithering away into the dark toward the big water. Rae straightened and backed away. She'd seen enough.

"Ow!" A nasty cramp in her calf took her by surprise. A dog yipped behind her. It danced around her, bowing and leaping. "Hey! Did you bite me? Where'd you come from?"

It was too dark to tell what kind of dog it was. The dog snapped again and got her on the calf.

"Ow! You're the biting kind, ain't you. Hey!" she said with more authority. "Quit it!" She stood her ground, knowing dogs well. No point in running. The dog prostrated itself before her and whined. "No, I ain't going to pet you, not after you bit me. Your master let you loose in this storm? For shame." A yip. More whining. The dog grabbed her dress in its teeth and pulled.

"You're addled, poor thing." The dog whined and made muffled, piteous noises. "Oh, all right," she grumbled, when it wouldn't let go. Her hand dropped to its head.

Its head was stone cold and hard under her fingers. Her palm felt funny where it touched the cold, hard dog. Lightning cracked across the air, blinding her. The dog tugged.

"Oh, all *right!*"

It tugged until she was walking obediently behind it, then it let go, herding her toward the construction site with feints at her ankles. She went willingly. After all, it was steering her where she wanted to go most in the world.

The bottom had fallen out of Davy's hollow in the nest. The rain came down harder than ever. He cried with fright, perched on the branches in his bare feet as best he could. He could hear trees and pieces of houses banging against each other in the water, banging the trunks of the trees under him. How close the water sounded!

The river did something big then, and the willow trees tilted, first one, then the other. Davy screamed. His feet slipped. One long leg slid all the way through the gap between limbs, and the other after it. He landed straddling a limb on his tailbone with a bump that made him weep. Big branches closed around his body, locking him in their yellow arms. The rain lashed down. The river threw foam high into the air, whitening the soles of his feet. His hair whipped around his face. His screams disappeared in his own ears. His hair stood straight up.

The willow trees began to walk.

Chapter Forty-Seven

Cracker passed out quite early, Alexander thought, for the sort of drinker he had taken the man to be. While Alexander sat on the cot with his beer, Cracker sprawled in the canvas chair, dead to the world. The whiskey bottle fell over and the liquor flooded away down a crack between the floor panels.

No matter. It felt companionable to Alexander to sit here with someone. He had plenty to think about.

The best news was that Rae still liked him. Whatever had been left unsaid today as they talked through the fence, he knew she still thought about him. So much that this fellow, her favorite lover perhaps, was here to give her away to Alexander.

The enormity of that gesture overpowered him. She didn't seem the kind of woman anyone could give away, yet apparently in some way Cracker felt he had a right, or at least inside knowledge. Alexander relived that handshake, and a huge joy that he had been sitting on finally rose up and filled him.

There was a crack of lightning outside, answered by a crack of splintering wood inside the trailer. The fluorescent light flickered. Alexander flinched. Rain hammered on the metal roof.

Would Rae come out to him in this storm?

The bald light of the fluorescent fixture fell on Cracker, half in and half out of his overalls, lending a silvery sheen to his skin. He flopped sideways. His upper body fell over the arm of the deck chair and lolled. He seemed to be shrinking. His legs looked shortened and swollen. His head dangled at a strange angle. He snored a wheezing, choking, whistling snore, painful to listen to. Alexander saw that Cracker's arms were shrunk to mere flippers that shivered bonelessly in time with his snores.

Alexander sprang up and fell over on his face. He shut his eyes, breathed calm into his belly, and shoved himself back up on his elbows for a look. His toes had burst out of his workboots and forced themselves into the crack in the floor where two plywood sheets joined.

He forgot all about Cracker.

His knife was in his tool bag across the room. Perhaps he could pull himself free and—oh, how much he cringed at the thought—he could make a cut, just a little cut to bring himself back to his proper shape.

Impossible. Down in the crawl space under the trailer, he could feel his toes already reaching for the mud. In a moment—he paused his frantic fretting to attend to just one toe, his whole mind aware of it dangling below in the crawl space, forking and reaching, reaching—in a moment it would touch the ground, and then—he shut his eyes while it happened—reaching—*yes.* There was water down there. His toe drank up water, and Alexander threw his head back at the thrill. *Another hundred thousand gallons of this, please. No ice.* His toes dove into the mud and spread, forking, drinking as they went.

After a long breath in and out, Alexander opened his eyes. Here's a pretty state of affairs. He struggled with the pleasure rising like floodwater in his body. Awkwardly he got to his feet, or his legs, or what his legs used to be—best not to look too closely—oh, lordy. What would Rae think?

Rae might come by for a visit tonight. I'll try, she had said. Joy burst out of its prison inside him and shook the world with music.

He stopped trying to think at all. When his eyes fell open again his legs had swollen so that his jeans were falling off his body, ripped apart at the seams. He pulled off his tee shirt and two flannel shirts and threw them in the corner with foot-long fingers. He knew an urge to tear the roof off the trailer with his bare hands. He refrained with an effort. Wait. *Wait.* Just *stop.* He flung his arms out until they touched the walls, then hugged himself as tightly as he could squeeze. His fingers shrank slowly. He rubbed them together, rubbed his torso all over. That's better. His eyes flicked around the room. Lamp, table, refrigerator. He panted, squinting hard at every homely object. Two thoughts would not go away.

What if he just gave in to it?

And: If only Rae would come.

That didn't help. Every time they occurred to him, these two thoughts stopped him, trapping him between two pleasures so intense that he forgot to breathe, one high and sweet, one low and hoarse, coaxing, insisting, drawing his mind away from business. He rubbed his arms and chest vigorously and came back to the fluorescent-lit room again.

How had he got here, he wondered, not fleeing or fighting, just waiting for this thing to overcome him? There was a reason that teased him just beyond the sound of that music, but he knew that once he gave in to the music he'd stop caring about reasons. Thinking was so hard. He had to breathe, he had to. When he did, he heard the music.

The harsh brassy note was retreating. Soon it would be almost gone, but not entirely, like a parade that swings away out of sight but never quite ends.

This is the sound of the sun, he realized. I can still hear it, even though it's all the way on the other side of the world.

And this note is the moon, pulling me out of myself, showing me the way into my full size. This was the one he could ride as he rode it last night, faster than the sun itself, looking down on seas and mountains and clouds. With a shudder, Alexander pulled away from that clear hollow sound, a sound like a single raindrop falling forever. The moon, he thought, throwing it back into the sky where it belonged and rubbing himself with both hands. It is *there*, and I am *here*. Now what?

Rae.

He had to get this Cracker out of the trailer. His business with Rae would not want witnesses. If he wanted to, if he tried, he could listen with his long roots and hear the river coming to him like a great honeymoon blanket to cover them up. If only Rae would come. He heard creatures fucking all around, as if to show this stupid fellow his business. They mated frantically outside the trailer, gnats above it, rabbits and mice beside it, worms below it, and the trees sucked up water all around, seeming to fill the air and the dirt with pleasurable groaning. Another five minutes passed. Alexander breathed and came back to his waking mind. He rubbed his arms and the small of his back.

The rain was making soup out of the ground outside the trailer, he realized. And he could feel the river rolling closer. There was not going to be a building in this place, not ever. In a few minutes, an hour at most, that river would be here. Alexander realized with surprise that he was calling to the river, gathering up the hem of its skirt and drawing it toward him. He had been calling it all night. And perhaps last night, too, and the night before. Soon he would be up to his chin in it—if not deeper. He wanted it and feared it.

He opened his eyes. His neck ached. His shoulders brushed the ceiling of the trailer, and his head bent down, showing him his swollen body and his legs running like brown and pink candle wax over the floor. His eyes had been closed for a long time, he realized. He had been thinking and seeing and hearing with—with those other parts of himself. He forced his eyes open in the harsh light in the office.

Cracker looked awful.

Alexander imagined that he could feel Rae, her heartbeat distinctive among the many gathered to share the night with him. Joy burst in his heart. He called to her. The sound rumbled in his chest and out along his roots. Something nearby answered.

Close. So close. *Oh, come to me.*

Chapter Forty-Eight

Under a hammering rain Walter Chepi drove his El Camino along US 31. This was probably not the best evening to come calling in the guise of land-grabber, but Mike Morse, his senior partner, was adamant: John Fowier had the right idea to woo the holdouts by the back door, and Walter was the man to pursue it.

Great, he thought, and switched his wipers and lights to high power. A bouquet of daffodils lay on the seat. He had considered a bottle of wine as well, but decided he didn't want to appear to come on too strong. The very thought of Gelia Somershoe's smile made him uncomfortable.

The windshield steamed up. He rolled the window down a crack, was instantly wetted, and rolled it up again.

A dog ran across the road. The truck in front of him swerved. Walter slowed. The truck righted its path and hit the gas, rear tires spinning and spitting spray onto his windshield.

"Crazy animal," he muttered. He peered to one side of the road, then the other. He was just about to speed up when the dog raced off the left shoulder and loped into his headlights.

He leaned on the horn. The dog was having the time of its life. It paced the car, bushy tail streaming out behind it, and yipped excitedly, every now and then lunging at the left front tire. "You crazy mutt!"

He played a tune on the horn, hit the brakes, skidded, bumped over something, heard a bang and a shriek. Oh, hell, he thought, I've hit it. The steering wheel dragged sharply to the left. The El Camino went into an extravagant skid.

The sky chose that moment to dump. For a timeless moment he gripped the wheel, staring at a white windshield studded with exploding waterstars while the car spun. He had no sensation of contact with the road. He kept the wheel absolutely straight. The left rear door smacked something good and hard, and his spin slowed. The car stopped. His heart started beating again. He had come out of the skid more or less straight on the road.

"Son of a gun," Walter muttered. The engine had conked out during the skid. He turned the ignition, got the El Camino started, put it in first gear, and inched it back into motion. Whew. At least it still drove.

His left front tire was gone. The site should be only an eighth of a mile ahead at this point. He tried to remember if there was a service station at the junction of US 31 and Route 64. He didn't fancy changing a tire in the rain.

The El Camino bumped forward lamely. This poor old car, he thought. Now there's something wrong with the right door. It sounded as if the chrome had come off and was slapping the side of the car. Every twenty or thirty feet something metal went pop! and the El Camino rocked a little. Maybe the trim was tangled up in the wheel. The rain increased violently.

Something swift darted into his headlights. He had just time to register relief that he hadn't hit the dog after all when this time he did hit it.

It was like running over a fire hydrant. The car lurched and jerked with a horrible clangorous ripping of metal. He could feel every foot of the El Camino's passage over the dog's body. Something cracked, something burst open with a hiss, something tore the muffler loose. The dog made hideous yi-yiing cries. Walter turned the key off and coasted bumpily to a stop.

He was not tempted to get out of the car to check the damage. Something was still making grinding noises in the bowels of the engine compartment. The windshield whitened with rain and his steamy breath. He sat there, sweating, listening to his car die, while rain came down like the end of the world.

Chapter Forty-Nine

King stood in the pouring rain talking to Gelia while Ernest and Ink towed the wagon to US 31. Willy had gone upriver looking for Davy, and King himself was behind times for searching. Nobody had tried yet to cross over to the far bank, to check Davy's favorite willow stand. Gelia was trying to talk him out of that.

"—And remember, if you don't find 'em on this side, never-you-mind about it because they'll be over t'other side and *that* won't flood tonight. River's coming *west*—y'hear?" The rain made Gelia's mascara run in black streaks down her cheeks.

"Gelia, that don't make sense. If it floods, it floods." King gnawed his lips. "Wish to hell I knew Cracker was safe."

Willy burst out of the weeds upriver. He gave the two of them a look and went on jogging past them to check the piece of riverbank that King was supposed to be checking.

King scowled. "Boy's like a sheep dog, and darned if I don't feel like a sheep," he muttered. "Wish I knew what the hell this was all about." Rain dripped off his cowlick into his eyes.

"Ernest and me will be at the Beard Hotel. Now get along. Don't dawdle," Gelia urged.

"Wish I knew where Mink and Davy is," King said, fretting.

Willy shouted from downriver. "I see him! He's in the willows! Oh, shit, King, we've got to get across right away!"

King loped to the water's edge. Willy half-knelt in the rowboat, gesturing with an oar. The boat wobbled crazily. He was frenzied with anguish. "Oh Davy, dammit, you crazy kid, oh dammit, oh *dammit*—"

"Calm down," King snapped. "Gelia, you got a flashlight in that mess?"

She was back with the flashlight before King had clambered into the rowboat. He looked up at her on the dissolving mud slope of the bank. "Keep an eye out for Cracker," he begged.

She was staring across the river, her eyes narrowed at the near-blackness of the willow sandbar. Davy was over there all right, waving something white.

"What? I'm coming, Davy!" King took the oars from Willy.

Gelia shook her head. "You take care of yourselves. That current's wicked tonight."

He hesitated.

Willy fidgeted on the edge of hysteria. "Let's go, let's go, let's go!"

King bent his back and got the boat moving. When they had pushed off, both brothers rowing furiously against an alarmingly strong current, Gelia hurried off after their caravan.

The Gowdy brothers wrestled their rowboat across the current. Rain strafed them southwest to northeast, plowing up little spurts on the troubled surface.

Tornado wind, King thought. He put his back into his stroke, and the boat skipped. The river had widened to almost half again its original size. Weirdly, it was as Gelia had said. The whole stream had shifted westward. The boat ran aground yards before the towhead where Davy usually moored. Willy leaped out and struggled across the exposed mucky river-bottom to the sandbar.

King dragged the rowboat to the towhead, sinking to his calves in silt, and tied off. "DAVY!?" he bellowed.

"Listen!" Willy yelled. King froze, perched on the towhead.

Not far away his brother's voice shrieked, "Willy! King!"

King pivoted slowly. His tennis shoes squeaked on the log. "DAVY!"

Something white flashed between the dark tree trunks. King scrambled down and dropped into the mud beside his brother.

They had to move carefully. The sandbar was coated with silt and the footing dropped off without warning from time to time, miring them in muddy shallows. Davy waved again. King saw him standing on a bit of high ground between a pair of box elders. There were two pale people with him.

Willy gasped. King splashed past him and stopped, gaping.

The storm lulled suddenly.

The woman standing next to his brother looked barely older than

King. "Mom," King said numbly. Her hair was black with rain. She wore Davy's tee shirt. She held a white bleach jug in one hand. Her other arm was around Davy. "Mom."

The man beside her, Davy's image, seemed younger still, bare-naked, his skin white and wet with rain. "I don't suppose," Carl said slowly, "you brought any extra pants with you?"

Behind King, Willy whooped and ran past him into their arms.

Davy watched, tall and proud. "I found 'em!"

King walked forward in a dream. "Mom," he said.

Gloria reached over Willy's shoulder and put out a hand. She said in a voice like running water, "I'm so glad you came." The hand touched him on the cheek.

King felt himself starting to crack. He turned from her to his father. "Why," he croaked.

His father met his eyes. "We've been trees for years, Son," he said solemnly.

King nodded. I've drowned, he thought, and this is my last dream. Well, I wanted to come home.

"Okay," he said numbly. It wasn't okay. He couldn't say so. Grievances clogged his throat. The miracle silenced him.

Davy pointed. "The boat's getting away!" He and Willy leaped after it.

Calmly King supervised the rescue of the rowboat, the boarding, the trimming of his mother's white bleach jug—where had she got that?—with a rusted half-bladed jackknife into a sort of bucket for bailing. Willy gave Carl his pants and got Davy into the boat. They sat, Willy shivering in his underwear, chattering and crying, Gloria with her arms around both boys.

King stretched his back over the oars and pulled for the near shore. It was the best position he could find, with his head turned to watch the shore—that way he didn't have to look at his parents, or the trailers on the west bank, or his brothers, who were loony with emotion. As long as he didn't see them, he didn't feel anything.

He could hear Willy talking in a giddy childlike voice with his mother. "Oh, Mom, I missed you! I missed you! Why did you stay away so long?"

"Well, we didn't mean to," Gloria said in that slow, unearthly way. "We got planted."

"Oh, Mom!" Willy cried again. The boat rocked, as if, behind King,

Willy had thrown his arms around her.

Davy shouted excitedly in King's ear, chanting out the progress of the river as it climbed the far bank and swamped the twins' house, then the smokehouse, then the Somershoe trailer. Then he shrieked, "They's burning, King! The trailers is burning!"

King heard Willy soothing his brother. "Somebody must have left a lamp on. It's okay, Davyboy. The river will put it out." The river would crush the trailers like Styrofoam cups, King thought, feeling terrible power in the current every time he dipped his oars. He couldn't spare it a thought.

Carl was silent. King resisted the urge to look back and make sure he was there. He pulled strongly on the oars. *This is the strangest feeling.* He couldn't bear it, yet he was feeling it anyway, as if his insides had done something odd, changed shape and color perhaps, and his head was slow to catch up. *I can't think of what to think.*

At that moment the boat struck a chunk of old concrete pier and cracked open. Carl took his wife by the shoulders and led her splashing through the last four feet of water to shore. Willy helped Davy disentangle himself from the seat board. It happened so quickly that King was left standing alone, up to his thighs in cold water, the oars in his hands, staring at how gently his father held his mother on the shore.

"I thought you killed her," he said.

Carl spoke low and slow. "Come out of the river."

King sloshed to shore. "How—" he said, his chest beginning to heave, the big sobs coming to the surface. He was shivering now. His mother came to him and put her arms around him. King shut his eyes. *No fair.* He had a right to be angry. *No fair. There's never any sense.* They led him up the bank. The cold sobs shook out of him like water off a shaking dog, on and on.

It was Davy who stuck out his thumb on the road and got them a ride into Rimville.

Chapter Fifty

The sky was dumping rain when Mr. Stass stopped running in the weeds outside an apartment complex south of the trailers. He bent over, sides aching, and grabbed for breath. Looking back, he found his view blocked by trees. Were the trailers burning? Two gallons of gas should have done it.

Well, he wouldn't go back. He'd had to wait nearly an hour for the residents to go away. Nobody'd told him they had a dog. His raincoat was torn and his arm ached where the beast had snatched at him. He would have shot it, only the damned gun was registered. He couldn't afford to have a witness, not even a dead dog with his bullet in it, right there on the property.

He stumbled out of the reeds into a parking lot. His rental car was parked back at a bar in Berne. To hell with that. He'd have to walk right past that dog again. He might go to the road, hitch a ride into town and get around the dog that way. The rain got colder with every gust. Icy water lashed him in the face.

A loud moan sounded directly over his head. He shied. The moan crescendoed, became a wail coming out of a big metal siren on top of a pole beside him. Fire department? He hoped he'd got 'em burning good. With a sigh he headed back toward the river. He could work his way farther north, away from the fire, maybe drop into a bar in Rimville until he dried off. The siren hooted for two solid minutes and then died miserably.

The rain was now coming almost horizontally, mixed with hail. Pellets of ice whacked his head and plonked on parked cars as he trudged across the lot. Behind him some deeper sounds rang like blows of steel pipe on pavement. He looked back. Under the light of cracked white light-globes, a gleaming doggy form loped toward him. He gasped, wheeled, and bolted north.

The parking lot gave out and he was up to his shoulders in cattails again. Someone behind him was beating on a car with a hammer, lots of hammers. Ahead, the cattails ended. He would be on smooth grass soon. Encouraged, he looked over his shoulder. Two beasts now followed him, one on the blacktop, one scampering over the hoods of parked cars.

He turned, hoping to get across the lawn before they should be through the cattails and able to see him again.

From where he ran he could see that he had two tennis courts and a picnic shelter to get past, then maybe a fence and then a factory building. The factory building appealed to him greatly. A yip behind him made him realize how exposed he was, and he quickly scrambled round a stand of shrubs, stumbled, sprawled. The grass was crisp with ice pellets that cut his palms. He was on his feet again in one jump. He ran.

He sprinted across two tennis courts, another strip of lawn, and a barbed-wire fence that tried to grab him. To his intense relief, there was a gravel alley on the other side of the fence.

He skirted the factory building. It was brick, with long casement windows looking out on the riverbank, and a railed wooden sidewalk. He stopped to try a window. The glass was reinforced with chicken wire, but he could see the latch was loose. As he tried to tear away the chicken wire, he heard a pattering of little hammers on the wooden sidewalk. The first dog came straight for him, bobbing its head and scrabbling its forepaws, so excited was it to reach him at last.

Well, I've got you, too, he thought, yanking his pistol out. Tail too long, he thought dreamily, as the beast leaped forward. He aimed, squeezed. Looks like a fox.

With a tremendous clang, the fox met the bullet and hurtled back against the sidewalk railing. It crashed through the railing and disappeared with a splash into the river.

Mr. Stass didn't wait. He pelted heavily past a footbridge, through the yards of two little warehouses. The railroad tracks closed with his path here. Twice he hopped through the rails and ties only to find them curving back into his path fifty yards on. He came to a street, crossed it, ducked around the back of a darkened supermarket along its bush-covered riverbank, clambered up a steep street, and found himself on the main drag of Rimville, panting, wavering between a little bar on his right and the welcoming terracotta front of the Beard Hotel across the street.

His heartbeat made an ungodly noise in his ears. Sounded just like someone pounding the concrete with a piece of pipe.

Pain lashed up his right leg. He snarled, whirling around. There was no way to tell if it was the same fox or a different one that danced around him, every footfall a blow of metal on stone. He took aim with his automatic, missed, aimed again and hit it squarely in the side. There was the same horrific clang. The beast tumbled over and over down the sloping street. Mr. Stass stood panting, holding his leg with his gun hand. Hot blood ran over his fingers. He watched the fox stop rolling, stand, shake itself, and come loping up the street again. Streetlight reflected off a tiny shiny spot on the fox's side.

He didn't know how long or far he ran. The foxes herded him away from the buildings, snapping with bear-trap jaws at his calves and ankles, keeping him running. The Beard Hotel's piazza overlooked the river. He crossed this, scrambled over the low wall at the other end of the piazza, and found a gravel parking lot. He ran through the parking lot with the river on his right and the foxes just off his flank in the road to his left.

To the right, the river boiled. Big tree limbs groped out of its folding currents and were sucked under again. Mr. Stass saw the earthworks of a railway trestle bridge looming up ahead. He started climbing.

It wasn't much of a bridge. He could run along one of two steel rails a couple of inches wide or take his chances on hitting the horizontal ladder of ties suspended sixty feet over the river. He looked down between his flashing white socks at black water moving toilsomely in whirlpools around the feet of the bridge. He slipped once. The gun fell from his hand. If he had waited to see it splash they would have had him.

Behind him, their feet pattering like the blows of ballpeen hammers on the rails, came the foxes.

Fifty yards later, on the other side of the river, he leaped over the rails and bowled head over heels down the north side of the railway embankment into a park.

He could see a riverboat thirty feet away, riding high over the submerged dock, bouncing against her moorings. His wind was gone. Fear and pain had stimulated him, briefly, to the terrible crossing on the open trestle, but now the last of his strength seeped out of him through the rip in his leg.

He had an inspiration. He staggered forward. When he came to the wooden dock he found it under two and a half feet of water. Only its guardrail showed. He splashed down the submerged dock to the rail, lost his footing, fell into the water, and was hurled immediately against the rail by a swift current. He didn't bother to try to find the walkway with his feet. He seized the rail and pulled himself hand over hand to the end of the dock. From there he could reach the stair rail that bridged the gap between dock and boat and, from there, the boat's low rampart.

He lay on the rampart, supported on his left side by the narrow shelf, half in and half out of the water. The water was shatteringly cold. The current pulled at his heavy clothes. An icy spot on his thigh told him where he was losing blood into the river. The foxes danced on the high ground above the water, yipping excitedly. He couldn't count on them falling, as he had, into water over their heads. Nightmarishly he wondered if they could swim, or even float. The foxes yipped on shore. The big, empty boat slewed and danced against the dock. Stalemate.

His hands were freezing into position where he gripped the rail. With an effort he clambered over the rail into the boat, broke a window in the door to the lower deck, and tumbled into the boat's parlor. The wind was working with the current to drag the riverboat over on her side. Inside the parlor he rolled on broken glass, feeling at the gash in his leg with cold, numb hands.

There was a jerk as the first forward mooring line pulled its cleat free of the rotting dock. Then the second cleat pulled out. The boat swung drunkenly until its port side was banging against the dock. The aft mooring lines stretched like taffy, rubbing back and forth against the gunwale.

Mr. Stass sat heavily. He lay down and laid his head on the floor. He could hear the wet rope rubbing on wood clear on the other side of the boat. The sound echoed deeply through the twin cavities of the riverboat's hull. It was like a bullfrog's voice, a remarkably peaceful sound. He closed his eyes. Warmth crept over him. He missed the snapping of the aft mooring lines. The boat drifted rapidly downstream, slowly righting herself, bumping shoulders with the trestle bridge abutments, shoving through the spiralling crowd of tree limbs in the whirlpools, and hanging up by her twin hulls on the brink of the dam.

From the Rainbow Ballroom at the Beard Hotel, the *Delta Queen* was clearly visible, a white building suddenly erected on the brink of the dam.

Gelia Somershoe pressed her nose to the window and framed her eyes with cupped hands to shut out the candlelight in the ballroom.

Driven from behind by ever-rising water, the riverboat tipped over slowly, slid forward on her hulls a few feet and hung up again on her wooden paddlewheel. Vane by vane the paddlewheel came apart. The last vane broke. The wheel gave. The *Queen* shot ahead, skidded over the dam, buried her nose in the roiling water below and backflopped. Glass and white banisters puffed away like crumbs.

Gelia thought perhaps the boat was too big a bite for the flood, but soon she realized the backflop had loosened all the *Queen*'s joints. The water hurried over the dam, gathered itself behind the old boat, and pushed. The *Queen* floated again. In a very few seconds she had drifted thirty yards downstream and broken into pieces against the Route 64 bridge.

Chapter Fifty-One

Mink circled the silver perimeter of the chain-link fence around the construction office trailer. There was no way she could squeeze her four-footed body under it. Something in there called to her. Mink had never taken orders from anyone in her whole life, but the silent voice from the trailer dragged her irresistibly forward. At the base of the fence she crouched, looked up, and whined. Seven feet is a long way to climb on paws. She backed up. Eyeing the fence a moment, she coiled herself. Then she sprang. Five feet up she hit the fence. Expertly she put her paws into its diamond-shaped gaps the way a cat or a child would, and climbed the rest of the way to the top. The fence had a nice broad pipe running long the top. She ran along the pipe, slipping in the rain and flattening her ears at thunder-cracks, until she was near a stack of lumber on the inside of the fence. From the fence she dropped to the lumber, then to the ground inside.

The screen door would be a bit more of a problem. She was very reluctant to leave the shelter of her new coat. Well, it would have to be done. Her nose couldn't tell her what was going on inside. Alexander, whiskey, beer, that was all right, but Cracker was in there, too, and something gamey. Who had called her? She snapped her jaws in frustration. Her paws dug into the mud. Slowly, with creeping horror at the itch buried half an inch under her skin, she wriggled inside out. Naked now and shivering in the rain, she ran to the screen door of the trailer and yanked at the handle.

It was locked.

Wailing, Mink hammered on the aluminum door. It was no good. She had to get inside, she *had* to. Snivelling, she circled the trailer until she found a long two-by-four. With this she pried the screen door open, then screamed with frustration again when she realized the inner door of the trailer was locked, too. She backed up and pelted forward, slipping in the muddy approach to the trailer, ramming the lock with the two-by-four. The impact knocked the two-by-four from her hands and sent her sliding across the gravelly mud.

A third blow sent the knob and lock shooting out of the door into the room inside. Mink climbed the wooden steps painfully and, putting her small hand through the doorknob hole, felt for the latch. Click. She let herself into the warmth and fluorescent glare of the office trailer.

The first thing she smelled was Cracker. Then she saw him. Asprawl across the chair nearest the door, he smelled feral and sour. She laid a hand on his shoulder. His skin was paper-dry, hard, pebbly, and slick. Dark blotches like shadows lay across his shoulder.

He still wore his overalls, lying draped over the canvas chair. His head dangled oddly over one shoulder. One leg of the overalls flopped empty, and a wad of folded papers lay fallen on the floor. She crouched beside the chair. Cracker's face was no longer human. Drunken snores wheezed out of the hard slit nostrils. Spittle collected on the tips of the fangs and dripped, smelling sourly of beer and whiskey, to the floor.

She stood up, heart thumping, and pressed one hand against her mouth. Her eye fell on the papers on the floor and she took them up, feeling them and sniffing them. Two days ago she would have stepped right over stray papers, never even have touched them. The world had changed, or she had.

A warm hand curled round her naked ankle. She started and looked up. The papers fell to the floor again.

Alexander was naked to the waist, bound to the floor by all his toes. His jeans hung in shreds around his waist. His body went up and up. He crouched, his neck bent against the ceiling. The room was littered with his roots.

He said in that unrefusable voice, "Hello."

To Alexander, Mink was a green flame full of curling, convulsing threads of light. He gathered his attention from all its many points and focused on her. "What's the matter?"

She just stared at him, her eyes getting bigger and bigger. One root had already curled around her ankle.

He pointed at it. "Better move. I can't watch all of it at once." Even as he spoke the root took another turn around her ankle and then inched slowly higher, tightening as it swelled.

She leaped away, hopping on one foot as she disentangled herself. "Are you going to be like that now?"

"Like what?" He cleared his throat. "I am going to be—like what?"

"The other one. Before they cut it down."

A long time ago in another life, Alexander had watched a big tree come down, not far from here. His whole body cringed along its length, the roots retracting, his belly going cold.

The child crept closer. She shivered. To Alexander's strange new eyes there was something wrong with the crackling lines of light in her flame. Inside her small body the green fire jumped and crackled and shorted out against her skin.

Mink knew that she was at last in the center of the place she had been looking for. She knew what was supposed to happen now. She was supposed to climb up in the tree and disappear for a while, the way Rae used to do.

The idea terrified her. She felt she was already vanishing, losing her shape, being eaten from the inside out.

She shrank from coming any closer to Alexander.

Her gaze traveled up his body, up and up to the ceiling where his neck and shoulders brushed the top, bent over. His dreads hung over his face like black roots, half-hiding it. His real roots cascaded away to the walls.

She pranced on tingly feet. It felt like standing in front of the power plant at the Berne dam. *I don't want to be here!*

Alexander was having trouble focusing on her. The colored flame drew him, as Rae might draw him. She was cracked inside, or disconnected, or something. He could mend that, perhaps—

Mink saw him reach for her. She skipped frantically out of range. This put Cracker between her and the door. Everywhere underfoot she tripped over yards of Alexander spilling across the room. His roots were beginning to climb the walls.

She tingled worse than ever. Her eyes rolled back in her head and she let out a long, wailing scream of fright and rage.

Alexander seized control himself with a huge effort. He wrapped his arms around himself and squeezed.

"Okay. Okay." Oh God, he had almost grabbed that little kid. He groaned. Where was Rae?

Outside somewhere. He could almost feel her. She was thinking of him. Not far. She was quite close, he could feel it in the ground. *Oh, please, Rae, come to me.*

The little girl clawed at her skin. "Can't you help me?" she shrieked.

"What happened to you, child?"

She snivelled and wiped her eyes one at a time, watching him. "You know."

"Talk. Tell me," he begged. "Talk to me."

"When I was down in the fish hole."

It was increasingly hard for Alexander to think about the past. Down in the fish hole. He remembered suddenly with extreme vividness putting his arm into a warm wet hole in the ground, and the sounds that pulled his head in after it. He could hear those sounds now, even louder. They had got into his bones this time. The sound of the music breathed when he breathed, the hoarse gold note roaring in, the cool silver note sighing out. In a panic he opened his eyes.

"I remember." He looked at her now with pity. "You are just a baby. You had better go away, little baby. I'm not safe now. And find Rae." *Yes.* The music in his bones grew louder, drowning the sound of his voice in his ears. He gathered desire into a command and flung it at her. "Find Rae. I need Rae!"

Her flame wavered and darkened as if he had blown on it. Where did she go? He narrowed his eyes: There—she was cowering against the back wall.

"Wait!" he cried. "I'm sorry—wait." He reached down to the floor, scrabbling at Cracker's insurance papers among his rustling roots. "Don't forget this. Take it to Rae. Tell her to come. Please."

He couldn't stop himself from commanding it. "Bring her."

Mink didn't want to come closer, but her feet moved. She reached for the papers. A gust of wind outside whacked the screen door against the wall.

She leaped, snatched the papers, and fled toward the door.

Alexander's eye fell on Cracker. *Rae is coming.* For a horrid moment even Cracker looked desirable to him, gray, deformed, and shrunken, bristly, slobbering, and passed out cold.

"Wait-wait! Take your kinsman out! Oh God, never mind, there is no time!" He wrung his hands.

Mink stood in the doorway, chewing her lower lip. "The river's coming. He'll drown."

"Go on, go, go, take the head of him, and I will push. I won't touch you. Just outside the door."

Cracker was an awkward load. Mink hated to touch him. There was little remaining of his arms, just a knobby place where his shoulders sloped down to join his body. The inside of his open mouth was white and soft, like a blister. She took him by his tail and hauled at him uselessly. She was too small. His head flopped wildly on his stretched neck.

With impossibly long arms, Alexander reached out and boosted Cracker off the canvas chair. Together they shifted Cracker out the door. The heavy, stinking body rolled down the steps and splashed onto the muddy ground.

Mink felt hardly any safer outside. Alexander's roots, she saw, were forcing their way between the wall and the floor of the trailer, oozing out and down over the cinder blocks.

"Don't forget the papers!" The folded papers sailed out the door. Mink snatched them up again, even as she ran for the lumber pallet. Behind her, the aluminum screen door swung on one hinge and banged back and forth in the wind.

It was colder outside now. Gratefully she resumed her fox's coat. She bounced four-pawed up the stack of lumber with the papers in her teeth, balanced for a teetery moment on top of the fence, and then she was down in the mud again, running slip-slop across a sea of mud and submerged concrete forms toward the sound of foxes crying.

Chapter Fifty-Two

Walter knew he was going to have to hoof it. He peered through his steamy windshield. The riverbank encampment was within sight now. Through the fringe of new-leafed trees around them, he saw golden lamplight in their windows. It wasn't even as if they had a garage. He had picked up the daffodils off the passenger seat before he remembered that the Somershoes also had no phone. He *had* to get a tow truck out here. His dead car was stuck in the middle of the road.

Then he remembered the construction trailer and Bob Bagoff's night watchman.

I'll just make a quick stop across the road. The watchman would let him call Triple-A. Gritting his teeth and ducking uselessly in the downpour, he dove out of the wrecked El Camino into the rain and splashed across the shoulder toward the construction office trailer. Within seconds, every stitch he wore was drenched. Maybe the tow truck operator would drive him across the road, too, he thought cravenly, as cold water pelted him in the face and cascaded down the back of his neck.

He grinned at himself suddenly, realizing the futility of knocking on the Somershoe trailer door in his good suit, with a bunch of daffodils in his hand, dripping wet, looking just like John Fowier this afternoon. He laughed out loud. But no, imagine the look on the night watchman's face!

The grin was wiped from his face when he realized that that silvery wall ahead was not rain, as his fancy had supposed, but a chain-link fence. Behind him, a dog snarled. He slipped, flailing, and almost fell in the mud.

The dog darted forward and nipped him sharply on the calf.

Walter yelped. "Hey!"

They faced off, dog and man, and he saw through the downpour that it wasn't the least intimidated by him. It wasn't even a very big dog. It crouched squarely between him and the fenced-off construction trailer and snarled, biting the air as if chewing on its anger. Walter looked around at the ground, hoping for a piece of two-by-four or pipe.

Then he looked behind the dog. "Oh shit," he said quietly. There were several dogs there, all ranged behind the one that had bit him, blocking his path to the office trailer. One of them had something white in its mouth. He squinted. Just like a dog carrying in the paper for Dad. The paper-carrier's lips curled over white teeth sunk in the white paper.

Get smart, he thought, and finally ran for it.

They herded him across the site in the battering rain. He dodged brick and lumber stacks and danced over rows of concrete forms, his shoes picking up more and more mud as he ran, weighting them night-marishly. The puddles were getting deeper. Did it seem that the dogs avoided the puddles? He didn't like the water much himself. Every time he splashed into a puddle, the mud slipped from his shoes and he felt winged for a moment, his heels kicking high, as if he splashed like a lit-tle kid for the hell of it. Then by the time he was out of the puddle, fresh mud would be grabbing him by the feet, climbing his ankles, dragging at his legs.

Once in a while one dog would start yiping and then they would all yipe. Like mating cats, Walter thought feverishly. You can't tell if they're laughing or crying. I'm getting giddy. His hands and face felt burning hot. Oh, brother.

They wouldn't let him get to the road. They didn't want him near the construction office, safe behind its fence. Maybe if he climbed a tree? He swerved again and headed upward, up the steep face of the ridge, scram-bling with hands and feet against weeds and stones and thorny raspberry canes, until he fetched up, winded, clutching a tree trunk.

The rain seemed lighter in amongst the trees on the ridge. He peered down the slope. The lights from 31 and from the site's temporary pole illuminated the street side of the construction office, leaving the ridge in deep shadow. A flash of lightning broke, and he saw four innocent-look-ing little dogs huddled only twenty feet below him on the slope, staring upward expectantly.

In the afterclap of the lightning he blinked hard, trying to keep a fix on them. The newspaper-toting dog disappeared just as another trotted up to join the group below.

Walter knew he had no more run left in him. He wrapped his arms around the leaning tree trunk and shinnied up it a few feet. This hurt worse than the raspberry canes. Groaning aloud, he shinnied up another foot. His inner thighs ached.

He thought he heard voices down on the site. He cleared his throat to shout.

There was a scuffle below. All the dogs turned and splashed away. Walter loosed his grip on his tree and slipped back to the ground, falling heavily on his tailbone to keep from tumbling headfirst down the steep slope. Through a gap in the underbrush he could just see the dogs loping away.

Rae followed the strange bitey dog out of the weeds and onto US 31, looking over her shoulder. Behind them, the river crept over the ground where she lived, then touched the edge of the railroad track. In the weak streetlight, in the rain, she saw now the long brush and sharply pointed face of her guide. Goosebumps rose on her arms and back. Fox. Cold, hard, bitey fox. Good lord, that's one of the foxes off the 64 bridge, she thought.

She followed the bridge fox across the road. Her feet touched the mud of the ruined meadow and she felt a thrumming, like a power line or a big truck nearby.

She crouched and touched the packed mud. It tingled under her fingers. She pushed, turning her wrist slightly, and the mud drew her arm in, clear up to the elbow. Erny's ley lines must be doing a dance number under here.

"C'mon, boy, what's the deal?" She hunkered down on her haunches. "Why you runnin' around when you're s'posed to be sittin' on the bridge, hmm? What was so all-fired important I had to come here?"

Alexander's over there. Her heart leaped, and she forgot about Mink, about the flood on her heels, the certain loss of her home. Alexander was sleeping not fifty yards away. Hope blazed up in her. She stood.

The fox feinted at her. "Darnit!"

Rain hammered down, the flow slacking off and renewing, pocking puddles around her ankles and beating a slurry of mud and sandy clay into her face and dress. Lightning sizzled, thunder cracked. When the lightning touched down, she felt a streak of heat shoot up between her legs, a glad welcoming.

The beast turned its glistening head. Its ears swiveled like the ears of a real fox. Something moved behind it. Rae noticed another fox standing stock-still, watching her. Its eyes were rusty-dull in the rain. And there, lying almost invisible in the mud, a third fox beside it. And a fourth with one broken ear, the break glittering like steel.

Across the soupy mud, another fox was splashing toward them. It had something in its mouth. It threw itself into the mud and writhed, its sopping wet brush flicking water from each hair. That one's a real fox, Rae thought with surprise.

In that moment its color turned a patchy gray and white. Its paws splayed out long-fingered, and it rubbed itself all over.

Not a fox at all. Mink, naked and mud-smeared, stood up and looked her in the eye, looking wilder and more critterish than Rae had ever seen her. Holy Moses. Look at the kid, Rae thought. No wonder Erny was worried about her.

Rae squatted and put her arms out. The child stepped forward cautiously. "Mink, honey, what's up?" she said.

Mink backed away. "Come on!" The foxes scattered and vanished, as if the sound of her voice had frightened them.

Rae held still. "Ernest tells me you're having a bad time."

"Come on!" The child pranced in the mud anxiously. Rae looked up at the ridge, then over her shoulder at the river. US 31 had disappeared underwater. The silvery flood crept toward them while she watched.

"I'm not moving til you talk to me," Rae said. "What's been happening to you?"

"Rae!" Mink cried exasperatedly.

"Ernest says you fell in that hole full of fish. How did you get in?"

Mink shivered, jerked her shoulders, rubbed herself between the legs, scratched her head. "We pulled them out. And then that man came and I fell in and then he got me out and he was growing and I felt itchy so I couldn't even stand it," she recited. Her body twitched from one end to another.

"I can't stay here," Mink whined, like a normal child. She raised her voice. "You're slow! Don't just stand there! Come on." When Rae only stood and looked at her, Mink threw an arm out to the advancing river. "Hurry!"

With pity, Rae watched Mink rubbing herself. The child was full of all that electric. Rae could see it wasn't working properly. Why not?

There. The gap she had found in John Fowier was here in Mink, too. Lots of gaps. Oh lordy. The poor kid wasn't wired together enough to handle all that electric.

Thunder rumbled overhead and the rain lashed hissing down on the puddles at their feet.

Rae murmured, "I remember how that feels."

She remembered all right. Everything had got too big and too close, as if every tree and stone and blade of grass had a voice and they were talking to her all at once. All her unfinished parts had straightened out at once. And then somehow they had got connected, by force.

By force. Rae shivered. She'd been fourteen when she crossed the road and found out who it was that brought out so much power in her mother.

Mink writhed miserably before her in the mud.

For the first time in her life, Rae felt really angry at her dead lover. He'd forced his way into her mind and body both, until all the connections ran like lightning through her. Didn't he know when a kid was too little? What happened to the mind that went with the power? Was it just a brainless force now, gobbling up kids and iron foxes and things, making a mess?

A clonk came from the direction of the advancing flood. Rae looked up to see the construction site's dumpster heel over slowly like a swamped rowboat and drift twenty yards. A moment later it sank in the advancing current. The river got closer every minute. She realized bleakly that their trailers were gone for sure now.

She bent to look the girl in the eye. "Mink, I've got to go to Alexander now. You go to the Beard Hotel. Wait with Erny and Gelia and your brother, hear?"

Mink didn't answer. She gave Rae a look.

Rae said more urgently, "I'll be there tomorrow, or maybe later tonight, I dunno." She struck quick, grabbing for the kid's wrist, but Mink danced out of her reach. "Just—just go to the hotel and wait, okay?"

Mink had known all along Rae would be no help. Rae *liked* feeling like this. She would go into the trailer and *like* disappearing into Alexander. A wave of despair flooded her. Ink was too young, Erny was too old, and Rae was just as bad as Gelia. Mink would just have to find the way herself.

Rae watched Mink heave a sigh so adult, so full of sorrow and disap-

260

pointment, that her heart squeezed. The kid picked up the envelope she'd been carrying, soggy and nearly black with mud.

"*He* says this is for you."

"Bring it to Gelia at the hotel upriver," Rae suggested. She saw refusal in the little face. She'd never tried hard enough to get through to the twins. Well, they were paying for it now. *Kids always pay for adult mistakes.* Full of guilt, she looked down at the child.

Mink looked back stoically.

Rae wanted to stick her arm down into the mud and send a blast of anger at somebody dead and gone, who didn't know when a kid was just too damn little.

Alexander wouldn't do a thing like that.

Coming out of his clothes. It came back to her again, what was happening in the construction office trailer.

"*He* says come *on!*" Mink urged.

Rae began to move blindly toward the fenced-off trailer.

Mink wheeled. *Come on,* she cried silently to the iron foxes in the shadows around her. *You gots to be my brothers now.* She took to her heels. On an afterthought she turned, loped back, snatched up the dirty envelope, and loped away again.

Chapter Fifty-Three

John Fowier crouched knee-deep in the river, watching Suzy dance. Rain came down in fistfuls as if the sky aimed for him personally, but if any of it was hitting Suzy she didn't seem to notice. The startling white curve of her backbone, the only unblackened part of her, came and went among the trees.

She cupped her mouth, dancing, leading with her pelvis. John couldn't hear her voice at first. Then she took her hands away from her mouth, and her singing came: shrill fluid wordless notes that shook him to the soles of his feet.

Her nude, mud-blackened body swayed. She limboed toward each tree, rubbing the insides of her thighs against it. She squatted lewdly and tossed her head from side to side, the hair whipping around her face, as if to toss her head off her shoulders. Her breasts flopped back and forth in time with her belly. Her voice rose. Her arms opened to the dark woods.

John hurried through the rising water, his pajamas clammy and hot against his skin. He would take her now. He felt strong enough to tackle anything. His bones burned.

She bent and embraced a tree. Her legs wrapped around it. She squeezed the tree obscenely between her thighs, pressing her innermost body to the bark. When she turned her face to the side, John saw by her expression what she was doing. Holy cow!

Just as he came up on the grove, she stopped dancing and threw herself down in a mud puddle. She rolled in the mud. She splashed mud around. She rubbed the mud between her legs and cried out. John was reminded suddenly of that crazy bitch in the outhouse yesterday. The thought made him light-headed. His hard-on swelled until it hurt.

Just as suddenly, the sickening smell of the mud hit him. It was everywhere: mud on him, on his pajamas, all over the ground, all over Suzy, mixing with her hot woman smell.

Just like that crazy bitch in the hole.

Uh-uh. No way. I can save myself a lot of hassle right now. He turned away and dove into the shelter of the water.

Then he knew he was asleep and dreaming, because he was swimming strongly against the current on the bottom of the river, surrounded by miraculous gray light. His groin ached stronger than ever. He felt a pang of sorrow. He wouldn't have missed Suzy's dance for anything, but if he was dreaming, it was over. New tastes, smells, and the most compelling horniness he had ever felt in his life swept the old dream downriver.

Ahead, something flashed over the sand. He wriggled and effortlessly overtook it: a catfish with drooping mustachios and a wide, wide sensuous mouth. He covered her, ignoring the current, and they spawned wildly, now swimming hard, now drifting with the current in the grip of cold passion, until they fetched up in an eddy under a bridge. There he joined her in the most trusting, guiltless, single-minded sexual act he'd ever known.

They weren't the only fish to think of this nook. His fat gray body was spent, but the water vibrated to the mating frenzy of a half-dozen other couples. John remembered that he was only dreaming. He laughed out loud.

In a flash he abandoned his body and took possession of the big gray male beside him, one long urgent muscle from whiskers to tail. The female churned the sand under him. He quickly came to his moment of truth and, before the last echoes of pleasure faded, leaped into the next fish. This time he stayed only until the explosion itself, and then, easily locating his nearest host by zeroing in on the exact note of its desire, rode its mounting hunger just to the edge of climax. There was a long time like this, and, dreamerlike, he seemed to follow with shut eyes from fish to fish, following the unmistakable sound or fibrillation of blind pleasure. Finally he thought of it as joy.

He came to himself some time later and noticed that he was above the surface, mounted on the back of a frog. They sat on a rubber tire rocking in fast water. While he probed her, the night sky whirled around and around above them. It seemed for a moment he would wake up. The tire revolved ceaselessly in the water. Rocking up and down on his partner while the riverbanks flashed by, he felt motion-sick. One moment he was a frog and the night was a pleasant blur. The next moment John Fowier was madly treading water, wondering how the hell to get out of here.

All in all it seemed a good idea to keep on dreaming that he was a frog, and he did. His lover tired and hopped out from under him. He knew there weren't any more frogs around. But somewhere on the bank something was mating; something shivered and burned with desire. He shot out of the frog, a spark in the rain, and homed in on that aching hungry vibration.

A turtle climbed his mistress's back, stubby legs clumsy as a two-year-old in a snowsuit. After the easy pairings of fish, this was slow torture. She was the wrong shape, or he was—his legs were short, his belly was armored and inflexible. He scrabbled against her shell, craning his neck at the clouds, frustration battling with a horror of rolling onto his back. With infinite labor he found her niche and drove home. Good God, he thought, when release had come and gone, there must be hundreds of these things here. I don't want to work this hard.

Too late. He helped twenty-one pairs of turtles fulfill themselves. With relief he plunged under the water, feeling spent to his soul, but the river creatures weren't done. Their horniness sucked him in. No sooner was one crayfish or mudpuppy delivered than he felt the high-pitched desire of crickets on the bank. When he realized that the singing of his nerves was the echo of mosquitos in lust, he panicked.

He woke up.

He still wore his satin pajamas. It was almost midnight. He was twenty feet under the surface of the river. After a brief struggle, he drowned.

Chapter Fifty-Four

Other half-dressed people crowded the Beard Hotel ballroom when King and his family draggled in. Someone found clothes for the Gowdys and put mugs of hot coffee into their hands. King caught sight of Gelia having a gay old time. Even Ernest Brown wore his usual calm self-possession, sipping coffee and answering questions. The mothers in the room made much of Ink, petting him and marveling at his blondness until he fled behind Erny's pants leg. King knew how the kid felt.

King's parents stood stillest of all. He could barely stand to look at them for more than a few seconds.

Every time he did, he was surprised by something else. They were young, he realized, just kids when they had had all those kids. And not a minute older now. King had whupped older and bigger men than Carl, in the army. Carl was now recognizable as a type King knew well, kind of weak, mostly drunk, meaning well but not having much luck with the machinery of life—a version of Cracker, he thought, only not lucky enough to run when the first gal got hold of him, and then he was tied down with kids. Just a punk. *This is so weird.*

Erny stood talking to them while King hung back. Carl didn't say much—how odd that was, how odd for him, old motor-mouth.

Every now and then Gloria said, "We were trees for years and years," in a vague, pot-head kind of voice.

Erny was saying, "But why didn't you *stay* that way?" to his mother, as if she had made a lick of sense. "There would've been no need to bring in that poor young fellow from the construction company at all."

"They was those two willows over there," Davy volunteered. "On the sandbar."

His mother petted Davy and Willy on the head, looking at them and around her like she was from another planet. Davy grinned like a cat, and Willy just closed his eyes and snuggled up to her. King felt intensely jealous. How could his brothers just *take* that crazy shit? Didn't they remember? Didn't they want some goddamned answers?

Carl said, "That's right. All the way across the river. We could feel it coming on," he said slowly, as if each phrase were hauled up from the bottom of a cistern in a bucket, "in the daytime. River coming closer." His eyes wandered off to some blissful thought. "And then at night it went away." He stopped. He seemed to have decided the conversation was finished.

Erny looked thoughtful. "The ley lines kept moving. You pulled them to one bank and that other young fellow pulled them to the other, but only while he slept there. Was that it?"

Carl just stood there kind of smiling.

It got to King. He felt desperately hungry for Raedawn's streak of reasonableness. He had begun to grasp that there just weren't going be any real explanations. They were just going to go on living as if nothing had happened, not because it *was* nothing, but because they didn't have any words for it. They were helpless in the face of their own ignorance, and they would stay that way, content with it.

The realization nauseated him. I thought I was through with all this. I just won't stand for it. He forced his way through a crowd that had somehow placed itself between him and his parents. Up close, Carl was even smaller. King shoved himself into his father's young face.

"Why did you do it?" he demanded.

"Do what, King?" Carl just stood there, incredibly solid and real and *different.* This wasn't the punk who had beat his wife and kids, got jailed for fighting, and drunk himself out of his worries. The inside and the outside of him didn't match. King looked Carl up and down frantically.

While he watched, Carl pulled himself together, as if noticing for the first time that his son stood there wanting something. It took a long time. King thought suddenly about trees pulling their leaves around to face the sunshine. When he had his father's full attention, King blinked.

Carl said slowly, "Well, we had to. We were told."

King covered his face with his hands. He would throw up. He would just go puke his guts out and get rid of this stuff, people making him feel things by saying just anything, lying and being pot-head goofy, like they could just say anything and those ten years wouldn't ever have happened. Rage tightened his stomach and his throat at the same time. He forced down bile.

He said, "Well, what about me? What about us kids?" His voice rose. "That son of a *bitch* Cracker drank all day and fucked around all night, we never had any *food* in the house! Those *babies* were on their *own!* Me and Willy and Davy were on our *own!"*

His mother looked distressed. "Oh, Son," she said in that same sappy, empty-headed voice. Her arms were still wrapped around Willy and Davy. "I'm sorry. We don't remember the past all that well. We were always watching," she offered, as if that made a bit of difference.

"It doesn't matter," Carl said. He was turning vague again, like he'd forgotten King already.

"It goddamned well *does* matter!" King bellowed. Some of the rich folks from up the hill turned their backs and sidled away, like they weren't really listening, but his old high school friends hung around. The snoops. Goddamn them, too.

He caught Willy's eye where he nestled in Gloria's arms. Willy sent him a quiet, sarcastic look. King felt shamed by that look. Hadn't he abandoned Willy, just like these two punks had? Davy was behind their mother, clutching her borrowed dress and burying his face against her. Hiding while the grown-ups fight. King had another flash of himself at Ink's age, hiding behind his mother when the yelling started. "Nothing changes, does it?" he said bitterly.

Carl looked at him. "I think we've changed." His voice seemed to come from deeper inside than King remembered.

It's true, King thought. He could barely stand to meet his father's eyes, remembering how much he hated him and seeing a stranger in the same man. Carl looked steadily back at him. Somebody in there knew King and was seeing him for the first time in years, looking at him the way Gelia and Erny had looked at him four days ago. The unfairness of it made him want to cry.

"But where *were* you?" he choked out.

"We were trees."

Enough of that shit.

King turned away. "Yeah, I heard you." He scanned the room, searching for Rae. *Please, somebody, anybody, talk sense to me.* He plunged off into the crowd without looking back. If he didn't find her between here and the bar, he'd go have a drink. The whole thing made him want to puke and scream until his throat bled.

He found the bar, which was jammed full. King elbowed his way to the counter and ordered beer. Why, he thought, why do they have to be weird on top of all this? It's bad enough they got so much to apologize for and they're not even gonna think about it. And then this *bullshit*. He downed his beer in two gulps and asked for a whiskey. The bartender's back was turned. King glared into the mirror and saw Willy squeeze up behind him, then next to him.

The beer settled his nerve, some. Okay, Willy now. What have we here? King's head was going round and round with seeing everything new, everybody different. His own eyes looked mean and narrow glaring into the mirror at his brother.

Willy stood quietly at his elbow, waiting to be noticed. King flinched from the naked boyishness in that face. There were hollows under Willy's eyes where riverbank life and, according to Cracker, liquor had made marks. It didn't seem right that Willy should be standing here with the grown men looking to drunk themselves up. He turned and took Willy by the arm.

"Come on. You're underage."

Willy stood, not resisting but not moving. King noticed how solid he'd gotten. Soccer team, Rae had said. Strong kid.

Willy caught his eye. King let go of him.

"Welcome home," Willy said.

It figured, Willy thought, that King's first real talk with him in five years would be a scolding.

King wasn't bad. He was just stuck in his own head all the time. Willy dove for an empty booth in the back of the bar and sat. The look on King's face was worth it, when he turned around with two whiskeys in his hands. King stared around the room, closed his eyes helplessly, then looked again. Willy couldn't remember the last time someone in his family had been anxious enough to look for him. He waved. King spotted him and came over.

"Hey," King said huskily. He sat, putting a glass in front of Willy.

"Hey yourself." Willy accepted the whiskey and sipped it. *Okay, so I'm a grown-up. Now what?* King looked really terrible. Big and strong and just beat to hell. Willy wondered if he would look like that someday. Probably not. King had Cracker's size and Gloria's yellow Coombs hair. Willy was all Gowdy, short, stocky, and black-headed. A kid brother for life. Willy made a face. King didn't say anything.

The ball was in Willy's court. "This is kind of weird for you, isn't it?" he offered.

King stared at him. "Isn't it? For you?"

Willy sipped his whiskey. "Not really." Studying his brother, he thought that King maybe had never known how weird it was to live here. Except the way any boy would, trying to go to school with the regular people up the hill and act normal. King's tolerance was lower, that was all. Willy remembered crazy nights trying to do his homework while washing out his underwear in the kitchen sink, while Cracker had a screaming fight in the next room with some girl or other, while Davy fed the twins whatever came into his head—peanut butter milkshakes sweetened with Coke, they used to like that.

King had never crossed the road. Come to think of it, he hadn't liked it much when Rae did. Throw in a couple of parents turned into trees—sure, King would fail to cope.

So that's where those two willows had come from. Willy remembered his last day with Eugene in that willow-tree nest and blushed all over. His mom and dad were right there all along. Probably got a good earful. He shrugged. At least there wouldn't be much explaining to do. His mom just seemed glad to see him. His dad just stood around and stared at everything. "I guess it is kind of weird," he conceded.

King was glowering across the room. "Well, I don't aim to stay long. I got a job offer in the North Sea. S'pose Cracker told you that."

Willy cleared his throat. "King, it's okay for you to go." It wasn't okay, but what could he do? King didn't fit in. He'd just be miserable.

King grunted. "Chasin' me out?"

Willy put his hand out. "No, no. I'm not. It would be—" He bit his tongue on a plea to King to stay. "It's just—well, it's easy for you to go. You're grown up now. You're—well—"

"I ain't as grown up as you think," King said.

"Well, a lot more than I am, anyway. I'm only sixteen. I *need* our folks." He hoped King would forgive him for that.

King jerked a thumb at the door to the ballroom. "Think those two's going to be any use to you?" he said harshly. "Hell, they were practically useless before—" He paused. "Before. Don't know what's got into 'em." He sounded a little awed.

"I don't know, King. I think they're settled down. They seem a lot more, more *steady*, don't they? Dad especially."

King said nothing. He stared into the middle distance, his lips twitching. "Well, they seem like goddamned space cadets to me. Or pot-heads or something." He tossed his whiskey down his throat. "*'We don't think about the past, King,'*" he mimicked. "God*dammit* that pisses me off. Where am I supposed to put these last ten years? Just stick 'em away in a sock? Changing diapers and ducking Cracker's temper and runnin' up and down river after Davy whenever he got scared of the shouting and took off?"

"I've been there," Willy said.

King met his eye. The steam went out of him. He looked down. "Yeah. I'm sorry about that." He fiddled with his glass for a long minute. "You ought to think about being a better student," he said, studying the shot glass. "'Specially in high school. Makes a difference when you get out.'"

"Even in the army?" Willy hadn't given much thought to the future. The past was too full of grief, and the present was full of these new parents, like the old ones but better maybe. Better so far. Please let them be better parents, he prayed. He couldn't think further ahead than going back to the ballroom to be held by his mother again. He fidgeted in his seat.

"Hell, yes," King said. "I'd of made corporal if I'd had better grades." He met Willy's skeptical look with a shamefaced grin. "Or maybe did less fighting." He glanced at Willy's glass, then his own. "You want another?" Something flickered in his eyes, as if he would take it back if he could.

"You know, I'd like to go out and be with Mom and Dad for a little while."

King's face darkened. "You do that."

"C'mon, King, they're my folks, too," Willy pleaded. "How—" He stopped. *How would you feel if you weren't afraid to feel?* But they'd already agreed, in King's abrupt Crackerish fashion, not to needle King for abandoning them. "How about you take a look around and see if Mink has turned up?"

King sighed a long sigh. "I guess. I got a bad need to see Raedawn."

CR

When King emerged from the bar he found Gelia first, standing by the long curve of French windows that let onto the hotel's riverside piazza. She was staring out at the night with her hands cupped against the glass while some guy was asking her about Cracker.

"Ain't seen him, Henry. Swept away, I guess," she said cheerfully, her breath making fog against the glass.

King came up behind Gelia and put his hands on her shoulders. "Boo."

She jumped. "Land! Oh, it's you, King." She slipped an arm around him and gave him a hug.

King returned it with interest. After an evening with his parents and young Willy, he felt positively like cuddling Gelia, who never changed. "'Tcha looking at?"

"*Delta Queen* just went over the dam," she said. "Oh good heavens!" She was looking past him out the French window.

"What?"

Gelia already had the latch open. Cold rain whirled in. "Get in here, child, you're stark naked and freezin'!"

A white form started back from the window. King recognized Mink. She flung something that smacked wetly into Gelia's dress and bolted.

Ink shrieked. Ernest seized and held him.

Gelia shouted, "Glory! Go get her, King!"

King gave chase. The kid ran like the wind. They raced across the Route 64 bridge in the rain and headed east up the hill, Mink dodging around cars and sometimes jumping over them, King pelting hard behind her, a painful stitch in his side.

There was a bad feeling in his belly, too, that had nothing to do with running. The kid had a look on her back that made him think she was running away for real. This wasn't playful flight, just a few inches ahead, a tease. The kid meant business. Always ahead, she doubled over and ran like a dog, grabbing at the ground with both hands at once and dragging herself onward in incredibly long, doggy leaps. As they crested the hill, King's lungs quit. Mink shot out of sight. He stood and panted on the crest. Rain blattered onto his head. "Damn," he panted. "Mink! MINK!"

He stood and yelled her name until the memory of the way she had run convinced him that she wouldn't come.

When he got back to the ballroom, Gelia was peeling long, wet sheets of paper apart and squinting at them. She looked up when King stepped back through the French window.

"Lost her," King said. "What's that?"

Gelia laughed shakily. "I'll be darned. It's them insurance papers Cracker was talking about. Here, Ernest, you look at 'em."

Erny took the papers.

King looked over Erny's shoulder. "Sure is insurance," he said. "Fifty thousand dollars." He shook his head, squinting at the fine print in the candlelight. Count on Gelia Somershoe to come up smelling like a rose. "Holy Moses, here's one here for Cracker, too. Erny, how come you got left out? Shit, Gelia, you're gonna have to marry him now. Your houses're all at the bottom of the river." He grinned. "Gelia, lookit."

While the better-dressed refugees in the ballroom raised their eyebrows, she read, looked up at King, grinned back, laughed again, then roared.

Chapter Fifty-Five

Suzy was dragging herself upstream toward the inn through howling rain when John Fowier's body washed up against her knees.

The river, so friendly when she had dropped out of her window, turned nasty. Even at knee-deep the current was wicked. Big chunks of floating garbage knocked into her, and the bottom was treacherous with old tin cans, unfriendly to bare feet.

She'd washed most of the mud off herself. That was a mistake. Now she was freezing cold and acutely conscious of her nakedness. Headlights flashed by on the east bank, and she crouched underwater.

Rain lashed down. Now and then lightning lit up the water. She felt miserable, cold, foolish, and triumphant. A furnace of inner power burned somewhere inside her chilled flesh, as if she had accomplished something. A lot of stupid decisions had brought her here. The only one she didn't regret was climbing out her window.

It felt like graduation. *So long to you jerks. I've done my time.* She would have to quit Atlas Properties. She'd like to get out of the city. Sell some stock, get a little capital together, maybe start a spa out here in bur-bland. With mud baths. She grinned.

Something heavy shoved her knees, nearly pushing her over.

In a panic, she splashed clear of the water and up the bank, where she crouched, huddling her arms around herself. At first she thought it was just somebody, some guy sneaking up on her. *Kill.* All the fine hairs on her body stood out like a cat's. She put her fists out.

Then she saw how fast the current was going, and how the body lay on its side, half-sunk and motionless. It tipped over slowly and slid on its back, sinking face-up into the shallows. She saw who it was. She gulped.

She tried to drag him clear of the water, but he was far too heavy. His skin was a horrid texture. His pajama top tore at the shoulder in her grasp, and she leaped back.

Her brain started working. Pajamas. Carefully keeping her eyes off that face, she worked the buttons on the pajama top. Turn him over, she thought, her teeth chattering. Pull the sleeves free. One at a time. Jerkily she slid herself into the clammy pajama top and buttoned it up. It felt indescribably nasty. Now the bottoms.

Suzy left him on his face. She didn't want to see his dick, cold forever now, while she took his pants. All her triumphant power seemed to have burnt itself out. Time to go home.

She pulled John Fowier by the ankle until he was submerged again. The current gave her some help with the heavy corpse. She had to wade deeper in, backing into faster and faster water. The bottom dropped away suddenly. John slid into the trench of fast current and disappeared.

Outside the inn, under her still-open window, she found a chunk of wooden fence bumping against the wall and used it to climb into her room. Now what? Pack. She packed naked by the faint light from the open window, dripping on the carpet. Everything went into her overnight bag. She shouldered the bag, wedged her purse into her armpit, and snuck out of the hotel by a back door.

Her clean, dry suit was soaked by the time she made the safety of Berne's main drag. The street was empty. A town like this wouldn't have cabs rolling around loose. She'd have to hitch.

As she turned her face to the eastward escarpment and marched uphill toward Chicago, she noticed a little dog with a pointy face following her. Sopping wet, scrawny, bedraggled, limping. It reminded Suzy of herself.

When a trucker finally stopped for her, she held the door open an extra moment. "Come on," she said, "you come, too."

Chapter Fifty-Six

Walter saw Raedawn Somershoe walk across the site toward the construction office.

The wind suddenly picked up. The hairs on Walter's head rose. Rae reached the chain-link fence and moved along with one hand touching it.

The noise of the river was closer now. The tracks and US 31 had disappeared, and the row of machines was a row of blockish islands. The water moved briskly only forty yards away. Soon it would swallow up the concrete forms. And then there would be nothing left but the construction trailer and a few loaded pallets in the ring of chain-link fence.

Down there, Rae climbed the fence. Walter hoped she knew what she was doing.

He turned and scrambled higher up the ridge. The children's path seemed to have dissolved in the rain and darkness. He bent double, grabbing hold of grapevines, thorny wild raspberry canes, saplings, and dead grasses that came away in his hands. Last year's leaves were slick with rain under his hands and feet.

Rae tripped over Cracker before she saw him. The power pole tipped over just then, dousing the lights inside the trailer. She squatted, groping in the dark. Her hands found his wet overalls. Drunk again.

"Oh, Cracker, did you have to? Tonight of all nights!"

The tornado was near. She could feel it all over her skin, lifting hairs off her arms and sucking the breath out of her mouth.

Lightning crashed and the body under the overalls moved and flexed. Gooseflesh came out on her arms. Rae held perfectly still. The overalls collapsed slowly under her hands, keys chinking in the pocket, and then they were empty.

In the dimness she watched the big snake slide to the fence. It nosed from side to side, seeking a way out. The wind rattled the fence, segments flopping loosely on their rabbit feet. She could feel Alexander in the trailer, calling her. His voice thrummed up through the mud under her feet.

Her mind worked slowly. Fence. Gate. Let Cracker out. It's locked, dammit. Padlock. Key. She fumbled in Cracker's empty overalls until she found a pocket, a set of keys on bathtub chain. The river was still rising. She could hear it growling on the road side of the trailer. Oh *damn* this fence anyway!

The lock on the gate was a common one such as she sold every day at the hardware store. *Let's see.* Cracker's key chain should have something useful. The snake's weight slid over her feet. "Just hold on," she muttered. There.

The gate swung open. The snake whipped past her. In spite of herself she gasped with fright, flailed for balance, fell and grabbed for the ground with both hands.

In that instant something lifted her into the air, smashed her into a million small fiery pieces, and then jammed them all back together so hard that she flew clean out of her body.

White light seared the air and split it. Walter looked back, and he saw Rae lying on the ground, face down. *Lightning.* She would drown, if she hadn't been killed outright. Should he go down there? Try to drag her up the hill?

The river surged closer. The edge of the chain-link circle was already wobbling as the river tugged against its rabbit feet. The horrid truth came to him. He'd never make it in time. Walter resumed his upward scrambling, faster now.

Rae woke reluctantly. Someone was tugging the end of her leash. Twitching it. Come back. Come here.

"You?" she murmured, and realized that she had come back into her body. Her cheek lay in half an inch of mud. "Ugh." All kinds of things were happening in her body, waves of stuff rushing from end to end, a big horny yelling up her middle.

Something warm slid between her fingers where they splayed in the cold mud. She opened her eyes. Blackness. The light-pole had fallen, she remembered now. The finger slid up her arm. Blind in the new darkness, she peered in the direction of the trailer until she could make out its gaping doorway. She stood carefully. Her feet clung to the mud like magnets.

When she reached to steady herself on the trailer's aluminum stairrail, she realized that she wasn't earthed. *Still fulla that electric.* As her fingers touched the rail there was a crackle and a spark. She jerked her hand away. Her ears hummed. Her body swayed like a cattail in the wind.

Didn't matter. She might lose her balance, but her feet would stay stuck to the ground. She plucked them up one at a time and climbed the steps.

It was almost pitch-dark inside the trailer. He smelled like mud, he smelled like musk. The floor was covered with him. The plywood splintered between his thousand toes. Rae took her tennis shoes off. One bare foot at a time, she set out over the lumpy carpet of his roots to find him.

Up on the ridge, the wind was so strong that dead leaves were beginning to spin upward from the sloping ground between Walter's feet. He could hear a freight train far off, coming fast. He knew there were tracks at the top of the ridge. Maybe he'd better go downhill a ways, he thought, in case the wind blows something off the top of one of the cars. He slithered ten feet downhill. There was a funny emptiness just above the roof of his mouth. He sat hugging a tree, cowering in the rain, and looked down on the site, waiting miserably for the river to swallow the trailer and Rae.

The sky roared.

A moment later the freight train came hurtling over the crown of the ridge. Walter clutched his tree. A cascade of dirt and leaves and gravel was flung over him, and the train followed, ripping up trees in its path. When it hit the bottom of the ridge a shower of water splashed as high as his place near the top. *Black.* Huge, Walter thought, and then, *tornado.* Something smacked him in the face.

The tornado tossed stacks of bricks and lumber at the rising wall of black Fox water as if to say 'Mine, go away!' The river drew back. Water whipped high into the air, churning up froth and flying spray. The silvery chain-link fence snapped into the air, unwinding itself from a ring into a broken bracelet as it went, and the temporary pole came with, tangling on its wire. Then the roof tore off the office trailer. Things flew out of it too fast and far away for him to see. The trailer sides tore away one by one.

An instant later the trailer and the noise and the enormous force of wind were carried away. Soon it sounded like a freight train again, and then there was nothing but ordinary wind and the flooding river, so soft to his ears now that Walter felt deafened. In that moment of silence, the black shining body of the river furled itself and swallowed what was left.

Alexander put his arms around Rae just as the tornado arrived. Her skin sizzled wherever they touched.

"Easy," she breathed. "I got to do a—"

She had one moment in which to throw all the lightning in her body out into one arm. She brandished that arm, clearing a safe space for them. The air pressure dropped hideously. Even inside her bubble of protection, she felt the breath being sucked out of her body.

Then the trailer roof ripped away. The refrigerator and table and cot and chairs and a cloud of papers hung for a moment in mid-air before they skimmed weightlessly through the roof-gap into a tower of whirling wind. The walls clattered and were gone. Then it was all gone. Outside their bubble, an avalanche of water smashed down.

Walter saw the river unfurl itself in the wake of the tornado. He scrambled to his feet and braced himself hand and foot against two saplings.

He held his breath. The river lay flat. Then it seemed to grow bulky without exactly moving, a terrifyingly silent swelling.

Snakelike, the river rolled over, spilling trees and bits of houses out of its insides as it rolled, then rolling over on them again. He felt it thunder against the ridge like a hundred thousand cannonballs hitting a castle wall at the same time. The ridge shook and shook. He clung to his saplings, feeling rain spatter down on his sodden back, then a handful of hail, then an unexpected warmth.

The rain passed. Walter clung to his trees until his shoulders and feet ached. The clouds thinned and raced after the tornado. The moon came out. Shoulders and hip joints aching, he pried his hands from the saplings.

Down on the site, the river was already pulling back. Its angry edge scoured the last of the asphalt off of US 31 and then retreated farther. Flotsam was caught in the railroad tracks beside US 31. Trees and boards stuck end-up in the gaptooth railless ties, for the water had scoured away the ballast and earth under the track, and the ties now lay tilted and fallen.

At the edge of the Somershoe property some trees still stood, showing where the edge of the tracks and the road had been. The place where Rae and her family had lived was a featureless plain of black water.

Walter looked away. Those poor people.

Rae clung to Alexander for an agonizingly long heartbeat, waiting for the big chunks to quit flying around them.

"Thirsty," he gasped in her ear.

He needed water. Tricky. She pulled her bubble in around her, so that she alone was protected. The river rushed in to fill the empty space, booming against his trunk and making him shudder. She couldn't tell how deep the water was. The river smashed against the ridge and returned. Rae felt its weight leaning against the force of her will. "Hurry up," she panted.

Wet all over! Finally! Alexander abandoned the last of his humanity in the cold sweet water of the Fox. The black waters foamed around his waist—where was Rae? Safe in his embrace, oh good. He clung tight to her. He needed water. He wrapped her up and, at last, threw the rest of his many arms over his head where they belonged, while the water swirled up around him, covering his face, his shoulders, his arms, his wrists, his fingertips, filling all the long hollows with sweet cold water, while he stretched the tips of his fingers toward the air.

It was a game. He stretched for the sky and broke the surface with his fingertips, then the water rose higher, bathing him, making him strong. And stretch again.

At length he won against the river, for it could only rise so high. The feel of the sky made him drunk. The music came back a hundredfold now that he was out in the air again, listening with every twig and leaf.

He felt green fire next to his heart. *Who are you?* he said to it.

"It's me, silly."

Rae relaxed, limp and swoony. Her hips were sinking into the body of his trunk. His wooden grip was hard. "Go easy on me, now."

Fuck me, Rae, for the love of God. "Are you here?" He was talking to her out loud, and sometimes silently, and the two mixed themselves up.

"You're all confused," she said. Her body half-buried in his, she could feel with him through his labyrinth of roots, now spread as far as US 31 and the ridge. She felt him taking up the muddy floody river water, felt the river's weight slide slowly eastward into its old bed, felt the air pressure change as the front passed, dragging the tornado winds after it.

"Here," she said. She added silently, *Don't grip so hard, I'm only flesh and bone.* She helped him shift his huge limbs to make her comfortable.

Bring me back. "Bring me back," he pleaded. She tried to show him the way, but it was all new to her. Her old lover had never wanted to be a man again. Still, they tried. She felt her way along his geometry, thinking about his lunchbox clattering open, showing him a picture of his hard hat, reminding him of the smell of a hamburger— And here he was, a human face and torso leaning out of the big tree, holding her in his arms.

"Great God," he gasped. "I don't think I can come back any further."

She became slowly aware of the moonlight and of a chilly wet wind on her skin. In the shadow of his branches she sought his face.

"Do you want to?"

"Listen," he said. "Do you hear the moon?"

She lay her ear on his chest. There it was. Such a pure cool sound. Her breathing slowed. The pull of that cool hornlike music called her blood up from her feet and pulled it straight up through her body to the top of her head. And back down. "Lordy." You feel it different than he did, she thought wonderingly. "What else is different about you?"

He laughed raggedly. "I don't know anything. Rae," he said in an urgent voice, more human now. "Stay with me. I'm not afraid if you stay here with me."

"Ain't going anywhere." She touched his dreadlocks. "You're all new."

I feel new, he said, and turned his face up toward the moon, pulling her closer in his arms.

Feeling new made him shout out loud, and the whole landscape shouted back to him. The music poured through him, feeding him, and through him feeding all the living things around. The more they drank from him, the bigger he felt.

"Rae." *Run with me,* he commanded.

Together they ran up his trunk and out his branches, fragmenting and spiralling along each twig, laughing as hundreds of new leaves popped out, waving at the moon. *Catch the moon with me,* he said. The cool pure sounds pulled them up and out until he had grown another ten inches all around, a thousand new twigs popping from their buds, making her sneeze with pleasure at the fresh, green smell. Then the long tones began to fall, harmonies crossing and tangling, making a dissonance, then a sweet chord. Rae and Alexander fell with them, sinking down his trunk into his roots, into the peace and darkness of the good black dirt, letting the sounds drain away. *Good thing you got all those toes,* she said. *Goes out quicker when it goes out a skillion little ends at once.*

Here it comes again, he said. Here it came.

Walter's eye found the place where the trailer had stood. In the moonlight something unaccountable and black rose out of the place, if that was the right place, for his sense of distance had gone wacky now that the office trailer was gone. Gone were the trailer's silver perimeter of chain link, the corralled lumber and masonry stacks, the yellow bucketloader, the Bobcat. No dumpster, no pump, no compressor, no rolling toolbox, no temporary phone pole, no piles of borrow earth. The place seemed larger without them.

And what *was* that, standing in the place where he thought the office trailer had once stood? A tree. Its branches stretched in a huge circle around it, bowed almost to the ground with dark heavy leaf. It seemed to grow under his eyes, reaching for the moon. The ground drank down the last of the river water and glistened in the moonlight, making the little acre glitter like a woman's beaded black dress. That tree must be almost as high as the ridge, he thought. How could he have never noticed it? He found the children's path at last and stumbled along it, trying to get closer. He couldn't take his eyes off the tree.

It was a tree for a warmer climate than this, surely. It looked bulky and royal. Its leaves were small shiny ovals. A fig? It can't be, he thought. A fig couldn't have survived a hundred of these winters, as this one must have done to grow so great. The bark was smooth. Long ropes hung from the upper tree, and the upper branches showered upward, heavy with leaves waving at the moon. Walter squinted in the moonlight. The tree stood on a platform of its own roots, which sprawled out from the trunk in an oddly rectangular mat before thickening and plunging toward the ground. In Cancun, Walter had seen banyan trees grow like that, or strangler figs so old that the host on whom they had first set root had rotted and crumbled, while their roots poured over the dead host like honey running down the side of the jar. That was it. It looked just like one of those banyans.

Wow. It's big.

Something white moved in the middle branches near the trunk. Walter squinted, lost his balance, slipped downhill a few feet, rescued himself with a quick grab at a sapling, steadied, and looked again. A naked woman was standing on a branch. No, it was an illusion. Moonlight fell on the branch through the clouds and fuddled his sight. She disappeared into the black tangle of limbs and leaves. A cloud passed. There she was again, in a different position. Walter sat down very carefully in the mud.

Under his palms, where he touched the wet mud for once without shrinking, he felt a tickling. A smell of incredible freshness rose like spring fog around him. A few blades of grass pushed up between his fingers.

They rode the music until the moon went down. There was a quiet space. Rae could feel Alexander waiting for something. In the absence of the music she began to separate from him, pulling first one arm and then the other free of his trunk. "Whatcha waiting for?"

His face emerged from his trunk. "Listening." His voice had changed, she couldn't tell how. Maybe it was just different from the way he sounded when he talked to her on the inside. Different, all new. She couldn't get over how different he was from the old one. Gentler, for one thing. More human. He *waited* for her.

He was waiting kinda too long. A hot wire still ran up the middle of her body.

His arms tightened around her. "Hear it?"

Listening, she began to slip back into him. Deep down she felt a trembling like the rumble of a truck going by. No, maybe it was way up there, a jet passing. It got louder, forked and split like the sound of lightning, making not a crack but a blazing brassy noise, like parades, like elephant voices. The hot wire in her middle trembled. "What is it?"

"The sun," he said. *The sun.*

"Let's do it," she said.

His body heated up against hers. He felt human now, and he smelled as horny as the Fifth Army Band. She would show him just what they could do.

"Kiss me quick," he said. "It is the last time, I am afraid."

"No, no," she reassured him. *That's not how it works,* she meant to go on, *I'll 'splain it all to you*—but her mouth was busy.

He spoke. *Give me your green fire.* She opened.

And in he came, everywhere at once, carefully, slowly, so slowly that she exploded in a whole new way. She felt every bit of her body like a web of fine-strung fire, and each fiery thread was a path between what she knew and what she felt. Look, she thought, there's dark places everywhere, and then the second pulse of pleasure burst, like the colored fireworks star inside the white star. While she tasted it she let trickles of fire run into the dark places in her body, waking them up. It seemed incredible that her old lover could have missed these places. Alexander—where was he?

I'm here. He was. He held her inside everything he was, and he was about to come inside her again. He was waiting for permission.

Rae snapped back into herself. She was buried up to the shoulders in his trunk. Her face was clammy with tears. There was a powerful smell of young leaves.

You aren't rushing me, she realized. She took a long moment to savor her options. He would wait until she was ready. Her old lover would have thrown her bodily into the sky and laughed while she squealed with fright and excitement. Alexander wrapped her around, lifted her, letting her see, letting her choose. *Oh, you are sweet.*

She breathed against the warm strength of his trunk, smooth as skin. Her eyes closed. Inside her, long lines of green fire brightened slowly, glowing stronger as her eyes got used to the darkness inside her head. Green fire ran from the roots of her hairs down through long open channels in her body, pooling and building, melting her from the inside out.

Ready? he whispered.

She felt like a salamander, melting-hot and bright in the furnace between their locked hips.

I guess.

He put one single twig into her hand, no, he wrapped a single strand of his light around hers, and he pointed. *Up.* She turned her face to the sky and stretched. The pathways of her body filled with green fire, melting, stretching longer and higher, pouring out a thousand fiery new filaments that burst from her hands. Together they wound their fingers into a net.

And caught the sun. It was far away, far around the planet's curve, but its music grew louder by the minute. Rae felt a shiver down all forty feet of her body, through her many hands and arms. The hoarse brass band of the sun ran like molten gold into pools in her shoulders, in her throat, in her heart, in her groin, making her scream aloud with pleasure. The sound

JENNIFER STEVENSON

poured down into her knees, her ankles.

Now, Alexander said. Oh, he was right with her. She felt his great hand under her foot. Cautiously, for fear she might explode with joy, she ran the sole of her foot down his long thigh. The music came in through the sole of her foot and pulled her like taffy, so that her legs stretched all the way down his trunk, twining among his thighs, diving for the safe dark dirt between his toes. Somewhere in the middle where all her legs joined, she felt Alexander enter her again. *Yes.* Harsh sweet music blazed louder and louder, filling the sky. *Soon it will be sunrise.* Together they gathered all that electric stuff into a knot between their legs and, when the first finger of dawn shot across the sky, they flung it out, through every toe and fingertip, out every root, every twig and leaf, shouting back at the brilliant sound stretching from edge to edge across the world.

The sun drowned their shouts in the roar of dawn.

Enough, he sighed.

Yeah.

Slowly Rae pulled herself back together until she was a single pink shivering thing in the cradle of his branches. He turned his big shoulders to the dawn and bent over her, cradling her. Just Alexander again.

She knew now that the music would always be too big for her to take it all in. What's more, she realized, Alexander knew it, too. Her old lover hadn't seemed to know. Had he grown selfish in his old age, she wondered? Or had he just grown so big and old that he'd begun to come apart? Like any piece of wood left out in the weather too long, maybe his pores had opened too far, and the light and sound came in and out at will, eating at his boundaries until he honestly hadn't known if he was in her or if he wasn't. If the sun shone here or on the other side of the world.

She lay quietly in Alexander's arms, letting her skin grow cool in the dawn mist, teasing his nipples and running her hands along his sides for the wonder of feeling the way his skin roughened to smooth, slippery bark. Up among the shiny new leaves in his crown his eyes shone black and human.

"Let's do that again," she said.

Chapter Fifty-Seven

A month later at four-thirty on a Tuesday afternoon, Walter Chepi descended the courthouse steps into Berne's main square. He'd been lucky. His firm carried malpractice insurance, but it hadn't been needed. The judge told Bagoff, Fimbeau and Juick to fight it out with their own insurance company. In the absence of John Fowier, Atlas Properties was helpless. Fowier's pretty protege had quit and could not be found to testify. The architect, the court ruled, could not be held responsible for acts of God.

There hadn't been much evidence left for the court to ponder anyway. The Fox River, changing its mind again after inundating the construction site for a scant ten minutes, had reverted to its original bed. Though the park and its ridge remained, there wasn't so much as a single cinder block left to show where the work had been done. Nobody would try to build there again.

Sweating, Walter wandered out to a bench in the shade. He was thinking longingly about an ice-cream cone when he saw Ernest Brown and Gelia Somershoe coming down the courthouse steps. Ernest wore a new tan suit. Gelia had on an airy knit dress that clung to her figure.

Walter raised his hand, and, when Ernest nodded back, he rose and came up to them.

"Howdy do, Mr. Chepi?" Ernest said.

"Howdy—how do you do, sir? Mrs. Somershoe," Walter shook hands with them.

"Mrs. Brown to you." Gelia surveyed his going-to-court suit with approval. "My, you look fine. We been getting married."

"Thank you. You look very well yourselves. Um—ma-married?" Walter tried not to sound stunned. "Congratulations."

"Thank you," Gelia said complacently. She extended her cheek. Walter pecked her and retired several feet away.

"Has your business in court prospered, Mr. Chepi?" Ernest inquired.

"My what?" Walter said, momentarily blinded by the diamond ring Mrs. Somershoe—Mrs. *Brown* was flashing in his eyes. "Oh. Yes, thank goodness. They tried about five suits with mine all at once. I forget how much damage was done along the river, between the two towns. Millions."

Ernest chuckled. "Act of God."

Gelia snorted. "Takes a judge and weeks of pussyfooting around to tell 'em so."

Walter congratulated her. "Oh, that's speedy, for a court matter involving so much money, Mrs.—Mrs. Brown. I imagine that with so many people left homeless they felt responsible for settling matters as soon as they could. Um, may I ask what, what prompted this happy event?"

"Well," Gelia said gaily, "you might say an act of God made us our fortunes. That insurance fellow that sold Cracker a policy? Didn't you hear 'bout that? Well, he did, and a nasty man he looked, but of course he died, and nobody looks their best thataway. Anyway, he sold one for the Gowdys to Cracker, rest the idiot, and sold him one for us—Rae and me, that is. Overlooked Ernest, of course, but what do you expect from a Yankee?"

"I hardly know," Walter said diplomatically. "So you were insured after all?"

Gelia laughed. "Yes! Ain't it a stitch? Lord knows if the tax man will try to take it all back next year, and I don't guess I care, but it seemed hard that Ernest here should get shut out in the cold when he lost the trailer, and the crawdaddy traps, and the truck garden and all." She shook her head over the losses. "A lot of work gone west with that garden. Twenty years, maybe more." She sighed.

Walter clicked his tongue.

"So we got hitched. I made a will in Ernest's favor, and he made an honest woman out of me."

The look she gave Walter with this remark was so spicy that he offered the only gallantry he could think of.

"Impossible, madam."

Chapter Fifty-Eight

Willy spent a feverish month getting to know his parents. His mother needed help with grocery shopping. It gave Willy so much joy to be in her company that he went to the store with her whenever she asked. They needed help picking out a new trailer, too. King kept arguing with them to buy a house off the damp riverbank but, as vague as Carl and Gloria could be, on this they wouldn't budge, which infuriated King.

Willy bridged the gap when he could. When he couldn't he turned his attention to Ink, who was inconsolable. There had been no sign of Mink since the storm. Willy looked for her, sometimes. He never found her. He thought maybe they never would, but he promised they'd go out in the world and look for her someday. Ink cried a lot and slept in Willy's room at the foot of his bed.

Carl worked around the place slowly but skillfully, hooking up the gas-tank fridges and stoves in the new trailers, helping Erny and Gelia rebuild the truck garden, and crafting new crawdaddy traps out of chicken wire and chunks of old storm fence. Mostly he stood by the river, or sat with Ink on his knee, his eyes closed and his face turned toward the sun.

They said very little. It drove King nuts, but Willy found it restful. They were always there in a very real and solid way. When they listened, they *listened*. Willy was oddly satisfied.

One afternoon he entered their room without knocking and found his parents standing fully dressed, twined together, motionless. The setting sun poured in the trailer window. Willy couldn't see their faces. After a long still moment of breathless watching, he noticed how long their arms were, how their knees seemed to cross and knit around one another. He heard a small tearing sound, like cloth giving way. Abruptly, he turned and slipped out the door again.

He closed the door gently and set his back against it, breathing hard. He'd spent weeks, he realized, being a little kid again. Avoiding things.

He heard a clank outside: King and Erny fixing up shutters.

King mustn't find them like this.

Quick as thought, he opened his parent's bedroom door a crack, slipped just his hand in, set the knob to lock itself, and pulled it shut with a click.

His heart gave two hard, aching thumps. Between those two heartbeats, he allowed himself at last to remember that there was a new tree growing across the road.

It's time for you, too, Willy-boy, isn't it? he thought. He drew a deep shuddering breath full of anticipation and fear. Now or never. He went outside.

The new tree was black against the sunset sky. Willy stood twenty feet away, feeling small and very lonely. He looked up and up. It didn't look a bit like the old tree. Its leaves were small, oval, shiny, a bright light green. The branches hung almost willow-like in a dense veil around the trunk. Shyly, Willy ducked under the veil and stepped into the deep shadow of the canopy.

Sure didn't look like the old tree at all. For one thing it stood on a big platform of its own roots which climbed like knees out of the dirt, inviting a foothold. Its limbs started close above the ground and grew in a rich peat-colored tangle, smooth as skin, inviting touch. The actual trunk of the thing was about as tall as a man's body. Well, a really big man's body. He stepped a giant step, up onto the platform of roots.

He began to climb.

Chapter Fifty-Nine

Rae got up and brushed mud off the knees of her jeans. The light was failing. Time to quit gardening. She was glad they had moved the garden nearer to home. She put the rest of the onion sets back in their net bag and tossed them into the wheelbarrow, then strolled down to the river to rinse her hands. I can put the tools away later, she thought, knowing Erny would do it for her.

King came out of the Gowdys' new trailer, a fifty-foot monster covered with chrome and oval windows, and crossed to where she stood at the river's edge. His duffel bag hung over one knotted shoulder. He looked at the water with her for a moment.

"You won't come with me," he said gruffly.

She shook her head, her eyes on the water. Fresh cattail reeds poked up a foot high and shed a faint rainbow of oil onto the surface. Something moved among the reeds. Rae turned and went toward her own trailer. King followed.

"Didja say good-bye to your folks?" she asked. He didn't answer. King hadn't said one word to her about the reappearance of his folks, but of course she'd heard plenty from Davy. As Davy told it, King yelled and his folks just stood there. They were a little odd now, but she was more tolerant than King, she supposed. Not like it was *her* mother who'd gone strange. She pointed. "Didja see? We gained nearly thirty yards of land!"

"Rae, it's mud."

She turned to face him. "It's ours."

"Why in hell's name don't you put up real houses, anyway?" he said exasperatedly. She just looked at him.

King followed Rae into her trailer, where she poured milk into a dish and carried it outside. She put the dish down by the front steps and backed away a few paces.

The reeds at the water's edge stirred again, and slowly, a foot at a time, a huge, thick-bodied cottonmouth snake crawled up onto the bank and worked itself across the mud toward them.

Hairs rose on King's nape. The snake ignored King and Rae and slithered up to put its head into the dish.

She laid a hand on his arm, a little timidly, he thought. "You want to come inside for an hour or so?" He scowled, and she removed the hand. "You don't have to grouch at me."

King hunched a shoulder, turning away. He felt ashamed of his rudeness. Without looking, he reached behind him for her hand. He surveyed the acre of their riverbank, of which so little now was familiar. He wanted to tell her something. Maybe at least that he still cared about her.

With his back to her and her roughened hand warm in his, he said, "I always loved this place." Emotion threatened to overcome him. He jerked his face to make it settle down. He had accomplished a lot, dammit. Found his parents and put them behind him. Checked in with the whole bunch. He'd even talked to Cracker before he ran off or got drownded or whatever.

And he had answered whatever question it was he had about Rae. Hadn't he? It seemed unkind to just leave her here. She deserved better than this.

"Rae," he said abruptly, "I don't want you to be trapped here. You don't have to be."

"King, I've got a place. This is where my—my strength is."

"How can you say that!" he burst out. "In Gelia's shadow all the time, how can you have any kind of a life? Get out while you can!" With an impulse he regretted even as he spoke, he added, "I'll take you away."

She smiled. "You don't mean that."

"She's a menace, Rae," King said out loud for the first time in his life. "She's not good for you."

"She's been jealous of me all my life. Everything she gave me, she put into a bag with a hole in it." Rae's face lightened. "But I've won two rounds in a row. History's been made. I think it's gonna be a trend." She grinned. "You ought to know Gelia's big secret. She's just human."

King shuddered. Never in a million years would he feel Gelia as only human. The woman hung too big in his sky, the moon of his youth. But there was Rae, too, who led him every which way, even somehow led him away, when the time came to git. Both of these women were too big. Too big to hold in your mind at one time— how could they be friends, or live in the same house? His heart hurt trying to imagine it.

At least they didn't have to live in the same house anymore. Gelia lived with Erny now, and Rae had a trailer to herself. He could leave with a clean conscience, he thought, not feeling any too clean yet.

As King frowned down at her, Rae felt a great easing. It was as if her edges had loosened. She waited quietly, feeling joy fill her up, one lap of the river at a time. Her happiness expanded as far as this tree here, then the next tree, then the next, clear across the road to the biggest tree of all. *My, I'm big*, she thought.

"I'm content, King. I have new work." She glanced over her shoulder across the road. "I'm gonna be busy."

King saw the direction of her glance and twitched. "I've got to go."

That's right, he wouldn't want to know. They walked up the bank toward the road with their arms around each other's waists.

At US 31 they kissed and let go of each other.

"I'll be back," he said.

She nodded as if that were true. He shifted the bag on his shoulder and swung away. The first twenty yards he moved slowly. After that his stride lengthened and in no time he was gone, heading south on US 31 toward the Berne train station.

She watched him out of sight and then walked home. The dish by the front door was empty, but the big snake lingered, half-coiled around the cinder block under the steps. She went inside and brought out a can of beer. This she poured into the dish. The cottonmouth slithered forward without waiting for her to back off. For a while she stood there, stroking the snake on the head with one finger and tipping more beer into the dish as it emptied. When she stood up, the sun had sunk behind the ridge.

Across the road where someone had once thought to put up a building, the ridge loomed. Its great black wall was freshening with new raspberry canes and grapevine, young alder leaves, ferns, mayapples, and bright green moss. Below the ridge, the meadow bloomed. Water stood in the meadow's low spots between clumps of new grass and prairie flowers.

A single tree, black-trunked, its branches stretching forty feet around in a circle of waxy leaves, covered the patch of ground where Bob Bagoff had placed his construction office.

She tossed the empty beer can under her trailer and started across the road.

At dusk, when Willy climbed down from the tree, he met Rae coming across the road. She stopped, cocked her head, looked from him to the tree.

Caught, he froze. He'd taken such care before, never to be seen climbing up or down. Years and years of sneaking around behind her and Gelia's backs. His feelings tangled. He felt smug because he'd got here first tonight, anxious that she might challenge him, weary at the thought of all the explaining he'd always avoided, and fearful with the crawling fear he'd felt since he was a boy—that she might turn the searchlight of her sexual curiosity on him and try to take him.

Oh well. Face it now. He felt too good right now to worry. He smiled and bowed low, flinging his hand out to the tree behind him.

"It's all in the family," he said mischievously.

Rae hesitated, blinking at him for a moment. Just then the tree seemed to catch her eye and she seemed to forget he was there. She walked past him, her face tipping higher and higher, her steps getting longer and quicker, until she was running into her lover's arms.

Jennifer Stevenson lives in Evanston, Illinois. She has washed dishes, shelved library books, repaired life-size rubber sunflowers, and groomed horses for a living. Crows follow her car, begging for peanuts.

With her husband of twenty-six years, she owns Hawkeye Scenic Studios, Inc., a scenery construction company located in Chicago. *Trash Sex Magic* is Jennifer Stevenson's first novel. She is currently working on a series of romantic comedies.

Her website is www.jenniferstevenson.com

Acknowledgments

It's been eighteen years since I first sat in the jury-duty waiting room at the Cook County Courthouse, roughing out some ideas for a book about a muddy bank along the Fox River. So many people have helped me with it that I know I must be overlooking some names. If you catch up with me, declare yourself, and I will remember and be abashed. I can never sufficiently repay such patient and generous friends.

In alphabetical order: To all the wonderful women of Chicago-North RWA for explaining plot to me once and for all, eluki bes shahar for encouragement at the right moment, Maggie Bodwell for saying Keep going, Rich Bynum over and over and over again, Farrell Collins for liking the sex, Chapter One for workshopping it first, John Crowley for doing it better, Julie Dreese for the crows, Kurt Engfehr for brilliant suggestions, Eugine Francis of the Bahamas Ministry of Tourism for expert advice, Gavin Grant for taking a chance, Theodore Halkin for liking the sex too, Nalo Hopkinson for being a goddess, Kim Hughes for herons and bees, Michael Kandel for cutting it, Donald G. Keller for early encouragement, Amey Larmore for swell notes, Mrs. Elich Lindon for honest answers, Kelly Link for loving it, Chris Lotts for reading closely, Kathy Oliver of the Bahamas National Trust for expert advice, Linn Prentis for persistence, Deb Sears for the deluxe critique, Kitty Slattery for listening mindfully, Caroline Stevermer (with extra sushi) for liking the trees, Michael Swanwick for thinking it didn't suck, Lois Tilton for sharp eyes, Gene Wolfe for the key lime pie, and for their patience and kindness, Sue Blom, Martha Bayless, Shira Daemon, Connie Downey, Claire Fanger, Margaret Gettings, Katherine Ross, Amy Shaefer, Delia Sherman, and Donna Slager, without whose virgin eyes this book could never have happened. I owe you all.